Going Out

Scarlett Thomas

FOURTH ESTATE • *London*

First published in Great Britain in 2002 by
Fourth Estate
A Division of HarperCollins*Publishers*
77–85 Fulham Palace Road
London W6 8JB
www.4thestate.com

10 9 8 7 6 5 4 3 2 1

A catalogue record for this book is available from the British Library

ISBN 1-84115-761-9

Book design by Geoff Green

Typeset by Rowland Phototypesetting Ltd,
Bury St Edmunds, Suffolk
Printed in Great Britain by
Clays Ltd, St Ives plc

For Tom

people have dirt in their houses, dirty dishes in the sink, clothes in the laundry basket.

Luke's floor is made of linoleum and all his furniture is plastic or MDF. He has nylon sheets and wears clothes made out of artificial fibres. He's sitting on his nylon bed next to Julie with his legs crossed, like some kind of yoga student. Julie is leaning against the wall, her knees drawn up to her chest. She finishes the Pot Noodle and puts the empty plastic container neatly to one side. Her insides feel warm and salty.

There's nothing on TV after the pop profile, so Julie gets up and scans the video shelf. She feels like seeing some American animation: dysfunctional families; dysfunctional robots; dysfunctional, offensive kids.

'I don't want to die,' Luke says. 'But I do want to live.'

Julie laughs. 'Oh please. Will you stop saying that all the time?'

Luke smiles too. 'At least it gets a laugh.'

'And will you stop talking about going out? It makes me feel anxious.'

'Look, I'm not going to do it, of *course* I'm not. Not now. I just like to think about it. Come on. I've never gone out just because I've talked about it.'

'Yeah,' she says. 'I know.'

Luke smiles. 'I'm not going to do it until it's safe – until I've been cured.'

At the millennium he swore that he'd be cured by 2001. It's October now. Julie pulls out a video and slides it in the machine.

'I'm worried about you,' Luke says suddenly.

'Me? Where did that come from? We were talking about you.'

He looks at the Pot Noodle. 'Have you eaten anything real today?'

Chapter 2

Luke Gale was born on 24 October 1975, during an episode of *Fawlty Towers*. In the year the Netherlands won the Eurovision Song Contest, the year of Wombles, Pong, Ford Capris and the Bay City Rollers, Luke was a miracle child.

His mother Jean had, apparently, always been unable to conceive, and the adoption agency she and her husband Bill approached had ruled that Bill was away too much for them to effectively parent a child. It didn't matter that half the women in the area were single-parent families with ten different men on the scene; Jean and Bill just weren't good enough for a child. Bill was away so much because his firm, a big insurance company, sent him to different locations for one, two or sometimes three weeks at a time. In the end, the savings fund that was supposed to provide private education for the adopted child they never had ended up going towards Brazilian herbal fertility treatments for Jean. A couple of years later, Luke was born.

The first time Julie saw Luke was some time in 1985. She was sitting in the removal van, half asleep. He was a face in a window that she at first thought belonged to a ghost. It was late – they'd been driving all day – and in the moonlight he'd looked pale, drawn and a bit deathly. Julie was ten at the time, and was going through a phase of thinking everything was a ghost and everything looked *deathly*, but there was something wrong about him even then. He wasn't looking at anything. He was just looking. As they pulled up outside their new home, she realised that he was going to be her new neighbour.

'I never thought I'd live in a cul-de-sac,' laughed Julie's mother.

'What's a cul-de-sac?' Julie asked.

'Like this,' explained her father. 'A road with a beginning but no end.'

The next day, after a night spent 'camping' in their new home, Julie's father started his first day in his new job as a lecturer at the local sixth-form college, preparing for the new term when he'd be teaching art. At about three o'clock, after spending the day unpacking, Julie and her mother went to say hello to the neighbours at number 17.

At first, Julie couldn't work out what was so weird about Luke. He didn't seem like a ghost any more; he seemed more like a child you'd see on TV or something – she wasn't sure why. When she thought about it a lot later, Julie realised it was because he had no scabs, no suntan, no insect bites and no dirt. He was the cleanest child she'd ever seen. They just stood looking at each other in silence, in what Julie later found out was the 'guest' lounge, in which she was never allowed again after that first day.

In the lounge, the funny-looking plastic blinds were drawn over the patio doors, although Julie didn't think this was particularly strange. For a few minutes, while Julie and Luke stared at each other, the mothers made small talk about the area, and Julie's mother, Helen, commented on Jean's display case and collection of glass-blown animals.

'I'll go and make a cup of tea, shall I?' offered Jean eventually.

'Thanks,' said Julie's mum, smiling nervously as her

daughter pushed her feet around the immaculate white shag-pile carpet, making little, meaningless patterns. 'Why don't you kids go and play outside?' she suggested.

There was a funny silence, and then Luke sort of sneered. 'Yeah, why not?' he said sarcastically. Then he left the room.

Julie couldn't believe that a child had been so rude to a grown-up. She was almost envious of the tone he'd taken with her mother; he'd sounded almost like a grown-up himself. Her mother looked at the floor and then fiddled with her earrings, the way she always did when she was nervous. She was wearing her clip-on dog earrings today, the ones she had bought on holiday in Cornwall last year. Julie suddenly felt cross with Luke for speaking to her mother that way and guilty that a few moments ago she'd thought it was clever. *Stupid little boy*, she thought, and wondered if he was a problem child like the ones on the estate in Bristol, near where she used to live.

'Why don't we go into the kitchen?' suggested Jean.

Julie and her mother followed Jean through the door and down the hall.

'Sorry,' said Julie's mother, who always apologised for everything. 'I hope I didn't say anything . . .'

Jean filled the kettle and put it on to boil in silence. Julie could sense a weird atmosphere in the room but tried not to think about it. Instead she wondered whether this was the sort of kitchen where you'd find Nesquik and Marmite, neither of which her mother bought, and both of which she'd always relied on getting at friends' houses. She'd already noted that there was no Soda Stream, which she was pleased about. Luke was too horrible to deserve one.

It was clear that Julie's mum was feeling uncomfortable.

'Can I help with anything?' she asked Jean.

'No, no,' said Jean, pouring water into the teapot. 'That's all right.'

'Maybe we should leave you to it. Get on with the unpacking . . .'

'I'm sorry,' said Jean. 'I'm sorry for the way Luke spoke to you.'

'I'm sure it's a just a phase,' Julie's mother said nicely. 'You should hear this one sometimes.' She pointed at Julie. This was something that really got on Julie's nerves. Whenever another child acted badly, her mother pretended Julie did too, to make the person feel better. This was unfair, because Julie hardly ever got into trouble.

'Luke hasn't been outside since 1976,' Jean said. 'He isn't usually so rude. I am sorry. He's having another assessment soon.'

Julie's mother seemed shocked. 'Assessment?' she repeated.

Julie wondered if Luke was a mad person.

'Yes. He's allergic to the sun,' explained Jean.

For the next half an hour, while the grown-ups carried on talking, Julie considered this. What did being allergic to the sun involve? She was allergic to wasp stings and swelled up whenever she was stung. Last time she was stung, she had to go to hospital for an injection in her bottom. She imagined Luke swelling in the sunshine, eventually exploding in a ball of yellow pus. She was aware of her mother making the sympathetic noises she always made when other adults told her their problems, which were usually something to do with an illness or 'trouble at home'. This time there were a lot of medical terms Julie didn't understand – apparently Luke was suffering from something called XP and various other allergies. Julie couldn't follow what the grown-ups were talking about and eventually started picking an old scab on her finger.

'He just watches TV in his room all the time,' said Jean. She looked at Julie and then back to Julie's mother. 'We got it for his birthday last year. Since then all he does is watch it, and we don't know what to do. He doesn't even read books any more – and he used to get through so many books.' She sniffed. 'It'll be nice for him to have someone of his own age to play with. Get him away from that box, anyway.' She's been crying a bit, and apologising a lot, like Julie's mum does sometimes.

'Has he got a TV in his room?' asked Julie. She had never heard of anything more glamorous in her life. No one she knew had TVs in their bedrooms, not even moneybags Joanna who'd had a bouncy castle on her birthday.

'*Julie*,' said her mother, embarrassed.

'What?' she said indignantly. 'I was only asking.'

Her mother gave her a look, and soon, after some fidgeting, sighing and more scab picking, Julie was taken home.

'That poor little boy,' Julie's mother said to Julie's father later that night, over dinner.

They were eating fish and chips in the half-unpacked sitting room. Julie's father had just been talking about his preparations at the college, and Julie's mother had been talking about all the reading she still had to do before her degree course started at the polytechnic. Now they were talking about that weirdo Luke. Julie was curled up on the brown sofa reading *Smash Hits* and pretending not to listen.

'What did you say he had again?' asked her father.

'XP,' said Julie's mother uncertainly. 'I can't remember what it stood for.'

'XP. Hmm. Never heard of it.'

'It's very rare, apparently.'

Julie's father flicked the TV on to BBC2. Julie held her breath. *The Young Ones* was about to start and if she held her breath there was a chance she wouldn't be noticed and would be able to watch it all before being told to clean her teeth for bed.

'She is a seriously odd woman,' commented Julie's mother. 'Crystal brandy glasses and a guest lounge,' she muttered to her husband and they both giggled before turning their whole attention to the TV. Just before bedtime, Julie overheard her father say something to her mother she didn't understand. It was about there probably being a lot of wife-swapping parties around here. It made them both laugh a lot, but it sounded very dubious to Julie. Who would want to swap their wife? She thought about the fat woman next door with her podgy fingers and gold rings and wondered if her husband might want to swap her. He probably would. That's probably what they meant. Smiling, having finally got the joke, she put on her My Little Pony nightie and went to sleep listening to her parents having sex.

Julie's school was a ten-minute walk from her new house. Compared to her last school journey, this was seen as too far for her to go on her own. Especially with Stranger Danger, and the industrial estate and the big fields that seemed to be the best shortcut to the school. The fields near the new house were yellow with tall grass and you got there by going down an overgrown alley next to a tyre factory. Julie enjoyed playing there. She found she could hide herself in the tall soft grass and make a little womb-like den where no one could find her. Then she overheard her mother telling her father that she was sure some kid would be found dead in those fields at some point. The next time Julie went there she lay in the yellow grass, perfectly hidden and still, and imagined being cold, pale and dead. Suddenly she didn't want to go there again.

She ended up walking to school with Leanne, the girl from number 12, after her mother went over and asked Leanne's mother if Julie could walk with her. Leanne already walked to school with Susie and Kerry, the twins from the next street. After some coaxing from her mother, she agreed to walk with Julie as well.

The night before the first day of school, while Julie was getting ready for bed, she'd seen Luke looking at her from his window. She knew his bedroom faced hers – they both looked down on the twin garages and drive-ways that separated numbers 17 and 18 – but he'd never actually looked at her before. When their eyes met, he'd made a funny face and she'd laughed. Then he'd smiled. Maybe he wasn't that horrible after all.

At 8.15 the next day, Julie found Leanne sighing and rolling her eyes at the end of the road. Julie was five minutes late.

'We're going to be late to meet the twins,' Leanne said crossly.

'Sorry,' said Julie, feeling stupid. The way Leanne spoke to her made Julie feel like she was stupid, big and clumsy like a monster or a sea creature.

'This is Julie,' Leanne said to Susie and Kerry, when they got to the next street.

'Are you new?' Kerry asked, looking Julie up and down.

Julie looked completely stupid compared to Leanne, Susie and Kerry. They had proper hairstyles – Susie and Kerry had French plaits and Leanne had bunches with proper bobbles. Julie had a boring ponytail that was already coming out.

'She's not allowed to walk to school on her own,' said Leanne.

'Why not?' said Susie.

'She's scared,' said Leanne. 'Her mum told my mum.'

'I'm not scared,' said Julie.

'Why don't you walk on your own, then?' said Leanne.

School was horrible. A small, south-facing modern building, with little Munchkin chairs and stupid exhibitions of pictures of fish created entirely with glitter, it was always too hot and gave Julie a headache every afternoon. Everything was supervised closely except playtime, which was supervised from a distance by a fat teacher in a long skirt with a bell. Leanne, Susie and Kerry turned out to be the most popular girls in the school. They spent a whole year calling Julie 'scaredy-cat', holding their noses when she went past and pretending she'd farted. The only time they left Julie alone was when they were playing gymnastics on the rail around the grass by the caretaker's house. When they did that Julie could keep away from them, and they'd be too absorbed to follow her; hanging upside-down on the rail, gripping with their knees and constantly arranging their skirts so their knickers weren't showing.

The boys were even worse. They all knew words that Julie didn't understand. At playtime they would come up to her and say things like, 'Do you know what *fuck* means?' and Julie would get embarrassed. She knew that 'fuck' was a dirty word but had never understood exactly what it signified, just that you shouldn't say it. When she said she didn't know, they teased her even more. After a while, Julie started pretending she did know what the words meant, but the boys were ready for her, either calling her bluff by making her define the words (she couldn't), or using made-up words in the first place so that when she said she understood them, they could laugh and say she was a smelly liar, and they knew because they'd made up the word.

All the kids at school loved *The Young Ones* and would spend the day after each episode quoting lines from the programme. But when Julie joined in, nervous and frightened of being laughed at, she got mixed up and said one of Rik's lines in Vyvyan's voice. No one laughed. No one said anything. No one even called her a flid or a joey; they just looked at her with this weird disbelief on their faces. How could someone be so stupid?

From her first day, she walked home alone but told her mother she walked with Leanne. Suddenly lying dead in the yellow fields didn't seem like such a bad thing.

Julie lost herself in books about planets and animals and maths because what she learnt at school wasn't very exciting. She became best friends with Luke. At eleven she moved up to the local comprehensive: a hard-gravel playground and sports field surrounded by cold Portakabins, bullies in mini-skirts, Cancer Corner, spitting competitions and – the place where most humiliation took place and where Julie once had to do PE in her knickers because she left her games kit at home – the sports hall.

Julie instantly became one of those kids who joined clubs because it meant she didn't have to go outside. She spent breaktimes and lunchtimes playing chess, doing chemistry experiments, playing Dungeons & Dragons, making models or, if there were no clubs running, doing her homework in a corridor or toilet somewhere.

If her homework was finished and there were no clubs, she would attempt maths puzzles set for her by Mr Banks, her maths teacher, involving challenges to trisect angles, square circles, double cubes or find the square root of -1. Mr Banks was very small, clever and sadistic, and always seemed as if he wanted to simultaneously reward and punish Julie for being so interested in his subject. Almost all the puzzles he ever set her turned out to be impossible to solve, or they'd be famous theorems no one had solved yet. But he did tell her how to work out square roots without a calculator, and how, with logic and time, you could solve almost everything – or at least explain why something couldn't be solved. Julie liked that. Everything was wrong or right; impossible or possible; unknowable or knowable. One or the other. You could be certain about maths.

Julie didn't have any friends, but she didn't really need any, since she had Luke at home. No one at school believed in Luke. One time, Julie told the other girls that her best friend was allergic to the sun and that's why he didn't come to school but they said she was a liar, and that she didn't have any friends – at school or anywhere else. They found her story doubly implausible: firstly, *no one* was allergic to the sun, and secondly, what boy would want to be friends with a girl?

School was shit. But it always is if you're different. Julie never worked out why she was different, she just knew she was. Maybe the people who stared, called her names or refused to be friends with her knew what was wrong with her, but they never told her what it was. No one liked Julie and she didn't know why; her best friend couldn't leave the house because of an illness no one understood. Mr Banks's puzzles, even the impossible ones, were a lot easier to work out than life was.

Chapter 3

The room is too hot. Luke switches on his fan. He's never been allowed to open the window, not even at nighttime. There's too much pollen, according to his mother, and moths, carrying poisonous dust on their wings, even in October.

Luke's reading. When he reads, he almost feels like other people because he can read books in exactly the same way other people do, even if he does have trouble picturing some of the scenes. He's never been able to play videogames, because all videogames seem to require you to travel on some sort of journey through vast improbable lands. Luke's only experience of travelling has been to the other end of the house and back. The first time he tried to play a videogame he felt anxious and lost as soon as the character moved from the starting point. Luke's never really experienced being lost and if being lost in the real world is as terrifying as being lost in a fictional one then maybe staying in this room isn't that bad. But then again, Luke would still give anything to go out.

The book he's reading now may as well be science fiction. It's set in an office and Luke's been having trouble creating the location in his imagination. Most of the time when he reads, he automatically places his most familiar image of, say, a house, or an apartment, or a field, into his imagination as required. But all his stock locations come from the TV or from films. If any action in a book takes place in an apartment, Luke's imagination accesses one of the apartments in *Friends*.

If anything takes place on a boat, Luke sees the inside of the *Titanic*. For Luke, there will always be several *Titanics* to choose from: an old black-and-white one, a Technicolor one with people in fifties clothes, one that keeps still like a photograph, and a huge Hollywood one with Oscars and celebrities. The idea that each of these images represents a real object that Luke can't see – well, if he can't see it, it doesn't exist. There is no real *Titanic*, just the pictures. Or: there are several real *Titanics*.

Luke doesn't use the word 'real' very often. He doesn't talk about the real world or things being realistic and he doesn't ever preface sentences with the words: *in fact*. Nobody really notices that he's weird, though, or, at least, not more weird than other people they meet. Maybe Julie notices but she's always been a bit weird herself. Luke thought for a long time that maybe other people didn't read books the same way as him. When he asked Julie she said she'd never really thought about it. He mentioned some book they'd both read recently that included a scene set in a hospital. When he asked her to describe her image of the hospital in the book, it was different to his. But when he asked if the image was similar to anything else – like, was it a hospital she'd actually been to, or maybe one from the TV or a film – she'd sort of gasped and said it was the set from *Casualty*, and she hadn't even realised. So maybe Luke isn't that weird.

Sometimes he dreams he's left this room. But the place he goes is a world made up of TV fragments, like a photo-fit, or those TV-clip shows they have on ITV: TV about TV. And after all, what else is he going to dream about? He's never seen the real outside, and you have to fill in the gaps somehow. If Julie ever played word-association with Luke and said the word 'car', he'd say 'Knight Rider', or 'Christine'. He'd never say 'street', or 'bus', or 'lorry', or 'motorbike'. So he dreams he's escaped into the TV, which is no escape at all. That's why he's reading more books, and that's why he wants to go out.

Julie once showed Luke a book that he couldn't understand, of paintings by Escher. He couldn't understand the outside world, or even his life; in the same way, he couldn't understand Escher. Julie tried to explain to Luke that Escher's paintings were 'impossibilities', or optical illusions, that stairs couldn't really do that: they couldn't really go up and down at the same time. Luke just thought, *Why not? Why couldn't stairs do that?* Julie got very frustrated with him at the time because she couldn't understand why he didn't see the impossibility. But if it turned out that every staircase outside this house was like an Escher painting, Luke wouldn't be surprised.

Luke's mind's still searching for an image of an office. The best it can do is the one from some American TV show about a lawyer, an open-plan mêlée of secretaries and computers and intrigue and people dressed in thin designer skirts. But it doesn't fit properly with the book and the chapter therefore feels uncomfortable, as the action fails to fit the location. The next chapter is set in a factory. Luke gives up. What's a factory? He can see big nineteenth-century furnaces and smoke and women in hairnets with cigarettes and children dressed in rags. Where would that image have come from? It's not right, anyway, so Luke closes the book. He'll look up factory images on the Internet tomorrow.

Yawning, he decides to go to bed. But before he does, he checks his e-mail. Apart from some of the usual crap, there's an e-mail from someone called Ai Wei Zhe, who says he's a healer staying in Wales. Luke's e-mailed Internet healers before, but he doesn't remember sending his details to this one. Maybe he's responding to one of Luke's newsgroup messages. There are lots of Luke's cries for help floating around out there on newsgroup servers, but it's very rare for someone to respond to one of them. This one says he may be able to help Luke.

Luke sends an e-mail straight back. Then, feeling suddenly more awake, he checks one of his newsgroups. While he's doing that, a second e-mail comes through from Ai Wei Zhe. He asks for Luke's phone number and for Luke to tell him when would be a good time to call. Luke immediately sends back a message with the number. He says he's awake now if Ai Wei Zhe would like to call him. Shaking slightly, Luke disconnects from the Internet and waits. Nothing. He goes to clean his teeth and change into his pyjamas, still shaking and still not feeling particularly tired. He checks he really is disconnected from the Internet and that his phone's not somehow engaged. Then it rings.

'Hello?' says the person on the end of the line. 'Is that Luke?'

'Yes, it is,' Luke says. 'Is that Ai Wei Zhe . . . ?' He has trouble pronouncing the name and makes *Wei Zhe* sound like *Wednesday*. 'I hope it's not too early or anything . . .'

'No, Luke. Don't worry. I always get up at dawn,' the voice says. 'And call me *Wei*.'

'OK.'

His accent sounds half American, half Chinese. 'You have an unusual problem?'

'Yes,' Luke says. 'I'm allergic to the sun.'

'The sun is yang. The sun gives life.'

'Not to me.'

'No.' Wei laughs. 'Have you seen a doctor?'

'Yes. A long time ago.'

'But not recently?'

'No.'

'Why not?'

'I just haven't. I um . . . I don't like the doctors, but that's not why.'

'Then why?'

'I don't know. They just haven't come. They stopped coming a while ago. I guess it's because this thing I have – XP – is incurable, so there's not much they can do apart from telling me to keep my curtains closed. This doctor my mother knows – he updates my medical certificates, but apart from that, nothing happens.'

'I see. And you've always been like this?'

'Yes.'

'I've never heard of this . . . XP before, but perhaps it's just terminology. I have heard of cases where people can't be exposed to sunlight, however; but I have not ever actually met anyone with this condition.'

'Can it be healed?' Luke asks.

'We will soon find out.' Wei laughs again. 'Perhaps you are too much yin.'

'What do you mean?'

'Well, being allergic to yang. This is fascinating.'

'Uh, yeah, I guess so.'

'Sorry. It probably isn't that fascinating for you, huh?'

'No.' Luke smiles. How can he put this? 'I want to dance in the fields,' he says.

'You do, huh? Then we must try to heal you.'

'You think you can?' Luke asks again.

'I don't know. If the problem is in your body, maybe. If not, well, maybe.'

'Oh. I think it is in my body.'

'Well, we'll see. Look, do you have a fax machine?'

'Yeah,' says Luke. 'Well, a scanner and . . .'

'Fax your medical documents. You have them?'

'They're in the house. I'll find them.'

'Fax them to me and we'll speak again on Monday.'

Chapter 4

The Edge is totally dead. Apart from the three members of staff – Julie, David and Heather – the only person in the restaurant is an electrician who's come to mend the electronic tills. Because the tills aren't working, it's impossible to take any orders. If there were customers, it would be a good idea to shut the shop, but since there aren't any it seems best to stay open.

Julie's topping up the salad bar with salad that David's just chopped up. In the evenings the chefs are too busy to make salad. There's usually some student washing dishes – too ugly or uncoordinated to be a waiter or waitress – and they do the salad then. Today Julie notices that the onion rings have less skin hanging off them than in the evenings and that there are no brown rotting bits in the tub of lettuce.

After the salad bar is done, Julie goes outside to write the 'specials' on the blackboard on the wall by the entrance. It's the same every lunchtime: all you can eat from the salad bar plus unlimited pizza slices for £6.99.

Along with some other shops – B&Q, Comet, Currys, Blockbuster, Staples and Homebase – The Edge is stuck a few miles outside Brentwood on a retail park. There, the big shops sit like fat kings with carpark courtyards, and their peasant subjects arrive in Ford Fiestas and Japanese people-carriers. At some point, some town-planning graduate must have created this concrete kingdom on a piece of paper, drawing the shops, carparks and of course the traffic-calming measures: voluptuous humps, little concrete kerbs (just like on real streets), a single mini-roundabout and various miniature hairpin bends.

Between the facing rows of carparking spaces there are concrete squares with off-green saplings growing in them. These prevent customers driving from their parking space into the one in front. The retail park is enclosed behind a wall made of browny-pink bricks and beyond that is the A12: twenty-four-hour noise and fast nighttime headlights. Beyond it are flat, scratchy-looking fields growing pale-yellow cereal crops.

The A12, a vast spectrum of greys, sits there as if a worm crawled on to an Ordnance Survey map and died with its head in London and its tail in Great Yarmouth. The section between Colchester and East London has more accident black spots than anyone can count, and the towns around it form the heart of Essex: Romford, Brentwood, Shenfield, Chelmsford and, further away, off the A127 or the A13, Southend, Pitsea, Basildon and Braintree. In each of these towns are houses with half-finished conservatories and patios; sunbeds, microwaves, satellite dishes and lock-ups where eighteen-year-olds fit huge stereos in their Ford Cosworths, Scorpios or XR3is. Inside the houses are bedrooms in which little girls learn how to do perfect French manicures and get thin like their friend Mandy or Danielle, and try to forget that for ten years any female who appeared on TV and said she was from Essex would get a raised eyebrow and a muffled, knowing giggle from the audience.

What's the difference between an ironing board and an Essex girl? It's easier to get an Essex girl's legs open. How does an Essex girl turn the light out after sex? She shuts the Cortina's door. What's the difference between an Essex girl and the *Titanic*? You know how many men went down on the *Titanic*. What does an Essex girl put behind her ears to make her more attractive? Her ankles. Julie's an Essex girl, but she's never had casual sex. Or *is* Julie an Essex girl? She's been here fifteen years. Is that enough?

Essex has a train line officially referred to as the Misery Line, and a regional accent – Estuary English – that no one thinks is remotely beautiful, lilting, romantic or edgy and that people all over the rest of the country put on when they want to imply that someone's thick. Julie speaks like that even though her mother used to tell her off for it. She probably speaks like that *because* her mother told her off for it. When you have only one identity available to you, you reach out and grab it, don't you? Whatever it is.

Before Julie writes today's specials on the board she has to rub off the specials from last night. *Spunk pizza, Gobble bread, Magic mushrooms, Fuck cunt.* The nighttime chefs and waiting staff always say it's the kids who skateboard on the retail park at night who change the specials board. But where would they get the white chalk? Without really thinking about it, Julie wipes the word 'Magic' off the board and replaces it with the word 'Garlic'.

Leanne has started coming over to The Edge whenever the new manager at Blockbuster lets her have a break. Her first break of the day is usually around 11.00 a.m. Today she turns up at five past. Julie's setting the tables for the lunchtime rush, although at the rate the till guy's going, they'll be shut at lunchtime.

'All right?' Leanne says to Julie.

Julie yawns. 'Mmm,' she mumbles.

'Keeping you up, are we?' asks Leanne, chirpily.

Julie once made the mistake of admitting to Leanne that she doesn't like to get up early, ever. Leanne gave her a slightly patronising lecture about late nights being bad for your skin and nails, and pointed out that Julie doesn't have to stay up late just because Luke does. Julie can't remember exactly but she thinks Leanne said something like, *If Luke threw himself off a cliff would you do it too, Julie?* Leanne's nowhere near the nightmare she was at school any more, though. In fact, Leanne's forgotten she ever bullied Julie at school, and gives the impression she thinks they've always been friends. Now she's standing here in her Blockbuster uniform unclipping her blonde hair and then twisting it back up in exactly the same semi-French pleat it was in before.

'So why are you still doing days, anyway?' she asks Julie.

Julie's the best waitress at The Edge, and her natural domain is the weekend: sweaty Fridays and perfumy Saturdays, couples who drink lots of Chianti, share a dessert, play footsie and tip quite well. But since another waitress went off sick a couple of weeks ago, she's been filling in. Almost everyone else who works here is a student or has another job during the day, so there wasn't anyone else to do it. The day shifts have turned out to be oddly relaxing. David, the chef, and Heather, the supervisor, are low-maintenance colleagues, and the haze of tiredness is actually OK, once you get used to it.

'Kerry's not back yet,' Julie answers.

'I heard she got pregnant by some biker from The Rising Sun.'

'I've heard loads of things. She probably just doesn't want to come back.'

Julie moves her box of cutlery and cleaning things to the next table. The plastic tablecloth looks clean, but still, Julie takes the little vase of flowers from it and places it on one of the chairs. Then she sprays cleaning fluid on the table, and wipes it with the cloth. Then she lays out two Edge napkins, two knives, two forks, and replaces the vase.

'Guess what?' says Leanne, following Julie to the next table.

Julie moves the flowers and wipes the table. 'What?'

'My cousin won the Lottery.'

'Yeah, right.' Julie's still in the school-days habit of not believing anything extraordinary that people tell her, in case it turns out to be a joke. When Leanne told her about Jill Dando being murdered last year Julie didn't believe that either. She puts out the cutlery and moves to the next table.

'Seriously,' says Leanne. 'Honestly.' She opens her blue eyes wide in the way she's always done when she's telling the truth and offended that someone thinks she's winding them up.

Julie looks up from the table and pushes some hair out of her face. 'How much?'

'Two million. She shared the jackpot with, like, three other people or something.'

'Two million's still a lot,' says Julie.

'I know. Guess what else?'

'What else?'

'She's buying number 14.'

'What, number 14 on our road?'

Leanne smiles deliciously. 'Yep.'

'Why? I mean, why would anyone want to live on our street?'

'Because Chantel always promised her mum that if she won the Lottery she'd get her a nice house, and our road is nice. Basically, right, Chantel – that's my cousin – her and her mum were living with this no-hoper guy in this, like, *shack*, near Basildon; you know, that Plotlands place that's always being condemned and stuff?'

Leanne makes a face, then unclips her hair and starts twisting it again, talking with the clip in her mouth. 'Anyway, her mum and my mum had a big falling out over this guy, basically. But now Chantel's mum, my aunty Nicky, right, she's ditched him and Chantel's won the Lottery and they're coming to live at number 14, like, next Tuesday. Chantel's like, "Oh my God, we're going to have *drains!*" They had a cesspit before.'

Julie tries to take in all this information. 'Do they know about number 14?' she asks.

'That's the thing,' says Leanne, putting the clip back in her hair. 'No one's allowed to tell them.'

'Won't they find out?'

'Not if no one tells them.'

Heather comes over and looks at the table Julie's just done. She touches her hair lightly as if she might break it.

'I suppose you want to go on a break,' she says. 'Hello, Leanne.'

'All right, Heather,' says Leanne. 'Hope you don't mind me popping in.'

Heather looks at Julie and smiles. 'As long as we get *some* work done today.' She doesn't really mean it – Heather's really chuffed to have Julie on her shifts. She's only twenty-two and this is the first supervisor position she's ever had. She wants to go into management eventually. She lives with her boyfriend in one of the villages near here. They've got a huge mortgage and Heather's got a pony she's had since she left school. Even though Heather's totally into The Edge and works really hard, Julie always gets the impression that she would rather be with her pony than here.

Leaving her cleaning box on a chair, Julie follows Leanne out the back. The back room at The Edge smells of cigarette smoke. There's also a smell of cold grease, like in the back rooms of every fast-food restaurant. No one would exactly call The Edge fast, but it's the same smell.

Leanne takes out a packet of Lambert & Butler. 'Want one?' she asks Julie.

'Yeah, cheers.' Julie takes one and sits down on a broken chair. 'So they're moving in next Tuesday?'

Leanne leans against the staff lockers. 'Yeah, that's right. And remember not to say anything to Chantel.'

'I won't. Anyway, I probably won't even speak to her.'

'You will. She's having a house-warming. She's inviting the whole street.'

'Oh. Well someone'll tell her, then, won't they?'

'Nah. I'm telling them all not to.'

'She'll find out eventually, though, won't she?'

'Yeah, but then they'll be settled in and stuff.'

Julie's not sure about this logic but says nothing.

'I saw Charlotte Moss the other day,' says Leanne, flicking fag ash into a McDonald's ashtray. She leaves a pause, perhaps for drama. 'I saw her in The Rising Sun.'

'What were *you* doing in The Rising Sun?'

'Looking for Charlotte Moss. It stunk in there. Fucking disgusting.'

Julie frowns. 'Why were you looking for Charlotte Moss?'

'To tell her to keep the hell away from number 14.'

David comes in. He's tall and a bit too thin for his height and moves around like he's a stray cat looking for food. He's from Romford and he's doing a law degree at one of the new universities around here. Everyone agrees he's the nicest chef, not that there's much competition. Once, a customer at The Edge groped one of the waitresses and the manager didn't know what to do. David just went up to the guy, picked him up by his shirt and threw him out into the carpark. Most of the waitresses like David.

He lights a fag with one hand. He's waving the other hand like he's burnt it.

'What's wrong with your hand?' Leanne asks.

'Burnt it,' he says. 'What's this about number 14?' he asks.

Leanne sighs. 'See? It's going to be well hard keeping this quiet.'

'Oh, you mean on your road,' he says. 'Everyone knows about that.'

It strikes Julie that yes, everyone does know about everything around here. It's not that it was in the papers, and it's not even that this is a particularly small town. Around here everyone works in shops and there's nothing to do except serve customers and talk about disaster, tragedy, and loss.

Mark Davies was the first person Julie had known who had died. He died last autumn, suddenly, in Lakeside, from a brain haemorrhage. He'd lived at 14 Windy Close all his life, except for his gap year and his time at university. When he came back from university a year early, having dropped out, he'd had this girl with him: Charlotte Moss. She lived there with him until he died and then she stayed on afterwards, looking after Mark's mother and father and doing the housework. She's actually the only remaining survivor of number 14 Windy Close. Mark's mother went mad, and his father killed himself, right there in number 14, the house opposite Luke's.

After it happened, Julie couldn't stop thinking about Mark. He must have died, just like that, while he was in the middle of thinking about what shop he was going in to next, or what he might like for lunch. He would have had no warning and no control. There would have been nothing he could have done to save himself. It was the most unfair thing Julie'd ever heard of. But also: if Mark could die like that, Julie could die like that too. She couldn't stop thinking about how terrifying his last few seconds must have been. Mark didn't deserve that. But these things are random, aren't they? And her sadness and fear about Mark eventually turned into one single thought: what if she's next? For several years Julie had been approaching life with a mixture of distrust and caution. Mark's death proved she was right.

Leanne stubs out her cigarette. 'She looked a right mess,' she says.

'What, Charlotte?' asks Julie.

'Yeah. And she smelt of that hippy stuff. Patchy-thingy.'

'Patchouli?' says Julie.

'She's well sexy,' says David. He stubs out his fag. 'Laters,' he says, and goes.

'What's she doing now?' Julie asks. She hasn't seen Charlotte for ages.

Leanne makes a face. 'Like I was going to hang around in there and ask her,' she snorts. 'Please.'

'Does David know Charlotte?' Julie asks.

Leanne shrugs. 'Puff-head, isn't he? Knows everyone.'

Heather comes in. 'I think we might have to shut,' she says to Julie. 'We still can't get the tills to work.'

'Can't you just write everything down?' suggests Leanne.

'What do you mean?' says Heather.

Leanne used to be a supervisor at The Edge before she defected to Homebase and then Blockbuster. 'Just make handwritten bills,' she says. 'The waitresses carry their floats anyway, right, so it's not like they have to put cash through the tills. You'll just have to trust them to write down what the customers order, give the orders straight to David on a napkin or whatever, and then put the written-down orders through the till whenever that man gets them working.'

'That could work,' says Heather uncertainly.

'Make sure David makes a note of what he cooks,' Leanne goes on. 'Then you can compare that with the bills the waitresses make and there's no room for them to fiddle the system.'

'I'm the only waitress here,' Julie points out.

'Yes, well,' says Leanne. 'You can't be too careful.'

'I think we might just close,' says Heather.

'Use my system,' says Leanne. 'I promise it'll work.'

'We'd better get back out the front anyway,' Heather says.

'I'm going back to Blockbuster,' says Leanne.

'See you later,' says Julie.

'Will you tell Luke I'll pop round later?' Leanne says.

'Yeah, but I think he might be busy.'

'Busy doing what?'

'I don't know. He said he was doing something tonight.'

'What, in his bedroom?'

'Yeah, of course.' Julie gets up and walks to the door. 'Why don't you ring him?'

'I always get his answerphone,' moans Leanne, following Julie through the door.

Chapter 5

The first time Luke tried to walk outside on his own he was about seven. It had been his favourite threat for a couple of years; the most effective way of blackmailing his mother and making her buy him more books and magazines. *Buy* Whizzer and Chips *for me, Mum.* 'No, Luke, you had two books yesterday.' *I'll walk outside.* 'Don't do this to me, Luke.' *I'll walk outside and I'll die and you'll wish you'd bought it for me.* 'Please, Luke, don't.' His mother always had a squeaky voice, pleading and whiny. And her hands always shook, even when there was nothing to be nervous about.

Eventually, of course, she knew she would have to call his bluff. She phoned a radio phone-in show for advice. 'Your son is spoilt,' the agony aunt told her firmly. 'Stand up to him. Show him who's in control.' So she did. On a sunny day in spring 1982, after one tantrum too many, she said, 'OK, then, walk outside if you want to.'

The argument took place in the kitchen on a weekday when Luke's father was in Yorkshire. Luke's mother called his bluff in the dark, orange kitchen, the morning sun turning everything orange through the heavy curtains, the dust hanging in the air, orange, like everything else.

Luke's small body felt even smaller.

His mother said, 'Go on, then, kill yourself. See if I care.'

He started to cry. He felt alone and cold; still in his Batman pyjamas, because he'd refused to get dressed.

His mother pointed to the back door. Her hand shook. She repeated her words but they didn't come out properly and she started to cry too. Luke didn't want to upset her, and really wanted a cuddle, not a fight. But he couldn't change his mind now. He would rather have died than let his mother win and have this control over him forever. He felt sick and small, as if he was shrinking. He had to do something before he disappeared altogether. He knew this was his moment of eternity. Nothing mattered beyond this moment; not today or yesterday or his life or anyone else's. He dimly remembered what today had been like before this moment and he wished he was back there but he wasn't. He felt even smaller. Everything around him seemed bigger. He ran the few steps to the back door.

At first it wouldn't open. He pulled at the handle and kicked at the door.

It must have been at the moment his mother realised that he was actually going to do it that she screamed *No!* and started moving towards him. The door opened before she reached him and Luke stumbled out into the spring morning, the air intriguingly cold and fresh, the gravel drive stinging his bare feet. As his mother reached to grab him they both fell. The last thing Luke saw was the amazing blue of the sky, purer than any colour he'd ever seen.

He was unconscious for half an hour. When he woke up in his bedroom, the doctor was there.

It was really crap being seven, wanting to go out and explore and make friends but actually being stuck in a dark, hot house instead. The only friend Luke had – and he was only a half-friend, really, because Luke didn't really like him, and he didn't really like Luke – was Mark Davies from across the road. Mark would come over sometimes with his dad. While Mark's dad and Luke's mum talked downstairs, Mark and Luke would play with the toys Mark brought with him – trucks and cars, mainly – and Mark would fantasise about owning a Scalextrix and Luke would find him slightly boring, but less so than his normal life. So Luke played along with Mark's fantasies, and was Robin while Mark was Batman, and explained time and time again why he couldn't go outside.

Luke spent a lot of time naked, especially during the long, hot, early-eighties summers when it was mainly just him and his mother in the house during the week and some weekends when Bill was at work. It bothered his mother, which was one of the reasons he did it, but she didn't challenge him very much after the kitchen-door incident. Luke hated his nylon and polyester clothes, even if he could make fireworks from them in the dark. It hurt, anyway, when he did that.

All Luke wanted were books and magazines. He needed lots of reading material, typically getting through six or so books a day, but of course he couldn't go to the library to choose his own books, so he had to try to explain to his mother what to get – and then threw tantrums when she failed. He became pretty resourceful. At six, he'd worked out how to phone children's publishers to get their catalogues, so at least he knew which books were coming out. He sometimes told the people who answered the phone (nice ladies, mainly) about not being able to go out, and sometimes they sent him free books, which was brilliant. His mother didn't believe he could read at such a great speed but he didn't care what she thought.

When Luke's dad came home on weekends, Luke would sit on his knee and tell him about the worlds he'd travelled to that week – the Faraway Tree, Narnia, Kirrin Island and all the others. At that age it was easy to travel to the completely imaginary worlds in children's books – it simply became harder as the books became more realistic. By the time they invented issues-based 'teen' fiction, Luke was watching TV more than he was reading anyway. He tried a couple of titles that one of the publishers sent him, but could find no way of understanding the broken families, bully-infested schools and general misery in the books. But when he was seven, books like that didn't exist and Luke had no TV. His world was full of magic.

On Friday nights, Luke's dad would drink a glass of Scotch or two, and the more of the dark-orange liquid he drank, the more interested he'd become in Luke's other worlds.

'You went through a wardrobe?' he'd say. 'Heh heh. Hear that, Jean?'

Luke's mother would sigh and ask when Luke's dad would be ready for his dinner.

The rest of the weekend, Luke would barely see his father, as he'd be busy working on the car, fixing things on the outside of the house or shopping in town with Luke's mother.

'He'll probably grow out of it,' the doctor said to Luke's mother.

'I didn't think people grew out of XP,' said Luke's mother.

'It's not necessarily XP,' he said. 'Remember, we talked about this.'

Luke was listening to the conversation with his eyes shut, pretending not to have come round yet. He didn't want to open his eyes and lose the incredible image of the blue sky he half-saw.

'Yes, but . . .' Jean stammered.

'We just have to wait and see. It could just be childhood allergies.'

Luke never saw that doctor again but for years he couldn't shake the hope that the doctor was right and he'd be able to go out one day. The next doctor he saw, when he was about eleven or so, was a friend of his parents' – Dr Mackay. He seemed excited to have a patient with XP and wrote a paper about Luke which none of the medical or scientific journals published even though he'd been sure they would.

Dr Mackay was still conducting allergen tests when the social worker, Mrs Murray, started visiting. Luke remembers her being a well-meaning lady with a sourness he later realised was just a lack of humour. She asked him questions about his friends, his home tutor, and his hobbies, and Luke said everything was fine because he'd got it into his head that he'd be sent to a home if he didn't say the right thing. Eventually the doctor and the social worker both stopped coming, satisfied that Luke's disease was incurable, that he was comfortable and, crucially for the social worker, that he wasn't likely to commit suicide or go mad.

At sixteen, there was one more doctor's visit, and after a brief examination of Luke's medical records, the doctor signed some forms that meant that Luke started receiving some sort of sickness benefit which he never understood. His mother applied for it, and she still collects it and puts half in the bank for Luke, and takes the rest for rent and food and bills. Occasionally she asks Luke to sign forms that always seem to come in the same A5 brown envelopes.

Luke hasn't seen his father for years. He's not even entirely sure what happened between his parents; all he knows is that one Sunday evening his dad went to Yorkshire and it was a few months before everyone realised he was never coming home again.

And apart from XP, and a couple of colds, Luke has never been ill in his life.

Chapter 6

Mice.

There are eight glass tanks, two stacks of four, in the pet shop window. The pet shop is on the High Street, a couple of doors down from Xoom Clothing, which is where Julie's due to meet David in five minutes. He's persuaded her to come and look at a jacket he's planning to buy. Because they left work early, it's not like Julie could have made an excuse or said she planned something else, because right now she should be plonking Pepperoni Passions on tables and wiping sweaty blobs of salad dressing off plastic tablecloths. And what else is there to do? Luke'll be asleep at this time of day and it's not like Julie has any other friends.

All the mice are asleep, apart from one that's moving around the glass cube with determination. It seems to be making a nest in the far right-hand corner; piling up bits of white stringy bedding probably made in a factory for exactly this purpose. Julie looks at the other tanks: the other mice all have nests in precisely the same corner, which is pretty weird, but then mice are a bit weird – like flies that only fly in geometric shapes.

Julie remembers once opening a cupboard in her old house in Bristol and seeing a biscuit packet with a perfect round hole cut into it. At first she thought it had been made by a machine. She was confused because who'd want to use a machine to make a perfect hole in a packet of Jammy Dodgers? Then she saw it. At the back of the cupboard, in the darkest spot, was a little ball of shredded paper – mainly bits of biscuit packet and most of a greengrocer's paper bag. Julie poked it with her finger, and there was definitely something warm inside, but nothing happened and she was kind of scared. She didn't poke it again. Later that night she saw a small brown creature run across the kitchen floor. The next day the nest was slightly larger, and the rest of the biscuits had disappeared.

Julie watches as the pet shop mouse tries to work out how to drink from the water bottle. She suddenly becomes aware that she is looking at a confined animal. How does she feel about that? Most people would look at an animal in a cage and instinctively feel that it should be set free. But this mouse seems pretty comfortable in the little tank, and seems to have everything it needs: food, water, a bed and some space to run around in. Julie wonders what choice the mouse would make if it was given one, if someone was able to communicate with it and say, 'Hello, mouse, would you like to be set free? It's a dangerous world out there, filled with predators, and you might starve or freeze to death or be eaten by a cat, but at least you'll be free. Alternatively, you could choose to stay in your tank, where you'll be kept safe, and cared for, and fed.' Would that mouse choose freedom, which, in Julie's opinion, is essentially a human concept (does the mouse know it's not free in its cage?) or would it instead think, 'No, my instincts lead me to safety and it's safe in here.' If there were no humans about and the cage was open, would the mouse even run away?

What would you prefer? A comfortable, safe, warm, cosy life in a cage; or an uncertain life of freedom? Julie would choose the cage, she suddenly realises, as long as her cage was safe; and fitted with a computer and modem, say, and satellite TV – and lots and lots of puzzles. She frowns, picturing herself in this comfortable cage. No matter how hard she tries, she can't think of any reason why she wouldn't want to live like that. In fact the vision of such a safe, comfortable life with everything provided for her suddenly makes Julie want to cry. It's so beautiful.

'All right?' says David.

'Oh, hi,' Julie says, blinking and losing her perfect image. 'I didn't see you coming.'

He's emerged from somewhere behind her. Now he's standing next to her looking through the pet shop window, breathing steam all over the glass. It's cold this afternoon, although they did forecast rain on the news this morning.

'What are you looking at?' he asks.

'Mice. I've never really looked at mice before. They're weird.'

David laughs. 'Hey, maybe we could do a raid on the pet shop and set them free.'

'Do you think they'd really want to be set free?' she asks.

'Yeah, of course,' says David. 'What's wrong with you?'

'Nothing. Come on, it's freezing out here.'

Xoom is one of those clothes shops that are kind of dark inside, with moody assistants and £200 price tags. Two local drug dealers own the shop and most of the clientele are already their customers and/or wannabe drug lords themselves; larging it in Stüssy and CP Company or whatever's in fashion now. Julie hasn't been in this shop for a few years but it hasn't changed much.

The men's stuff takes up most of the rail space: shiny shirts and slightly flared jeans and huge, fluffy, hooded tops. There is one rail of girls' clothes, on which there are tiny T-shirts and dresses that you could almost imagine using to dress a doll rather than a person. Julie prefers Miss Selfridge and Top Shop for clothes. Her favourite style, at least to look at, is probably that recycled look with clothes from charity shops. It always looks great in magazines – suede jackets, frayed jeans, wool bags, second-hand jewellery and cowboy boots – but there's no way she could wear something that belonged to a dead person, or, worse, something that someone could actually have died in. Whenever Julie goes into Oxfam, all she can think about is someone crying as they bundle clothes up – a mother usually, crying over her dead daughter's things. The last time she went in, there were rails full of club-wear – rubber dresses, PVC trousers and little sequined tops. These clothes had obviously all belonged to the same person and Julie obsessed for about six months over what must have happened to her.

'All right, mate,' David says to one of the assistants.

'Yo, bro,' he says. He looks at Julie. 'All right?' he says.

Julie looks at him. 'Uh, hi,' she says.

'It's Julie, isn't it?' he asks. 'Haven't seen you for a while.'

David looks confused. 'You know each other?' he asks.

'School,' says Will. 'You used to go around with, um . . .'

'No one,' Julie reminds him. 'I went around on my own.'

Will looks uncomfortable. 'Oh, right,' he says.

David looks weirded-out. Julie knows that as far as he's concerned she's always been a bit of a loner and strange in some way. Maybe he's freaked out to imagine her at school – at the same school as Will, who's one of those guys that other guys seems to adore in a bizarre way, waiting for him to acknowledge them in the street, to nod his head or call out a *Yo! Bro*, or know their name or who their friends are. Maybe David's just shocked because Julie's not trying to be cool with Will. But Julie doesn't want to be cool. She doesn't want to belong to a social group like some sort of ant or insect and text message people and call them *m8* and pretend to do drugs or know the right word for dope (it was 'draw' last time she checked, but that was about three or four years ago). She just wants to be on her own, or with Luke. A glass tank would be pretty good right now but it would have to be the sort of glass you can't see through.

'Didn't you used to be blonde?' asks Will.

'No,' Julie says.

There's silence for a couple of seconds.

'So anyway, what can I do you for, mate?' Will asks David.

Fifteen minutes later, David has a new jacket. It's grey and sort of shiny.

'Do you want to get a drink or something?' he asks Julie.

She looks at her watch. 'I'm not sure . . .'

'Come on, don't be boring.'

Julie looks down at the pavement. 'I like being boring.'

'Yeah, I can see that. Go on. Just a quick one?'

'Oh, all right. Rising Sun?'

David makes a face – it's too grungy to be his kind of place – but they start walking in the direction of The Rising Sun anyway.

Chapter 7

When Luke wakes up it's getting dark. His room has a deep-blue glow, and occasionally, when a car passes outside, there is a yellow streak across his ceiling, a muffled engine sound or the squeal of a fucked clutch. Then nothing. The cul-de-sac is usually quiet – it's one of the reasons for the high house prices around here. But at about four every weekday afternoon, the shift workers at the local industrial estate use it to turn in because you can get on the A12 better going the other way. These cars are like Luke's alarm clock and the approaching darkness is his dawn.

His curtains, which he can open only when it's fully dark, are heavy enough to keep out all the light and most of the shadows. Since about January, though, Luke's been experimenting; leaving a tiny gap in the curtains so that there are more shapes and shadows in the room. He read somewhere that his condition – if it is in fact XP, which no one ever really found out for sure – is dangerous only in direct sunlight and that it would be perfectly acceptable to have his curtains open in the day with special filters on the glass. But Luke's mother told him that was rubbish and made him vow to keep the curtains completely shut. He did, for years, but now something's making him slightly rebellious. Probably this 2001 deadline, this kill-or-cure feeling he's got.

Another day; still alive. Luke's been waking up with headaches lately, that's the only thing. Of course, that could be down to the cable they're installing in the road outside. It's pretty hard to sleep when a load of guys are drilling just beneath your bedroom window.

The air in the room is heavy and stale despite the various air filters and ionisers. After getting out of bed, Luke switches on his fan and starts his exercises, which he hates but still does every day. He doesn't hate the effort, just the empty feeling afterwards, the adrenaline rush that never has anywhere to go. The feeling goes with the territory, he knows that. He knows he's ill, and it could be a lot worse than this – if he was bedridden or contagious or didn't have a TV or computer, *that* really would be hell. This isn't so bad, he knows that.

After Luke ran out of the house for the first time on that bright, cold spring morning, his mother installed window locks and turned the house into a prison, with everything that was lockable firmly locked. If she was going out she usually shut Luke in his room, a practice she reluctantly gave up a year or so later when a neighbour pointed out that it was a fire hazard. After that she went out less often and gave up her nursing job to keep a proper eye on Luke. When Luke threatened to open his curtains and kill himself that way she got his father to paint the outsides of the windows with silver paint, which came off after about a month. Keeping up with Luke's new and sometimes ingenious ways of threatening to kill himself took its toll on Jean, until she had an ingenious idea of her own.

'I think I might kill myself,' she said thoughtfully one night. Luke was about nine. They'd just watched *Dallas*, and everything was normal until she said that.

Luke's eyes filled with tears. 'Mum!' he wailed. 'You can't say that.'

'It's how I feel,' she continued, in a faraway voice, like a radio drama.

Luke started crying. 'Why are you saying this?' he sobbed.

'I think I might gas myself. Or maybe I'll cut my wrists. What do you think?'

'Stop it! Please.'

However much he begged her, she wouldn't stop.

'Maybe I'll chuck myself off the roof. Oh, I know. I could hang myself.'

'Please don't, Mum. I love you.'

'Well . . .' She pretended to think.

'I'll do anything.'

Tipping her head to one side, she pretended to think some more.

'I'll be good,' Luke promised. 'I know I've been difficult . . .'

'Maybe if you give up all this talk of going out . . .'

'I will. I swear.'

'Good. Then I might be able to carry on living. But Luke?'

He looked up at her with big eyes, hoping this was all over. 'Yes, Mum?'

'One more word about going out, and . . .' She paused. Luke's heart squeezed in on itself. 'You know what I'll do, don't you? I won't warn you, I'll just do it. Do you understand?'

'Yes, Mum. I promise I won't say anything ever again . . . I promise. I promise. I promise . . .' His tears prevented him from saying any more. His mother held him as he sobbed, and then she put him to bed with a low-fat chocolate drink and a hug.

It's eggs for breakfast today. After breakfast Luke goes into his en-suite bathroom to wash and shave while his mother airs the room. He hears her moving things about and then the clunk of the window lock and the click as the small window opens. He imagines the cold, clean air entering his room and the bad, hot air leaving. His mother lets the air circulate for five minutes or so before Luke hears the sound of the window closing and the lock being fastened. He has asked his mother to stop locking the window, to trust him to do it or even not lock it at all but she always says that it needs locking and she might as well do it when she airs the room.

After the window lock is fastened, Jean sprays anti-bacterial air-freshener around the room to kill anything that may have come in with the air. Then she goes downstairs to watch TV. Luke waits until he hears the annoying *Countdown* music before he comes out of the bathroom. He tries not to see his mother more than necessary because, lately, he doesn't know what to say to her, and whenever he does say something it's wrong, or she accidentally says something wrong and they end up arguing. Without even thinking about what he's doing he connects to the Internet, just as he does every single day. Maybe if he could talk to his mother in a chat room things wouldn't be so hard. In chat rooms you can use emotions to show that you're only joking, or that you mean something in a nice way, or simply to prevent people from misunderstanding and, ultimately, flaming you. If Luke could pepper his conversations with his mother with happy smiley faces, or cute, regretful unhappy ones, things might be easier. And if he used text rather than speech, his mother could never complain about his 'tone'.

Luke half expects something to have come from Wei, but there's nothing. He scans his Outlook Express inbox. He can see that there are three unread messages in his 'Crap' folder, ten in his 'Mailing List' folder and two in his 'Personal' folder. He clicks on this folder first. One of them is from Leanne and the other is from Charlotte. For a minute, Luke has to think. *Charlotte?* Then he remembers. It must be Charlotte Moss. No one has seen or heard from her for ages. He clicks on her e-mail first.

> Hey,
> Have you heard about number 14? Some trailer-trash cousin of Leanne's has won the Lottery and bought it. Fucking hell. That house is cursed. That whole fucking street is so Jerry Springer – even now I've left. :-) Anyway, I expect you know all about the rich cousin and everything since you're getting jiggy with Leanne. Yuck! (Yes, she told me everything.) What has got into you? I'm coming to this party, by the way. I'll pop in and see you too if that's OK. Sorry I haven't been in touch for ages. Oh – I told a friend about you and he said he'd be in touch. Hope that's OK. Say hi to Jules.
> Charlotte xxx

Then Leanne's:

> Dear Luke
> I have tried to phone you but I can't get any reply. How are you? My cousin Chantel is coming to live at number 14 and no one is allowed to tell her about what happened there. If Charlotte gets in touch with you before I see you can you tell her that too? I did go and see her but she was a bit out of it and I don't think she really understood how important this is.
> I really want to see you, Luke. I'll drop by later today (Friday) after work. I finish at 6.00 p.m.
> Lots and lots of love
> S.W.A.L.K. Leanne

Then another from Charlotte.

> His name's Wei, by the way. He's really nice. C xxx

Chapter 8

Inside The Rising Sun it's dark and damp-smelling and warm. Radiohead's new album is playing loudly. It sounds like videogame music; funny little electronic melodies. There are about ten people in the pub: two guys who always claim they can sort you out with a firearm; three women who have tattoos and piercings and tarot cards and a load of kids at the primary school over the hill; a huddle of four grunge-kids drinking snakebite & blacks; and the homeless guy who sits in here all day, waiting for students to buy him guilt-drinks. Charlotte isn't here, not that it matters.

'You're weird,' says David.

Julie's drinking Coke. She specifically asked for no ice and a straw. She is terrified of ice in drinks in pubs: she's seen too many people scrape up ice with glasses rather than plastic scoops – a practice which is illegal because the glasses often break this way and the glass gets in the drinks. Inexperienced bar staff never know the rules.

By the way David's been looking at her you'd think she was trying to be cute by having a straw. Now he's saying she's weird. He wouldn't really know either way; they hardly worked together before Julie started doing days.

'In what way?' Julie feels in her pocket for the pack of Superkings she picked up in The Edge. They're probably Leanne's.

David studies her as if her weirdness is imprinted on her on a barcode that he could scan if he could find it. 'Eh?' he says.

'In what way am I weird?'

'I don't know. That's what I'm trying to work out. Leanne reckons you dropped out of school. It was some big drama.'

'She can't talk. She dropped out of college in the first year.'

Julie's heard rumours that David isn't doing so well on his degree course. One time she overheard him telling the general manager of The Edge, Owen, that he needed a couple of days off to do an essay or he was going to get chucked out. Owen said no. When David came out of the office his eyes were red. Julie had started liking him a bit more after that. Previously he'd just been another annoying chef as far as she was concerned, making jokes about anal sex and blow jobs the whole time, asking each waitress if they reckoned they could take his cock *and* balls in their mouth at once. Mind you, all the chefs piss around like that, in the same way that all the waitresses talk about cystitis and diets and how many calories there are in a small pizza. It's just part of the job. David always was the nicest chef, even if he did always seem like he was up to something.

'You're still weird,' David says. He makes direct eye contact with Julie but immediately looks away as if it's uncomfortable. He turns the beer mat on the table through ninety degrees three times. Two hundred and seventy degrees, Julie thinks.

'How, though?' she asks.

'Well, all that lot at The Edge seem so retarded. You seem different but I can't work out why that would be.' He looks at her again. 'You're not a student. Only students and retards work at The Edge, or so I thought. And you aren't either of those, and you don't seem to want to leave The Edge and do anything else. Why is that?'

Julie smiles. 'Maybe I am weird,' she says.

David frowns. 'Huh?'

'Isn't that reason enough?'

'Not really. Come on. How long have you been at The Edge?'

'Um, I suppose about three years or so. Something like that.' Julie starts twisting a section of hair around her fingers, then realises that she read in a magazine that this is something you can do to let a bloke know you fancy him, so she stops, and plays with the straw in her drink instead.

'And you're not looking for another job or waiting to go to college or anything?'

'Nope.'

'For fuck's sake, Julie. Why? Do you like it or something?'

She shrugs. 'Yeah, kind of. I dunno. It's simple, you know. I go there and it's not like it's a real effort or anything, because it's pretty close to where I live, and when I get there I can do a good job without it being too demanding. I like the customers and the other people that work there, and it doesn't, you know, take over my life or anything. When I get home I can go and chat on the Internet, or see my friends, or listen to music and it's not like I'm having to prepare a report for a scary boss or worry about having to go abroad for a meeting or whatever. Life should be a lot simpler than people make it.' She fiddles with her straw some more. 'People sometimes forget that work is just something you do to get money. It's not your life. If you spend your life working or getting qualifications to work, or just stressing about it generally, you totally waste it.'

'Really? Is that what you think?'

'Life isn't a videogame, is it? It's not about how many points you can get or how many possessions you can collect, or how many levels you can complete before you die. Life's this real thing that everyone wastes and . . .'

'You're not wasting yours by working at The Edge?'

'No, I'm not. It gives me time I use for other stuff.'

Julie can feel that her face is going red. She didn't mean to say all this.

'You don't even like pizza, do you?' David says.

'Not really.'

They both laugh.

'Leanne said you were a freak.'

Julie smiles. 'I bet those were her exact words.'

'Yeah.' David frowns. 'She said you were a freak and she told me about this guy . . . Your next-door neighbour or something. He never goes out.'

'Luke? Yeah. So?'

'I thought you were just shy, or boring, or quiet or whatever.'

'Thanks.'

'Yeah, but then I'm hearing about this weird neighbour, and you dropping out of school, and now all these mental reasons why you work at The Edge . . .'

'Yeah?'

David stops talking and plays with a beer mat. 'I dunno.'

Julie feels a bit like she's being interviewed by the worst interviewer in the world, for a purpose neither of them is really sure about.

Then she sees the expression on David's face.

She frowns. 'This isn't actually about me, is it?'

Chapter 9

'Move over, Luke.'

Leanne's been sitting in Luke's armchair for the past fifteen minutes, talking about Chantel, cesspits and Charlotte. Now she's zeroing in on his bed.

'I, uh . . .' Luke looks at the rest of his bed. How can he convince her that there isn't any room? He crosses his legs as a preliminary measure. He's wearing a nylon T-shirt he ordered from some clubbing website last year and a black fleece top with black fleece tracksuit bottoms. The top and bottoms are new – they're only about £5.99 each from Matalan, and although he doesn't usually like it when his mother buys him clothes, he's happy for her to buy him as much cheap fleece as possible. What a great invention. So soft, so comfortable, and totally artificial. In fact, he's hardly been able to listen to Leanne while she's been talking because he's been busy secretly stoking the arms of his new top. This material is addictively soft.

'Don't be shy,' Leanne says. 'It's not like I've never been on your bed before.'

She's been on it – or, more accurately, in it – seven or eight times in the last couple of months. She decided she fancied Luke some time at the beginning of the summer and pursued him relentlessly. He was flattered at the time. Now it feels like it's all gone a bit too far.

Leanne crawls onto the bed next to Luke and sits with her legs out in front of her, crossed at the ankles. They are tanned and shiny, with little tiny pinprick-holes all over them that you can only see up close.

'What's this music?' she asks.

'*Dark Side of the Moon*. Do you like it?'

Luke doesn't really like it. He's hoping Leanne won't either and that she'll go. The last thing Luke feels like is sex. He's thinking about Wei and the possibility of being healed. On TV sitcoms characters don't tell someone to go; they drive them out with amusing tactics. That's what Luke's trying to do with the music. It hasn't worked yet.

She cocks her head. 'Hasn't this got something to do with the *Wizard of Oz*?'

Luke strokes his arms again. 'Has it?' he says. He's also got new socks today, also 100 per cent polyester. They're thick and fluffy and when he walks around on his floor with them on it makes the floor feel different – spongy like a cake, which is wonderful when you've had the same floor to walk on for over twenty years.

'Yeah, I think so. Unless I've got it muddled up with something else.'

Glad of the excuse to get off the bed, Luke pads across to his computer and types in a URL. 'Yeah,' he says after a few moments looking. 'Pink Floyd wrote it as a sort of alternative soundtrack or something. Oh, hang on, here it says they didn't, but apparently it still works as a soundtrack. How do you know this?'

'We're having a *Wizard of Oz* week at Blockbuster next week. It's like a special promotion. Lloyd – that's the new manager; I've told you about him before – he's doing loads of special promotions: all with, like, classic film themes. Except we're all supposed to call films *movies* now but I keep forgetting. Anyway, I didn't know how many fil– uh, *movies* are, like, remakes of the *Wizard of Oz*. I don't even know why someone would want to use someone else's story for their film. But anyway, that's how I know.'

'Cool,' says Luke, tapping away on the keyboard. Leanne sits there examining her split ends until he stops.

'Luke, did you just go on the Internet?'

'Yeah. Why?'

'You didn't dial in.'

'I've got my own line, and an unlimited-connection deal, so I leave it connected all the time.'

'No wonder I can't ever get through to you on the phone.' Leanne says. 'I thought you were avoiding me.'

'Just e-mail me if you want to get in touch. I've told you that before.'

'But what if I want to make a booty call?' giggles Leanne.

'A what?' says Luke.

'A booty call. You know.'

'That song by All Saints?' Luke sings: '*It's just a booty call.*'

'Yeah. The song's about booty calls.'

'Which are?'

'God, Luke. It's when you phone someone because you want sex. But it's, like, sex in a fun way; not in a commitment-sort-of-a-way. Like casual sex.'

'So you want to be able to call me to ask for casual sex?'

'Not when you put it like that.'

'Oh.'

She sighs. 'I *so* don't know what I see in you sometimes.'

Luke wonders where Julie is. 'So, what other promotions are you doing at Blockbuster?' he asks Leanne.

Leanne's pouting. 'I don't know.'

'Are you cross with me?'

'No.'

She obviously is.

'I'm sorry I didn't know what a booty call is,' Luke says, sitting next to her again.

'Will you stop going on about it. I'm embarrassed enough.'

'Oh. Sorry. Um . . . Shall I put the TV on?'

'OK. Have you got satellite yet?'

'No. I told you I'm not allowed it.'

'So is it just normal TV, then?'

'Yeah. But *Top of the Pops* is on.'

'Great,' mutters Leanne.

Chapter 10

When Julie walks through the back door of number 17 Windy Close, Luke's mum is cooking in the kitchen.

'Hello, Jean,' says Julie.

'Julie,' says Jean sharply.

'What's wrong?' asks Julie. 'Is Leanne here?'

'I'd give them a minute if I were you,' says Jean. She puts up with Luke's sex life but it obviously makes her uncomfortable. 'Cup of tea?'

Julie shakes her head. The kitchen smells like gravy.

'I might just go up anyway,' she says. 'Take my chances.'

'Common little slut,' Jean says, and Julie knows she's talking about Leanne.

'Hello, Julie,' says Leanne when Julie walks into the bedroom. 'Fancy seeing you here.'

Leanne's sitting on the bed and Luke's in his armchair looking like he's got new clothes. There's some weird music playing.

'What's this?' asks Julie.

'Pink Floyd,' says Luke, grinning. 'We watched *Top of the Pops* but now there's some gardening programme on. Leanne didn't like it.'

'Can't we watch *The Bill*?' Leanne asks.

'No,' says Luke. 'I already told you. I can't follow *The Bill*.'

'Can I check my e-mail?' Julie asks, sitting in Luke's computer chair.

'Haven't you been home yet?' asks Leanne.

'No, I went to The Rising Sun with David.'

Leanne raises an eyebrow. 'You and *David*, eh?'

'No,' says Julie firmly. 'Not *me and David*.'

'Isn't it about time you got laid?'

Luke laughs. Julie sort of smiles. 'Yeah, I suppose it is, really.'

'Well, you keep your hands off my Luke.'

Luke turns away, making an oh-my-god face.

'I seem to have managed it for the past fifteen years, Leanne,' Julie says. 'But then again, if I got really desperate . . .'

'Stop trying to wind me up. Luke, tell her.'

But Luke's still trying not to fall off his chair laughing. There's a ding from the computer. 'E-mail,' says Luke. 'Better see what it is, Jules.'

Julie's been looking at her Hotmail account. There's an e-mail from Luke saying: *Help! Where are you? Come and rescue me from Leanne.* She grins, closes the browser and sees that something has just been filtered into Luke's 'Personal' inbox. 'Charlotte,' Julie says. 'Shall I open it?'

'*Charlotte?*' says Leanne. 'Are you two still in touch with her?'

'I haven't heard from her in ages,' says Julie.

'Me neither,' says Luke. 'Until today. She sent me a couple earlier.'

'Yes, well, it is Friday the thirteenth,' Leanne says.

'Leanne!' says Julie.

'Sorry. Anyway, I'm going home,' says Leanne, getting off the bed and smoothing down her skirt. 'Have you got Charlotte's e-mail address? I think I might e-mail her to, you know, impress on her how important it is for her to stay away for a while.'

'She's already stayed away for a year, though,' Julie points out. 'If you hadn't said anything she probably wouldn't ever have come back. It's not like she's got happy memories of living here. But I bet you've wound her up now and she'll want to come and see what's going on. You know what Charlotte's like.'

'Yes, well,' says Leanne. 'I'd still like to e-mail her.'

'I'll give her your address if you want,' Luke suggests.

'Yeah,' says Julie. 'We'd better not give her address out without asking her first.'

Leanne gives Julie a look and leaves.

'I miss Charlotte,' says Luke, after Julie's read him the e-mail. It said: *By the way, I also forgot to say I'm doing yoga now. It's really cool.*

'Yeah, me too.' Julie minimises Outlook Express and turns around. 'Leanne is so mental.'

'Leanne's scared of people like Charlotte.'

'What did she say in her other e-mails?'

'Not much, just stuff about Leanne, and this party and everything.'

Julie looks down at her fingers. 'I looked for her today, in The Rising Sun.'

'What, Charlotte? Really?'

'Yeah. She wasn't there.'

'Why were you looking for her? Has she e-mailed you?'

Julie shrugs. 'No. I haven't heard from her for ages. I don't know why I was looking for her really. Probably because I was talking about her with Leanne and then I saw these mice, and this guy from school and . . . I just wondered how she was doing, I suppose.' Julie is silent for a moment.

'You haven't been to The Rising Sun for years,' says Luke. Julie used to go to The Rising Sun with Charlotte and Mark. She hasn't been there since Mark died.

'I know. It wasn't as weird as I thought it would be.'

'Why did you go there, though? Were you just looking for Charlotte?'

'No. I told you, I went with David.'

Luke looks surprised. This isn't the sort of thing Julie normally does.

'Who is David?' he asks.

'One of the chefs. He's doing a law degree or something.'

'Why did you go for a drink with him? Do you, you know . . . ?'

'What, fancy him? No. Don't be stupid.'

'So how come . . . ?' Luke says.

Julie shrugs and swivels around absentmindedly on the computer chair. 'We had to shut early at The Edge and he asked me to go into town and help him choose a jacket. Then we went for a drink.' She stops swivelling and frowns. 'It was a bit weird, actually.'

Since Leanne left, Luke's ditched his weird music and now the TV is on. When the BBC News starts, there's a report about a huge flood in Uckfield, East Sussex. Apparently some schoolchildren were performing 'Captain Noah and his Floating Zoo' when the heavens opened, flooding the small town.

'Very biblical,' comments Luke.

He and Julie stop talking to listen to the report.

'So what was weird?' Luke asks when it finishes.

'What, about David? Um . . . Well . . . To be honest I thought he was trying to pull me at first, especially since he kept asking all these questions, like he was trying to get to know me in five minutes or something . . . Then it seemed like he just wanted to talk about how weird I am – Leanne told him loads of stuff, apparently – and about you and stuff. And then he just completely freaked me out. He told me something . . .'

'Which was?'

'Well, he's this normal, nice guy . . . And we'd just been shopping at Xoom and he always seems all cool and together and everything . . . You know, like, just *healthy* and young and stuff. Anyway, after we'd established how weird I am, which, incidentally, I didn't enjoy at all, he looked at me and told me that he's um . . . He's got cancer.'

'Fucking hell. Cancer of what?'

'The testicles. He found out a few months ago or something, and he's had treatment but they're not sure yet if it's spread. He hasn't told anyone about it – not even his parents. He knew he had to tell someone but of course all the guys David knows are insensitive apes, and he doesn't know any women apart from his ex, who hates him, and his sister, who's in the middle of a divorce and stuff – oh, and Leanne, and it's not like you'd tell her anything confidential – so when he found out I was weird he decided to tell me.'

'What, just because you're weird? I don't get it.'

'He probably thought someone else might laugh, or tease him.'

'They wouldn't, though, would they?'

'Of course they would. People around here are pigs. I think he wanted to find someone who was similarly afflicted, and then when he couldn't find anyone who was actually dying or terminally ill, he chose me, because I'm weird, and around here that's almost the same as being terminally ill, and I suppose because I don't have anyone to tell and because he probably thinks I'm extra sensitive because I'm a loner and, well, just *weird*.'

'What does cancer of the testicles involve?' Luke asks.

'I don't know. Let's look it up on the Internet.'

Dawn's not there when Julie goes home. She sometimes is around late at night, because she's got some sort of insomnia. Dawn says it's stress but what's stressful about making sandwiches for a living?

Julie's father has been married to Dawn for about five years now but Julie still feels funny around her. Maybe it's to do with not growing up with someone, never seeing them naked, never having them read you bedtime stories . . . And then having to pretend, as an adult, that you are related. When Julie's mother still lived here, the house had a bohemian edge; purple walls and second-hand furniture. Dawn got rid of all that when she moved in. Now the sitting room looks like something out of a mid-nineties Argos catalogue, with display cases, mass-produced ornaments and those chairs that go up, down, backwards and forwards, like the ones Joey and Chandler have on *Friends*. The whole room's designed for optimum TV viewing: comfortable chairs all facing the TV, footrests, occasional tables and about three different universal remote controls.

Julie picks up one of the remote controls and presses the number 3. There's a chat show on. The host is talking to a man who is in a relationship with his ex-wife's sister's child, who is sixteen. The man is about forty. He left his wife for her sister's daughter. He is sitting there holding hands with the girl, and her mother is sitting next to them.

'How could you do this to the family?' the girl's mother asks her.

'You can't choose who you fall in love with,' she replies.

They bring on the man's daughter, who is about seventeen.

'Why did you take my dad away?' she asks forlornly.

'You can't choose who you fall in love with,' repeats the girl.

Everyone hates her. Julie can't help feeling sorry for

her. She's never met the girl – an art student, apparently – who helped break up her own family. She could never hate her, either; it's not like it would be fair to hate the girl. This hasn't stopped Julie wondering about her, though. She went to Ireland, apparently.

'He'll beat you like he beat me,' says the ex-wife.

It's time for bed but Julie's not tired, and this chair's too comfortable. She sits here every day after coming home from Luke's, like *déjà vu* or a recurring dream. Every night it's hard to get up from the chair. Every night Julie gets sucked into late-night TV and thinks she may as well have stayed at Luke's for an extra hour. But even if she did stay for longer, she'd still sit here for an hour after getting home. It's her routine.

Chapter 11

When Julie wakes up on Saturday, something weird happens. *One day*, she thinks, *I'm not going to wake up. The world will go on and I won't be here.*

Her body does something peculiar in response to this thought. It seems to shrink from the inside, and with a little fizz and a little pop in her stomach, Julie immediately wants to cry. She feels like a little girl again.

She can't even sit up; she just lies there in bed feeling disorientated. All her life, Julie's seen death as failure: failure to be careful; failure to eat the right things; failure to notice that fishbone or that strange man following you or the car coming too fast down the road you're about to cross. It's always been as though life was an equation you could solve, or a multiple-choice test that, if you got all the answers right, would go on forever.

Is life a test? That's what Julie was taught at school. She remembers her RE teacher, a little lady with white hair, explaining how God tests people – how bad things might happen to you but they're just a test and if you pass you can go to Heaven. Somewhere during her childhood, Julie stopped believing in Heaven and God, but she still retained the idea that life was somehow a test that would just carry on until you failed. On some level Julie thought that if you just kept making the right decisions, you could live forever. This wasn't conscious thought. But in any case, it's a thought she suddenly doesn't have any more. She could do with something comforting in her unconscious but it's too late. She's just realised that there's no such thing as immortality.

Julie thought she had death under control but she doesn't. She thought that, if she drove slowly, avoided motorways, didn't eat food with bones, never went down dark alleyways and never took risks, she could live forever. But now she understands: she's going to die whatever she does. She's an organism, like a worm or an aphid, and organisms die. One day she's not going to be able to control her existence because she literally will not exist any more.

When Julie was about twelve her mother's friend Rosa was diagnosed with a terminal disease. Julie picked up that much from overhearing her mother on the phone to various friends from the poly but she never worked out what disease Rosa actually had. A few weeks later Rosa left her husband. Then she moved in with Julie's family.

Helen and Rosa decided between them that the disease could be cured with herbs used by tribal cultures, and meditation and cannabis. Keeping Rosa alive became a twenty-four-hour occupation and it seemed like every time Julie went into the kitchen her mother was blending yet another high-potency drink. Either that or Rosa was lying on the table smoking a joint while Julie's mother stood there giggling and trying to remember how to balance Rosa's chakras. The one thing Julie could never understand was the way they seemed to be having so much fun all the time. Weren't you supposed to be sad when someone was dying?

In the end Julie's dad got pissed off with having Rosa around and said that although he felt sorry for her his house wasn't a hospice or a tribal meditation centre. He took Julie to stay with his parents for a few days, and when they got back Rosa was gone. Julie never found out what happened to her, or if all the herbs and potions worked.

Now she thinks about it she realises she'd always assumed that they had worked. The whole process had seemed so scientific at the time (although obviously, now Julie looks at it with grown-up eyes, it wasn't). But mainly it seemed that you couldn't try that hard at something and fail. It wouldn't be fair. Julie's RE teacher taught her that God rewards hard work. Even though Julie stopped believing in God ages ago she still felt that hard work should be rewarded – not by a made-up man in a beard, but at least by the results. You couldn't work hard and have no results, could you? That's science: fuel in, energy out. Energy doesn't just disappear; it creates change. So if you wanted to live, and you wanted it enough, you could make it happen. People who died clearly just didn't want to live that much. As a child, Julie wasn't scared of cancer or MS or AIDS, because she knew that if you tried hard enough, you could make yourself better.

That's why Julie's devoted her life to avoiding accidents. Car accidents, plane crashes, choking on a fishbone, getting stuck in a tall building that catches fire, accidental poisoning, food allergies, Toxic Shock Syndrome. The theory: you take away risk and end up with a non-risk activity. That's maths. But now Julie realises that life isn't a non-risk activity or even a low-risk activity. Life ends in death no matter what you do. It's high risk.

She manages to sit up. She looks at all the mess in her room and imagines it all being boxed up and thrown away. Her books and clothes would probably be sent to Oxfam and the rest would just get thrown out and end up in some landfill somewhere. Julie imagines all her pieces of paper becoming pulp and her pencils decomposing. Then she sees all the plastic things in her room. They're not biodegradable. And then she realises that her plastic ruler, her biros and her calculator will actually exist for longer than she will. They're not biodegradable. She is. When she's dead and forgotten her ruler and pens and her calculator will still exist. They're artificial. They never lived; they can't die. When Julie dies the rest of the world will carry on and she'll never get to see it. And her calculator will still be there at the bottom of some pit somewhere but no one will ever use it again. It won't work any more and the metal parts will have rusted away but the place on the plastic where she carved her name with a compass will never disappear. This is the saddest thought she's ever had.

Julie imagines telling Luke about her revelation, and she sees him laughing.

'You thought about death?' he's saying. 'Hey, what a surprise.'

But this isn't the way Julie normally thinks about death. She goes straight over.

Luke comforts Julie while she cries.

'It'll be OK,' he says, stroking her hair.

'I don't want to die,' she says.

'You won't die until you're very old. I promise.'

'But I'll be old before I know it and . . .'

'Old people don't mind dying,' says Luke. 'They're prepared for it.'

'What, the ones on TV, you mean?'

Luke's face falls. He moves away from Julie. 'I . . .'

'Oh, God, I'm sorry,' Julie says. 'Luke, I'm so sorry.'

'It's not my fault I've only got the TV. I do try to understand life.'

'I know.'

'I want to go out and discover all this myself.'

'I know.'

'I hate the way everything I know is filtered through that fucking glass screen.' He points at his TV. 'Or that one.' He points at his computer. 'Fucking, goddamn screens. I hate it, Julie.'

Now Julie comforts Luke. He doesn't cry, though. He seems to be trying to find the right words to say something.

'At least we're not like David,' he says, in the end. 'Poor David.' And then Luke does start to cry. 'Poor David,' he keeps saying. He doesn't even know David but that doesn't seem to matter.

'We're going to get you out of here,' says Julie softly. 'We'll find a way.'

Chapter 12

On the day her A levels started, Julie still wasn't sure what she was going to do about all her university offers. Her dad had been pleased; her mum was thrilled – separately, obviously, since they were no longer together when the offers all came along.

Julie was eighteen, and still at that stage where every detail of her education could still be monitored. She knew that if she got her predicted four As for her A levels she'd have very little control over her future. As if she was one of the molecules she studied in chemistry, everybody would watch what she did next, and *help*, while she weighed up her options and chose which university to go to. Her parents would help her prepare for going away; her dad would give her financial advice, and her mum might help her pack, or at least give her a lecture on being a successful, strong, in-control woman. Her dad would drive her to the university, not allowing her to drive herself in the clapped-out Mini, and her mum might wave, if she was there.

She sat down to her first exam – physics – imagining this moment. All she could see was Luke at the window, the same way he'd been when she first saw him, waving goodbye to her. That song, 'Say Hello, Wave Goodbye', had come to her as she looked at the unopened physics paper and she'd lost herself in the lyrics as they came into her head. She'd never even realised she knew the lyrics to that song. Julie loved exams, and she'd studied for this one for two years. But she failed it on purpose, because there wasn't anything else she could do.

At first, failing the exams was difficult. She'd revised like mad – not that she needed to, and it would have been easy for Julie to get As in all her subjects. It was far harder to fail pitifully, to quell her urges to impress the examiner and do her best, things she'd always excelled at in the past. But she had to fail. If she failed she could be there for Luke. If she failed, she could get her life back and breathe again, rather than live through the shallow-breathing head-dizzying hell of student grants and halls of residence and other people and everyone being so proud but expecting so much. Julie knew she was doing the right thing. In some warped way she knew she'd be moving back on the right side of the microscope if she did this. She felt like a hero. She had to feel like that, because it was the only thing that gave her the courage to do what she did.

By mid-June, Julie had thrown away her future. She still had the last chemistry and maths exams to go but what she'd already done – her life's great work – was enough to ruin all her chances of a place in any scientific department of any higher-educational institution in the country. Each time Julie failed another exam, she walked out of the exam room defiant, rebellious, and feeling only slightly sick. Her failure was her secret, for the time being, and she sank into it like a huge blanket, comforting and secure. The only times this feeling evaporated were on the horrible, chilling mornings when she'd wake up and think it had all been a bad dream; that she'd just woken up from a nightmare in which she was throwing her future away. But instead of waking up and finding it was all only a dream, she was waking up to find that the nightmare hadn't been a dream at all; it was actually her life.

Every morning during the exam period Julie would see an image of her mother, colourful and proud on

Greenham Common, or in her old polytechnic student bar, talking about feminism and education and how proud she was to have a daughter who was brave and strong and who could run the world one day if she wanted. She'd see her mother and know she should be succeeding for her but then she'd remember that her mother was the one who'd left her, right in the middle of her last year at school, and that she couldn't care if she'd done that. Maybe failing would make her care again but anyway, perhaps in the end Julie's mother didn't matter to her as much as her only friend, who could look out of the window only at night, and probably wouldn't even be able to see her off if she did leave to go to university because she'd have to leave in the day, like normal people do.

For a few years after the exams, Julie went to imaginary evening classes in her head just before she dropped off to sleep and got the four As that she deserved. In the dreams, she did it in secret, just for herself, so she could go to university once Luke was cured. In her head, a man in a white coat came to her front door one day and demanded to know what happened to her all those years ago – the brightest applicant he'd ever encountered. In the fantasy, she cried into his shoulder and explained that she'd deliberately failed her exams because her friend needed her, and he was so shocked, so stunned, so impressed by her admission, that he demanded that she accept an offer to do research at his institution, which was always either Oxford or Cambridge, right away. When Julie said she still wouldn't go because of Luke, the man insisted that Luke came too, so that he could be studied, cured and ultimately set free.

But the only person who ever came to Julie's door was the postman, and all he ever brought her were catalogues that she didn't want, which she only got because she couldn't say no to the women with the clipboards on the High Street.

Perhaps the worst thing was that her parents weren't totally shocked when Julie failed. She'd spent every day since her exams crying, certain she'd done the right thing but feeling inexplicably sentimental, already missing the future she would never have. She knew that when she picked up the envelope from the school, her life would change – for the better – and everyone would leave her alone. She had done the right thing, hadn't she?

It was too late. By the time the results came, Julie's certainty was stuck to her like a frozen smile and she couldn't question it any more. When she showed the contents of the envelope to her father, he just shook his head and said, 'I'll run you into town on Monday and we'll find you a job.' Her mother had looked at her father in a strange way and looked at Julie and looked at her hands and said, eventually, 'Julie can find her own job, can't you?' And that was pretty much that.

And Julie was free.

Chapter 13

By Monday morning, the tills at The Edge are working again.

Lunchtime is quieter than usual on the whole retail park and Julie's pretty bored by the time Leanne comes over at about three. It's raining so hard that Leanne's usually perky blonde hair is hanging in spiky tendrils around her face when she walks into the restaurant. Julie's dying for a fag but she finishes topping up the salad bar while Leanne talks about Chantel, who's arriving tomorrow.

'. . . totally fucked with all the floods,' she's saying.

'What?' says Julie. She's been thinking about David all day, and his testicles, and the cancer inside them. It's the first time she's been able to think about a disease without being terrified she might get it herself. It's a weird feeling. David must be so scared. It's horrible.

'Had to come a totally different route and everything.'

'What did?'

'The removal van, stupid.'

Heather comes out of her office. 'Julie?' she says.

'Yeah?' says Julie, tipping blue-cheese dressing into its little pot.

'Can you come in here for a minute?'

'Can't she go on a break?' says Leanne.

'It won't take a minute,' says Heather. 'Then she can go on a break.'

Heather's office isn't really her office at all. She shares it with the other supervisors and managers at The Edge.

As a result, the room has an anonymous atmosphere, like a waiting room or a bus stop. There's a lot of clutter on the single desk, and bits of Edge uniform lying around – blue T-shirts and braces – mostly still in plastic wrappers. Heather gestures for Julie to sit down opposite her at the table.

'OK,' she says. 'I've got a little test for you.'

She opens the drawer and pulls out something that looks like a job application.

'What's this?' Julie asks.

'A test, like I said.'

'OK.' Julie likes tests. 'Cool.'

'Aren't you going to complain?' says Heather.

'What? No. Why?'

Heather shrugs. 'All the others did.'

'Oh.' Julie looks at the test. 'Do you want me to do it now?'

'Please. I've got to stay here and watch, to make sure you don't cheat.'

'OK.'

'It's not that I think you would – or even really that you could, because it's not that sort of test, but still, those are the rules.'

'OK.'

Julie takes her pen out of her bum-bag – heavy with her float – and opens the test paper. Most of the questions on the test are about food hygiene, food and drink preparation, customer service and The Edge rules. They're all multiple choice. Julie finishes the test in about seven minutes.

'I'm done,' she says to Heather, who's reading a magazine.

'Blimey,' says Heather, startled. 'It wasn't some sort of race.'

'I wasn't trying to . . .'

'You can go on a break now,' she says, sighing. 'Tell David to watch the restaurant.'

David's hardly said a word to Julie all day, as if the conversation they had never happened. She hasn't known what to say to him, so it's been a pretty odd day. He hasn't even told any sex jokes, or quoted any Eminem lyrics, or anything. He's just had the radio on in the kitchen, and has turned it up whenever any cheerful pop song comes on.

'So how's it all going?' Julie asks Leanne, once they're out in the back room.

'All right,' says Leanne. 'I'm moving on.'

'Moving on?'

'Yeah. I'm going to tell Luke it's definitely over.'

'Why?'

'Well, we can never go out anywhere. And he's been distant lately, too, you know, totally wrapped up in his own world.' She sighs. 'It's hard getting through to him when he's like that.'

'Oh, I see.' Julie doesn't know what else to say. Leanne gives her a Lambert & Butler. She lights the cigarette and gets dizzy instantly. She hasn't had one for about four hours.

'I'm going out on the pull with Chantel later,' Leanne says.

'I thought you were saying she'd been held up in the floods?'

'Nah.' Leanne draws on her cigarette. 'Removal company has, though. Chantel came early and left her mum to get on with it. She's been hiding out in a hotel in Shenfield while they sort out all the stuff. Not that they're bringing much of it, of course, it's mainly her gran's stuff they're keeping for sentimental reasons. Everything else is being chucked out, and they've got this designer working on the new house ready for them to move in, and Chantel's like, "Now I'm a millionaire I'm not helping the removal men move my stuff; I just want to go in there when it's all done." I'd be the same. I hate moving.'

As far as Julie knows, Leanne's never moved.

'What's she like?' Julie asks.

'She used to be really fat,' says Leanne. 'I don't know. She's all right.'

'Is she nice?'

'You'll see tomorrow, won't you?'

David sticks his head around the door. 'Heather says can you come out?' he says to Julie. 'I've got to do a test or something.'

'Sure,' says Julie.

Leanne puts out her fag and goes back to Blockbuster.

Julie's meeting Charlotte Moss after work. It'll be the second time she's socialised with someone other than Luke and Leanne in one week, which is pretty remarkable considering that the last time she went out so much was before Mark died. Since their little group – Mark, Charlotte, Julie and Luke – broke down completely, Julie's hardly been out at all.

The e-mail Charlotte sent Julie, late on Friday night, was so chatty that it almost seemed as though nothing had happened. But then Charlotte's the sort of person who'd send a '*Hey, nice to see you yesterday*' e-mail even if she was referring to the day you told her you'd thought seriously about killing yourself.

Chapter 14

While Luke sleeps he can't help but hear the day outside. He has, at most, two clear hours of uninterrupted sleep each night, then, inevitably, when the world starts without him, he finds himself half-dreaming of birds, doorbells, vacuum cleaners, pneumatic drills and cars. He almost wakes when he hears the little bleep from his computer each time an e-mail comes through or the tone that tells him he's been disconnected from the Internet. Each time this happens, he opens his eyes and through his thick, hot, nylon head he wants to get up and check out what's going on but he can't because he's nocturnal, because although he probably wouldn't instantly fry if he got up in the morning, it just wouldn't feel right.

On Monday morning Luke's semi-unconscious dreams are enhanced by a new group of sounds that he hasn't heard very often in his life – the sounds of someone moving into the street. At what must have been about eight o'clock something very large with a deep, growling engine pulled into Windy Close. Since then there has been a lot of banging and male voices and counting to three – and the rain, of course, which hasn't really stopped since Friday night.

Usually, Luke plans his day around what's on TV, filling the rest of the time until Julie turns up with Internet chats, keeping up with his newsgroups and checking his e-mail in between the times it automatically checks itself, which is once every five minutes. Today Luke has no plans. After breakfast, he reads a bit more of his incomprehensible book while he waits for Wei to phone. He didn't give a time, and Luke forgot to ask for one. Luke barely manages to go to the toilet all day, thinking the call will come the minute he does. He doesn't get dressed, either. Frustratingly, he also can't connect to the Internet, or his phone will be engaged when Wei calls.

The next chapter of the book, after the one with the factory setting (tiled floors, broken fans, sewing machines, women with babies on their hips, tyrannical supervisors, men with guns, mosquitoes), features a woman wearing something called a 'sarong'. Luke can't look this up on the Internet, so he spends the whole chapter thinking it's a hat, until she rips it off to have sex with some guy whose name makes Luke think of fishing and wasps.

The call eventually comes at about 6.00, during a trailer for a TV documentary about the *Big Brother* contestants and what they're doing now. One of the reasons Luke became so obsessed with *Big Brother* over the summer was because it was the first piece of TV he could actually relate to, and because it was so easy for him to follow. He knew what it was like to be trapped in one house, not really knowing what was going on outside, waiting for experiences to be presented to him. He used to hope that something would happen and the last housemates would never leave the house, because then there would always be some people like Luke out there, and it would be like a special soap opera just for him, and he wouldn't feel like such a freak.

When Luke's phone rings, it does so through some software on his computer. He can set it to make animal noises instead of simply ringing, so when Wei calls, the phone roars like a lion, three times.

'Hello?' says Wei, when Luke picks up.

'Hi,' says Luke. 'Wei. Thanks for calling.'

'Have you had a good day?'

'OK. I've been reading.'

'Anything good?'

'Just a novel. It's OK. Hard to follow.'

'Why hard to follow?'

'It has all these places I don't recognise. Also, the story is a bit . . .'

'A bit what?'

'It doesn't seem to flow properly.'

'A non-linear narrative?'

'Something like that. It keeps going into the past, then the future.'

'You should stop reading it.'

'I don't have anything else to do. Well, apart from watching TV – but I'm feeling a bit sick of TV at the moment.'

'You could think, surely?'

'What, and do nothing? I'd go mad.'

Wei laughs. 'I can see how it may seem like that but it may be worth remembering that weaker men than you have endured lifetimes in solitary contemplation with no TV and no friends . . . Just their thoughts. It is possible.'

Luke can't imagine that. 'But surely they go mad?' he says.

'On the contrary. These men – and women – have done the greatest thinking in the world. They consume little – not much food, no entertainment, no sex – but they produce great truths.' Wei laughs softly. 'But you need to go out and experience life before you can learn and think to that extent. You have to see the world you are thinking about. And anyway, maybe you don't want to spend your life learning. Maybe you want to climb mountains. The world also needs mountain climbers.

There's that saying: *If everyone was a thinker, who would fetch the goats?* I think it's Swedish. Anyway, I take it you'd rather be a mountain climber?'

'Yes,' Luke says instantly. 'I'd love that. I'd give anything to climb just one mountain. Or even just to look at a mountain . . . That would be enough for me, more than enough.'

'You have friends?' Wei asks.

'One. Julie. And another girl who lives nearby, but . . .'

'Many girls.' Wei laughs again.

'No! Not like that. Well, one of them, Leanne, she and I . . .'

'You have sex?'

'Yes . . . But we're not very compatible. It's a mistake.'

'And Julie?'

'She's my closest friend in the whole world.' Luke pauses. 'I used to have some other friends, not quite so close but, you know . . . Anyway, one died, and one moved away. Now it's just me and Julie.'

'And she helps you?'

'Yes. She comes here every day. I don't know what I'd do without her.'

'OK. And she is normal?'

'Normal? Julie?' Luke laughs. 'No. She's . . .'

'She goes outside?'

'Oh yes. But she'd rather live like me, I think. Outside is too much for her.'

'Perhaps she is the thinker and you are the mountain climber.'

Luke thinks. 'Perhaps. But . . .'

'But?'

'I'm so worried about her. She probably needs healing more than I do. She *is* a thinker but she never went to university. She ended up staying here. She won't eat anything natural. She's scared of nature, and dirt and anything organic. She virtually lives on Pot Noodles and soup, which she supplements with sweets and Lucozade and Ribena, because even though she's scared of eating, she's more scared of fainting or wasting away. It's hard to explain . . .'

'She is afraid of the earth?'

'Yes. Dirt and earth and . . .'

'And you are allergic to fire. Interesting.' There is a tapping sound and then Wei's voice comes again. 'Can you fax me some details about Julie? I have to go now but we can speak again tomorrow evening. OK?'

'Yes. Great. Oh – before you go, could you tell me what time you'll get in touch tomorrow evening? I don't mean to try to pin you down or anything, it's just . . .'

'No, not at all. What is a good time for you?'

'Um . . . Eleven? I know it's a bit late but Julie will definitely be here then and . . .'

'Yes, it would be useful for me to speak with Julie as well. OK. Eleven it is.'

Chapter 15

The night before Mark died.

It was going to be a normal Friday. As usual, Julie, Charlotte and Mark were planning to hang out in Luke's bedroom, watching videos late into the night. Fridays were never for going out; always for staying in. There used to be good TV on Friday nights. Charlotte, Mark and Luke would pig out on music shows, sitcoms and offensive animation, waiting for Julie to come back from work with the pizzas and videos, which in those days they actually had to pay for because Leanne still worked at Homebase. Julie thinks about how different it was then, and she remembers that Leanne wouldn't have given them free videos then anyway even if she had worked in Blockbuster. She never exactly approved of their little group.

Charlotte lived at 14 Windy Close for about two years. Like the older, badder supporting-role girl in coming-of-age films, her few scenes were intense – never just there, she was totally, enormously *there*. And when she left, it was like a power cut, or when someone turns off the radio when your favourite song comes on.

First of all, Charlotte was beautiful. Secondly, Charlotte was impossible to ignore. It wasn't just Julie; no one could stop looking at Charlotte. And it wasn't because of her beauty, because a lot of the time Charlotte did nothing at all with her natural looks, preferring to go around with unwashed hair, chipped nail-polish, cheap sunglasses and charity-shop clothes that would look shit on anybody else. Charlotte just had something, and Julie spent a lot of time trying to work out what it was. Before they were even introduced, Julie would watch for hours from her front window as this girl lay there in the sun toasting her tits in the front garden, reading angsty books in the sunshine, playing dumb while people got offended.

'You've got a crush on her,' Luke said, on that particular Friday, just before Julie left for work. 'I've been wondering what it is, and that's it. You're obsessed with her.'

'What? With Charlotte?'

'Yeah.'

'Luke, I'm *so* not. *God*. Fucking hell.'

'You've read all her favourite books.'

'So have you.'

Charlotte's arrival had, among other things, been a bit like a travelling library pulling into the street and then staying for a couple of years. Luke and Julie were able to discover authors like Douglas Coupland, Haruki Murakami and young London-based writers whose work wasn't even available on Amazon. Charlotte was a walking twentysomething crisis with all the books to match and her crisis was so compelling that everyone wanted a part of it. And since she never talked about it, whatever it was, the books were the only way in.

Julie'd never read an actual life-changing book before but after *Generation X* she added supermarkets to a long list of places she wouldn't ever go. After reading *Generation X*, Julie knew that if she walked into a supermarket the world would end. *Girlfriend in a Coma*, which still reminds Julie of the first full summer Charlotte spent at Windy Close, made the supermarket problem a lot worse.

'Maybe you're the one who's obsessed,' Julie continued. 'Maybe . . .'

Luke interrupts: 'Julie, look at yourself. Look at your hair, your make-up, your clothes. You're becoming her. You even speak more like her now – all those *likes* and *sos* and *totallys*.'

'And I couldn't have got that from you? That's not my obsession with Charlotte, that's your obsession with American TV shows – no – *programmes*.'

Is there anything more embarrassing than being caught imitating someone you really admire, by someone who knows you really well? Apart from being caught taking a shit in public, maybe not. *Taking a shit*. That was one of Charlotte's favourite phrases as well.

Julie fumed all the way to The Edge. How could she be trying to *be* Charlotte? How could Luke think that? Julie was herself, not some Charlotte-a-like, and she liked herself. That was the other thing, Julie didn't *want* to be someone else. There was nothing wrong with her. All she was doing, if anything, was trying to inject a little tiny bit of Charlotte into herself, to take the parts of Charlotte that were compelling and add them to her mix so that she'd still be Julie but an enhanced, souped-up, better-than-new Julie. Julie + x, where x is that bit of magic that Charlotte has and Julie doesn't. It's like when you take a gene from one plant and add it to another. The second plant doesn't *become* the first plant, it just takes the properties that are useful to it. All Julie was doing – and she wasn't even doing it consciously – was a bit of harmless genetic modification, and, regardless of what people actually thought of GM in practice, as a metaphor there was really nothing wrong with it.

So she had a suntan for the first time in her life? Big deal. That wasn't so much from wanting to be Charlotte as from wanting to be with Charlotte, since Charlotte sat in the sun the whole time. OK, so maybe Julie could have been a bit subtler with her make-up experiments. Maybe she shouldn't have tried doll-style pink blusher just because Charlotte somehow got away with it, and maybe she shouldn't have stopped washing her hair because it suited Charlotte in that weird way, and maybe the asymmetric blobs of Michael Stipe blue eye-shadow on an otherwise unmade-up and unwashed face was a mistake too, but all girls make mistakes with cosmetics, and it wasn't like Julie had even had a proper female friend before. Maybe she was just catching up on stuff she should have done when she was, like, ten, or something.

Thing was, whatever Julie had done, whatever the germ of Charlotte-ness had given her, it was working. People didn't ignore her so much at The Edge. The other waitresses asked Julie to join their Lottery syndicate, and sometimes they invited her to go out with them – not that she ever went, because she was always too busy with Luke and Mark and Charlotte. Maybe it was just the extra confidence Julie had from having a friend but something about knowing Charlotte put Julie in the world again. Something about knowing Charlotte made Julie realise that it's OK to be a bit weird, thoughtful and quiet – you can, somehow, be cool too. How could Luke hope to understand all of that? It wasn't like he'd ever been in the world himself, having to take his identity out and show it to people, waiting for them to judge him.

By the end of her shift, Julie had worked out what she would say to Luke after Mark and Charlotte had gone home that night. She'd point out all the differences between herself and Charlotte, like the way they both felt about the weather. Knowing Charlotte hadn't exactly made Julie fear the weather less. So, she sat in the sun more – that didn't mean she wasn't still terrified of rain, fog and, particularly, storms. Charlotte loved extremes of weather and experiences – Julie was the total opposite. Charlotte liked motorways; Julie would rather die than go on a motorway. Charlotte hated TV; Julie loved it. So they were hardly the same person.

To this day, Julie has never seen *Happiness* or *Pleasantville*, because they were the films she'd picked up for that night. When she got to Luke's everything seemed different, and Charlotte wasn't there.

'Charlotte's not here,' said Luke, when Julie walked in.

'I'm sorry,' Mark said, looking at the floor. 'Things aren't, I mean . . .'

'What's going on?' Julie, putting the videos and pizzas down on Luke's bed.

Luke looked at her in a funny way. 'Charlotte's at your house.'

'Oh.' Julie glanced at Mark. He seemed sad. She looked at Luke, and he looked back at her, and she knew something wasn't right between them but she didn't know what was going on. 'Why's she at my house?'

'She said she'd see you there,' Luke said.

And even though something in his voice was daring her not to go, she still did.

'I'm breaking up with Mark,' Charlotte said simply.

She'd made herself at home on Julie's bed and was drinking a cup of tea.

Julie sat down at her desk and looked at Charlotte, then, seeing tears in her eyes, looked away. Through her bedroom window she could half-hear and half-see movement in Luke's room. A few moments later Julie saw Mark leave, cross the street and walk into his house.

'Does Mark know?' Julie asked.

Charlotte shook her head. 'No. He suspects, but he doesn't know.'

'Are you leaving?'

'I guess I'll have to.'

'Wow.'

'This sucks, Jules. I've fucked up bad.'

'Is there someone else?'

'Maybe.' Charlotte looked at her in a funny way. 'I just don't know . . .'

'What do you mean?'

'Things have got pretty stale with me and Mark, you know.'

'I didn't know,' Julie said.

It was never easy to know how Charlotte was feeling. You always told her everything without realising she'd told you nothing. In all the time Julie had known her, Charlotte had never been this open about anything. Sure, their friendship had become deeper lately but they never really spent a lot of time alone together. They were always either at Luke's, with Mark, or somewhere like a pub where Charlotte would spend most of her time just being Charlotte – making her unique observations on the world, looking out rather than in, never talking with anyone about herself or her perfect relationship. That's the thing: her relationship seemed perfect. Mark and Charlotte used to go around together barefoot sometimes or wearing matching sunglasses. They liked the same music and he sometimes let her put make-up on him and it seemed like they'd be together forever.

Now Charlotte sighs. 'Talking's boring, sex is boring. If it wasn't for you and Luke, I'd have gone ages ago. You know I only decided to live with Mark because I didn't have anywhere else to go? I wouldn't exactly have chosen to live with a guy and his parents under normal circumstances.'

'So why . . . ?'

'When I went to university, my parents pretty much told me not to come back. They threw out all my stuff and gave my room to my sister. I met Mark at university and we made it to the second year before we thought we should split. The whole thing was doing our heads in. We were living in this shitty student house with bitchy girls and no hot water, and our course was mind-numbingly boring. We wanted to do something rebellious. It was winter, so we drew out all the grant money we had left and went travelling, trying to find somewhere hot. When we ran out of money and came back to the UK we didn't really have anywhere to go apart from Mark's parents' place.'

'I never knew that.'

After a minute Charlotte said: 'Jules?'

The way Charlotte said that made Julie shiver.

'Yeah?'

'Can I tell you something really fucked up?'

'Uh . . . Yeah. Go for it.'

'You know we have a special connection, right?'

Julie's stomach flipped. They did have a special connection, or at least, Julie hoped they did but she never thought Charlotte would be the one to point it out. Julie herself had been trying to work out what that connection was long before Luke accused her of having a crush on Charlotte; she just hadn't been doing it in a particularly conscious part of her brain. At least she had his answer now. *No, Luke, it's not a crush, it's just this special connection we have.*

'I, uh . . .'

'We do, right? I mean, I haven't just imagined it?'

'No. I mean yes. We do. Of course . . .'

'I'm so scared you're not going to like me any more . . .'

'Why? Charlotte, I won't ever stop liking you.'

'The thing is . . .' Charlotte put her mug of tea down on the floor. 'I think I might like, you know, uh, like *girls.*' She looked at Julie as if to check her reaction and then carried on speaking, a bit faster, as if to cover up what she'd just said. 'At least, that's what I'm going to tell Mark. I'm going to tell him that I want to explore this, to see if it's just some passing obsession, or whether it's something real.'

'Wow. I . . . How would that make me stop liking you?'

'I dunno. Do you . . . do you know why I'm telling you this?'

Julie's mind raced. She needed to hit the pause button so she could assess what was actually going on here. Just as she was about to answer – and she wasn't even sure what she was going to say – a light flashed into her room from the house next door. Luke's special signal.

'I've got to go,' she said, automatically.

Charlotte looked hurt. 'Oh. I'm sorry if I . . .'

'No – it's Luke. I have to . . . Can we talk tomorrow?'

'Sure,' said Charlotte.

But Julie didn't get to speak to Charlotte the next day, because when Charlotte woke up at about two in the afternoon, someone was telling her that Mark was dead. Two months later, after refusing to speak to anyone in all that time, Charlotte left Windy Close.

Julie hasn't actually spoken to Charlotte since the night before Mark died.

Chapter 16

For some reason, Charlotte's arranged to meet Julie in the café above Littlewoods.

'You can smoke in here,' Charlotte explains when Julie sits down opposite her. 'And it's weird.'

There's only one other clean table in the café. The rest are strewn with the remains of elderly people's lunches and bits of denture-friendly afternoon teas.

'How are you supposed to order?' Julie asks.

'You have to queue up over there.' Charlotte points to the long cafeteria-style counter. 'Get us a coffee.'

When Julie pays for her bottled mineral water and Charlotte's coffee, the cashier tells her that the shop is closing in twenty minutes, and asks her to make sure that she and her friend have gone by then.

Julie looks at Charlotte properly as she walks back to the table and sits down. She's put on a little bit of weight, which she needed, but otherwise she's the same. She's wearing tight jeans, a blue vest top with red bra straps showing, a duffel coat and – she insists on showing Julie – Hello Kitty socks and white kitten-heeled shoes.

'So . . . You still like places because they're weird?'

'Not everything changes,' Charlotte replies, taking her foot off the table.

'Sorry about Leanne hassling you.'

Charlotte sort of snorts. 'She's not your responsibility. She never liked me.'

'She never liked me either. I don't know why she does

now.' Julie smiles. 'It's an unexplained phenomenon.'

'And this thing with her and Luke . . . That's totally fucked up.'

Julie laughs. 'I know.'

'How the hell did it happen?'

'I don't know. After you left, she started coming around more. Girls have always gone for Luke. I suppose it was just a matter of time.'

'Yeah, and she's getting old now, isn't she, not to be married?'

'Leanne? She's my age.'

Charlotte laughs. 'Yes but in Leanne's world . . .'

'Oh.' Julie laughs too. 'I see what you mean.'

'I bet she doesn't like staying in with Luke all the time.'

'No. In fact she says she's going to dump him because they never go out.'

Charlotte's still laughing. 'Fucking hell. Still it's not like he'll care, will he?'

'No, I don't think so. It was a sex thing, really. So anyway . . .'

Charlotte looks down at her coffee and stirs in some more sugar. 'Yeah. Anyway . . .' she says softly.

Lots of stuff runs through Julie's mind. She wants to ask about those weird few months when everything went wrong in Windy Close, about what Charlotte did when she left, about how she never got in touch, about what she did and whether she thought about everything and why she's been acting like none of it ever happened.

'I can't believe I haven't seen you for so long,' Julie says in the end.

She opens her bottle of water and drinks from it.

'I've missed you,' Charlotte says simply.

Julie's stomach suddenly turns over, just like it did in her bedroom a year ago. She's not comfortable with this kind of statement anyway, but from *Charlotte*, just like that? Charlotte never says things like that. Charlotte's the queen of sticking a smile on, hiding your feelings and hoping for the best, a strategy Julie was sure she'd even use through a nuclear war. But . . . Charlotte *missed* her. That means she thought about her. That means she thought about what happened. God.

Instead of saying, 'I missed you too,' Julie just sort of blushes.

Charlotte pulls another Marlboro Light out of her packet.

'So what have you been doing, you know, this year?' Julie asks her.

'Oh, stuff, you know. I had a bad few months just after I left.'

'Where did you go?'

'A squat in Chelmsford for a while. Then Europe.'

'Europe?'

'Yeah,' Charlotte says quickly. 'It was weird. I'm glad to be back.'

'So what are you doing now?'

'A bit of bar work at The Rising Sun. Not much, really.' She pauses. 'I did love Mark, you know.'

'I know you did. Why are you saying that?'

'Just because I wanted to leave him doesn't mean I wanted him to die.'

Julie almost puts her hand on Charlotte's arm but then doesn't.

'Charlotte . . . Of course you didn't. I mean, nobody thinks . . .'

'I thought you'd think I did. I couldn't face you. I had to leave.'

The woman from the counter comes over to clear the cups away. 'We're closing now,' she says. 'So if you could finish up.'

It feels weird walking down the stairs and out of the shop. Julie doesn't feel comfortable continuing such an intense conversation now that she and Charlotte are on the move, not that she'd know what to say next anyway. There's almost too much to say. What did Charlotte do in Europe? What's she doing now apart from bar work? Did she end up liking girls or not? Julie doesn't know if this is it – if she's expected to just say goodbye and go home now, with nothing really having been said.

'Do you want to go for a drink?' Charlotte asks, once they're out on the High Street. 'I mean . . . a proper one, you know . . .'

'Yeah,' says Julie. 'Sure.'

On the way to The Rising Sun they walk down the High Street in the rain. The High Street is a mess of mobile-phone shops, McDonald's, Burger King and a dirty-looking café with a homemade 'No Dogs' sign illustrated with a clip-art picture of a lion. Further down, on the pedestrianised section, there's a stall that hasn't been there before. In fact, you don't usually see stalls on the High Street on a Monday, especially not in the rain – most of the dodgy traders just set up for a bit on a sunny Saturday afternoon, selling puppets with invisible strings, plastic dancing hot-dogs or knock-off designer clothes until the police move them on. This guy looks different from the usual shell-suit wide-boys. Dressed in old jeans and a cagoule, he seems to be packing up, taking bottles of greenish liquid off his small table and putting them in a cardboard box on the street. A slightly tattered laminated A4 sign flaps in the breeze, stuck to the table with sellotape. *Live to 130!!!* is printed on it in bold sans-serif type. As Julie and Charlotte walk towards him, he stops packing away for a second, watching them. Then he smiles and holds up one of the bottles.

'Hello,' he says. 'Would either of you be interested in a longer, happier . . .'

'Fuck off,' says Charlotte.

Chapter 17

'You've been out with *Charlotte?*' Luke says.

It's almost ten o'clock and Julie's only just made it over to Luke's. He was in the middle of an intense Internet chat when she walked in, so she used his loo, walked around the room for a bit, washed her hands, and then frowned at herself in the wardrobe mirror for five minutes. Now they're both sitting on the bed. Julie's drying rain off her hair with a towel, and Luke's fiddling with his socks.

'Yeah. And David was there, and Leanne.'

'I wondered where Leanne was,' Luke says.

'Hasn't she rung you?'

'No.' Luke shakes his head. 'No one's rung or anything.'

Julie looks sad. 'Sorry,' she says. 'I should have rung you. I just . . . It's the first time I've seen Charlotte since, you know . . . and . . .'

'Hey,' Luke says, smiling. 'You don't have to explain. I'm not your jealous boyfriend or anything. Anyway, I was connected to the Internet almost all night.'

'I don't like thinking of you on your own for ages.'

'I was OK. I went on some chat room for a while, then that *Big Brother* follow-up show was on and I've just been watching TV since then.'

Julie takes the towel back to the bathroom. 'I wanted to watch that *Big Brother* programme,' she says on the way back.

'It wasn't that good. I don't like thinking of them all out in the world.'

'Hmmm.' Julie sits back down on the bed. In the background, the BBC News is on.

'Why's the news on now?' Julie asks.

'They've moved it to ten o'clock, silly.'

'Oh, yeah. I forgot that was tonight.'

There's another big report about the floods. Then a short item about some job applicants who went missing last September – they still haven't been found, so the search has been scaled down.

'So you haven't heard from Leanne at all?' Julie asks.

'No. I thought she'd come round demanding sex as usual but . . .' He shrugs. 'Nothing.'

'Oh.'

'So anyway, how's Charlotte?'

'The same. Still sort of elusive. We didn't get to talk in that much depth. First we were in this weird coffee shop that we got chucked out of, then we went to The Rising Sun and immediately bumped into Leanne and David.'

'I thought Leanne didn't go to The Rising Sun?'

'I know. David isn't exactly part of that crowd either. It was strange.'

'But she was OK? Charlotte, I mean.'

'She seemed OK. She was being quite funny about Leanne, actually. I mean funny ha-ha, you know, not weird or anything.'

'I think it's hilarious that we're only back in touch with Charlotte because . . .'

Julie laughs. 'I know, because Leanne's so mental. Charlotte thinks so too.'

'So did she say anything about, you know . . .'

'About Mark and everything? Not really. Not beyond saying she loved him and she didn't want him to die – like we didn't know that anyway.'

'Poor Charlotte.'

'I know. She said she couldn't face us.'

'Really?'

'Yeah, because she said she wanted to leave him and then he died. She said she thought we'd think she wanted it to happen or she'd betrayed him or something. That's why she left.'

'God. Poor Charlotte.'

'I know. She seemed OK in the end, though. I think it'll be nice to be back in touch with her, don't you? She was a pretty good laugh when she was around.'

'Yeah. I've really missed her. So is she . . . Is she going out with girls now?'

Luke remembers all those weird, semi-whispered conversations last year when Julie told him, bit by bit, what Charlotte said to her the night before Mark died.

Julie shrugs. 'I don't know. She didn't mention that at all. That last conversation we had – it was like we never had it, you know?'

'Weird. Um, Jules?'

'What?'

'I never asked you . . .'

'Yeah?'

'Was anything ever, you know, going on between you and Charlotte?'

'*Going on?* No, don't be silly. Of course not.'

'OK. Just asking.'

'I like boys, Luke.'

'I know, I just . . .'

'I'm going to make a cup of tea. Do you want one?'

While Julie's downstairs, Luke checks his e-mail. There's one from Wei: *Don't fax details – fax broken. Send by e-mail to this address.* Then he gives an address, perhaps not realising that he doesn't need to since it's the same address he's sent the e-mail from.

'You know when you asked me if I had a crush on Charlotte, ages ago?' Julie says when she comes back upstairs.

'Yeah – I'm so sorry about that, I just . . .'

'No, don't worry.' Julie puts down her tea. 'I sort of think I did, a bit.'

'I never meant it in the way you thought,' Luke says. 'I never meant to say you were copying her or anything. I could just tell that there was something . . .'

'*Going on.*'

'Yeah, sort of.'

Julie shrugs. 'That night, when she was over at my house . . . she said we had a special connection. I never told you that bit.'

'You did have one, though, didn't you? Everyone could see it.'

'Could they?'

'Yeah, definitely. Um . . . There's something I never told you as well . . .'

'What?'

'That night.'

'Yeah?'

'Mark asked me directly. He said, "Is Charlotte fucking Julie?" That was when you were both over at your house. In fact, I think that's the last thing he ever said to me.'

Julie covers her face with her hands. 'Fucking hell.'

'I know. I didn't want to say because . . .'

She doesn't move her hands but Luke can see her face is red underneath them.

'Yeah. I know. Fucking hell. *Jesus.*'

'I know.'

'I feel a bit ill, now.' Julie finally takes her hands away and puts them on her stomach, as though it hurts.

'Sorry. I . . .'

'No. I am glad you told me but . . . I didn't think two girls could, you know, *fuck*.'

Luke's embarrassed. He shouldn't have said anything. 'Look, it's just an expression, isn't it? I don't suppose he actually meant like *that*. He just meant were you having a thing, or whatever. I'm only telling you because it was that obvious to everyone that you had *something*. There was just something intriguing about you when you were together, like you had a secret you weren't telling anyone else.'

'People say that about us,' Julie says. 'Me and you, I mean.'

'Do they?'

'Yeah.' Julie thinks for a minute. 'God, I'm totally freaked out now.'

'Just forget it.'

'Yuck. Mark thought *that*. God.'

'Forget it, Jules. It doesn't matter. Mark was a bit of a dick anyway.'

'Luke!'

'What?'

'He's dead.'

'Yeah, I know. I still think he was a bit of a dick.'

Julie giggles for a few seconds then stops. 'I never realised he thought there was something going on between us, though.' She looks directly at Luke. 'You do believe me don't you? There really wasn't. We were just friends. And she was only a bit less fucked up and weird with me than she was with everyone else.'

'Maybe it was just all the stuff she said when you weren't there.'

'Like what? What stuff?'

'Oh, *Julie's so cool*, stuff like that. She talked about you a lot.'

Julie raises her eyebrows. 'Really?'

'Yeah, totally. I mean, she really, really liked you.'

'Really?' She sighs. 'God, all this stuff is just a bit of a mystery to me . . . I've never had a female friend before, so I don't really know how it's supposed to be. I thought it was all normal, I mean as normal as it could be with her being weird and me being . . .'

'Weird,' Luke finishes. He laughs. 'You had a lot in common.'

'We didn't, though, really, did we? She's the travelling, outdoors type and I'm obviously . . . well, not. Maybe that's why I was so drawn to her. Maybe I wanted to be a bit more like her, not in the obvious ways but just, you know, to be less scared of everything.'

Luke looks at Julie. 'I thought you were happy the way you are.'

'Sorry?'

'You're always going on about how you're the only one who's sane and it's everyone else that's mad. I thought you said all your fears were logical.'

'Yeah, they are.' Julie shrugs. 'It's just if I was a different sort of person I wouldn't use logic to dictate how I lived my life, I'd just, I don't know, do stuff because it's fun, or because everyone else does, or whatever. Not choose my activities based on whether or not there's a hundred per cent chance of survival.'

Luke laughs. 'I see what you mean.'

'I don't think other people think about dying as much as I do. I think they just sort of assume they're not going to die, even if they do go in a plane or bungee jumping or whatever. They focus on the fun and maybe . . . Maybe they think the fun's worth it, and maybe they sort of don't really mind if they do die. If that makes sense.'

Luke fluffs up his pillows and gets comfortable lying back on the bed. 'Sort of. How do you mean?'

'Well, sometimes, especially when I was a kid, I'd

get caught in those moments on a fairground ride or something, and it would be going really fast and it would be totally thrilling, and somehow the thought of doing something dangerous enough to kill you was exciting. It made me feel brave, and cool, and on the edge and . . . I guess all that stuff people say about "living dangerously" and everything. I do understand the attraction of that, but nowadays I just can't let go enough to get caught in any of those moments. Now I wouldn't go on a fairground ride because I'd look at it and realise how unsafe it is and just not physically be able to take that risk. Nowadays feeling on the edge just wouldn't give me a thrill; it would terrify me. I guess because now I know the edge is real.'

'But you wish you could go back?'

'Where?'

'Well, to a time when you didn't think about all this.'

Julie pauses. 'I don't know. I think about all the things I did so easily when I was a kid. I travelled in cars with other people driving – on motorways, even – and I didn't ever think about crashing. I used to eat fish from the fish and chip shop, and I didn't think about bones. Of course, when you're a kid, grown-ups are in charge and they don't let you do anything that isn't safe and you sort of trust them. If my dad was driving, or my mum, I'd just think they wouldn't crash, because they were my parents, and because crashes happened to other people and . . . And I mean, when you're a kid and your dad tells you to watch out for fish bones, you don't even listen, because you don't really believe someone could actually die from eating something. I don't know. Maybe I just don't trust grown-ups any more, maybe because I am one, and I know they're not very trustworthy.'

Luke thinks back to the summer when Julie got her A level results. She was due to fly to Barcelona with her mum; their first holiday together since she and Julie's dad split up. On the train on the way to meet her mum in London, Julie had just sort of freaked out. She'd rung Luke from Liverpool Street station, crying, saying something about a storm, and the train going too fast and feeling dizzy at the thought of going up in a plane. Nothing Luke said could calm her down and she came straight home – not on the fast train, but on slow, local trains, building up her journey like a spider's web, slow, safe and time-consuming. Luke thought at the time that Julie was stressed about her exams – she'd been so totally weird through the whole exam period – and then she got her terrible results and the whole thing seemed to get worse.

The more Julie simplified her life, and the more logical and safe it all seemed, the more distance she seemed to put between herself and the rest of the world. Of course, all Julie says is that her life is real, and that commuting a hundred miles a day isn't real and that she likes her 'simple' job and her 'simple' life and that if everyone lived like her the world wouldn't be so messed up.

Julie cuts into Luke's thoughts. 'You know the funny thing? When I was a kid, dying – or, you know, almost dying – seemed fun and kind of glamorous. It would mean time off school and a scar maybe, and loads of people asking how you are and bringing you sweets, and life not being so *boring*. The one thing I remember about being a kid is how structured and monotonous everything was, with grown-ups deciding everything, and having to go to school every day for like thirteen years and just thinking how good it would be for something different to happen for a change.'

'I feel like that all the time,' says Luke. 'I wish something different would happen to me. I wish my life would change.' He thinks of Wei. Could he be that change?

Luke wonders briefly if now is the moment to tell Julie about Wei getting in touch, but he wants to be sure first. He knows what Julie will say anyway, if he just tells her. She'll say the whole thing's mad. Maybe it'll be better if she just speaks to him directly herself tomorrow night, when he rings.

Julie looks at him. 'You know, if I could do something to change everything for you, I absolutely would. I mean, if someone came along now and said I had to eat, I don't know, a half-cooked chicken or something, or fly to Australia in a plane, or anything, really, and you'd be cured, I'd do it, just like that. I'd do anything to make you better.'

'I know, Jules. I'd do the same for you.'

'But there's nothing wrong with me.'

'No . . . Obviously. I just mean I *would*, if there *was*.'

Chapter 18

When Julie leaves the house for work on Tuesday morning, she sees something she's never seen in Windy Close before: cats. One, a greyish tabby, is dancing around a tree outside number 14 trying to catch a bird. The other, small, lean and black, wanders in front of her before casually sitting down outside Luke's house and washing itself slowly. The sky is clear and blue, which is nice, since it rained all night.

'What on earth is going on out here?'

It's Luke's mother, still in her dressing gown. She's obviously seen the cat.

Julie can tell that Jean's pissed off. She would be, after all. Luke's allergic to animal fur. But even if there were no cats and Jean was pissed off about something else, Julie would still be able to tell. Jean doesn't show emotion easily but Julie can read the smallest twitch in her grey eyes; the small shake of her hands she gets when she's worried or angry.

There's no one else who can handle Jean really, apart from Julie. Dawn goes to bingo with her but doesn't actually handle her very well. She drives at the speed Jean dictates and parks where Jean suggests. Jean chooses where they sit and Dawn just goes along with it. Jean's main objective is never to sit near anyone she knows. Julie used to think that Jean was a snob who hated other people. Now Julie realises that she's just terrified of being judged.

When Julie thinks of Jean she can't help thinking of her in terms of the word 'handle'. It's not that Jean's actually delicate, though. When Julie thinks of the way she is with Jean it's like an animal handler: a lion-tamer or someone who works with difficult horses.

Even Charlotte could never handle Jean. Charlotte's never been scared of anything but when she used to come and visit Luke she'd edge past his mother like she was walking on a high window-ledge in a suicide scene in a film. Jean would always look her up and down and sort of frown. 'Old cow,' Charlotte always used to whisper as she and Julie walked up the stairs together to Luke's room.

But Julie can handle Jean. Julie knows how to talk to her about her favourite subjects – celebrities, illnesses, the paranormal and romance novels – and occasionally Jean will pass Julie a thick book with a wink and say: 'Nice and steamy, this one.' Julie never reads steamy novels but she always takes the book anyway. She likes Jean, even though no one else does.

'What on earth . . .' Jean says again, staring at the cat.

'Good morning, Jean,' Julie says.

'Where did this cat come from? Is it a stray?'

'I don't know,' Julie says.

Jean tries to shoo it away but the cat just sits there looking at her. When she stops trying to shoo it, it resumes washing itself, its back leg stuck in the air like a mast.

'It's got a collar on,' Julie points out.

'Can you read it, love? I don't want to bend down.'

Julie bends down to read the cat's collar. As soon as she touches it, the cat rolls on its back and starts purring. 'There's a phone number,' she says. 'It's a Basildon code.'

'Basildon? Leanne Straw's cousin is coming here from Basildon, isn't she?'

'Oh yeah. Of course. They must be her cats.'

'Didn't someone tell her not to bring cats into the street? For goodness' sake. Well you'll have to have a thorough wash before you come round tonight. We can't risk getting cat hairs near Luke. I don't believe this. I'm going to phone the council.'

'What can the council do?' Julie says.

'Hopefully condemn these lowlifes before they even move in.'

A man dressed in a turquoise suit walks past. 'Good morning,' he says.

Jean ignores him and walks back towards her house.

The Edge is flooded. When Julie gets there, David is putting sandbags against the doors, but it seems to be too late.

'Floor tiles are fucked,' he says cheerfully. 'Glue dissolved.'

'Bloody hell,' Julie says.

'Heather's on the phone to Head Office. We might have to close.'

Julie looks at the sandbags. 'Do you want a hand?'

David grabs another sandbag and drops it by the door.

'Nah,' he says. 'Done now. All we need now's a fucking ark.'

'It isn't even raining any more, though.'

'Fucking pissed down last night, though, didn't it? More coming tonight.'

'God.'

Heather comes out. 'Hi Julie,' she says. 'OK, Head Office say we can close but only while we get cleaned up. So we're hoping to open again by tonight, or failing that, tomorrow morning. Right, um . . . Can you both help clean up inside? We need to take up all the floor tiles and sponge up the water underneath, then the tile people are coming to re-lay them this afternoon. We also need to work out what's been ruined in the store cupboard and the walk-in, throw out the wet stuff and make a note of everything that's been ruined so Head Office can claim it back off the insurance. And I want to know who stored all the sweets for the ice-cream machine on the floor, because you've been told so many times not to do that . . .'

'Wasn't me,' says David, looking at Julie.

'Or me,' Julie says, looking at David.

'Probably night staff,' says David.

'Yeah, probably.' Heather sighs. 'Right. Let's get on with it. You two start with the floor tiles and I'll start doing the stock. When you've finished doing the tiles, you can come and help me. Oh, also – could one of you put up a sign saying we're opening again soon? Cheers.'

Inside, there's a funny smell, and the floor feels sort of spongy.

'Can't the floor-tile people pull up the floor tiles as well as putting them down?' Julie says. 'This is going to take ages. I bet they've got special machines or something.'

'They're probably more expensive than us,' David points out.

Eventually they settle down with tea towels (to go under their knees), knives (to pull up the tiles) and cappuccinos from the machine.

'This really is going to take forever,' David says, scraping away with the knife. 'They're not going to come up that easily.'

'Is this even in our contracts?' Julie says.

'Probably not, but we'd better get on with it.'

'Did you lot stay long at The Rising Sun after I left last night?'

David shrugs. 'Until last orders or something. Chantel came after you and Charlotte left.'

'Why was Leanne there? I thought she hated The Rising Sun.'

'She does but Chantel wanted to get some puff, and Leanne asked me if I'd get it for her so we all met up in there.'

'What's Chantel like?'

'Really nice. And very hot. Everyone fancied her.'

Julie laughs. 'Bet Leanne was thrilled about that.'

'Yeah. Fucking hell, this tile won't come up.'

'Here, let me have a go.'

They both chisel away at it with a knife, but it doesn't come up.

David puts down the knife. 'Fuck this. Have you got any fags?'

'We can't go out the back now.'

'Fuck going out the back.'

'We can't smoke in here, though.'

'We're not open, so it doesn't matter. Fuck it.'

'But the restaurant's non-smoking now . . .'

'Who cares? Come on. Even Heather smokes out here when we're shut.'

Julie frowns. 'Really?'

'Oh yeah. She has one in here before we open in the mornings, while she's doing the floats. She says the table in the office is too cluttered or something.' David comes in earlier than Julie because he has to warm the oven and prepare pizza toppings.

'Oh, OK then,' Julie says, putting the knife down.

David finds a pack of Rothman's in one of his pockets and gives one to her.

'I really should give up soon,' he says.

Julie doesn't know what to say for a moment. Agreeing with someone who has cancer that, yes, they should give up smoking seems a bit weird.

'How are you feeling?' she asks in the end.

'OK. Still waiting to find out about my lymph nodes.'

'Oh.'

There's an awkward silence which is broken by Leanne coming in.

'It stinks in here,' she says. 'Hello Julie, David.'

'All right?' says David. 'Hungover?'

'What, me? No. Drank loads of water, didn't I?'

'Did you go back with that bloke?'

'Who? Oh, Martin. Yeah, for a bit.'

'Have you spoken to Luke yet?' Julie asks her.

'No, not yet.'

'Don't you think you should tell him, you know . . .'

'That it's over? Yeah. I'm not sure it is yet, though.'

'How do you mean?'

'I might give him another chance. Dunno yet.'

David gives Leanne a cigarette and she leans against the meet-and-greet station. All the tables and chairs are stacked outside.

'Anyway, just wanted to make sure you're both on for this party tonight. At Chantel's. Her house-warming thingy.'

David sort of shrugs. 'Didn't know I was invited,' he says.

'Well you are, so you'd better come. Julie?'

'Yeah, of course. Oh, does Chantel have cats?'

'I don't know,' Leanne says. 'Probably. Why?'

'They were in the street this morning. Jean was going mad.'

'Oh. Stupid cow. They're not going to kill him, are they?'

'Well, maybe. He is allergic to most things like that.'

'Oh well, we'll soon find out, won't we?'

'Leanne!'

'What's going on?' David asks.

'They reckon Luke's allergic to cats,' Leanne explains.

'Don't you think he is?' Julie asks Leanne.

'Look, all that other stuff he's supposedly allergic to – perfume, cigarettes, dust – he just isn't, is he? You smoke there, don't you?'

'Not really,' Julie says. 'Not any more.'

'I do,' she says. 'And I wear perfume and all sorts.'

'I've never worn perfume round there,' Julie says.

'Yeah, well, I reckon his mum's a bit paranoid, don't you?'

'I'd be paranoid if my kid was allergic to the sun,' David says.

'It is better to be careful,' Julie agrees. 'He is allergic to some pretty weird stuff. I've seen him have a reaction. It's really horrible.'

'Yes, well,' says Leanne. 'Seven at Chantel's. And don't tell Charlotte.'

'What's all this about Charlotte?' David says, once Leanne's gone.

'Leanne thinks she'll tell Chantel about the stuff that happened at number 14.'

'Oh yeah. I forgot we weren't supposed to say anything.'

'I told Leanne – everyone'll forget, and someone's bound to tell Chantel eventually. I mean, I don't think anyone's going to come out and say it at the party or anything but once Chantel's been living around here for a while she'll just pick it up, won't she? It's local folklore now. I don't see why it should make that much difference anyway. Every house has had someone die in it at some point.'

'Suicide's different, though, isn't it?'

'Is it? I haven't really thought about it.'

'Would you want to live in a house someone had topped themselves in?'

Julie shrugs. 'I suppose not.' Not because of superstition. It's just good science to avoid unlucky or 'cursed' places. Often, places with a reputation for being unlucky really are unlucky because they're downwind from a toxic-chemical plant, built on a site where something poisonous was buried or under a huge electricity pylon.

Heather comes out. 'Bloody hell, you haven't done much,' she says.

Between them, Julie and David have uprooted about three tiles.

'It's really difficult,' David says. 'They're stuck down.'

'I thought the glue had dissolved,' says Heather.

'Yeah, around the edges, but not in the middle. See?' David pulls one of the tiles and the edge rips, leaving the rest stuck to the floor by a patch in the centre. 'It's well fucked.'

'Oh God,' Heather says. 'I can't ring Head Office again.'

'What do you want us to do?' David asks.

'Just keep going. Can you use lighter fluid or something?'

'Could do. Be a bit of a fire hazard, wouldn't it?'

'Suppose so. Oh, I don't know.' She looks like she might cry.

'You should ring Owen or someone,' David says. 'You shouldn't have to deal with all this on your own. Get him to come down here and sort it out.'

'I've tried him, he's not in.'

'Oh. Well . . .'

'Just keep going with the knife. Whatever's left the tile company will have to do. Julie, can I have a word in my office?'

'Oh, OK.' Julie gets up. 'Is something wrong?'

She's worried about smoking in the restaurant. She shouldn't have let David convince her it was OK. After all, the health and safety regulations say that no one should ever smoke in a designated No Smoking area.

'No,' says Heather. 'Just a word, if you don't mind.'

Julie follows Heather past the take-away counter and out into the back area.

'So . . .' Heather says, once they're in the office. She seems less stressed now she's out of the main restaurant area. 'How do you think you did on that test the other day?'

'Um, I don't know.' Julie shrugs. 'OK, I suppose.'

'Well . . . I was going to pretend you didn't do very well – that's what Owen said I should do, for a laugh – but I'm not very good at that sort of thing.' Heather smiles. 'OK. Well, you got a hundred per cent. Every question right. Not only were you the only person here to get all the questions correct – no one's ever done it before apart from managers.'

Julie smiles. 'Oh. That's good.'

'So how do you feel about going into management training?'

'Huh?'

'That's what the tests were for, to see who's in the right jobs, who needs extra training and, like in your case, who goes forward for management.'

'So I'd be a manager?'

'Yep.'

'Like you?'

'No, I'm just a supervisor. No, a manager like Owen, of a whole restaurant.'

'God.'

'Are you pleased?'

'I don't know. I think so.'

'It's good, isn't it, because you're not a student or anything, and you wouldn't have to give anything up to do it.'

'No. I suppose not. I'd never really thought about . . .'

Heather carries on. 'So anyway, Owen's going to have a chat with you himself tomorrow or something, and give you the forms to apply for the management training. Most trainees have degrees but you've got loads of experience and the test result so it's pretty straightforward. You'll definitely get it, basically.'

'God,' Julie says again.

'Right. Well, I thought you'd be pleased. Maybe it'll make those floor tiles come up a bit quicker, eh?'

Back in the restaurant, David's still struggling with the same tile he was trying to get up when Julie and Heather left.

'What was all that about?' he asks.

'Oh, nothing,' Julie says. 'How are you getting on?'

'Fucking shit,' says David.

Chapter 19

'Your dad'll be pleased,' says Dawn.

Julie's home from work early because of the floor and Dawn's just got up from her nap.

'He was saying to me the other day, "Julie's not going to be a waitress forever, you know" – not that I was saying anything about you being a waitress at the time.' Dawn yawns, her eyes puffy from sleeping for most of the afternoon. 'You *will* tell him when he gets home, won't you?'

Dawn goes to bed for her nap when she gets home from doing the sandwiches, at about half past eleven. By then she's not only made the sandwiches, but also driven around all the industrial estates in the Brentwood, Shenfield and Ingatestone area selling them: bouncing into the prefab offices in her pink trainers, matching lipstick and ash-blonde highlights, doing the hard sell on pork and pickle or egg and tomato. Dawn does pretty well with her sandwiches on the industrial estates: the people who work on them rely on services like hers because they can't get anything to eat at lunchtimes otherwise. All the industrial estates are in the middle of nowhere.

Julie read somewhere that retail parks and industrial estates were intended to work in harmony together. Concrete communities far away from everything else; the idea was that people would work on one concrete slab and go to the gym, see a film, buy furniture or get lunch on another. Trouble is, most people who work on industrial estates get paid fuck all and retail-park prices are ridiculous. Who can afford five Edge meals or Old Orleans bar lunches in a week anyway? No one Julie knows, certainly. The retail parks were slower to grow than the industrial estates anyway, and with half-built slow-food outlets offering nothing but dust and arse-cracks, the sandwich makers moved in. Now they're as much a part of the work day as Radio 1 and mild sexual harassment.

When Dawn gets up from her nap, usually at about four, she drinks strong tea, eats a Kit Kat and watches her programmes – *Fifteen to One*, *Countdown*, *Pet Rescue* and *Neighbours*. She usually videos *Celebrity* and *Wheel of Fortune* (which clash with *Pet Rescue* and *Neighbours*) to watch after that. She used to watch *Home and Away*, until Channel 5 bought it and it was taken off ITV, but *Celebrity*, its replacement, is pretty good. Somewhere between *Neighbours* starting and the videoed programmes ending, Dawn puts the oven on and gets dinner in, usually a ready meal from Tesco: Indian, Chinese or Tex-Mex.

When Julie's dad comes in, he and Dawn eat from the plastic cartons in front of the *Channel 4 News*, which, along with *Newsnight*, is the only TV news Julie's dad trusts. There's less washing up when they eat out of the plastic cartons, which is good because, although Dawn doesn't mind cooking dinner, she says she refuses to wash up for any man. She wants to get a microwave but Julie's dad says that microwaves are just part of the government plot to melt everyone's brains, so she doesn't. She's always offering to cook for Julie, but Julie always eats her own food.

Dawn stirs sugar into her tea and takes it through to the sitting room. 'You are going to do it, aren't you?' she says.

Julie follows Dawn and sits down. The room smells of vanilla. It's the stuff Dawn uses to polish the wood and the cabinets. She always does the polishing late, when Julie's dad is in bed. It's weird.

Julie shrugs. 'I don't know.'

'Retail management's a really good area to get into,' Dawn says. 'My friend Toni started off working in a corrugated-cardboard factory on an industrial estate in Chelmsford, just assembling boxes or something. But she wanted to work with the public, so she went for a job at Stead & Simpson, which was horrible, all smelly feet and climbing up ladders only to find out you've run out of that size or that colour or whatever – I should know, I started in shoes before I moved on to sandwiches. Anyway, then she moved to Bay Trading as an assistant supervisor, which was all right but she didn't get on with her manager. Then there was a supervisor vacancy at All Sports which she got and within a month they put her on one of those courses and she earns really good money now. She manages an All Sports up in Manchester. It's a good laugh, and she gets loads of staff discounts, which is good with her having the three boys and everything.'

'I'm not sure I'd be any good at management,' Julie says. 'I'd have to do budgets and ordering and bossing people around. I wouldn't like that.'

'It might bring you out of yourself.'

'I suppose so.'

'And you can't live here for ever. Not that we wouldn't want you to,' Dawn adds quickly. 'It's just you'll be wanting to move on at some point, and everything's so expensive now and once you're in management, well, it's a career, isn't it?'

'Yeah. Um, Dad hasn't been talking about me going again, has he?'

'Not really. But I mean, you are twenty-five, and we do wonder if you'll ever leave home.' Dawn laughs. 'But people do stay at home for longer now, don't they? And you've got Luke next door and it's not as if Jean's going to want him to leave. That's what I tell your dad. I say, "When *he* leaves, *she*'ll leave." When Luke goes, you'll be fast behind – but not before. I don't really understand why he can't leave home, myself. It's not like his bedroom is the only place in the world with curtains.'

'I suppose for him it doesn't matter where he is,' Julie says. 'Since he can't go out anywhere. He may as well stay in the same room forever.'

'Depressing thought, isn't it? Imagine what it would be like, living in the same room forever. Poor Luke. No wonder Jean worries so much. She's very good to him, you know. She could have gone back to work after her hip operation but oh no, she stays there looking after him, day in, day out. You're good with him too of course, everybody thinks so. Mind you, you should watch out that you don't get, you know, too involved. You wouldn't want his life. You should remember that.'

'Dawn, I've been *too involved* for the past fifteen years. And I'm his best friend, not his home help, so it doesn't really matter how involved I get.'

'Maybe this management course is just what you need. They're residential, you know.'

'Oh. Really? God.' In Julie's mind, a big barracks-style building appears, with landscaped grounds surrounded by unfamiliar motorways, A-roads and – the only roads Julie can drive on – B-roads. She can't travel by train any more, so how would she get to a place like that? And why is she even thinking this? It's not like she's ever going to do the management-training course anyway. She doesn't really know why she told Dawn about it, either. It just seemed like something to say.

'Oh yeah,' Dawn says. 'It's sort of like, you go away

as a normal person and you come back as something else. Like magic really.'

'Oh. Well, I'll have to think about it.'

'Not much to think about if you ask me.'

'No. Oh, Dawn?'

'Yes?'

'Why are you up? Aren't you usually still in bed at this time?'

'Yes, well, I'm trying to re-thingy myself.'

'Realign?'

'Something like that. Your dad and me have fallen out over my late nights again, so I'm trying to get back to normal. It's strange, though. I just can't sleep properly at night. But we never have sex any more and I'm always disturbing him and he says he can't sleep without me . . .'

Julie's blushing.

Dawn laughs. 'Oh – too much information? Sorry.'

Dawn's got the TV on mute but Julie can see *Watercolour Challenge* finishing.

'No, it's all right.' Julie gets up. 'I'm going to go and check my e-mail anyway, then go next door.'

Julie has a laptop she bought with her tips from The Edge last year. She has her own phone line in her room – some BT special offer that her father couldn't resist, even though he couldn't immediately think of a use for a second line.

'Julie can have it,' Dawn had suggested.

'I suppose so,' her father had said. 'As long as she pays the bill.'

Julie's got one of those free-connection deals, the same one as Luke, so her phone bill never comes to very much anyway. It's not like she ever phones anyone.

She hits 'connect'. While the computer dials her ISP,

she looks over at Luke's bedroom. The curtains are drawn and there doesn't seem to be any movement inside. Apart from some spam from an American company offering Julie a university diploma, there's no other e-mail. Remembering the party tonight, Julie pulls off her work uniform and goes to have a bath. Afterwards, while she's putting on a skirt and jumper, she hears the familiar scraping sound of Luke's window being opened, then the hiss of the antibacterial stuff his mum sprays around every day. Good. That means he's up and Julie can get over there as soon as she's dried her hair.

When she gets downstairs, her dad's home early.

'. . . water everywhere,' he's saying.

'Really? So they're closing the college?' says Dawn.

'I'm just going next door,' Julie says to them both.

'Hang on,' Julie's dad says. 'How come you're home so early?'

'Floods,' she explains. 'Floor's knackered at The Edge.'

'The same thing's happened at the college,' Dawn says.

Julie's dad raises his eyebrows. 'Dawn told me about your job offer.'

Julie looks at the floor. 'Well, it's not a job offer, really.'

'What would you call it?'

'Well, it's a training programme.'

'Same thing these days. What would your salary be, as a manager?'

'Don't know.'

'Didn't you ask?'

'It wasn't that sort of conversation. Heather – the supervisor – she just told me I'd done well on this test and that they're recommending me for the management thing. She made it sound like I'd won a prize or something and I had to pretend I was pleased. It wasn't the right moment to start asking how much I'd be getting paid.'

'This is exactly how people get exploited. What have I told you? *Always ask what the salary is first.*'

'Yes, Dad.'

'Anyway, why were you only pretending to be pleased?'

'It was just a stupid catering test at The Edge.'

He fixes his eyes on her. 'And?'

'And, well . . . A lump of wood could have passed it. It's not exactly a big deal.'

'Shame a lump of wood couldn't have sat your A levels for you, then, isn't it?'

'Doug!' Dawn says. 'Stop bringing up her bloody A levels, for God's sake. It was years ago. She tried her best. Leave her alone.'

Julie's dad's laughing, as usual. The A level thing is like one big joke to him now. He stopped being cross almost immediately and turned the whole episode into a comedy routine instead, telling mix-and-match jokes that usually started, *My daughter's so stupid she . . .* or *There was an Englishman, a Scotsman and my daughter . . .* If there was a joke with an Irishman, a mother-in-law or a dyslexic, Julie would find herself stuck in it in place of them. Her father's humour has always been strange. One minute he's all politically correct, bring-back-trade-unions, power-to-the-people and so on; the next minute he's laughing at a cripple joke, in a totally ironic way of course, thinking that because he's so politically correct there's something extra funny about him laughing at unfunny or un-PC jokes.

'Well, see you later,' Julie says, walking towards the door.

'I thought you liked The Edge,' her dad says. 'You're

always saying, *I like being a waitress, it's simple.* So what's wrong with being a manager? Not *simple* enough for you?'

'At least I don't fuck my students,' Julie says, not quite loud enough for anyone to hear, as she leaves the house.

Chapter 20

Luke's still doing his exercises when Julie walks into his room.

'You're early,' he says, looking up from a crunch.

Julie explains about the floods.

'Do you think we'll get flooded here?' he asks her.

'Don't think so. It hasn't ever flooded here before, has it? Why?'

Luke laughs. 'I'd be fucked if we did.'

'Nah,' Julie says. 'You're upstairs. If it flooded this high, we'd all be fucked.' Julie sort of slumps on to the bed, looking annoyed.

'So, what's wrong?'

'Wrong?'

'Yeah.' Luke gets up off the floor and walks over to his computer and checks his e-mail. 'You seem all . . . I dunno, all thingy.'

'Oh, my dad pissed me off . . .'

Luke smiles. 'Tell me something new.'

'Yeah, and I did this stupid test at work and now they want me to become a manager. It's so boring I don't even want to talk about it. But for some reason I told Dawn, and she told my dad, and now they're both like, *It's a career*, and I'm just totally not interested.'

'Wow.'

'Yeah. I just wish it had never happened. I don't even know if I can keep working at The Edge as a waitress now.'

'Why not?'

'I don't know. Because I've been noticed or something. I just want to do my stuff without anyone *noticing* and trying to fast-track me to something else.'

'Maybe you're just good at everything.'

'Try telling my father that. He still thinks I'm the world's biggest failure.'

'He's a dick.'

'Yeah, I know.' Julie laughs. 'My dad's a dick. Huh.'

What would happen if today was the season finale for a TV drama? Luke ponders this question after Julie leaves for Chantel's party. He reasons that today couldn't actually be a season finale – everything's too unresolved. This is more like an episode-before-the-penultimate-episode or something; the setback before the resolution. Mind you, there hasn't been any setback, really, or not any particularly dramatic setbacks. Only Julie would see a job offer as a setback. (Although Luke can understand why this is, it doesn't work so well as narrative.) Luke's whole life is a perpetual setback, and it's not like anything can go more wrong for him. Leanne's probably going to dump him but that's what he wanted, so that's hardly a setback. He will miss the sex, though. Someone succeeds and that's a setback; someone gets rejected and that's not. Luke's life needs more narrative drive, somehow – it's just not TV enough at the moment.

The thing about Luke's life: if it isn't TV, then what is it?

One of the only arguments Luke and Julie ever had was over some story she told about her day at The Edge a year or two ago. Her story wasn't neat enough for Luke, and when she finished it, he'd said something like, 'Is that it? Didn't anything else happen?' and he hadn't meant to offend her, but she'd started crying, in this weird way that seemed frustrated as well as sad.

'Real life isn't the way you think it is,' she'd said, eventually.

'How do I think it is?'

'Like TV.'

'I don't think that . . . I don't actually know anything about real life, at least, not outside of my room. I've always admitted that. I know TV isn't real, I just don't know what is. You and me in here – that's all I know about reality. And I don't think we're like TV,' he added.

'It's not the content . . . it's the structure,' Julie said. 'It's that whole beginning, middle and end thing in narratives. What do they call it? The three-act structure or whatever. Everything you see on TV – every A, B and C strand of a sitcom, every plotline in a soap opera . . .'

'Everything happens for a reason,' Luke said.

Julie stared at him. 'Huh?'

'In TV, everything happens for a reason. That's how you can predict plots so easily. You know, like in soap opera – if two characters who aren't normally in scenes together suddenly are, you know that they're going to have a relationship or that one is the other's secret son or something.'

'Yeah, exactly. But in real life nothing means anything. Stuff happens and there just is no structure.'

Luke sighed. 'I know that. But . . .'

'What?'

'I'm not in real life, am I? I wish I was in real life but I'm not. I'm stuck in this shitty *Truman Show* world and TV narratives are all I've got. Jules, I'm really sorry I said that thing before, about that story you told . . .'

'It wasn't a story. That's my point. It was just an event.'

'I know. I just . . .'

'Not all events are stories. That's what I'm saying.'

Luke thought for a moment. 'Yeah, but people make events into stories. Stories give events meaning, or at least they do for me. I understand stuff better if it's a story – if it's edited to make sense, so characters get introduced properly and storylines are identified and resolved, you know, *neatly*. Like *Big Brother* – you know how I couldn't follow the twenty-four-hour Webcam thing at all; I could only follow the actual edited TV show? It was because it was cut together to make a story. Sometimes I worry that even if I did get out of here, I wouldn't be able to follow what was going on, because, I don't know, because it would be like someone who knew how to sit in a garden thinking that meant they could trek through a jungle or something. Maybe I can only understand things through stories, and I can only understand characters on TV – not real people and I'm better off staying in here with my TV because of that.'

'No, Luke. You're going to get out of here one day.'

'What, resolve my story? My plotline? Yeah, right.'

'It's more like TV out there then you think,' Julie said. 'People talk like on TV, dress like on TV, get highlights in their hair like on TV, and tell each other stories because, well, the language of TV is stories. Everyone our age talks like they're on *Friends* and they have these meaningless conversations with each other that are so, like, you know, almost acted out as if they were on a sitcom. And they're just covering up their shit lives by doing that. You're not the only person who sits in front of the TV all the time, you know.'

'Oh.' Luke smiled, sort of sadly. 'I'll feel right at home, then.'

'Look, it's just me,' Julie said. 'I just can't turn events into stories – or, well, I can, but I just don't like it. That's why I got upset, because I thought you wanted me to do that. Thing is, I prefer moments. You know, like when things happen and they just *don't* mean anything. When I did English at school the teacher said that fairytales, myths and even the Bible were all just ways of arranging moral code, safety advice and reflections on the world into stories, so that people could understand the messages better, so the messages were more easily digestible and compelling and meaningful. And I get that, I totally do. It's just that I don't want life packaged into stories for me, like those stupid ready-meals Dad and Dawn eat.'

'Hang on,' Luke said. 'You eat Pot Noodles. What's the difference between a ready-meal and a Pot Noodle?'

'Pot Noodle doesn't pretend to be real,' Julie said. 'It doesn't claim to be authentic. It just is what it is.'

Luke doesn't know what he doesn't know, but he knows he doesn't know it. He feels normal because, to him, he is normal. But he sort of assumes that nothing he does could be normal – that people outside would be different by definition, that they wouldn't imagine they're in a TV commercial every time they clean their teeth, or pretend they're starring in a fitness video when they work out, or think that, someday, someone will make a film of their life and it'll look just like this. So Luke's life *is* TV. That's just how it is.

Knowing his life has an unnatural connection with fiction actually comforts him, though. Because if his life is a story, then his illness will have to be cured – there's no point in it otherwise. In stories, problems are only there so they can be solved. And after all, why have a story about a boy who's allergic to the sun if he doesn't get cured? That would be stupid.

Chapter 21

'Shit,' Leanne hisses into Julie's ear. 'What's *she* doing here?'

The party hasn't gone well so far. One of the waitresses – they are all wearing themed outfits, although Julie can't tell what the theme is – has tripped over, dropped a tray of canapés, sprained her ankle and had to be taken to Casualty by one of the cocktail waiters. Chantel's mother has had to start handing things out herself. A DJ organised by Leanne hasn't shown up. And now Charlotte's walked in wearing a long lacy skirt, a bra top, a fake-snakeskin jacket and an old pair of Dunlop tennis shoes. By the look on Leanne's face, her arrival is the biggest setback so far.

Everyone is mingling in the new sitting room – redecorated by Chantel's mother and the man in turquoise who's been hanging around Windy Close the last week or so. The old sitting room had just a sofa, a couple of armchairs, a mantelpiece, a stereo and a TV. The new one has a leather floor, a water feature, a curved, waiting-room-style seating arrangement, also in leather; some hanging shelves with glass ornaments, plants sitting in coloured glass rather than earth, and silver blinds.

'Hey, Jules,' says Charlotte, walking over.

'Hiya,' says Julie.

Leanne sighs loudly.

'Hello, Leanne,' says Charlotte.

'How did she know about the party?' Leanne hisses.

'Julie invited me,' says Charlotte.

On the far side of the room, a large man is setting

up a karaoke machine. Meanwhile, someone's put *Smash Hits Mix '97* on the large silver CD player, and in the centre of the large room, some little girls in sparkly dresses and big earrings are dancing to 'Wannabe' by the Spice Girls, bouncing on the leather floor, doing a routine that must have taken hours to work out.

'Who are they?' Charlotte asks.

'Cousins and stuff, I think,' Julie says. 'From Dagenham.'

'You'd better not cause any trouble,' Leanne says to Charlotte.

'Which one's Chantel's mum?' Charlotte asks Julie.

Julie looks around. 'I'm not sure,' she says. 'I don't really know what she looks like.'

'There's her,' says Leanne, pointing to a slim woman with a blonde bob, a black dress and a plate of prawn dim-sum. 'But don't talk to . . .'

Charlotte walks off in the direction of Chantel's mother.

'For God's sake,' Leanne says to Julie. 'She's so going to mess everything up.'

Julie smiles. 'She won't. She's just winding you up.'

'She'd better be.'

As Julie predicted, Charlotte doesn't talk to Chantel's mum at all. Instead, she takes a dim-sum from the silver tray, then walks straight past her and out of the sitting room.

'See,' says Julie. 'She's just winding you up.'

'Hmmm.' Leanne sips some white wine. 'How's Luke?'

'He's fine. You know. Normal.'

'Upset that he can't come to the party?'

'No, not really. He's used to it.'

'I suppose he is. Oh – there's David.' She waves. 'Hi, sexy.'

David comes over. 'Where's Chantel?' he asks.

'Dunno,' Leanne says. 'Maybe she's still getting ready.'

'How are you feeling?' Julie asks David.

He gives her a shut-your-mouth look. 'Fine,' he says. 'How about you?'

'See!' says Leanne. 'I knew there was something going on between you two.'

'Leanne!' says Julie.

'Fucking hell,' says David. 'Jesus.'

'You do fancy each other, though, don't you?' says Leanne.

'No,' says Julie and walks off.

The kitchen, like everything else in the house, is different. A long time ago, Julie used to come in here to cook Findus Crispy Pancakes with Charlotte. She would stand there trying not to get in the way or be noticed, while Charlotte got in Mark's mum's way – usually on purpose – making a mess. When Charlotte and Mark lived here they paid board to Mark's mum in the form of small amounts of cash and large amounts of housework. They cooked for themselves because food wasn't part of the deal. They had their own half-shelf in the fridge, a corner of the coffin-style freezer and their own plates, mugs and glasses in half of the highest cupboard in the kitchen. They did their own shopping most of the time although sometimes Mark was allowed to add a few items to his mother's list. Charlotte never was. If Charlotte was working, or away, Mark's mother would cook for him – some 'it's your favourite' extravaganza involving frozen peas and gravy – as if he'd been away for a long time, possibly in the wilderness, and had just returned home. At that time Charlotte never seemed to eat anything but microwave food and Findus Crispy Pancakes.

Even Julie would eat Findus Crispy Pancakes – not

that she's eaten them since Charlotte left – and after they were cooked, she and Charlotte would take them into the garden where they'd sit on the grass by the pond and break them in half, opening their mouths wide to catch the long strands of melted cheese. Charlotte, as always, was less inhibited than Julie, who always looked for wasps and wished she was inside. But it was still fun; more so as a nostalgic reflection than at the time, of course. The past is always more fun for Julie than the present. The one thing Julie knows she'll always survive is the past.

In those days the kitchen floor was tiled in mint-coloured lino, and powered by practical, function-over-form white goods – a fridge, kettle, microwave, chip fryer and toaster that looked like they had been entirely moulded from the same piece of cheap plastic. But now these items have been replaced with expensive-looking chrome versions. The fridge looks like a spaceship or some kind of nuclear weapon. The kitchen surfaces are now finished in marble, and the breakfast bar – which Mark's family used as a place to store letters, old copies of the *Daily Mail* and seedlings – is now a tasteful collage of tiny silver-and-white tiles.

Chantel's mother is poking around in the fridge and a waiter has just left the kitchen with a tray of drinks. Julie suddenly gets the feeling that this kitchen is out of bounds; that this isn't one of those parties where you help yourself to beer from the fridge and hang around listening to people talk about drugs, sex and how the party's so crap and embarrassing and the music so shit that they have to stand in the kitchen to get away from it. Julie's head is starting to spin. It's raining hard outside again.

'Are you all right, love?' Chantel's mother says to her. 'Are you lost?'

'Oh, sorry . . . No. I was looking for . . . It doesn't matter.'

Chantel's mother shuts the fridge and walks over to Julie.

'Are you sure you're OK, love?'

Julie grabs the breakfast bar with both hands. She can see she's leaving fingerprints on the little tiles but that doesn't really matter now she's dying. Her head feels like it's swelling. Oh, shit. Her hands go numb, then her forearms, then her neck.

She tries to smile at Chantel's mother, pretending that nothing's wrong.

I'm not dying. I can smile. If I can still keep up appearances, I'm OK.

'Sit down, love, come on, at the table.'

But she thinks I'm ill. Maybe I look bad. I must look bad, and this is going to be it. Is this a brain haemorrhage? What should my last thought be?

'Come on, love.'

I want my mum. I want my mum. I want my mum.

'Would you like a glass of water?'

Julie shakes her head. She sits down at the table and puts her head in her hands, her eyes closed. Everything's still spinning and the music from the other room sounds like it's been slowed down or distorted. Still keeping her head down, she runs her sweaty fingers through her hair.

'I'll make you a nice cup of tea, then.'

The dying feeling starts to pass, but Julie's still shaking. Now that she's not dying, she notices how much she's shaking, and she feels stupid, and washed out, and exhausted. *I'm not going to die*, she thinks. Then she thinks: *touch wood*. And then she does – she touches her little wooden lion keyring that she's had since she was about ten or maybe longer: she had it when her family first moved to Windy Close. It doesn't even look like a lion any more, it's been touched so many times.

Julie doesn't believe in fate but she started the *touch wood* thing before she realised that. And it's always worked, which makes it almost scientific. Then again Julie isn't into that sort of science. Not since she learnt about Bertrand Russell's Inductivist Turkey. Just because you observe something happening the same way over a period of time doesn't mean it's always going to happen that way. The turkey thought because he was fed every morning at nine a.m. he always would be. And he was, until Christmas Eve. Still, Julie's carried on touching wood because it makes her feel better, and because it takes her mind off feeling like she's going to die. In that sense, it does work.

Chantel's mother puts a cup of tea in front of Julie, along with a sugar bowl.

'I'm Nicky, by the way.'

'Thanks,' says Julie, putting two sugars in the tea.

'This must be weird for you. It must look so different in here . . . I heard you had to move out in difficult circumstances. I heard . . . Well, Chantel's not supposed to know, but I found out about what happened here. You poor love.'

'Oh, God . . .' Julie realises that Nicky thinks she's Charlotte. How embarrassing. Nicky thinks she's upset because she's Charlotte, and Charlotte has every reason to be upset, and Julie doesn't have any reason and . . . 'I'm sorry. I . . . I'm not . . .'

Nicky frowns. 'You used to live here. Your boyfriend . . .'

'No. That's Charlotte. I live at number 18, down the road. I'm Julie.'

'Oh. So . . . ?'

'I'm sorry. I just wasn't feeling very well. I was looking

for Charlotte, actually. We're friends. I just, sort of, um . . .'

'You're not on, you know . . .'

'Drugs? No!'

'Is it like an anxiety thing?'

Julie looks down at the table. 'Maybe.'

'It could be an iron deficiency,' says Nicky. 'You look pale.'

'Could an iron deficiency make me feel dizzy and weird?'

'Oh yeah, definitely. You should get it checked out.'

'I will.'

'Unless . . . You're not pregnant, are you?'

'I don't think so.' Julie sips some tea. 'No. Definitely not.'

Nicky raises an eyebrow. '*Definitely* not?'

'Definitely.' Julie smiles. 'Unless it was by osmosis.'

Nicky laughs. 'Maybe you just need to get laid, then, love.'

Her laugh sounds like she just smoked a hundred fags, one after the other.

Julie laughs too. 'Yeah, that's what Leanne always says.'

'Bless her. She thinks everything can be cured by sex or a manicure.'

'Yeah, I know.'

'Has she told you much about us? We didn't used to be rich, you know. We lived in a bungalow that wasn't much more than a shack, really, before we came here. One day Leanne came to visit – she only ever came once; no one ever came more than once – and she took one look at the place and our horrible rugs and how we had a goat inside, and she rushed straight out to the car for her manicure kit. "It'll cheer you up," she said. But that's Leanne for you. She'll never talk about her feelings or do anything that makes her uncomfortable, or do anything practical like washing up or ironing – but she'll give you a manicure at the point when you're so depressed you don't care if your hands fall off. It did make me feel better, though. What? What have I said?'

Julie's smiling. She likes Nicky. 'A goat? In the house?'

'Billy. Yeah, well, he didn't like the cold. Rob, my ex – it was his goat. Rob used to live in a caravan,' she explains. 'They all had goats. Billy used to like cigarette-ends. He used to eat them when they were still alight. Ate the curtains – which was a good job, really; they were horrible – and anything you put on the washing line. In fact, even if it was warm it was better to keep him indoors so he couldn't eat the washing. Washing out: goat in. Washing in: goat out. You get systems going in these situations.' Nicky sips her tea thoughtfully. 'I'll bloody miss that goat.'

'This is a really nice house,' Julie says.

Nicky looks around as if she's seeing it for the first time. 'Do you like it? Yeah, I suppose it'll grow on me.'

'Don't you like it?'

'Yeah, of course. It's lovely. I think I'm just a bit overwhelmed by it all. It's too nice, almost. I mean, when Chan won the money, I was like, Oh my God, new curtains. But I never expected this. I'll have to get used to living near my sister again, though. Might be a bit tricky. Me and Michelle don't see eye to eye on everything.'

Karaoke's started in the sitting room. Nicky pops a pill in her mouth and washes it down with her tea as someone sings the last few lines of 'Angels' by Robbie Williams. There's some clapping, then the first few bars of another song. Oh, God, it's 'Smells Like Teen Spirit'. That means . . . Yep. The next thing Julie can hear is

Charlotte's voice, low, rasping and desperate, and several people shouting for her to shut up.

It's nice in the kitchen. The red Aga is warm. One of the cats is sitting on it, slightly wet, just in from the rain. Little lights illuminate the work surfaces. It feels like Christmas in here. Julie realises she's taking up Nicky's time and Nicky is probably only talking to her because she's worried – and because she thought Julie was Charlotte – and that the polite thing to do would be to go back to the party and let Nicky get on with whatever she was doing.

Julie gets up and puts her mug in the sink. Nicky gets up too.

'Thanks for the tea,' Julie says.

'Are you feeling better now?'

'Yes thanks.'

'Well you can help me clingfilm these, then,' Nicky says. There are various plates on the breakfast bar; each one has a few sweaty-looking canapés left on it. 'These'll do for tea tomorrow. And then I want to show you something upstairs.'

The bedroom is fluffy and clean. It makes Julie feel sleepy. She sits on the edge of the peaches-and-cream bed and the cotton is so crisp she just wants to rub her face in it, and roll on it, and breathe the clean, new smell forever.

'Here,' Nicky says. She hands Julie a photograph. 'That's me.'

Julie doesn't know what to say. 'It doesn't look like you. Wow.'

The thing in the picture looks like it's on its way to suck up a small American town in a fifties B-movie. It looks barely human – let alone like Nicky.

Nicky looks proud. 'Know how old I was then?'

Julie shakes her head. 'How old?'

'Fifteen. Two years before I had Chantel.'

'God. You look twice that. This is incredible.' Julie's only recently understood diet-photo etiquette. It's OK to say the person looks like a fat blob, as long as the picture's pretty old, and they've had such a dramatic weight loss it's impossible for them to ever gain that weight again.

'Mad, isn't it? Little me, used to look like that.'

'Wow.'

'Keep that,' Nicky says.

'Keep it? Thanks. I mean . . . *Why?*'

No one's ever asked Julie to actually keep one of their diet photos before.

Nicky laughs. 'I like you. Look, I'm giving you this to remind you of what I'm going to tell you now. Right? Now look – I *did* this. I went from that to this and it wasn't easy but I did it. And I'm not exactly Miss Willpower. I drink. I smoke. I went out with a dodgy bloke who treated me like shit for years, so I'm far from perfect. But I solved the biggest problem in my life because I decided to. You can do that too.'

'How do you know I've . . . I'm . . . ?' Julie asks.

'You virtually collapsed in my kitchen, remember? And you're not ill, are you?'

'No, I don't think so.' Julie pauses. 'No, I'm not.'

'You're fat, just like I was.'

Julie looks down at her stick arms and stick legs. 'Thanks,' she says, smiling.

'Not fat with weight, but fat with anxiety, problems.' Nicky taps her head. 'It's all in there. I've seen it before. So you take this photo and you remember that you're as fat as I was, just not with weight but with fear. And you're going to get rid of it all, just like I did.'

To be normal. To be thin and normal and attractive

and have no baggage . . . For what? To be normal, so you can go to normal pubs and have normal experiences and dodgy blokes can fuck you and use you because you're so pretty and normal and they just want to break you? Nicky looks like a Barbie doll that's been barbecued, or put in the oven, slightly small and burnt, like you'd run out of Shrinky-Dinks and just done Barbie instead, because you fucking hated her and wanted to hurt her, and melt her perfect plastic skin . . . But Nicky's nice, and what she's saying not only makes sense, it's also probably the most profound thing Julie's heard all year. But Nicky would have been just as nice if she was fat.

'How did you lose it?' Julie asks. 'The weight, I mean.'

'Slim Fast,' Nicky says. 'Milkshakes. It was easy.'

'Shame you can't get those for fear,' Julie says.

Nicky laughs. 'I like you,' she says again. 'You're funny. Now, let's go and find Chantel. I haven't seen her for hours.'

Chapter 22

Chantel's at Luke's. She's been there all night.

'So you're not going to your party at all?' Luke asks.

It's almost ten and Chantel looks like she's settled in for the night. She's taken off her trainers and curled up on the bed. Luke's sitting on his armchair trying to work out whether Chantel's about to jump him or not. Luke's not that good at reading women – at least, not real ones who actually exist. He has no trouble anticipating what a character on TV is about to do but he simply has no idea with real people, particularly not women. Luke's had four sexual partners in his life. The first, somewhat inevitably, was his home tutor, Violet, a sexy, kind woman in her early thirties. Having taught Luke to read and write and add up, she eventually took pity on him and taught him how to fuck. He was sixteen then.

After that, Luke immersed himself in a distance relationship with a pen-pal he found on Teletext. Luke had various pen-pals at the time but they all fell away when he discovered Chloe. The relationship ended after Chloe came to visit Luke for the first time. They had sex, and afterwards Chloe was oddly silent and withdrawn. Then she left and never answered Luke's letters again. He always wished she'd told him why, and what he had done wrong, but she never did.

A year or so after Chloe, Luke met Paula, a mature student from Plaistow, on the Internet. Paula had three kids, a sick mother and the degree course to keep her busy, and she would joke that Luke was the perfect boyfriend: 'Low maintenance, always know where he is, never goes down the pub.' She wasn't easy to read, though. Some days she'd come over in a skirt and high heels and want to giggle, have sex, and talk about her dreams and the future. Other days she'd walk in slumped with her face pinched and drawn and want to talk about her kids and how tired she was. Luke could never tell which Paula he was going to get, and although the clothes should have been a clue, sometimes she'd start crying even when she was wearing a skirt. Luke had no idea how to read her at all.

Paula came over quite a bit in the few months they were together, but in the end she couldn't deal with the whole situation any more. Luke just wasn't very worldly, she explained. Her life was just too full of brutal realism to be understood by someone who'd been educated by TV drama. And she couldn't deal with Luke's mother. Luke's mother had a habit of reminding her to have a bath before she came round. Who could deal with that?

And then there was Leanne. Luke's thing with Leanne is the nearest he's come to an actual relationship, in the sense that they see each other often, they have normal enough sex and Leanne doesn't cry all the time. But the relationship is still deeply flawed by the fact that he doesn't really like her and they don't have anything in common.

Chantel wrinkles her nose. 'I might do. Maybe later.'

She has small freckles over her nose and her voice is husky and cracked.

'What about your cousin?' Luke asks.

'Leanne? She'll be having plenty of fun without me being there.' Chantel looks a bit uncomfortable suddenly. She sits up. 'Look, do you want me to go?'

'Go?' Luke looks at his TV screen. He can't hear what's going on, and he's confused, until he remembers he muted it. Chantel brought some cans of beer with her and, feeling reckless, he's drunk about half a can. He's never drunk alcohol before. While he's been drinking it, Chantel's been talking about how much she loves surfing. 'Why would I want you to go?'

'You keep asking me about my party.'

'I just don't know why you'd rather be stuck here in this room with me than at your own house-warming, that's all.'

Chantel shrugs. 'You're more interesting.'

'How can I be?' Luke asks. 'I haven't done anything. I haven't done anything at all with my life apart from sit here reading books and watching TV.'

Luke thinks about all the people who've turned up here to see the amazing freak – TV BOY! – the same way you'd look at a fish in an aquarium or a weird bug someone's caught in a jam jar. He feels like a freak show, not because of Chantel exactly – she seems OK – but because of the years of having to receive strangers here, of having to be witty and amusing and answer questions in crowd-pleasing detail about how exactly he would die if he came into contact with sunlight, how fast his skin would shrivel up and whether he'd turn red or black afterwards. Those dicks who came here never wondered if Luke got bored with all that crap – for them it was always the first time.

Chantel cocks her head to one side. 'So you're really boring, then?' she says.

Luke laughs. 'I felt like a freak show for a minute just then – it's a long story – but yeah, I am pretty boring.'

'What's your favourite colour?' Chantel asks suddenly.

'Uh, orange.'

'See, you're not boring. Boring people don't choose orange.'

'How do you know?'

'I read it in a magazine. Anyway, half the people I

know live the same way as you; the only difference is that they go to work during the day. I can't believe you think you're a freak. You seem really normal to me. Not boring-normal, just normal-normal.'

'Thanks, Chantel.'

'Call me Chan, please. Otherwise I sound like a stripper.'

Luke giggles. 'OK.'

Chantel starts looking in her bag for something. 'Anyway, I'm a bit shy at parties – especially if it's, like, my party and everyone wants to talk to me and stuff. I'm sure no one'll notice I'm not there. Anyway, I did want to meet *all* my neighbours properly.'

'Sorry?'

'Well, you're the only one I haven't met yet. Oh, apart from Julie.'

'She'll come here later.'

Chantel seems to be pulling everything out of her little rucksack: hair-glossing creme, hairbrush, plasters, deodorising wipes, a diary covered in little furry elephant stickers that Luke asks to touch because he's never seen stickers like that before ('Wow, they really *are* furry; how do they do that?'), a Salt Rock purse, a Kangaroo Poo keyring with a few keys on it, a toy elephant ('It vibrates, look') and, finally, a little address book and a little birthday book, both with pictures of female surfers on them. These seem to be what she's looking for, because once she's found them, she starts putting all the other stuff back in. Luke wonders if she got it all out just so she could show him, because it can't be that hard to find two small hardback books in a bag that size.

'I'm glad you came, actually,' Luke says.

'So you should be. Especially now you've seen my vibrating elephant.'

Luke laughs. 'Everyone's been talking about you for

ages – Leanne wouldn't shut up about you. I wanted to see you for myself. I was very curious.'

'Leanne was going on about me?'

'Yeah, totally.'

Chantel frowns. 'I see. So she's not embarrassed about me any more, then?'

'What do you mean?'

'Never mind. Oh, I used to be fat, and really poor. When's your birthday?' Luke tells her and she writes it in her birthday book. 'Address? Oh, actually I know that already. Phone number?'

Luke gives her his number. 'I'm always on the Internet, though,' he says. 'No one ever gets through on the phone. Do you want my e-mail address as well?'

'Um . . . Go on then. I haven't really worked out e-mail yet, though.' Chantel frowns with concentration as she copies it into her book. 'So what's the long story, then?'

'Huh?'

'Before. You said you felt like a freak show.'

'Yeah.' Luke sighs. 'Oh, it's just that I've had a lot of people come here just to look at me, like I'm a creature in the zoo.' Of all the things outside that Luke can't understand, a creature in the zoo is one he reckons he's come closest to. 'I don't mean you or anything – you're my new neighbour – but sometimes people come here and they just want to ask me question after question about what my life's like.'

'Do you get a lot of people around here, then?'

'Yeah, quite a few. Maybe not so much any more but a few years ago this place was crawling with . . .' Luke searches for the word. In American it's 'stoners', but what's that English expression Julie and Charlotte use? Oh, yeah. '*Puff-heads*. You know, all these people would hear about me down the pub or something and come round and smoke loads of dope and watch Cheech &

Chong films – which, incidentally, were completely unintelligible to me – and then talk about the meaning of life and what it would be like to be me and it was funny the first few times but my God it got boring.'

Chantel's laughing. 'Did you get stoned as well?'

'No,' Luke says. 'I'm not allowed. Allergies.'

'So you're trapped in the house with a load of puff-heads, being forced to watch Cheech & Chong when you're not stoned? Fucking hell. I didn't even think people still watched Cheech & Chong. I thought those films were like a relic from my mum's youth.'

'Sadly, they still do.'

'You poor thing. Do you . . . Oh, this might sound like a weird question, and tell me if I'm out of order, but do you get much sex, you know, being trapped in here?'

Luke looks at Chantel and tries to assess whether this is an I'm-interested-in-the-answer question or an I'm-going-to-jump-on-you question. Her face looks open, like it's just a question.

'Yeah. A bit,' Luke says. 'It hasn't ever been a huge problem.'

She doesn't jump on him.

Luke gets the impression that Chantel would like to ask him more questions, and actually he wouldn't mind talking about this – he could answer Chantel's questions then ask her questions of his own about girls and where she thinks he may have gone wrong in the past, and how he could somehow sort out this situation with Leanne. But now he's made a fuss about feeling like a freak show maybe Chantel feels scared about asking him more about his life. In any case, she doesn't, and instead asks him if he can show her some sites on the Internet.

Chapter 23

Leanne's trying to find someone to duet with her on 'Summer Nights' from *Grease*.

'I'm fucking out of here,' David says.

'Me too,' says Charlotte. 'I've had enough of karaoke. Jules?'

'Yeah. I'll just say goodbye to Nicky. Then shall we go to Luke's?'

'Is that the guy who's allergic to the sun?' David asks.

'Yeah,' says Julie.

David makes for the door. 'Sorted,' he says.

When Julie, Charlotte and David get to Luke's, Chantel is there. She looks healthy – Julie wouldn't often describe someone as looking 'healthy', but Chantel is almost glowing with it – tanned and fit. Her shiny chocolate-Labrador-colour long hair is tied in two plaits that come down over her shoulders. She's wearing a long skirt, a hooded skating-logo top, and there are some blue trainers with two white stripes on each of them lying on the floor. The hoody has a little kangaroo pouch on it, and Chantel has one of her hands in it. Her legs are crossed at the ankles, dangling over the edge of Luke's bed. She's drinking a can of beer.

In the background, Luke's TV is on, as always, but with the volume switched off. *Eurotrash* or *Ibiza Uncovered* is on; Julie can't tell which. All she can see on the screen is a huge pair of breasts.

'You must be Julie,' Chantel says.

Julie smiles. 'You must be Chantel.'

'Yeah. Call me Chan, though.'

'I like your skirt,' Charlotte says to Chantel. 'What is it?'

'Hooch,' Chantel says. 'Nice, isn't it?'

Julie suddenly feels like two popular girls at school are having a conversation and she's just eavesdropping. She doesn't even know what Hooch is, but she assumes it must be a surfing or skating clothes brand of some kind.

'What do you think, Jules?' Charlotte says. 'Cool skirt, isn't it?'

'Uh, yeah,' Julie says. 'It's nice.'

David shakes hands awkwardly with Luke. 'All right, mate?'

'This is David,' Julie says to Luke.

Luke looks like he's going to say something but Julie indicates for him not to.

'Hi,' he says instead.

David circles the room looking for somewhere to sit. Charlotte's settled down on the armchair, and Julie's just sitting down on the computer chair. Eventually David sits on the floor by the bed.

'Where's Leanne?' Chantel asks.

'Singing "Summer Nights" at your place,' explains Julie.

'That's why we left,' adds Charlotte.

'Also, she's avoiding Luke,' Julie says. She looks at Luke. 'I think your tactics worked. She's been going on about letting you down gently. Must have been the Pink Floyd.'

Charlotte laughs. 'Oh my God. I still can't believe you did it with her.' She starts rolling a cigarette.

'Chan's into surfing,' Luke says, quickly changing the subject.

'Luke's always wanted to surf,' Julie explains to David. 'Where do you go surfing?' she asks Chantel.

'My mates go down Cornwall,' David says.

'I've never actually gone,' Chantel says. 'I want to, but . . .'

'You've never been?' says Charlotte. 'How do you know you're into it?'

'I just do. It's just a feeling, like . . . I don't want to sound like a wanker, but you know when you feel like you've been born to do something? I could never afford to go before, and now I can, but I'm scared. It's so blokey and stuff. I just need to find someone to go with me. It'll happen. I'm only nineteen.'

'Isn't surfing really difficult to learn?' Charlotte asks.

Chantel shrugs. 'Nah. Not when you're born to do it.' She smiles. 'Anyway, I've read all the magazines. How hard can it be?'

David laughs. 'Good attitude,' he says.

The music stops and Julie gets up to change it.

'So what's happened to you?' Luke asks Charlotte.

She lights her roll-up. 'What do you mean?'

'You've gone all hippy.'

'Fuck off. I haven't gone all hippy.'

'You're smoking roll-ups.'

'Yeah,' Julie says. 'And doing yoga.'

'Yoga's cool. Don't fuck with my yoga.'

'What kind of yoga are you doing?' Chantel asks.

Charlotte relights her roll-up. 'Ayurvedic.'

Chantel nods. 'Cool,' she says.

'You what?' David says.

'Ayurveda,' Charlotte says. 'It's Indian.'

'How does Ayurveda work?' Julie asks. 'Is it just yoga or a whole mind-body thing?'

Charlotte draws both her legs up and crosses them underneath her on the armchair. 'It's a whole thing.'

'It's the one with *doshas*, isn't it?' Chantel says.

'That's right. Every person is born with a particular

constitution, and that's called a *dosha*. There are three: *vata*, *pitta* and *kapha*. Each one has a distinct diet that balances it, and certain forms of yoga that are more beneficial than others.'

'I'm *pitta*, apparently,' Chantel says. 'Fiery, oily and competitive.'

'What are you?' Luke asks Charlotte.

'*Vata*,' she says. 'Small, cold and neurotic. Why are you laughing?'

'How do you know about all this?' David asks Chantel.

'My mum did it,' Chantel explains. 'She's done everything like that.'

'Does she still do it?' Charlotte asks.

'No. It was just another fad with her.'

'So you're really into this?' Julie asks Charlotte.

'Yeah. It's no big deal, though. I mean, I may be a fucking vegetarian pacifist who eats rice pudding for lunch and can never eat or drink anything cold, but I feel better than I have in ages.'

'Rice pudding?' Luke says. 'Why?'

'My *vata* is unbalanced,' explains Charlotte. 'I have to eat warm things.'

'I hate all that New Age crap,' David says.

'It's not really New Age,' Charlotte says. 'Well, I mean, the New Age people do Ayurveda but I'm not exactly one of them.'

'You know what I don't understand about the New Age thing?' Chantel says.

'What?' asks Charlotte.

'Well – not meaning you or anything, Charlotte, because what you're doing sounds really cool and Ayurveda is really good – but, well, you'd think that all these people – the New Age people, I mean – having discovered all these ways of living longer and beating cancer and detoxification and all that, well, you'd think they'd be a bit more happy, wouldn't you? They should go around looking contented with huge smiles on their faces the whole time, laughing and singing and telling jokes, but they don't, do they? They just look really depressed and ill the whole time, and their hair's always thin and stringy and their skin's always grey and they never smile, and they never laugh and, well . . . Who'd want to be like that? I paid for my mum to get in one of those New Age life coaches and she was a right nightmare. Bad breath, bad hair, weird food . . .'

David laughs. 'Fucking right,' he says.

'I think they're all so unhappy because they've given up smoking and drinking and caffeine,' Charlotte says. 'I'm not quite there yet.' She looks at Luke. 'Anyway, what's with you?'

Julie's noticed too. Luke seems different. He's more talkative; more direct.

'I gave him some beer,' Chantel says. 'Sorry.'

'You what?' Julie says, spinning around in the computer chair and staring at him. 'God, Luke, are you OK?'

'I'm fine,' he says.

'Aren't you supposed to drink?' David asks.

'No.' Luke giggles. 'I'm not dead, though.'

'Shit,' Julie says. 'This has to stop.'

She can feel her face getting red, but she doesn't care who's here, or what they're thinking. Luke's been taking risk after risk lately, and it's stupid. All this idiotic stuff about going out; it's like a constant pressure in her head all the time. *Is my friend going to die today?* How many people think that when they wake up? *Is my friend going to kill himself because he wants to be free?*

'It's OK, Jules,' Luke says quietly, looking down at his hands. 'Don't worry.'

'Are you really allergic to loads of things?' David asks.

'Yeah,' says Luke, without looking up. 'Since I was a baby.'

'I didn't realise you couldn't have beer,' Chantel says. 'Shit. It's a good job I didn't skin-up as well.' She looks at Julie. 'I'm really sorry. Oh, God. Could he have got really ill or something?'

Julie shrugs. 'We don't know. Alcohol is just one of those things that he's never tried, you know, because he's *probably* allergic. Because all his childhood allergies fitted a pattern – he was badly asthmatic, had a terrible peanut allergy and so on – we just assumed he wouldn't be able to tolerate alcohol as an adult. These things all come in groups, you know, like headache triggers.'

Julie gets up and bustles around Luke, feeling a bit like a nurse. She puts her hand on his forehead to feel for a temperature then takes his pulse. It's hard to find his pulse with her own going so fast, and her fingers are sweaty as she presses them first to his wrist, then his neck. Then she looks at his tongue and asks if he feels tingly anywhere. She's known this routine since childhood. While she's doing all this, she can feel everyone else in the room watching her. She wishes they'd talk among themselves or something.

'Is he OK?' Chantel says.

'He looks all right,' says Charlotte.

'Can I do anything?' says Chantel.

'He's OK,' Julie says, giving Luke a look. She sits back down at the computer. Something's flashing on the screen, but she ignores it and connects to Hotmail, just for something to do. There's nothing there. How could there be? All her friends are here.

'So Luke, mate,' David says. 'What's it like being allergic to everything?'

'I don't know,' he says.

'Huh?' says Chantel. 'How can you not know?'

'I can't know what it's like, because I don't have anything to compare it with. It's like me asking you what it's like to be normal. If I asked you that – or if some alien came and asked what it's like to be a normal human being – you'd probably say it was kind of crap, and pretty lonely sometimes, and that you wished for all these things that you can't really have, and that you want more money and more freedom and someone to love you, or at least to shag occasionally. That's what I'd say, too, but our lives obviously aren't the same. If you want to know what it's like being stuck in my room all day, I'd have to just say it's normal. It's what I always do. It's OK, but it's a bit shit too. I get bored, just like everybody else. I get excited sometimes, like if I'm going out with someone nice, or if there's something really good on TV.'

'Chantel wouldn't wish for all those things, though,' says David. He looks at Chantel. 'Didn't you win the Lottery or something?'

Chantel frowns. 'Yeah, I did.'

'So you've already got half those things, then.'

'Nope,' says Chantel. 'Just the money.'

'Did you get all six numbers?' asks Julie suddenly, looking up from the computer.

Chantel nods. 'Yeah.'

'What were they?' she asks.

'Um . . . 6, 11, 14, 19, 40 and 45.'

'Birthday?' guesses David.

'Yeah, sixth of November.'

'What about the others?' asks Charlotte.

Chantel blushes a bit. 'Fourteen was . . . the age when I first had sex. Well, kind of sex.'

David sort of smiles.

'What's "kind of" sex?' Charlotte asks.

Chantel smiles, but ignores her. 'And I'm nineteen now.'

'What about 40 and 45?' asks Luke.

'Oh, I . . . I just thought they looked pretty,' she says.

Julie understands why Chantel would have chosen numbers because they looked pretty. Maybe it's because of their colours. Julie's seen numbers in colour all her life; maybe everyone does. The number 1 is white; 2 is yellow and 3 is blue; 4 is dark red, 5 is orange, 6 is white – almost like 1, but with a small hint of blue; 7 is red or blue, depending on Julie's mood; 8 is dark orange and 9 is black.

She's sometimes wondered if other people see numbers in colour or not, and how they see numbers in their minds in general. In Julie's mind, they form a definite pattern that she could draw if she had to – a diagonal line stretching from about minus 100, which sits in the bottom left-hand corner of her mind, up to 100, which she can see in the top right-hand corner. Zero is in the middle. If Julie needs higher or lower numbers, she scrolls up or down to them, her line of numbers always scrolling from bottom left to top right, moving upwards or downwards like an escalator. Beyond a million, the line gets a bit dim; the lights aren't so bright up that high. As for infinity, the infinity point doesn't sit inside her mind at all – the human mind cannot ever contemplate infinity, just as it can't contemplate the size of the universe or the true meaning of life.

Double-figured numbers have some unexpected colours. For example, the number 40 is black, although it is made up of 4 (red) and 0 (translucent); 45 is a sort of plum colour. That's the thing with mixing numbers: it's not like mixing paints; you can't always predict what you're going to get. The number 32 is turquoise, for example, and the number 17 is pink, as is the number 15; 28 is brown, and 37 is blue. Pi is light blue, and e is navy. Julie's favourite number, i, is cream.

Julie prefers odd numbers to even numbers, and she is suspicious of whole-number squares, but not their square roots. In the end, any number can be a square root; any number can be a square. And whole-square numbers are vain, like club singers or mobile DJs – not as sexy as they think they are; not as sexy and remote and beautiful as prime numbers, which manage to be remote even though, to the naked eye, there are more of them. (In fact, of course, there are an infinite number of both.)

Luke is slowly falling asleep with his head half on and half off Chantel's knee. As Luke becomes more sleepy, everyone becomes more quiet. Now the room's silent except for the hum of the computer and the sounds of everyone's breathing. After a few minutes Chantel gently moves her leg, and Luke's head lolls on to the bed. David gets up from the floor and yawns.

'Better make a move,' he says softly.

'I'd better go too,' Chantel whispers. 'Sorry about the beer.'

'Don't worry,' Julie says. 'Sorry I freaked out.'

'If there's anything I can do . . .' Chantel says.

Julie smiles. 'Thanks. It was really good to meet you.'

'Shall we all go for a coffee sometime?'

'Sounds good to me,' Charlotte says.

Julie nods too. 'Yeah. We should do that.'

David looks at Chantel. 'Did you say you had some draw?' he asks her.

'Yeah,' she says. 'Do you want to come round mine for a smoke?'

'Yeah, wicked,' he says, grinning. They leave together.

When David and Chantel have gone, Charlotte and Julie put Luke to bed.

'He's fucked,' whispers Charlotte.

'I know.' Julie's voice is choked.

'Hey, babe? What is it?'

Julie wipes her eyes. 'Don't worry about me.'

Charlotte puts her arm around Julie's shoulders. 'Hey. Come on.'

'You don't know how stupid and crap I am,' Julie says.

'Why? Oh God. Let's get you home.'

'You'll have to stay at mine anyway,' Julie says. 'It's really late.'

'Yeah, and you're going to tell me everything.'

'I'm so worried about him,' Julie says, looking at Luke.

Charlotte looks too. 'I know.' She pulls Julie towards her and cuddles her, smoothing her hair down.

'I missed you,' Julie says.

'I missed you too.'

As they leave, Julie remembers to switch on the air filters to get rid of the last of the cigarette smoke in Luke's room.

Chapter 24

It's almost six o'clock and Julie's supposed to be going home but hardly any of the night staff have turned up at The Edge. Everyone's been talking about the big train derailment that happened at Hatfield yesterday but now they've turned their attention to the crisis of there being no staff tonight. It's Wednesday, and Wednesdays are usually quiet, but lots of bookings seem to be coming in for some reason that no one understands.

'For fuck's sake,' says Heather.

'Jesus fucking Christ,' says Owen.

'Shall I try ringing Stewart again?' asks Heather.

'Yeah,' says Owen. 'Tell him if he doesn't come in, he's sacked.'

'I can't do that. It's illegal.'

'I don't fucking care.'

Stewart is usually the weekend night-chef.

'I'm not staying,' David whispers to Julie. 'They can fuck off.'

They're all standing at the counter where people place their take-away orders. Heather goes off into the office, presumably to make more phone calls.

'Looks like it might be a long night for you two,' says Owen, smirking.

David goes out the back. Julie follows him.

'I can't fucking stand any more of this,' David says.

'They can't expect us to stay,' Julie says. 'We've been here all day.'

It's been a shit day as well. Heather's been on her back about the management thing, not understanding why she isn't excited about it. And Luke phoned, which was weird. He phoned, and he said something about having a plan. Charlotte was there with him, and they had a plan, but he didn't say what the plan was. Julie's tired. She didn't get any sleep last night. She told Charlotte about the panic, and the fear, and Luke, and The Edge, and Charlotte said 'Mmm' a lot, and Julie felt more dirtied than cleansed by her admissions. It was only afterwards that Julie remembered she never wanted Charlotte to know about her mess inside; that Charlotte had given her a kind of normality, because she believed she was normal, and, incredibly, sort of cool.

'I feel ill,' David says, suddenly.

'Ill how?'

'I dunno.' He sits down on a plastic chair.

'What do the doctors say?'

'I'm on a waiting list.'

'What for?'

'I dunno.'

Owen comes in. 'Right, well you can forget about going home tonight, you two.' He laughs. 'Cheer up. It's not that bad. Julie, you're going to have to take sections C and D. Fern's coming in and she's going to do A and B. It's not ideal, but it'll have to do.'

'Fern can't do two sections,' Julie says quietly.

Usually two waitresses share one section, which comprises roughly ten tables, each table seating between two and ten people. On a busy night a section could have between twenty and thirty people all wanting another drink, a different sort of garlic bread or a clean fork; or to know where their pizza is or why their garlic mushrooms are still frozen in the middle. On a busy night a waitress will be taking orders for drinks and starters one minute, giving other customers their bill the next and trying to keep up with cleaning and resetting tables as well. Julie's the only waitress at The Edge who can handle one section by herself. Two is going to be a nightmare. In her head, and without meaning to, she starts developing a strategy. She and David could use sign language instead of the computerised tills . . . That could speed things up. Or . . . Julie's tired. Her brain isn't working properly this evening. She was looking forward to going home.

'You can help her,' Owen says.

'Julie can't do two sections and help Fern,' David points out.

'She'll have to.'

'Why?' David asks, getting up. 'Why will she have to?'

The atmosphere in the small room changes. You don't openly question managers and supervisors like this. Conversations at The Edge are usually a swirl of self-deprecating jokes, good-humoured grumbling, bitching, or just having a laugh. *Great here, isn't it? On holiday? Chance would be a fine thing. It's all right for some. Heather should watch Phil when he does the salad – he throws so much away. That's it, Owen, I'm leaving – only joking! Friday night? You're taking the piss, aren't you? It's my sister's hen night. Well, only if you're really short.* At The Edge, you never ask anyone why anything is the way it is – you wouldn't; you're just there to do a job, and you know it's a bit shitty, but if everyone has a laugh then it's all right. And anyway, *why* is the exclusive domain of children, hippies, students and losers. Everyone knows that.

'Why?' David asks again.

'There's no one else. That's why,' Owen says, confused.

'Why don't you just shut, if there's not enough staff? Or shut more sections?'

'We can't. You know we can't.'

'Why not?'

'Because we'll lose money.'

'Who's going to get all the money we're not losing, then, Owen? I'm not. Julie's not. You're not. Why don't you pay Julie double if she's covering two sections?'

'You're being ridiculous,' Owen says. 'You know we can't pay her double.'

'But you'd usually have two waitresses. Why not?'

'You know why not. What's wrong with you?' Owen looks from David to Julie and smiles uncomfortably. 'Students, eh?' he says. 'Always have to question the bloody obvious.'

As Owen finishes his sentence, David punches the wall.

'Fuck you,' he says. 'Fuck your exploitation. I'm trying to do a fucking degree and I work here part time, in this shitty, meaningless job, so I can pay a bit of my rent, and put a bit of money on my electricity key, but you actually want this – this *shit* – to take over my fucking life.' David starts emptying his locker, throwing loose change, fag packets and old newspapers into his sports bag. His hand is bleeding where he punched the wall. 'And her life.' He points to Julie. 'And even your life, Owen. And the poor fucking customers – they pay too much for what we do for them and we get paid too little for doing it. Who gets the fucking money we're all generating? Why is it against company policy to give doggy bags? Why do staff have to pay for their meals? Why can't we do half-and-half pizzas? Why can't we be more fucking human?'

'You're sacked,' Owen says. 'And this is fucking great, because I don't have a chef, and I've only got two waitresses . . .'

Julie's putting her coat on.

'Julie?' says Owen.

Julie looks at him. 'Make that one,' she says.

As they leave, David looks Owen in the eye. 'I've got cancer, by the way,' he says. 'And it really gives you some fucking perspective. I'd get a life, if I were you, before it's too late.'

The rain falling on the carpark looks orange, because of all the lights. Half the shops are shut at this time, but their lights are still on, and the carpark has little yellow streetlamps illuminating all the geometrically perfect, space-efficient parking bays. If you screw up your eyes and look at the retail park from certain angles, it looks like an alien spaceship.

'Well, we're fucked now,' David says.

'What you said was right,' Julie says. 'We did the right thing.'

Beyond The Edge and past Homebase, the A12 pulses like an electric current through a circuit board of roundabouts, lay-bys and slip roads. Yellow lights, white lights, blue lights, hazard lights, fog lights, bull bars, noise. The noise is wet tonight. An urgent, relentless wet noise punctuated with lights.

'I suppose I'll be dead soon, anyway,' David says. 'What are you going to do?'

'You won't be dead soon. Anyway, there are other shit jobs out there.'

'Where shall we go now?'

'Huh?'

'Well, we are going somewhere, aren't we?'

'I forgot McDonald's went No Smoking,' Julie says.

'I left all those ashtrays at The Edge,' David says regretfully.

They're sitting upstairs in Burger King, smoking, looking at the rain. Julie'd suggested McDonald's: it had seemed appropriate somehow, under the circumstances.

But she'd forgotten that David used to work there and that it's No Smoking. So they went to Burger King instead. It's dark outside but there's too much light everywhere. The retail-park lights were bad enough but Julie's used to them. The lights in Burger King make her feel like she's in a huge sunbed.

Apart from David and Julie, there are some kids in the other corner, shredding plastic cups, straws and cartons. One of them, a heavily made-up girl, is eating a cheeseburger. The others are flicking the shredded bits of plastic, and bits of lettuce, at her.

'I wonder what they're doing at The Edge,' Julie says.

David shrugs. 'Dunno.'

'I wonder if they'll have to shut.'

'I hope so.'

Julie smiles. 'Me too.'

David sips his coffee. 'Ow. This is fucking hot.'

'Maybe you should sue them,' Julie suggests.

Some of the kids at the other table get up to leave. One of them, a thin, scrawny boy with messy orange hair and a big chain hanging from one of his belt-hooks, nods at David as he walks past.

'All right, mate?' he mumbles.

'Yo, man,' says David, sounding a bit hip-hop. 'Sorry about that,' he says to Julie, once the kid's gone.

'Who was he?' Julie asks.

'Just some kid. His older brother Anthony had to leave town recently.'

'Leave town?'

'Yeah. Because he was going to get killed.'

'Killed? Why?'

'Selling fake gear, wasn't he?' David laughs. 'Moody puff. Do you know what it turned out to be?'

Julie shrugs. 'What was it?'

'Bonsai-tree fertiliser.' David laughs.

Julie laughs too. 'God.'

'It was fucked up. How stupid's that? Those little fertiliser pellets . . . I'd never seen them before, but they do look like the real thing . . . Just taste of earth, that's all. You know Jesus, that guy that deals in The Rising Sun?'

'Who?'

'Jesus.'

'Seriously? A guy called Jesus?'

'Yeah, you must have seen him. He looks like, well, like Jesus, hence the nickname.'

'Oh, that guy.' Julie can vaguely picture a guy with long mousy hair, a mousy beard and dirty clothes who often drinks in The Rising Sun. She didn't know he was a dealer. 'Yeah. What about him?'

'He bought a load of this moody gear off Anthony, but the thing is, Jesus actually has bonsai trees and so he recognised what these pellets were. He said he was going to kill Anthony, so he left. Charlotte knows Anthony,' he adds.

'Charlotte knows everyone.'

'She's all right, isn't she? She was showing me some yoga move the other night in The Rising Sun, to help with my headaches.'

'She hasn't always been like that. Luke was right last night – she is way more hippy now compared with what she was like when she lived in our street. She used to eat Findus Crispy Pancakes and shoot an air rifle in the back garden then.' Julie realises she's talking too quickly. 'Are you having bad headaches?'

'Yeah. And nausea. It hasn't been too good this week.'

'Is it to do with . . . ?'

'Yeah.'

'Shit.' Julie looks at the table.

'I went to the hospital yesterday. I've got some weird

complication that I don't really understand. There's some treatment I can have, but you have to be worse than me to get it. This thing I need – they've got two machines in the country or something but there's more in America. All I can do here is have one of my balls removed and hope for the best.'

'What if you go to America?'

'Could cure it. I'll never know.'

'Does it cost loads?'

'Yeah. There's no way I could afford it. Got my passport, though, in case I win the Lottery, but there isn't much chance of that.'

'God.'

'Yeah. Anyway, it's not that bad. At least I don't have to have my dick cut off.'

David catches Julie's eye and for some reason they both laugh.

'They should protect people from this,' Julie says.

'How do you mean?'

'Well, all the money they spend on space travel and consumer research and making things more efficient . . . You'd think they'd try immortality first.'

'*Try immortality first?* What the fuck are you going on about?'

'You know, if they valued life above everything else – they could find a cancer cure instead of sending people to the moon. Or instead of developing cars that went faster, they'd make safer cars. Instead of developing aircraft, they'd make ships one hundred per cent safe first. I don't know. It seems stupid to me that cars are made of this really thin metal so that when you crash there's maximum damage and maximum injury. It's stupid. Why not make cars out of rubber, or put magnetic forcefields around them so they repel each other or something?'

David shrugs. 'People aren't that into safety, are they?'

'And these train disasters . . . They make me so angry.'

'Yeah. That's privatisation, isn't it? Profit first, safety second. I agree with you there. I'm not sure about rubber cars, though.' David laughs. 'You're so fucking mental.'

'Trains are terrifying,' Julie says. 'I don't understand why they go so fast. I'm sure people would rather get to work alive than fast.'

'Do you think so?'

'Of course. Don't you?'

'I don't know.' David lights another cigarette and draws on it hard, holding it between his thumb and index finger. 'It's not that simple, is it?'

Julie thinks for a second. 'All right, imagine there are two train lines. One runs really slow trains. It takes, say, an hour to get to London from here, but you know you'll definitely get there safely. There's a hundred per cent chance of survival. Right, so there's another line, with faster trains that get you to London in fifteen minutes, but on this line there's only, say, a ninety-six per cent chance of survival. Wouldn't everyone take the slower train? I would.'

David's laughing. 'Julie. No one would. You'd be on that train on your own.'

'But why not? I don't understand.'

'People take risks all the time. People don't think in terms of percentage chance of survival. They just want to get to work quickly.'

'But why don't they think about survival?'

'They just don't. If you thought about survival all the time you'd . . . I don't know. You'd just go fucking mental, wouldn't you? You just don't have that level of control. You've just got to live with it.'

'Why? What if you don't want to live with it?'

David shrugs. 'I suppose you'd just never go out, or

do anything.' His phone starts playing an electronic version of 'Guilty Conscience' by Eminem and vibrating across the table. 'Hang on,' he says, picking it up. 'Don't know who this is going to be.' He flips it open. 'Yo,' he says into it. 'Oh – all right? How did you get my number? Huh? Yeah, it's true. Julie? Yeah, she's here.' He covers the mouthpiece. 'It's Leanne,' he says to Julie. 'Burger King,' he says into his phone. 'Do you want to speak to Ju– Oh, right. OK, then.' He flips his phone shut. 'She's coming here,' he says.

Chapter 25

When Luke woke up on Wednesday morning he had that feeling like he'd forgotten something important. It was a weird feeling, because Luke's never really forgotten anything in his life. There's not exactly much for him to forget. All his memories are collected around him in this room. Luke's never out; rarely unavailable. He may well be the most organised person on earth. At least, he may well have been, before he decided to drink beer.

If an e-mail comes through, the computer makes a noise. If someone wants to speak to Luke on the phone, the computer makes a noise. When Wei tried to get through on the phone at eleven last night – as arranged – the computer didn't make a noise. Luke had muted the sound when Chantel was looking at websites because she didn't like the music. Then he got drunk and forgot to put the sound back on.

Charlotte came over soon after Luke woke up, looking like she'd just got up herself.

'I've fucked it up,' he said to her. 'I've let Wei down.'

She made a phone call.

'We're going to see him,' she said. 'In Wales.'

It was as simple as that.

Then she showed Luke how to do the Hero, the Tree, the Cobra and the Cat instead of his usual exercises. While Luke stretched himself into these positions he considered the possibility not only of leaving the house, but also of going to Wales, wherever that was, and felt oddly sick at the thought of everything.

It's almost nine when Julie rings. It's dark and raining. Charlotte's gone home.

'We're on our way over,' Julie says.

'We?' says Luke.

'Me and David.' She sounds breathless. 'We left The Edge.'

'What, as in . . .'

'As in walked out.'

'Why?'

'The manager was being a dick. David told him he was exploiting us.'

'Good for David.'

'We've got Leanne with us as well.'

'Lucky you.'

Julie doesn't say anything. Probably because Leanne's there.

About ten minutes later, David walks into Luke's room alone.

'All right, mate?' David says.

'Oh – David. Hi. Where's Julie?'

'Out in the car with Leanne still. Leanne's having a "mare".'

'A what?'

'A nightmare. A crisis. She said she had to talk to Julie.'

'Maybe she's broken a nail or something,' Luke says.

David laughs. Luke motions for him to sit down.

'I've had a bit of a weird day,' Luke says.

'Join the club, mate.'

Luke's breathing feels funny. There's an unfamiliar uncertainty swirling around inside him like clothes in a washing-machine in one of those whiter-than-white commercials. Julie's not here. David's here and Luke likes David but he doesn't know him very well. He's not sure what to say to him. Julie's not here. She's late. She's left her job. How is Luke going to tell her that she's got to go with him to Wales? Where is Wales? Luke sees a street sign in his head, like the ones in American films: *You Are Now Leaving Essex – Welcome To Wales*. Will it take ten minutes to get there? Half an hour? It can't be longer than that, surely. If it takes ten hours to get to California, then it can't take that long to get to Wales. Maybe fifteen minutes.

One of Luke's favourite programmes is starting on BBC2. It's this thing about a group of people connected to a new Internet company. Luke found the first episode a bit tedious, then got hooked. He understands the Internet-related elements of the plot, and the narrative drive is very strong. They should have more TV shows based on the Internet, or people shut in houses. Usually, Julie would be here, and they'd watch the show together, in silence, like they always do, with their agreement – more than ten years old now – to discuss a show only after it's finished. One of the many things they agree on is that if you discuss something while it's happening, you miss it. Luke suddenly wonders if journalists feel they don't experience the events they report because of this. He thinks of mentioning this thought to Julie, but she's not here, and David is.

'I hate this fucking programme,' David says. 'Sad fuckers.'

Luke switches over. A Will Smith film is on. There are aliens.

'I like this,' David says. 'Bang! Shit! Fucking kill it!'

Luke sets the video to BBC2 and presses the record button on the remote.

'Where's Wales?' he asks David.

'Down the M4, mate.' David stares at the TV. 'Behind you! Fuck! Kill it!'

'What's the M4?'

'A road.' David looks confused for a moment. 'Shit, I forgot. You wouldn't know about roads and stuff, would you? You've probably never been on a road, have you?'

'No.'

'Why do you want to know where Wales is?'

'I'm going there.'

'Seriously?'

'Yeah. But don't tell my mother.'

David laughs. 'Yeah, OK. But . . .'

'What?'

'Isn't it like . . . Won't you die if you go out?'

'I'm going at night.'

'Oh. Do you usually go out at night, then?'

Luke remembers when he was a kid and his mother joined an XP parents' support group. One time they sent through some leaflets advertising something called the Moon Kids Club where children with various photosensitivity problems went out and had picnics and played in sandpits late at night. Luke nagged his mother for weeks asking to be allowed to go: he tried to be really good; then, when that didn't work, he resorted to being really bad, throwing several tantrums a day. But the answer was always no. 'It might be all right for those other children,' she'd said. 'But your disease is more complicated than theirs.'

Luke looks at David. 'No,' he replies. 'I've never gone out at night.'

'Shit. So you still might die?'

'Yeah. But I probably won't. I'll make a . . .' Luke looks at the TV. 'A space-suit or something.'

David can't seem to keep still. Every time something

happens on screen he flinches, says *ouch* or leans forward a bit more, gripping the sides of the chair. Luke watches him, and the TV, alternately for five minutes or so.

'You're ill, aren't you?' Luke says eventually.

'Yeah. Cancer, mate.'

'I'm really sorry.'

'Yeah, well.' David keeps looking at the TV.

'Why don't you come with us?'

'Who?'

'Me, Julie and Charlotte.'

'Where?'

'To Wales.'

David thinks about this for a few seconds. 'Yeah, why not? I haven't got anything better to do. No fucking job, anyway. And the college is flooded so there's no lectures for a week or so. Yeah, all right.'

'We're going to see a healer. Maybe he can help you.'

'Yeah? I doubt it, mate. But I'll still come, though. It'll be a laugh.'

Chapter 26

Leanne's freaking out.

'It's all my fault,' she says for the third time.

'What is?' Julie asks.

Her car is completely misted up, and it's not going to get any better, because Leanne's crying almost as hard as it's raining outside. It's like sitting inside a cloud. The car is parked on the street outside Luke's house. Leanne refused to go to her house, or to Julie's, or into Luke's. So they stayed in the car.

'Everything. David, Chantel . . . The rain, even.'

'Huh? Leanne, I don't understand. You have to explain better.'

'I made Luke love me. Well, not love me, but I made him want to shag me.'

Julie still doesn't know what Leanne's talking about. 'How?'

Leanne ignores the question. 'And I made Chantel win that money, and I made it rain, and I made David ill – but I had no idea until tonight that he was ill . . .'

'How did you find out?'

'Owen spread it around. Everyone knows.'

'Oh. Anyway, I still don't understand. How is any of this your fault?'

Leanne blows her nose. 'I didn't mean it.'

'Leanne, for God's sake, just tell me!'

'Do you watch *Sabrina*?' Leanne asks.

'*Sabrina, the Teenage Witch*?'

'Yeah.'

'I've seen it a couple of times . . .'

'Well, I saw one where they did love spells and I thought I'd try one out on Luke.'

'You tried out a love spell from *Sabrina, the Teenage Witch* on Luke?'

'No. I got the spell from a book.'

'Where did you get the book?'

'Crystal Ball.'

'*You* went into Crystal Ball?'

Crystal Ball is a shop on one of the small streets off the High Street. It sells whale-music tapes, feng-shui videos, and books on visualisation techniques, Jungian discourse, recovering from abuse, disciplining your inner child, balancing your chi and Tantric sex. As well as that, it has an extensive range of books on Wicca and Paganism, lots of boxed sets of Harry Potter novels, stickers that say *Neighbourhood Witch*, and a flotation tank.

'I wanted a book of love spells, didn't I?' Leanne says.

'But it's really weird in there. I thought you hated stuff like that.'

'I've been in there before,' Leanne says, slightly defensively. 'Someone got me a flotation-tank voucher for my birthday last year. They do hypnosis and stuff too – you can get tapes that you play while you're asleep to help you give up smoking, or become more popular or . . .'

Julie can suddenly see Leanne lying in her bed, surrounded by soft toys, falling asleep listening to a disembodied, calming voice telling her she's popular, and everyone likes her, or whatever they say on those hypnosis tapes. She must know she isn't popular any more, and that the last time she was really popular was when she was about eleven. Poor Leanne. She must be incredibly lonely. Julie bets all Leanne's soft toys have names, and that Leanne would be embarrassed if people knew that.

'Anyway,' Leanne says. 'The spell worked.'

'What, the love spell?'

'Yeah.'

'How do you know it worked?'

'Well, Luke was never interested in me before. Then he wanted to shag me.'

'I see.' Julie smiles. 'What about the other stuff?'

Leanne starts crying again. 'I gave David cancer. I didn't mean to, and I didn't really know that whatever you give out you get back three times – have you seen *The Craft*? – anyway, I was really fucked off with him one day. I came in to see you at The Edge and he was really rude to me . . .'

'Rude? How?'

'I asked for you, and he just sort of sang at me: "You can suck my dick if you don't like my shit." I know he was only messing around, but it really embarrassed me. He did it about four times – whatever I said, he just sang it at me. I think it was a lyric from some Eminem thing or whatever and I know it was just a joke but it was really doing my head in. So I stormed out, and after work I went to Crystal Ball and got a new magic book. Then I cursed him.'

'Cursed him? Hang on – I thought they only sold good-magic books in Crystal Ball.'

'They do. I modified a good spell. I didn't mean to. I was just angry.'

Julie sighs. 'When was this?'

'About six months ago.'

'Leanne, I'm sure you didn't give David cancer. He would have had it before that.'

'Would he?'

'I don't know. Probably. Cancer takes a long time to develop.'

'Oh. But what about Chantel, and the rain?'

'What do you mean?'

'Did you know that Chantel gave me money?'

'No, I didn't know that.'

'She gave us all money. She got her mum the house, of course, but she gave me and my mum ten grand each.'

'Wow. That's a lot. That's really nice of her.'

'Yeah, but about two months before that I did a whole ritual where I asked for money. You have to be really careful with those spells, because although you usually get what you ask for, you sometimes get it in a way you don't expect. Like, you could ask for money, then get it in the form of inheritance when someone you love dies. So instead of making it about me, I made the spell about Nicky. I knew if she got rich she'd give me money . . . As it was, she got a house because Chantel got rich and I still got money. So it worked.'

'Well, what's wrong with that?'

'It proves I'm a witch! And after that worked, I got really freaked out, so . . . When you were a kid, did you ever wonder if God really existed?'

'Yeah, of course.'

'Did you do that thing where you said: *God, if you're there, make it rain so I know you exist, then I'll believe in you?*'

Julie smiles. 'Yes. Everyone does. It didn't rain when I did it.'

'Me neither. But when my magic seemed to be working, I decided to test it the same way. I found a rain spell and performed it. The next day, this rain started, and then everything flooded, and the rain won't stop.'

'Leanne, you didn't cause the floods.'

'How do you know?'

'Ordinary people can't control nature.'

'Witches can.'

'Not to that extent.'

Leanne shrugs. 'Maybe I'm a powerful witch. Anyway, I'm scared.'

'What of?'

'This . . . power I seem to have. I never thought any of this stuff would work.'

Julie wants to laugh. This is ridiculous.

She fiddles with her car keys. 'Have you tried to reverse any of these spells?'

'You can't reverse magic. It doesn't work like that.'

'Can't you do a spell to make it stop raining?'

'No. You're not supposed to mess around with the weather.'

'But . . .'

'Obviously, I didn't know that when I did the rain spell.'

'Oh.'

'Also, I don't know a spell to make rain stop.'

'Have you looked on the Internet?'

'Yeah. People must like rain, there weren't any rain-stopping spells.'

'I suppose no one wants a drought,' Julie says.

'Oh yeah. I never thought of that.'

When Julie walks into Luke's room, something's different. David's there but that's not what it is. David and Luke are watching a film Julie and Luke have seen before. What is it that's wrong? A smell – patchouli. But Charlotte was here, wasn't she? Luke said so when he rang. Maybe it's this plan; the one Julie doesn't know about yet. She knows there's a plan, and in some way the room feels like there's something new in it, like a plan, like too much electricity before a storm.

'You were a long time,' David says.

'What was wrong with Leanne?' Luke asks.

Julie sits on the computer chair and logs on to Hotmail. 'Nothing, really,' she says. Leanne made her promise not to tell anyone about her special powers. 'Just some girl thing. Nothing to worry about. So what's been happening?'

'We're going to Wales,' David says.

Julie looks up from the computer. 'What? Who is?'

'We are,' David says. 'You, me, Luke and Charlotte.'

'That's the plan,' Luke explains. 'The one I told you about. David's coming.'

Julie's skin prickles. 'I don't understand,' she says.

David looks at Julie, then at Luke. 'Laters,' he says, getting up.

'Hang on – how are you getting home?' Julie asks, confused by everything.

'Walking. It's not far.' He smiles. 'I think I'd better leave you two to it.'

When he's gone, Luke's body droops. 'Sorry,' he says.

'Sorry? What for? I don't understand what's going on.' Luke doesn't reply. 'Luke?' Julie says. 'What the hell's going on?'

'I wanted to talk to you about it first. I . . .' He gets up and walks across the room, stands in front of his bookshelves for a second then turns and walks back to the bed. 'This healer – Wei. Charlotte put him in touch with me. She's due to go to India to do some Ayurveda course or something, and the people she's going with know this guy and they said he was really good, apparently . . . Anyway, he got in touch and he asked me all these questions and said he could heal me . . .'

'He said he could heal you?' Her body goes cold. 'Bloody hell, Luke. God.'

'Yeah. But I wasn't sure about him at first, and I didn't want to get your hopes up by telling you about him . . . But after I'd spoken to him a couple of times, he said he wanted to speak to you as well, and I thought . . .'

'Me? Why?'

'I don't know. I may have mentioned that you don't like travelling and stuff. Anyway, I'd arranged to speak to him last night, with you there – after the party – and I wanted to find out what you thought and everything but I drank that beer and I forgot and this morning I felt so bad. Charlotte came over from your house and I was in such a state, feeling like I'd let Wei down, and that this was my only chance of being cured, but that I'd stuffed it up. So she rang him, and they decided we should go to see him in Wales. How far away is Wales?'

'A long way away. Why can't he come here?'

'I'm not sure.'

'Didn't Charlotte ask?'

'I don't know. Sort of. I . . .'

'Oh, shit. Have you got her number?'

'Charlotte's?'

'Yeah.'

Luke goes to his computer and pulls up the address file for Charlotte. There's a Brentwood number there. Julie dials it. There's no reply.

'Hasn't she got a mobile?'

'She doesn't believe in mobiles. They unbalance her *doshas*. Why do you want to phone her anyway?'

'I want to find out what's going on – why this guy can't come here to see you; and if it's because he can't be bothered, maybe we could persuade him or something. We could pay him, I've got tips saved up.'

'He can't drive,' Luke says. 'I heard Charlotte say that he can't drive – and neither can her friends.'

'Oh, shit. The trains.'

'Huh?'

'They're not running – you must have heard about that big crash in Hatfield yesterday morning. That'll be why. The trains aren't running and there's no other way for him to get here. Maybe we can put it off until he can come here on the train.'

'That's not really fair, though,' Luke says.

'It's not really fair that you have to travel to Wales, considering you're not supposed to go out of the house.'

Luke looks at the floor. 'And he's leaving the country next week, apparently. He's only here for a while.'

'Oh God.'

'Julie?'

She gets up and walks to Luke's small bathroom and looks at herself in the mirror. Her pale, smooth skin, her boring hair – never highlighted or bleached or dyed. Her eyes are big and blue, but glazed with fear. She is used to seeing her face in this mirror, or in the one at home, or in the one in the Ladies' at The Edge – not that she'll be seeing it there again. She feels like her face wouldn't fit anywhere else; that she wouldn't look right outside of those places. She pulls half of her hair to one side, and plaits it. Then she plaits the other side. That's how Chantel had her hair.

Chantel wouldn't have a problem going somewhere, Julie thinks. Maybe if Julie keeps her hair like this she won't feel like herself, and if she doesn't feel like herself, she'll be able to do this. Fuck it. She's going to have to do this anyway, because she always promised she would. She needs to find out about this healer – but if Charlotte's recommended him and he says he can help then there's not much more to find out, really. She'll have to get a map, that's the main thing.

She'll have to get a map and find a way to get there without going on any main roads. And she'll have to think of a reason to tell Charlotte that she's doing that. And David. How the hell did David get invited along? Luke probably asked him to be polite, and David said yes because people like David will always join in with anything if it sounds like a laugh. This doesn't sound like a laugh to Julie. But there's still only one thing she can say.

'We are going to have to go there, aren't we?' she says, walking back into Luke's room. 'This is insane.'

'I know. I'm scared. But you'll look after me, won't you?'

'Of course I will. I just . . .' Julie walks across the room and sits on the bed, slouched over with her elbows on her knees and her head in her hands.

Luke looks at her. 'What?'

She looks up and smiles weakly. 'Nothing. Everything feels different, that's all.'

'Like you can't go back?'

'Yeah. Like you can't go back.'

'I feel weird inside,' Luke says.

Julie wants to say she feels weird too, but she can't. 'Weird how?' she says instead.

'I don't know. This has all happened so quickly. Jules?'

'Yeah?'

'Why aren't you saying that we can't go?'

'What do you mean?'

'I thought you'd say it was mad and that we couldn't go.'

Julie shrugs. 'Things feel different today. And anyway, we have to go. This guy's the only person who's ever said he could help you. And I promised that if we ever found a way to cure you, I'd do anything to make sure it happened.'

The only problem is that the last time Julie left Essex, seven years ago, she crawled home in tears. And another problem: what does this Wei guy know that no doctor in the world does? Julie doesn't believe in healers any more than she believes in ghosts or magic. Why would she? But Luke wants to go out, and he wants to try this, and at least Julie can look after him if she goes with him. She can't say what she really thinks about the idea of healing. If she did, then she wouldn't be able to go with Luke, and if she doesn't go it's fairly likely that he'll just go without her, with Charlotte and David. And anyway, maybe it is about time Julie and Luke left Windy Close, even just for a day or two. And maybe this healer does know something that other people don't. And maybe a small part of Julie still believes that if you try hard enough you can cure anything.

Chapter 27

There's a low hum, then the sound of something falling out of the sky. It sounds like a plane about to crash.

It's about eight in the morning. The sound of falling gets worse, until the house is vibrating with noise overhead. Julie scrambles out of bed, remembering news reports; eye-witness accounts of people who saw planes falling in their back gardens or the fields opposite; or the stories of the people who came home to find their roof mashed in by a wing or a cockpit saying how the packet of fags they went out for just saved their life. She's always hated the sound of planes flying overhead – they always sound like they're falling even when they're just flying – but this one sounds like it really is falling.

In the couple of seconds it's taken her to process these thoughts, Julie has jumped out of bed and run out into the street. She always does this when there's a loud noise overhead, the logic being that you can't be crushed to death in your house if you're not in the house. Also, you get a chance to see what it is and where it's falling and run in the opposite direction. This is Julie's flying-object drill: *Stay calm, get out of the house*. It's quite simple. Most complex is her storm drill: *Stay calm, change into rubber-soled shoes, close all windows, take off all metal jewellery, switch off everything electrical, don't touch water, don't go out, sit in a cupboard if possible*. Staying calm is the bit she needs to work on in these situations.

Shaking, she looks up at the sky. It's not a plane at all. It's actually a huge, military-style helicopter, almost right above the house, hovering. It's so loud that if Julie shouted right now she wouldn't be able to hear herself. It's making her ears hurt, and she's tired, and the vibrations are making her dizzy. There's still a chance it could fall.

'Go away,' she says softly. 'I can't handle this today. Just go away.'

After about five minutes it moves off over the A12 towards Chelmsford. But Julie can still hear a hum in the air and there's a chance it could come back, screaming overhead, falling – or at least sounding like it's falling. She stays where she is, sweating, trying not to think about the palpitations in her chest.

'What are you doing?' asks Chantel.

Julie didn't see her coming. 'What? Uh, looking for the postman,' Julie lies.

'Why?'

'I'm waiting for a parcel.'

'Oh. Are you OK?'

'Yeah, of course.'

'Is it true you need a camper van?'

'A what?'

'To go to Wales. Charlotte said . . .'

Julie feels nauseous. 'Can I talk you to later?' she says. 'I'm feeling a bit . . .' She runs into the house and into the downstairs toilet, gasping for air, begging her body not to be sick. Julie hasn't been sick for almost ten years. Her diet is supposed to prevent her from vomiting: no food-poisoning, no bacteria, no bugs. Julie starts her sickness drill: *Stay calm, think of clean things, breathe properly, run the taps.* She thinks of waterfalls, and green meadows, and ice-cubes, and then she switches on the taps in the bathroom. The feeling passes after a few minutes, but Julie's still sweating, and her heart's still going at a mad pace, and her breathing still feels jerky and shallow. As far as mornings go, this is about as shit as it gets. And she hardly got any sleep last night because she was worrying about having to go to Wales. She needs a cup of tea.

Her dad's in the kitchen, reading the *Guardian*.

'What's wrong with you?' he asks. 'Why are you running around?'

'I just . . . It doesn't matter.'

Julie grips the edge of the kitchen work-surface until she's breathing properly again. Then she puts the kettle on and tries to avoid looking at her dad.

'You look like one of the girls off the heroin leaflet,' he says.

The heroin leaflet is one of a series being produced by the art students at the college, under the supervision of Julie's dad. Their knowledge of class-B and -C drugs, their substandard mastery of DTP (Julie's dad objects to computers on the basis that corporations are using them to take over the world) and some warped but enthusiastic airbrushing have combined to produce roughly what you would expect: supposedly anti-drugs leaflets with an unmissable pro-drugs subtext, printed on card just thick enough to use for roaches.

'Thanks, Dad.'

'That's it! You're a heroin addict. That would explain everything. Maybe that's what the helicopter was here for – they must be on to you.'

'Yeah, very funny. It's eight o'clock in the morning. Heroin addicts don't get up at eight in the morning. You can put that in your leaflet under "tell-tale signs".'

'We don't do tell-tale signs any more. We just tell people how to sterilise needles. Anyway, you probably would get up at eight if the Feds were on to you.'

'I'm still pretty sure we don't have Feds in this country, Dad.'

Julie's dad always says *Feds* instead of *police*. He probably thinks it's funny or ironic. Or, more likely, his green-haired students say it, and they make it sound funny so he copies them. It's not actually his most irritating habit, but it is up there on the list. His top three most irritating habits include singing along with Slipknot and Limp Bizkit when they're on *Top of the Pops*, and taking his packed lunch to work in a Thunderbirds lunchbox because it's retro and he's trying to be cool. Actually, now Julie thinks about it, that's actually more sweet than it is irritating. It just becomes irritating when he does it.

He ignores her. 'Or if you were a doctor or something. Did you know that professional people are the biggest heroin users?'

Julie makes her tea. 'Is the college still flooded?' she asks.

'Our site's not so bad. London Road's had it. What's happening at The Edge?'

'It's OK now, I suppose. We had to have the floor tiles replaced.'

Julie hears the front door slam, then Dawn walks in wearing a frosted-pink bomber jacket and white leggings.

'Hi guys,' she says. 'You're up early,' she adds, to Julie.

Dawn usually stops for a cup of tea on her way to the industrial estates. 'That manager from The Edge phoned last night,' she says. 'He said he'd un-sack you if you went back before seven, or something.'

Doug laughs. 'Sacked?' he says, looking at Julie. 'You?'

'I wasn't sacked,' Julie says. 'I walked out.'

Dawn's eyes widen. 'Walked out? Why?'

'Owen was being really crap. A couple of us walked out, actually.'

'So you're unemployed now?' Doug asks.

'I'll get another job.'

'When?'

'I don't know. Don't give me that look, Dad. It was the right thing to do. We were being exploited.'

'Exploited?' Doug says, when he stops laughing. 'What the hell do you expect, working as a waitress at The fucking Edge? You were the one who always said you liked it. You were the one who always said it was . . .'

'Simple, yes, I know. Stop going on. I just changed my mind.'

'You join a union. You don't walk out. You get the union to negotiate for you.'

'I'll get another job.'

'You can't live here for nothing.'

'I don't live here for nothing. I pay rent, bills . . .'

'What are you going to pay them with now you're out of work?'

'Doug,' Dawn says. 'Leave it. She'll get another job. Oh – Cerise at the ceramics place is looking for a packer. Shall I see if I can get you an interview?'

'Thanks, Dawn, but I think I'll get another waitressing job.'

Doug gets up. '*Waitressing*. My daughter's ambition in life is to be a *waitress*.'

'She's not hurting anyone,' Dawn says. 'If that's what she wants . . .'

'I fathered a retard,' says Doug, heading for the door. 'Bloody hell.'

When he's gone, Dawn says: 'He doesn't mean it.'

'Yes he does,' Julie replies.

Later, after lunch, Julie knocks on Chantel's door. Nicky answers, dressed in tracksuit bottoms and a T-shirt with the words *Love is War* on the front.

'I've got my pilates video on pause,' she says. 'Cup of tea later?'

'Yeah, that would be nice. Is, um . . . Is Chantel in?'

'Up the stairs, down the hall, on the end.'

'Thanks.'

Chantel's room is a lot smaller than Nicky's. One whole wall is covered with pictures of elephants. Another has surfing posters – girls with blonde hair and wetsuits in some scenes; in others, androgynous figures riding pure blue waves. By the bed is a picture of a group of people with wet hair sitting by a fire on a sunset beach. Another wall has transparent shelves covered with ornaments. It's much tidier – and more homely – than Julie's room, which is more of a tangle of wires for her stereo and laptop and TV and a load of clothes, and bits of paper covered in numbers in a heap on the floor. Everything in here seems to be in the right place. A blue dressing gown with little elephants on it hangs neatly behind the door while ten different pairs of flip-flops are lined up under the bed. About fifty bottles of nail varnish are arranged on the dresser like a colour palette, moving from shades of red to shades of blue, darker colours at the bottom, lighter colours at the top. Around them sit several toy elephants, an electric toothbrush (still in its packaging) and some letters with unfamiliar-looking stamps. In the middle of all this, on the bed, Chantel is arranging photographs in an album. She's listening to Radio 1 – Julie can hear Mark and Lard making some sort of joke about the weather.

'Hello?' Julie says, knocking at the open door.

Chantel looks up uncertainly. 'Oh – hi, Julie.' She gets up and turns the radio down, then sits back on her bed with her pile of photographs and albums.

'I'm sorry about before,' Julie says quickly, walking a few steps into the room. 'I was having a bad morning. I thought I'd better come round and apologise, or explain or something. I must have seemed really rude, running off like that.'

'When? Oh – in the street. No worries. Do you want to sit down?'

Julie sits awkwardly on the edge of the bed. There isn't anywhere else.

'How's Luke?' asks Chantel.

'He's fine. Oh, he's pretty freaked about going to Wales, though.'

'Has he really never been anywhere?'

'No.'

'Charlotte told me about Wales, by the way,' Chantel says. 'I mean, that's how I knew . . . I haven't told anyone. She told me not to.'

'Thanks. What were you saying about a camper van before?'

'She said you wanted to borrow one. Charlotte did, I mean. I thought you'd know what I was talking about. I mean, I haven't actually got a camper van yet, but I was telling Charlotte I'd like to get one, to use for going surfing, once I pass my test. She said it's a shame I didn't have one I could lend you now, because she said Luke will need more space than you've got in your car, when you go to Wales, because he can't lie down and be covered on the back seat of a Mini.'

'That's true,' Julie says. 'David's coming as well, now, so there definitely won't be room.'

'David?'

'Yeah.'

'He's nice, isn't he?'

'I suppose so,' Julie says. 'Anyway, when were you talking to Charlotte?'

'She was here last night. She came here from Luke's.'

'Oh.' For some reason this makes Julie feel weird. 'Why?'

Chantel looks confused. Julie realises that this seems like an odd question to ask.

'We were just talking about things, you know?'

'Yeah, of course. I . . .'

Chantel smiles. 'She's nice, isn't she?'

'Yeah. She is.'

'She was telling me about when she went to Europe and stuff.'

'Oh.'

Julie wanted to ask Charlotte about that but never found the right moment. Now Chantel knows all about it before she does and she's known Charlotte what, five minutes? Julie tries to shift slightly to get more comfortable on the bed, although she doesn't know why she's still here. Outside, the drizzle turns into full-on rain and a strong wind blows raindrops at Chantel's window. For a second, it's like someone has sprayed the side of the house with a huge power-shower nozzle.

'I love rain,' says Chantel. 'I bet there are some amazing waves on the coast.'

Julie thinks of big surfy waves with soapy foam but her mind won't accept this picture and turns the waves into big walls of water out of control . . . tidal waves, mega-tsunami that could wipe out whole coastal towns. Her heart thumps as the rain gets heavier outside. What if the rain came so strongly out of the sky that everything was suddenly washed away? Julie wants to feel safe. This rain isn't making her feel safe.

Chantel's still organising her photo albums. She picks up a photo of a goat.

'This is Billy,' she says, handing Julie the picture.

Then there's a flash, and a huge bang in the sky. Julie drops the picture.

'Oh, shit,' she says.

'Julie?'

Julie's looking at her shoes. Trainers. That's OK. Can she ask Chantel to shut the window? Probably not. The radio? How mad will Chantel think she is if she asks her to switch off the radio? She could leave, except she can't go outside when there's lightning. She's got to keep safe, but seem normal. Oh, God.

'Are you OK?' Chantel asks. 'Are you afraid of storms?'

Julie forces a smile. 'Yeah. Silly, aren't I? Oh – sorry, I dropped your photo.' She picks it up from the floor. 'I was just a bit, you know, startled by that lightning.'

'Yeah, me too. It sounded like it was right overhead.'

There's another flash, and another bang. The lights go out for a second. The bed's right in front of the window, which is still open. Julie's way too close to the storm. She gets up from the bed and walks over to Chantel's shelves, pretending to look at all her ornaments. In the space of one day, Chantel's seen her losing it first over a helicopter and now a storm. This is stupid. She tries to pull herself together, but by the time the next flash comes, she's almost crying. She just wishes the world would leave her alone, that she could go and live in a hole away from all this crap.

Chantel looks concerned. 'Julie?'

'Sorry. I'm . . . Not good with storms.'

'Would you like to sit in a cupboard or something?'

'Is that OK? Would you mind?'

Chantel laughs. 'I was sort of joking. Mind you, it is a bit mad out there, maybe it's a good idea. Come on, we can both fit in here.' She gets off the bed and opens the doors to the huge built-in wardrobe. There's another flash and Chantel sort of pushes Julie into the wardrobe, giggling slightly.

'Come on,' she says. 'Get in.' There's another clap of thunder and she squeals. 'Quick, come on, before we get fried.'

It's dark and warm inside the wardrobe, and Julie instantly feels safe – almost irrationally so, as if she'd still be safe in here even if the house took a direct hit from the lightning and crumbled to the ground. There's a clean smell of clothes, and a leathery smell of shoes and trainers. For a few seconds, all Julie can hear is her own breathing as she nestles between Chantel and the back of the wardrobe. Then Chantel giggles again.

'What are we like?' she says.

Julie laughs too. 'I'm so pathetic,' she moans.

Outside there's a loud crash and a much dimmer flash of lightning.

'I'm glad we're in here,' Chantel says.

'Me too.'

'It's getting worse from the sound of it.'

'Yeah.'

'My hair feels all staticky.'

'Really? God.'

'I might be imagining it, though.' Chantel laughs. 'What are we like?' she says again. 'I'm glad we're not on a golf course.'

'Why?'

'That's where most people get struck by lightning. Stressed-out accountants with pacemakers and stuff apparently. You know I read somewhere that if you are stuck out in an open place and a storm starts, you should lie on the ground and stick your bum in the air.'

Julie laughs, but makes a mental note. 'How does that help, though?' she asks.

'I can't remember. Something about being a small target.'

'Oh.'

Chantel shifts slightly and her leg brushes Julie's. 'I thought you hated me, by the way,' she says.

'No,' Julie says quickly. 'Course I don't. Why would you think that?'

'Because I gave Luke beer and stuff . . . I felt really bad about that.'

'No, it's not that . . . Oh, God. I've given you totally the wrong impression.'

'Don't worry,' Chantel says. 'I'm oversensitive. That's probably it. It's just this morning, out in the street, you couldn't get away from me quick enough.'

'That's why I came to apologise,' Julie says. 'It wasn't you at all.'

'Oh. Cool.' Chantel sounds relieved. 'No worries, then.'

Julie sighs. 'It was . . .'

'You don't have to tell me.'

'No, it's all right. Look, you know how I'm scared of storms?'

'Yeah. I am too when they're like this.'

'Well that helicopter this morning . . . I was scared of that too.'

'Yeah, it was mad, wasn't it? I came out to look at it as well.'

Julie frowns. 'Really?'

'Yeah. It was well scary. Why didn't you just say that this morning?'

'I didn't want to seem like a total . . .'

'Muppet?' suggests Chantel.

Julie laughs. 'Yeah. I don't like admitting when I'm scared.'

'I know what you mean. I don't think anyone does.'

'Some of the stuff I'm scared of is really stupid, which doesn't help.'

'Everyone's scared of stupid stuff, though,' Chantel says. 'My mum's scared of newspapers.'

'Newspapers?'

'Yeah. The print. When she was a kid she put newspaper in her hamster's cage and it died, because the print was toxic. Anyway, since then she won't touch newspapers of any sort. She thinks if she reads enough newspapers over a long enough period of time the print might be toxic enough to kill her too. How stupid is that?'

'It's quite logical, in a way.'

'Yeah, but you can take logic too far, can't you?'

It's warm and secretive in the wardrobe. Julie feels safe in there.

'You OK?' Chantel asks.

'Yeah. I feel much better.'

'It's still bad out there, though.'

'We'd better stay in here, then,' Julie says. 'Unless . . . ?'

'No, I'm cool. I like it in here, actually. I've never sat in a wardrobe before.'

'Me neither. I've sat in cupboards, of course.'

Chantel laughs. 'You're mental. You remind me of my granddad.'

'Your granddad? How?'

'He was scared of planes, storms, any loud noises in the sky. It was because of the war. He died about five years ago but when the Gulf War was on he insisted we turn off all the lights. He thought we'd have to have another blackout, and even though we explained it wasn't that type of war, he still insisted on keeping all the lights off at night. Imagine, though, thinking every plane that flies overhead is going to bomb you or something. That's what his life was like for about fifty years. It was like the world moved on but he couldn't. Well, I suppose if you'd seen the things he'd seen, how could you?'

Julie thinks every plane that flies overhead is going to

fall out of the sky. She can almost imagine what that would be like. But she doesn't have a reason like he did. She has no idea why she finds planes so terrifying. Julie finds planes so terrifying that when she cried at the end of *Casablanca*, it was because she thought the plane the Laszlos left in was going to crash. In the wardrobe, though, it feels almost like planes don't exist, and it's like wartime in here, but a special wartime with no planes and no actual war: a cosy bunker, underground.

'I don't even notice planes going overhead,' Chantel continues. 'But he noticed every single one. I think the worry almost sent him mad.' She looks really sad. 'He was such a great bloke, you know? I loved my granddad so much. You know how people sometimes say things like, "All old people go on about the war all the time," like it's boring? I hate people like that. It isn't boring. Some of the stories Granddad told me were things I'll never forget. And also, we're only all here living in freedom because of what our grandparents did. I just can't understand why people our age wouldn't show those people some respect because of that, because they were so brave and did all that stuff people do on their PlayStations now – but actually for real, and actually for a reason. How many people of our generation would actually see someone get killed? And if you did, you'd get shoved into grief counselling or something. In the war, you just had to get on with it. Do you know the saddest thing?'

'What?' says Julie, pushing her hair back.

'Soon there won't be anyone left who remembers the war, and people won't go on about it, and no one will complain about old people talking about the war any more, because there won't be any of that generation left. Don't you think that's weird? All my life, old people have talked about the war. But I realised that soon you'll have a new generation of old people who'll just talk about DIY and cruises or something. They'll have been too young to have been in the war. I suppose maybe some of those people would have lost their parents in the war, so they might talk about it a bit. Then there's us, and even though our parents and grandparents might have been affected by it, we don't talk about it much, and then there'll be our children, who'll be like, "What war?" It's sad, isn't it?'

'Yeah. When you put it like that . . . It really is.'

'My granny was a lesbian during the war,' Chantel says, almost proudly.

Julie laughs. 'Only during the war?'

'Pretty much. She loved my granddad loads but they didn't have sex before marriage in those days, I don't think, and in the end they were more like companions. I think she always wanted to be with a woman. She used to hint at it, but she never really did anything about it. I don't want to be like that.'

'Like what?'

'Not experiencing the things I want to experience.'

'Oh.' Julie laughs. 'I thought you meant you didn't want to go through life not being a lesbian.'

Chantel laughs too. 'I do want to try it out,' she says. 'Seriously.'

'Try what out?'

'Doing it with a girl. I was telling Luke the other night.'

'I bet he loved that.'

'Oh, he did.'

They both laugh.

'Maybe everyone's just bisexual anyway,' Chantel says. 'I read that somewhere.'

'Yeah, I've heard that, too.'

Chantel shrugs. 'Could be true, I suppose.'

'Have you ever fancied a girl?' Julie asks.

Chantel wrinkles her nose. Julie can only see her vaguely in the dark of the wardrobe. 'No, not really. I'm still trying. Maybe Drew Barrymore.'

'Hmm.' Julie couldn't picture herself fancying Drew Barrymore.

'What about you?' Chantel asks.

'Huh? Me what?'

'Have you ever fancied a girl, you muppet.'

'Oh. Yeah, I did once, actually.'

Chantel squeals. 'Really? Truly?'

'Yeah. And, well, don't tell anyone this . . .'

'I won't.'

Julie takes a deep breath. 'It was Charlotte.'

'Wow. Did you ever tell her?'

'Not exactly. I think she knew but nothing ever happened.'

'Are you glad?'

'Maybe. I'm not sure we'd still be friends if . . .'

'Yeah. Doing it with friends is never good.'

'I know. Charlotte was really confused at the time as well. She thought she might be a lesbian because she wanted to leave her boyfriend. Then he died. I don't know what she thinks now.'

'She isn't. A lesbian, I mean.'

'Oh. How do you know? Did you talk about it?'

'Yeah. Last night. I was going on about it again – you wouldn't think I'm actually quite shy, would you? I can't remember how it came up in conversation in the first place . . . Oh, yeah, we were saying you were pretty, and then we wondered if that made us sound dykey, or at least I was wondering about that – well, sort of hoping, actually. Charlotte told me about how she went around Europe after she stopped living here – she was trying to find herself or something. She was hitching, and she ended up doing a few hundred miles with a lesbian truck-driver. I think that convinced her that the whole thing wasn't her scene.'

Julie's still blushing from the idea of two girls finding her pretty. Obviously Charlotte didn't mention that there was any possible connection at all between her finding Julie pretty and ending up going around Europe. But now Julie thinks about it, there probably wasn't.

'In what way?' Julie asks.

'She said she couldn't stand the thought of having to be all girly or all blokey. And she kept going on about mullets, about how all dykes seemed to have mullets.'

'That sounds like Charlotte.'

'Yeah.' Chantel laughs. 'So . . . Have you ever liked any other girls?'

'No, I don't think so. With Charlotte I think I was just caught up in a moment. I never could have done anything sexual with her.'

'That's the key, isn't it? I mean, I can fancy girls if I really try, but I can't ever really think about kissing one. Maybe it's because I've been with so many blokes. I don't know. I'll have to keep trying.'

'Why, though? Why's it so important? Can't you just give up trying?'

Chantel sighs. 'This is going to sound stupid.'

'Go on.'

'Well, just before I won the Lottery, my gran died . . .'

'Oh, I'm sorry,' Julie says.

'Yeah. I was devastated. Still am, actually. I was much closer to her than I am to my mum. I mean, my mum's all right but we don't totally get each other. She wants to be normal and I don't . . . Or I do, but our ideas of what normal is are a bit different, if that makes any sense. Anyway, my gran seemed to have everything so sussed out. She loved my granddad, but she obviously had – or had at some point – this secret life. Not just the girl thing but other stuff, and I so wanted a way into knowing about it. If you gave her sherry, she'd hint at it, you know? But I never found out exactly what she'd done or what sort of person she'd been when she was young. But I've always wanted to be like her. And so far, I'm turning out just like my mum. I don't want to be common and shag loads of guys and use my money to buy a pub and loads of gold jewellery. I know this makes me sound like a snob, but . . . I want to do something different, or interesting. I thought if I started shagging girls I'd be able to be different to Mum, and more like Gran. It's stupid, really.'

'Maybe you should just stick to surfing,' Julie says, smiling.

'Yeah, maybe.'

'By the way,' Julie says. 'What's with all the elephants?'

'Huh?'

'I noticed that you've got loads of elephants in your room.'

'Oh, yeah. I like them. They're my favourite animal.'

'Why?'

'They never forget. And they don't mind being fat.'

The storm passes eventually and Julie has to come out of the wardrobe, although she felt better inside it than she's felt anywhere recently. The sun's shining through the dark-blue clouds outside, and although it's still raining, it looks like it could brighten up soon.

Chantel's smoothing down her skirt.

'Do you want to come to Wales?' Julie says suddenly.

'OK,' says Chantel, grinning. 'I'd love to. I could do with an adventure. So what do you want to do about this camper van?'

'Well, I suppose we definitely won't all fit in my car . . .'

'We'll go van shopping tomorrow, then. My treat.'

'And we're going to have to make a space-suit,' says Julie.

Chapter 28

No one can think of anyone who can sew, apart from Leanne.

'Please, no,' says Charlotte. 'Anything but that.'

'We don't really have any other choice,' says Julie.

'Maybe I can learn,' Charlotte suggests. 'We've got all day today and most of tomorrow.'

It's Friday now. The plan is to leave as soon as possible after it's dark on Saturday night.

'We need a sewing machine anyway,' Julie points out. 'And Leanne's got one. We're going to have to ask her. There's no other way.'

'Can't we just buy one?' Charlotte suggests.

Chantel shakes her head. 'No one would know how to use it, would they?'

Charlotte, Julie and Chantel are in Julie's bedroom. David, who's been on a silver-foil-gathering mission since just before midnight last night, is still missing in action. His plan involved breaking into The Edge, stealing all the silver foil and then pissing in Owen's office. No one knows if he succeeded but Julie's hoping for the best because the foil is going to be one of the main parts of Luke's space-suit. David was supposed to be here an hour ago. This is the first official meeting of the Going Out Committee.

Charlotte's flicking through *Auto Express*. 'There are loads of camper vans in here,' she says. 'So that bit shouldn't be too difficult.' She looks at her watch. 'We should think about going to see some of them before too long.'

'So who's going? What's the plan?' Julie asks.

'Well, you're the only one who can drive apart from David and he's not here. I think he's banned anyway, so you'll have to go look at the camper vans and test-drive them,' Charlotte says. 'And I'm not staying here on my own sewing with Leanne, so I'll come with you . . .'

'Hang on,' says Chantel. 'If we all go and get the van, who's going to make the space-suit?'

'Leanne, apparently,' Charlotte says. 'And Luke, when he wakes up.'

'We'll have to help, though. And we've still got to go and ask her if she'll do it.'

'Well, how long will it take to get a camper van?' Charlotte asks.

Chantel and Julie both look blank.

'It can't take that long, can it?' Charlotte says. 'Leanne and Luke can start off the suit and we can all help tonight. And David, if he ever shows up again. I'll start ringing these numbers while you two go and ask Leanne. Can I use your phone, Jules?'

'Sure,' says Julie.

Leanne isn't at home. She's at work.

'I hope David's all right,' Julie says, as she drives into the retail park.

The Edge looks funny now, a place Julie knows she'll never go to again.

'I'm sure he's fine,' says Chantel.

Blockbuster has changed. The usual carpet now has a piece of yellow brick-effect linoleum looping across it, joining the 'Manager's Choice' section to the popcorn and then around to the tills, where there's a backlit display of *Wizard of Oz*-inspired films, including *Wild at Heart*, *ET*, *My Own Private Idaho* and the *Back to the Future* series.

'Hi, Chantel, hi, Julie,' Leanne says. 'Do you like our yellow brick road?'

'It's nice,' says Chantel uncertainly. 'Why are you dressed like that?'

As well as her usual Blockbuster uniform, Leanne's wearing bright-red shoes, blue ankle socks and has her hair tied in two bunches. She is also wearing blue eye-shadow, and has painted several freckles across her nose with what looks like brown eyeliner.

'I'm Dorothy,' she explains.

Chantel looks her up and down again. 'Dorothy . . . ?'

'It's *Wizard of Oz* week, dummy.'

Julie tries not to laugh. 'We wanted a favour,' she says.

'I did wonder what you were doing here,' Leanne says. 'Owen's not happy with you. I'm surprised you'd even show your face on the retail park now . . .' Julie makes a face and Leanne pauses. 'So anyway, what's this favour?' she asks suspiciously.

'You can sew, can't you?' Chantel says.

'Yeah, course I can. You know I can. Why?'

'We've got a sewing project,' Julie says. 'We need your help.'

A customer comes up to the counter with three children's videos and a PlayStation game. Leanne glares at Julie and Chantel and they move away from the counter. The man cheerfully places his choices on the counter and hands over his blue-and-yellow laminated membership card, smiling. Leanne scans the card and sort of tuts.

'Oh dear,' she says. 'We've got some outstanding fines here.'

'That's OK,' the man says, still smiling. 'I think I dropped a couple of late ones in the box the other night . . . The kids always want to watch their films at least three times. I can't understand it. I'll be glad when these floods are over and they can get back to school. It's driving me nuts . . .'

'The fine is £12,' Leanne says.

The man looks shocked. 'Twelve quid? Wow. Are you sure?'

'Yes. *Lolita*. It was four days late.'

'*Lolita*?' Now the man looks really confused. 'Are you sure?'

'What would you like to do, sir? You can pay by credit card, cheque or cash. I'm afraid I can't let you have these videos until you've cleared the fine.'

'Look,' he says, nicely. 'The fine isn't the problem, I just . . .'

'If you can't pay the fine, sir, I'm afraid I can't allow you to take any more videos out until it is cleared,' Leanne says. She picks up the man's videos and his game and places them out of his reach behind the counter, as if he's about to run off with them.

The man looks pissed off now. 'I didn't say I couldn't pay the fine,' he says slowly. 'I am just saying that I don't understand how it got there. Sure, I'll pay it, if it's mine, but I'm not sure it is, that's all. And I don't particularly like being spoken to as if I'm a . . .'

'I'm sorry, sir, but you'll have to clear the fine before you can take . . .'

'I can pay the bloody fine,' he says loudly, as if Leanne can't hear him. 'That's not the issue. I've just never taken out – what was it? – *Lolita*. I only ever use this place to get stuff for the kids. My kids are six years old, eight years old and ten years old. Why would they want to watch *Lolita*?'

'I'm sorry, sir, but the computer clearly says . . .'

'Are you suggesting your computer knows more about what I do than . . . I do?'

Leanne doesn't answer. 'I'm sorry, sir,' she repeats, 'but you're going to have to . . .'

He takes his wallet out, frustrated now. 'Are you a robot?' he asks.

'The computer says that . . .'

'Here.' He throws a selection of credit cards at her. 'Take your fucking pick.'

'I'm sorry, sir, but I'm going to have to ask you to leave.'

The man takes a deep breath. He seems like the kind of person who's never been ejected from any establishment in his life. 'OK, look. I am going to pay this fine and then – rest assured – you won't ever see me in here again. I'll be using Videos Videos Videos on the High Street from now on. And you'll be hearing from my solicitor about this.'

Leanne sighs. 'I'll clear this fine,' she says. 'But I'm afraid I can't allow your membership here to continue. And I won't be able to give you back your card.'

'Can you not even lip-read?' the man says. 'I just said I'm never coming in here again. You can stick my membership card up your . . .'

'Which credit card would you like me to use?' Leanne asks.

'Take your pick,' the man says again.

'I'm sorry, sir, but you'll have to choose one. I'm not authorised to . . .'

The man holds out his hand and Leanne gives him back his cards.

'Forget it,' he says. 'Fucking sue me for the twelve quid. I can't stand any more of this.' He puts his cards back in his wallet and leaves the shop, his face red, looking like he might cry with frustration.

'Nice customer service,' Julie says.

'Firm but fair,' says Leanne.

'Where's Lloyd?' Julie asks. 'Don't you have to ask him before you can cancel a membership?'

'Strictly, yes. But he's out buying bunting.'

'Bunting?'

Leanne shrugs. 'More promotions,' she explains. 'Lloyd's promotion-mad.'

'I'm surprised you've got any customers left to promote anything to,' Chantel says. 'Is this Lloyd as heavy-handed as you are?'

Leanne laughs. 'Lloyd? He's a pussycat. He would've wiped that fine and probably given the guy a free rental to make up for the "mistake". But you can't be too soft on these people. You get customers clocking up ridiculous fines, then they tell you that their mother died, or they left the tape in their car and it was stolen, or the car was stolen with the tape in it, or they accidentally put it in their wedding-video case and packed it in a suitcase and it went to Barbados or something – they're really inventive sometimes but it's all lies, and it's all to get out of paying a fine. It's just theft, and it has to be stamped out. We're running a video shop here, not a charity.'

Julie and Chantel look at each other but say nothing.

'Anyway, what's this thing you're sewing?' Leanne asks.

'It's a . . .' Chantel begins.

Julie nudges her. 'We'll tell you later,' she says to Leanne.

'I'll need a pattern,' Leanne says. 'That's if I decide to help.'

Chantel sighs. 'I think we're going to have to invent the pattern. It's a bit unusual.'

'I might not be able to do it without a pattern,' Leanne says.

'Didn't you do fashion at college?' Julie says.

'Yes. You know I did. Until I left.'

'Well surely you know how to design your own patterns?'

'A bit. But they always went wrong. That's why I left.'

'I'm sure you'll be fine at this,' Julie says.

'I don't know.' She sighs. 'When does it have to be done by?'

'Tomorrow afternoon.'

'Tomorrow?' Leanne shakes her head. 'No. I'm working tomorrow.'

'We were planning to work on it tonight,' Chantel says. 'At Luke's.'

'Definitely not, then. I'm trying to avoid him. I think we need time apart at the moment. You know we definitely split up? I told him that . . .'

'Come on, Leanne,' Julie says. 'We really need your help.'

'You're the only person we can ask,' Chantel says. 'Please?'

'I don't know. Have you got fabric?'

'A lot of it's going to be tin f–' starts Chantel.

Julie cuts in. 'No, not yet.'

'You'll need to buy the fabric.'

'Of course,' Julie says. 'How much should we get?'

'How am I supposed to know? You haven't even told me what it's for.'

'It's kind of a body-suit,' Julie says.

'Maybe a bit like a wetsuit,' Chantel adds.

'I can't make a wetsuit. The fabric's too thick to fit in the machine.'

'Not with wetsuit fabric,' Chantel says. 'Just that shape.'

'Just get loads, then.'

'What's loads?'

'Ten metres? I dunno. Whatever you think.'

'Is ten metres a lot?'

'Yes. Probably too much, but we'll need to leave room for error.'

'Why?'

'I might be a bit rusty,' says Leanne. 'And I've only ever made skirts.'

'You've only ever made skirts?' Julie says.

'Yes. I could never work out how to do sleeves.'

'Oh God,' says Chantel.

'That's fine,' Julie says quickly. 'It'll be fine. We'll all help.'

'Try to get some sort of pattern if you can,' Leanne says as they leave. 'And thread for the sewing machine, and pins – I'm almost out of pins – oh, and Julie, I need to speak to you as well, later. I need a favour in return for this.'

'I felt really sorry for that guy,' Chantel says in the car, on the way into town.

'What, the *Lolita* guy?'

'Yeah. I hate the way shop assistants speak to you – like you're insane – just because you've got a fine on your video membership or something.'

'I know,' Julie says. 'Leanne's like Hitler dressed up as Dorothy. It's disturbing.'

Chantel laughs. 'She's not the only one, though. One time, just after I won the Lottery, I'd been on this big shopping spree, mainly getting surprises for Mum, and a few bits for Michelle and Leanne, and some treats for Billy. Anyway, I stopped off at Tesco on the way home, because I was going to do a big shop for Mum – she always had to buy the economy brands, and never had any luxuries, so I thought I'd surprise her with strawberries and champagne and chocolates and bubble-bath and whatever. So I had my basket piled up with all this stuff, and I went through the checkout and put it all in bags – I remember I chose those recycled "bags for life" which are 10p each, because I thought they were such a good idea – and when it came to paying I just handed over my debit card that I'd been using all day and kind of daydreamed as the girl put it through the swiper. Anyway, I could hardly believe it when she asked me if I had another form of payment because the card was being rejected. I asked her to try it again – assuring her that I had plenty of money in my account – and I sort of laughed and made a joke about how I always used to worry about my card being rejected, because I was always so close to my overdraft limit, but that this time I wasn't worried because I had loads of money in my account. So she tried it about three more times, and said it was still being rejected. She suggested that I should go and draw out cash from the cash-point machine, because I didn't have any cash . . .'

'Why didn't you have any cash?' Julie asks.

'Oh, I'm scared of carrying cash. I've always been scared I'll lose it. I think it's because once when I was a kid we went shopping, and I had twenty quid that I'd been saving for about a year or something, and I lost it – it must have dropped out of my pocket or something – and Mum couldn't afford to replace it and I had to start saving again. I think I spent that whole day crying, searching the pavements in Basildon and just crying, I suppose. If ever I do carry cash nowadays, I check every five minutes or so to see if it's still there. It's almost obsessive.'

Julie smiles. 'Presumably you didn't explain this to the Tesco girl?'

Chantel laughs. 'No, I just said I didn't have any. But I don't have a cash-point number for my debit card – there's no point, is there, because you can pay for everything by card, and get cash-back if you really need cash, and anyway, I can never remember those numbers – so I was totally screwed. I made another joke to the girl about how I'd just won the Lottery recently and how ridiculous this was, considering I had about two hundred thousand pounds in this particular account, but she just looked at me like I was mad and said there was nothing she could do. I asked if I could speak to the supervisor so she sort of sighed and called her over – and all the other people in the queue were getting so pissed off. The supervisor did that whole Leanne routine on me, not listening when I tried to explain anything, just repeating this phrase over and over: "I'm sorry, madam, but I'm afraid if you can't find another method of payment there's nothing we can do. It's not our problem, it's the bank. If their computer says you don't have the funds, we're not authorised to override it . . ." Blah, blah, blah. I tried being nice to her – even though by this point I knew I was going to have to leave my shopping behind – because I was feeling so humiliated, and I just wanted her to sympathise with me, but every time I started saying something friendly, like, "Oh, well, I suppose this must happen all the time", or, "Silly me, I should have brought more cards with me", she just repeated the same phrase, as if I was trying to con her into letting me steal all this shopping.

'It upset me so much, I just ended up leaving in tears. It was that brutal brick-wall attitude that got me. It completely spoilt my whole day. And the bank said there was no problem with my card, and that it was probably the Tesco machine that was at fault and that the girl could have just typed the number in instead, but she didn't, she just kept trying to swipe it. When I rang up Tesco Customer Services to complain, they did explain that they get people trying to rip them off all the time, sometimes with real sob-stories, and that's why they adopted the brick-wall strategy, but I told them I thought that was stupid. If that manager hadn't been so blinkered and so into thinking I was just out to con them, maybe she'd have tried punching in the number. But she just didn't bother. The Customer Services people were quite good about it, actually, but I haven't been in Tesco since.'

Julie turns the windscreen wipers up a notch because it's suddenly raining a lot harder. She's got to find somewhere in town to park the van, then they've got to go and buy all this fabric.

There are no spaces to park on the High Street, so Julie drives around to the carpark behind The Rising Sun.

Chapter 29

By seven o'clock, Luke's room is covered in pins, bits of fabric and tissue paper but no one actually knows what they're doing yet. Leanne's still getting over her shock at being told the plan.

'I still can't believe you're doing this,' she keeps saying. 'Jean's going to go mental.'

'I wonder how Julie and Charlotte are getting on,' Chantel says.

Julie and Charlotte are out buying a camper van with some cash Chantel got out of the bank in town. She's already explained to Luke about Blockbuster, and her shopping trip with Julie afterwards, and how there was no such thing as a sewing pattern for a body-suit (apart from for babies), and about how they had no idea about what fabric to get, or really how much, and how Julie kept worrying about where David was and how much of a nightmare Leanne was going to be. Chantel decided in the end that she'd be better off at Luke's helping with the space-suit while Julie and Charlotte got the van, and Luke was grateful because he had no idea what had already gone on today. Also, he didn't really like the idea of being stranded on his own with Leanne.

Since then, David's turned up with fifty rolls of tin foil, a motorcycle helmet and a strange don't-ask-what-happened expression, and Leanne's emerged with her sewing machine and a bit of an attitude that Luke can't work out, but seems to be something to do with the fact that she was the last person to be told what's going on, and that she's only been included because she can sew.

'I can't believe you didn't get any sort of pattern,' Leanne complains.

'They only had ones for babies. I told you that,' Chantel says.

'You should have got one of those, then. We could have scaled it up.'

'Yes, I know. You already said that.'

'Right,' says David. 'I reckon Luke should lie on the floor on the fabric, and we can just draw around him. Then we just cut out the pieces and sew them up. Sorted.'

'What about zippers and stuff?' Leanne says. 'You know, a way in and out?'

The others are all sitting on the floor, looking at the fabric with puzzled expressions. Luke's sitting at his computer, looking up space-suit designs on the Internet. He's feeling more excited then he's ever felt before, and this is making him cheerful. The more cheerful he gets, the more pissed off Leanne seems to become.

'Hey, look at this,' he says. 'SpaceProps.com. We could have hired a space-suit from them. Well, if we'd known we were doing this about a month in advance, we could have.'

'Shut up, Luke,' Leanne says.

'I'm only joking,' he says. 'They're replicas. They wouldn't work, would they?'

'Let's have a look,' says Chantel. She stands up and looks over Luke's shoulder at the picture on the screen. 'Wow, that looks well complicated.'

David has a look too. 'It doesn't have to look like that, though, does it?' he says. 'It just has to perform a function. All we have to do is make a body-suit then stick all the tin foil on it so it reflects the sun.

'Just find me a pattern,' Leanne says.

That's what Luke's supposed to be doing on the Internet. He searches again, for the phrase 'making a space-suit', and is directed to the NASA site, which has several interesting space-suit-making projects intended for schools, involving balloons, hacksaws, sewer-pipe and gloves. 'Gloves,' he says suddenly, looking at the screen. 'We'll need gloves, won't we? You know, to connect to the sleeves. Unless you can make them.'

'I'm not making gloves as well,' Leanne says.

'I'll ring Julie on the mobile,' Chantel says. 'I'll tell her to pick some up.'

'Where will she get gloves at this time of night?' David says.

'Supermarket? I don't know.'

'There's other stuff on here,' Luke says. 'But I don't know what any of it is.'

David has a look. 'Oh, I see,' he says. 'Look, that tubing stuff is for flexibility. They should get some of that. And Duct tape as well, to join those bits together . . . Shit, where're they going to get all this stuff? We should have thought about this earlier.'

'What about one of those DIY shops on the retail park?' Chantel suggests, dialling Julie's number. 'Hi,' she says into the phone. 'How's it going? Oh, cool. Well, we've got a bit of a shopping list developing here – yeah, I know.' She laughs. 'Yeah, she is, a bit. Anyway, shall I just read this stuff out to you? Sorry? Oh, a DIY shop. One on the retail park? I know, sorry. Oh, OK. Speak to you then.' She flips her phone shut.

'Aren't they getting it?' David asks.

'Yeah, they are, but they don't have any paper or a pen, so they're going to ring me back when they get to the shop.'

'Print that out,' David says to Luke. 'And we'll see what else we can find, before they ring back.'

'Can someone at least measure Luke?' Leanne says. 'We're wasting so much time.'

'Why don't you do it?' David says.

'I'm not touching him,' she says. 'He might get excited.'

'I'll do it,' says Chantel, sighing, and picking up the tape-measure.

Luke gets up. 'I haven't been measured for ages,' he says.

'Oh, look,' David says, sitting down at Luke's computer. 'They've got a list of average measurements here. Well, biggest and smallest. We could use measurements in between those. Luke's seems like average build.'

'It has to fit properly,' Chantel says.

'Yeah, but there are over a hundred measurements to be taken.'

Chantel looks over his shoulder. 'Blah, blah . . . Elbow-to-elbow distance, blah, blah . . . Foot width, foot length . . . Shit! What are we going to put on his feet?'

'Moon boots?' Leanne suggests sarcastically.

'Wellies,' says Chantel. 'It'll have to be. We'll have to attach them to the fabric the same way as the gloves, then wrap them in loads of foil.'

'You're pretty good at this,' David says.

'Cheers, mate.'

They smile at each other, then go back to looking at the screen.

'Glue!' says Chantel suddenly.

Her phone rings. She puts down the tape-measure, which she's been waving around, and picks up the phone. 'Oh, hi,' she says into it. 'It's Julie and Charlotte,' she says to the others. 'They're in Homebase.' She puts her finger in her ear. 'What? Oh, cool, have you got a pen now? Good. All right. We need a pair of wellies . . . Shut up! You can't laugh, or we'll never get this done. A pair of wellies, loads of Duct tape, a ten-foot length of sewer-pipe. No, I don't know what it is, really. Hang on . . .' Chantel looks at the computer screen. David scrolls to the picture. 'Oh, OK. It's like, um . . .'

'It's like the thing you have on vacuum cleaners,' David says. 'Those – fuck it, what are they called? – the, fuck it . . . the *hose*. Yeah, like the hose bit on a vacuum cleaner.'

'Did you hear that?' Chantel says to Julie. 'Like the long hose bit on a vacuum cleaner. But you don't actually want a vacuum-cleaner hose, you want a sewer-pipe. That's what it says here, yeah. Like, I dunno, just like a long, bendy pipe with corrugated bits. Yeah? Cool. OK, we also need strong glue. No, not Super Glue, I can see us having an accident with that. Oh – David says they wouldn't sell it to you anyway because you look like a pair of glue-sniffers and – what?'

David's laughing too much to say anything else.

'They do have all the tell-tale signs,' Leanne says seriously. 'I used to work in Homebase and we couldn't sell solvents to anyone who looked dodgy in any way. We had training.'

'Bloody hell,' says Chantel. 'Did you hear that? Hitler-Dorothy used to be Homebase-Hitler and refuse to sell solvents to anyone who looked dodgy. Can you imagine that?' She's laughing, but Leanne gives her a look, so she stops. 'OK, sorry, Leanne. Anyway, gloves. I don't know. What sort of gloves?' she asks David.

'Rubber?' he suggests. 'I don't know what kind of gloves you can get at Homebase.'

'Gardening gloves,' says Leanne.

'I reckon rubber,' says David. 'They shouldn't be breathable in any way.'

'Did you hear that?' Chantel says into the phone. 'Good. Right, we also need . . . Oh, it says here now that we do need vacuum-cleaner hose. David got it wrong.' She smiles, and David pretends to hit her and she ducks. 'Turns out the reason it looks so much like vacuum-cleaner hose is because it is sodding vacuum-cleaner hose. Yeah, I know. David, do we need the sewer-pipe as well? Oh, he says we do, but I don't know why. No, I don't know what it looks like now; I thought the vacuum-cleaner hose was a sewer-pipe, so . . . Just ask one of the assistants. But the hose is the important thing. We also need hacksaws, sandpaper, scissors. Oh, hang on. No, we've got scissors. Oh, but hang on again . . . Leanne says we can only use her scissors for fabric, so you'd better get some others for the tape and stuff. You got all that? Great. I think so. Yeah, I'll call back if there's anything else. OK. See ya.'

'Did they get the van?' Luke asks.

'Yeah,' Chantel says. 'They got a VW Camper. They're driving it back here after they finish at Homebase.'

'Cool,' says Luke.

'You're all a load of nutters,' Leanne says, shaking her head.

'Why?' says David. 'We're only going to Wales.'

'What about the floods?' she asks.

'We'll manage,' Luke says. 'We'll have to.'

'They're telling people not to travel, though,' she says.

'Except in emergencies,' Chantel points out.

'And?' says Leanne.

'This is an emergency,' Luke says. 'This is pretty much a matter of life and death.'

Chapter 30

Charlotte's been singing the *Scooby Doo* song for the past half an hour as if she still thinks it's funny. Julie's trying to remember everything she's been told about the indicators, the headlights and the soft ('you really have to stamp on them but they do work') brakes. Still, she hasn't quite got the hang of it yet, and every time she wants to turn a corner, she puts the windscreen wipers on. Whenever she wants to stop, she has to think about it a few seconds in advance. She keeps thinking of those anti-speeding adverts that illustrate, with an image of a kid being run over, how stopping distances change depending on how fast you're going. Julie wonders if you could ever get this bloody van to stop.

'I'm not sure this is safe,' she says.

'It's probably just a case of getting used to it,' Charlotte says.

'You're sure it's not dodgy?'

'Yeah. That couple were totally genuine.'

Julie thinks about the two people who sold them the van. The woman, pale and thin, had been holding a baby and a tea-towel. The guy had about three days' stubble, a beer gut, and a mobile phone clipped to his belt. He'd said that if they didn't take the van now, he'd have to sell it to a lady from Maldon who said she'd be back for it the following day, when she could get cash out of the bank.

'How do you know they were genuine?' Julie asks.

'Mark used to do up cars, didn't he? We were always out buying wrecks. You sort of get a nose for this kind of thing.'

'What, for wrecks?'

'No, you dickhead, for genuine people.'

'Do you think Chantel will like it?'

'Huh?'

'Well, it is hers, strictly.'

'Yeah, she'll love it. Well, she will if she likes Scooby Doo.'

'Are you sure the Mystery Machine was orange? I don't think it was.'

Charlotte thinks for a minute. 'Maybe it was blue and orange.'

Everything's been fun today: the Going Out Committee meeting, then hanging out with Chantel, now this weird, surreal shopping trip with Charlotte. They almost got chucked out of Homebase for laughing so much, and for trying to do wheelies with the un-steerable trolley, and for generally being loud about space-suits and rubber gloves and hoses. Now it's dark and it's raining and Julie suddenly gets a stabbing feeling of loneliness and nostalgia, like she's desperate to go home but she doesn't know where that is any more. Something's still bothering her.

'What's this Wei guy actually like?' Julie asks Charlotte.

Charlotte shrugs. 'Really nice. He's a friend of Jemima's husband.'

'Whose husband?'

'Jemima . . . This hippy friend of mine. She's a good laugh, actually. I met her on that yoga retreat I told you about.'

Julie laughs. 'I still can't imagine you on a yoga retreat.'

'Why not?'

'I don't know. Maybe it's the word *retreat*.'

'How do you mean?'

'Well, I don't know, retreat implies going backwards. I've never been able to imagine you like that. You know, needing to retreat.'

'Huh?'

Julie can feel her brain starting to do the logic thing it always does: connections and equations fireworking around her head, turning the world into maths. Still, what she's thinking does add up.

'Weakness,' she says. 'All the New Age stuff. It's all about weakness, isn't it? Retreats, victims – of abuse, or pollution or chemicals or whatever – dependency. And you know the way those Crystal Ball types act like they'd die if they inhaled the smoke of one cigarette or got within brainwave distance of a mobile phone or a microwave. And all those words like "wellness". Why can't they just say *health* or something? The whole thing is just too bloody gentle, like the people who are into it are just too delicate to be able to handle anything else.'

Charlotte laughs. 'Yeah, well, that's part of it,' she says. 'But you can do something like yoga and not be like that. To be honest, that's how me and Jemima gelled, really. Some of the people on the retreat were total wank-brains and we used to go off for sneaky fags together to get away from them. So, how did you get so worked up about the New Age thing anyway?'

'I don't know, really,' Julie says, indicating and turning right towards the High Street.

'You're usually Miss I-Don't-Have-An-Opinion.'

'I know. I don't usually say what I think.'

'That doesn't answer the question about what got you all worked up about New Age stuff,' Charlotte says, rolling a cigarette on her knee.

'I'm just worried about Luke. I don't want to put him in the hands of some freak.' One of the gears jams.

There's a horrible tearing sound. 'Jesus,' says Julie. 'This is so hard to drive.'

'Just chill, babe. It'll be OK.'

The van rights itself again, and Julie hopes the gear thing was a one-off. 'So this woman Jemima. She's all right, then?'

'Yeah, she's great. Really down to earth about the whole thing. Definitely not a freak.'

'And you're going to India together?'

'Yep. In fact, I'm going to stay with her and her husband in Wales until it's time to go. So I won't be coming back with you.'

'Oh, OK. That's cool.' Julie remembers which side the indicators are on and signals left. It feels weird being this high up, looking down on the tops of cars rather than straight in the back of them. 'So is Wei into Ayurveda as well?

'Nope. He's a Taoist.'

'A what?'

'A Taoist. Tao. It's a Chinese thing.'

It sounds to Julie like these people just go to the local take-away to get their religions. All of this is still sounding too Crystal Ball for her liking. The trouble with all those people is they're too busy fucking around with alfalfa sprouts and carrot juice and weird allergies and phobias that they wouldn't know a real illness if it came up and killed them. At least Julie admits – even if only to herself – that she's afraid. But however scary the world is, Julie knows the answer isn't carrot juice. The one time she went into Crystal Ball recently, she was asked to leave when her mobile phone rang. She'd gone in there to see if there was a book about getting over fear – she'd gone through a phase of thinking maybe she should try to face some of her problems. Then her stupid phone had rung – it was Luke, needing her; he's the only reason she even has the phone at all – and the manager accused her of bringing harmful vibes into the shop and asked her to leave.

'Anyway, Wei isn't a freak,' Charlotte says, looking at Julie. 'He's the real deal.'

'In what way?'

'Well, he actually is Chinese for a start.'

'And?'

'Well, a lot of these people who get into Tao or Zen or Buddhism aren't the real deal, are they? They're just guys with beards from Surrey who want to expand their minds and stuff. It's sweet but you wouldn't trust them. I heard about some guy who set himself up as a Chinese herbalist basically because he'd read a book on it and he wanted to set up his own business because he'd had some kind of breakdown and had to leave work for, like, ever . . .'

Julie interrupts. 'That's another thing about all the New Age people – they're all self-employed. Why is that?'

'It's because they're too fucked up to hold down an actual job,' Charlotte says.

Julie laughs. 'I thought you'd become one of them.'

'Come on, babe. I'm just into yoga. Get worried when I stop smoking. Anyway, this guy, the one who had to leave his job, he almost killed someone with Chinese herbs. He misread one of his books – either that, or the Chinese had been mistranslated – and he totally fucked up.'

'God. This isn't exactly making me feel better. So what makes Wei different?'

'He's totally . . . I dunno. He's just . . . The real deal, like I said.'

'Hang on – I thought you hadn't met him?'

'I don't actually *know* him; that's what I said. I did meet him for a couple of minutes once.'

'And?'

'It was like someone had switched the light on and I hadn't even realised it was dark. Honestly, Jules, I wouldn't have put him and Luke in touch if I hadn't thought he'd actually be able to make a difference. He really is something else.'

'How does your friend know him?'

'Her husband Walter's editing a book called something like *Motorway Meditation*, or *Concrete Karma* or something. It's all about how you can use New Age thinking to ease away the stresses of modern living. Wei is contributing a chapter. That was how I got to hear about him in the first place.'

'Is he a writer, then?' Julie asks.

'No, I don't think so. He's more known for his lectures. Walter approached him to do the book, and I think he said no originally, because it was too commercial. Then Walter promised he'd donate a load of the profits to Free Tibet or something and Wei was in. They flew him over do to it. It's pretty amazing that Luke can see him. Wei's pretty famous, you know.'

'Flew him over?' says Julie. 'What, from China?'

'No, he got chucked out of China. From America.'

'Oh. Well I suppose that sounds better than if he was just some beardy-weirdy English fraud.'

'You really hate New Agers, don't you?'

'Yep.'

'Why?'

'You never knew my mum, did you?'

'No. She left, didn't she?'

'Yeah. She got into New Age stuff in a big way, although it wasn't called New Age then, it was just kind of, I don't know, hippy, or something. I got so sick of mung beans and sunflower seeds and chick peas and having to eat coriander with everything . . .'

'I like coriander.'

'I don't. The smell of it makes me want to gag.'

'You're really pissed off with your mum, aren't you?' Charlotte says.

Julie sighs. 'Oh, I don't really want to go into it.'

'You don't want to channel your anger or anything?'

Julie laughs. 'Sorry,' she says. 'I'm really going on about this. I'll stop now.'

'Don't worry, babe. It's cool.'

'So, tell me how you got into Ayurveda, then.'

'Not if you start accusing me of being New Age.'

'I won't. I know you're not like that.'

'OK, look, I don't think I ever told you this – but I was really caning it after I left Windy Close, too much coke and booze and even a little bit of smack . . .'

'Charlotte!'

'I know . . . Anyway, I needed to find something else, or die, basically.'

'God. What did you do?'

'I called the Samaritans.'

'Because of the drugs?'

'Actually, no. Well, kind of. I thought my house was being invaded by flies.'

Julie can't help laughing. 'Flies?'

'Yeah. The lady said I was stressed out, and suggested I learn meditation.'

'I thought they weren't supposed to suggest things.'

'I don't think you can go wrong with meditation, Jules.' Charlotte smiles. 'So anyway, the flies incident was the last straw and I knew I was on the verge of flipping out completely, so I went along to some meditation class in the Adult Education centre and then they had yoga afterwards, so I stayed for that – mainly because I was feeling weird after the meditation and couldn't move and also because the teacher looked really horny. Anyway, a couple of sessions later, I was starting to feel better. I asked the teacher if it would help to change my diet as well – I don't know why, really, it was just something to say, because I knew I was going to be told to give up booze, caffeine, fags, chocolate and chemicals, just like in any fucking diet, but this guy just looked me up and down, and said, "Try this for a week: eat porridge for breakfast; rice-pudding for lunch; rice and butter for dinner; and a selection of sweet fruits and honey afterwards – and don't watch TV while you eat." I thought he was raving, but it sounded quite nice, so I tried it. After a few weeks, I felt so much better and I asked him what exactly I'd been doing and he explained the basics of Ayurveda to me. Then I went on the retreat, met Jemima and she was the one who told me about this thing in India. You can learn for free but in return you also have to pass on what you teach. It's cool.'

'You really have turned into a hippy,' Julie says, shaking her head.

'Cool, isn't it? The new me is definitely better than the old one.'

By three in the morning, the space-suit is almost made.

'I can't believe we've actually done this,' Charlotte says.

'You haven't done anything!' Chantel says. 'You've just sat there smoking roll-ups all night.'

'Yeah, well,' Charlotte says. 'I've been supervising.'

David's insulating the boots with Duct tape and silver foil. 'Sorted,' he mutters.

'When are we going to see this van, then?' Leanne asks.

Julie and Charlotte parked it on the industrial estate so as not to arouse suspicions in Windy Close. Since they got to Luke's, Julie's been studying a map and Charlotte's been sitting in the corner of Luke's room making various impractical suggestions about the space-suit. Leanne's been quietly stitching all the bits she's been told to stitch, and it's been hard to tell whether she's in a mood or not. Chantel and David have done most of the actual work, while Luke's become more and more excited about actually leaving the house.

'You can all come and see it after this, if you want,' Charlotte says.

'Luke could test out his space-suit,' Chantel suggests.

'No,' says Julie. 'Jean'll know. We can't risk Luke leaving until tomorrow.'

'So what's the plan?' Chantel asks. 'How are we going to get away tomorrow?'

Julie looks up from the map. 'We've still got to work all that out,' she says. 'We should do it now. It shouldn't be too hard, though, because Jean's going to bingo with Dawn and Michelle tomorrow night, so we can slip out while they're gone.'

'Are you going to leave a note or anything?' Charlotte asks.

Luke looks unhappy suddenly. 'I really don't know,' he says. 'Mum always said . . . Oh, it doesn't matter.'

'She always said what?' says Chantel.

'She always said she'd kill herself if I went out.'

'What? Fucking hell, that's insane,' Charlotte says. 'That's total emotional fucking blackmail.'

'It was ages ago,' Luke says. 'She did it for my own good . . .'

'I can't see how that would ever be for your own good,' Charlotte interrupts.

'Come on,' he says. 'You weren't there.'

'You never told me this,' Julie says, suddenly, to Luke.

'It was before you moved here. It was because I kept

trying to, I don't know, *escape*. I was about seven or eight or something and I was always coming up with plans to get out – at that age I didn't really understand death, and I therefore didn't care if I died, I just wanted to go out into the world and not stay inside any more.'

'Well, that's pretty understandable,' Charlotte says.

'Your mum must have been really worried,' Chantel says.

'She was,' says Luke. 'That's why she did it.'

Charlotte looks like she might say something else, then doesn't.

'Bit fucking brutal, though,' David says, wrapping a final bit of Duct tape around one of the wellies.

'Yes, but I needed a shock. I was going to kill myself.'

'I guess she thought of the only thing you cared about more than yourself,' Chantel says.

'Exactly,' says Luke. 'I think she was brave, to be honest.'

'Where was your old man?' asks David.

'Yorkshire. He worked up there.'

'Does he still work there?' Chantel asks.

Luke shrugs. 'I don't know. He used to come home at weekends but then he just stopped coming back.'

Everyone's quiet for a few minutes. No one seems to know what to say.

'So what's the plan?' Luke says eventually.

'Can I say something?' David asks.

'Sure,' says Charlotte. 'What?'

'This plan, right? Tomorrow night Luke's mum's at bingo, yeah? So Luke puts on the space-suit and we leave. That's it.'

'Very inspired,' says Chantel.

'Thanks,' says David, smiling at her.

'What about the floods?' Leanne says.

'We'll be OK,' Charlotte says. 'It's only water.'

'What about *her*?' Chantel says, pointing at Leanne.

'What?' Leanne says. 'What about me?'

'We're going to have to take her with us,' Chantel says. 'We can't leave someone behind who knows where we're going, especially if it's this big secret and Luke's mum can't know.'

'Yeah, that's true,' says Charlotte. 'Jean'll interrogate her.'

'I'm coming anyway,' Leanne says. 'I have some issues to resolve. I could do with some time away. I'll take a couple of days' holiday. Lloyd won't mind.'

'*Issues*?' says Charlotte. 'Oh, never mind. Right. What else?'

'The route?' suggests Chantel.

'Down the A12, round the M25 and then shoot up the M4,' says David. 'Easy.'

'It's going to be a bit more complicated than that,' Julie says.

Chapter 31

'The yellow roads?' says David, looking at the map Julie's given him.

'Yeah. The B-roads,' Julie confirms. 'We're going on B-roads.'

'Is there any reason for that? It'll take fucking weeks.'

'It'll be fun,' Chantel says. 'Lighten up, David.'

It's Saturday night. Everyone's preparing to go. David gives the map back to Julie, shaking his head, then he and Chantel get out of the van to do something with oil. Julie, Leanne and Luke are in the van, sheltering from the rain, waiting for Charlotte. Luke's sitting on the bed at the back, Julie's sitting on the chair behind the passenger seat, and Leanne's sitting primly on the little sofa. It's smaller in here than Luke thought it would be, and his feet are getting caught up in everyone's bags.

'Where's Charlotte?' asks Julie, looking at her watch. 'We've got to go in a minute.'

'She's probably taken too many drugs and forgotten,' Leanne says.

When Luke and Julie were about fifteen, they used to play a game called Trust. Julie would fall backwards and Luke would catch her, and vice versa, or one would blindfold the other, and then give the blindfolded person instructions on how to walk around some obstacles placed in Luke's room.

Leaving the house felt like the Trust game multiplied

a thousand times. As Julie helped Luke towards the same back door through which he tried to escape all those years ago, he'd suddenly had a sensation of not being able to breathe; and he imagined collapsing again like he'd done when he was seven, like in a film, shot from every angle. As he walked towards the door, with Julie touching his arm, all he could think of was that day: the gravel, the cold air, and then waking up in bed.

Once he could breathe again – they'd had to rest in the kitchen for several minutes while Luke mentally prepared himself – he found he wasn't sure if he was more scared that he was just going to wake up in bed again like last time, or that he wasn't. He never thought this would actually happen. Going out was unthinkable. Luke had spent years fantasising about what lay behind the kitchen door, and now he was finally going to see what was really there. He'd had that one glimpse of blue sky years ago and it had been like being able to feel a Christmas present but never open it.

Luke's mother always used to put his presents under the tree on Christmas Eve. Luke was never allowed to touch, shake or feel them. He was only allowed to look. But one time he couldn't help himself. He crept up to the tree and squeezed a small, intriguingly shaped package. It was so soft. A toy! It had to be a toy. A soft, furry toy he could love and stroke and hold. He'd never had a soft toy for Christmas before. Usually his presents were electrical items or clothes. All night, Luke fantasised about unwrapping his toy. On Christmas morning he was allowed to open one present from his pile before breakfast. He chose the small soft package, of course. It was a pair of socks.

So far, being outside is like socks. Socks, when Luke expected a soft toy.

He walked out of the door with Julie sort of pushing

him and there was no magic; no vast Technicolor world in which he could dance naked. There was just the sound of rain, the smell of someone's dinner cooking and a greyness he could barely see. Then Julie hurried him into the van, which had been parked on the gravel driveway, almost right by the door. She had an umbrella. He didn't even feel rain on his face. Not that he would have anyway, because of the helmet he's wearing. It's a shame. He always wanted to feel rain on his face.

Now he's sitting in the van while the others come in and out, preparing things, arguing about the route and complaining about Charlotte being late. Luke's looking through the steamy, smeared window at his house. It feels like an out-of-body experience; like he's a snail looking at his shell. It's the strangest sensation he's ever experienced. He never ever thought he'd be here in this van, and that he'd be leaving his home and going somewhere else. He couldn't picture it at all. Now he's actually here his life seems pictureless, because there's no storyboard in his head for what might come next. Luke's scared. He shuts his eyes. The van smells mouldy inside; wet and sort of dying, like a cup of coffee you'd left under your bed for a week.

In the back of the van, Leanne's whispering to Julie. 'You said you'd do something,' she hisses.

'I have done something,' Julie hisses back.

'What, exactly?'

'I don't know. I mean, I do know, but . . . Look, I had to tell Charlotte.'

'You *what?*'

'Only the bare facts, don't worry.'

'I can't believe you'd betray me by telling Charlotte.'

'Calm down, Leanne.' Julie sighs. 'It's not a big deal.'

'That's easy for you to say. I'll never live it down.'

'She wasn't like that. She knows it's a secret. Don't worry about it.'

'She'll laugh at me.'

'She does anyway. Look, I think she thought it was pretty cool, to be honest.'

'Really?'

'Yes, really.'

Luke hasn't got any idea what they are talking about. He keeps his eyes shut. Everything sounds different. Maybe it's the effect of the wind, the rain or the temperature, or maybe just the infinite space of outside. That could be it. It used to be that Luke's whole world was carpeted and had walls and curtains. Now he doesn't know what it is but he knows it goes on forever. Luke lies down on the little bed and covers himself with one of the huge fleece blankets that Chantel and Julie brought along. It's probably better that he stays hidden. And maybe it's best for him not to look out of the window at his house any more.

David's been doing something to the engine of the van, and the metal sounds that he's generating – the squeaking and scraping of the bonnet opening, and a circular, twisting sound of things being unscrewed and screwed back again – are clean and crisp, even through Luke's foil-covered crash helmet and the blanket. As well as David's metal sounds, Julie's whispering voice and Chantel's occasional giggle, Luke can hear the echoey spatter of rain on the van roof and, faintly, the last part of the *Coronation Street* music, which, after the sound of a key being turned and a door being opened, suddenly becomes louder.

There's the crunchy sound of gravel.

Then Julie's dad's voice: 'What the hell are you doing now?' It sounds like he's laughing.

Julie's voice: 'Nothing. Moving something from Luke's.'

'Who the hell owns this heap of junk?'

Chantel's voice: 'It's mine, Mr King.'

More sounds of gravel. It sounds like Leanne's getting out of the van.

Julie's dad's voice: 'You lot are doing something dodgy, aren't you?'

Chantel: 'No, Mr King, we're just moving some things Luke wants to sell and . . .'

There's the sound of Julie's dad laughing. And his voice again: 'Do I look like I care? It's about time my daughter did something interesting, anyway. Of course, knowing her, you're all doing exactly what you say you're doing. Boring, boring, boring.'

There's some more crunching, a slammed door, and then the TV is quieter again.

Luke can't open his eyes; he can't move the blanket. He prefers to put images to sounds inside his head; they seem to make more sense that way. Also, he can add whole scenes. He can create an image of David chasing after Julie's dad and pinning him up against the wall of his house and telling him not to ever speak to Julie like that again. He can see Julie's dad slump to the ground like a man in a film, with his shirt all scrunched up and his tie coming undone. It's a satisfying image. One of the reasons Luke can't open his eyes is because he won't see fiction if he does. He stays under the blanket.

'Where the hell is Charlotte?' Julie's saying now.

'Taking her time, isn't she,' says David.

'We've got to get a move on. Luke's sitting in there on his own.'

'I'll sit with him,' says Chantel. 'This rain's getting worse.'

'Me too,' says Leanne. 'My hair's going frizzy.'

Inside the van it suddenly sounds as though someone's throwing small hard objects on to the roof.

'Fuck it, it's hail,' says David, and everyone gets in the back of the van with Luke.

Chapter 32

Charlotte arrives in a taxi with a woman who looks like a witch.

'This is Sophie,' Charlotte announces. 'She's a witch.'

'Hi,' says Sophie.

'I said we could drop her off at Epping Forest,' Charlotte says.

Charlotte settles in the main passenger seat at the front of the van, next to Julie, and Sophie gets in the back with the others. 'So where's the guy in the spacesuit?' she says. Luke's still under his blanket; Julie doesn't know why.

Leanne's looking confused and slightly pink. She's looking backwards and forwards from Julie to Charlotte but neither of them says anything. Chantel looks slightly nervous and even David looks a bit freaked out. It could be because Sophie really does look like a witch. Dressed all in black, with a black shawl, black lace gloves and a pentagram-shaped pendant around her neck, she also has rather piercing black eyes and a large mole on her forehead. If it wasn't for the facial features and the pentagram, she'd just look like a Goth. As it is, she looks like a witch. The only thing that's remotely un-witchlike about her is the black Reebok holdall that she chucks on top of all the other bags in the back of the van before sitting down next to David and Chantel.

Julie starts the engine and reverses out of Luke's drive. 'David?' she says.

'Yeah?'

'Have you still got the map there?'

'Yeah.'

'Oh – hang on a sec . . .' Julie puts the windscreen wipers up a notch and uses an old cloth from the dashboard to wipe the inside of the windscreen. All the windows are misting up with the rain and everyone's breath. She can hardly see anything as she turns in the cul-de-sac and drives out of Windy Close towards the road into the town centre.

'You OK?' David asks, after they've been driving for a few minutes.

'Yeah. I need you to find a route to Epping Forest.'

'On B-roads?'

'Yeah. On B-roads.'

'For fuck's sake.'

'Just stop complaining, David,' Chantel says. 'Julie's scared, OK? And since she's the only one who can drive, we have to do it her way. It'll be fine.'

'You're scared of roads?' Sophie says to Julie. 'And you're going to Wales?'

'Yes and yes,' Julie says. 'We have to go there for our friend. It's important.'

The road joins the High Street, and the van passes McDonald's. Luke hasn't said anything for ages, and when Julie looks at him in the rearview mirror, all she can see is a lump under a blanket in the back of the van. This must all be too much for him.

'How do you know she's scared?' David asks Chantel.

'She obviously is.'

'I had a big car accident,' Julie suddenly says. 'On a motorway. That's why.'

'God, why didn't you say?' says David.

'I didn't know about that,' Charlotte says. 'Wow, babe, that's rough.'

'I don't like to talk about it,' says Julie. She hates lying but maybe the others will leave her alone now.

'I could charm the van, if you like,' Sophie says.

'Cool,' says Charlotte. 'Can you do it now?'

Sophie shakes her head. 'When we stop at Epping. There's no energy here.'

David laughs and Chantel elbows him. 'Just read the map,' she says.

He turns it upside down and around a few times. 'There aren't any B-roads going to Epping,' he says eventually.

'There must be,' Julie says.

'Nope. There are these non-roads that don't even have a colour . . .'

'Can you see a route to Epping, David?' Julie asks. 'On these *non-roads.*'

He sighs. 'Kind of.'

'Good. Let's go, then.'

Julie's heart is beating in a weird way. It would be really terrible to have a heart attack now with all these people in the van. Still, if she goes slowly on the B-roads, it'll be all right. At least if she does crash it won't be fatal.

'So, what's in Epping Forest?' Chantel asks Sophie, as the van moves slowly down the High Street.

'My coven,' she says.

'You have a coven?' Chantel says.

'Of course. You can't be a witch without a coven. Well, actually, come to think of it, you can, but most witches are part of a coven.'

'What's a coven?' David asks.

'It's a group of witches, stupid,' Leanne says. 'Everyone knows that.'

'How many witches are there in a coven?' he asks Sophie.

'Thirteen,' she says. 'But we've only got twelve.'

In the back of the van, the conversation about covens continues loudly. In the front of the van, Julie's still getting to grips with the gears and the brakes and the steering and her weird heartbeat. Charlotte has found a way to sit with her legs up on the dashboard, crossed lazily at the ankles. She's smoking, and vaguely saying something about finding a radio station to listen to on the stereo that doesn't really work.

'Where did you find her?' Julie half-whispers, half-mouths to Charlotte.

'Sophie?'

'Yes, Sophie.'

'In The Rising Sun,' Charlotte says.

'Do you know her?'

'Not really. Jesus does.'

'The drug dealer?'

'Yeah. They get their drugs from him.'

'Who?'

'Her coven.'

'Witches use drugs?'

'Of course they do. Well, herbs anyway. Jesus can get anything.'

'And this is going to help Leanne how, exactly?'

'Wait and see.'

The car in front of Julie stops at a mini-roundabout even though the way ahead is clear. Julie wasn't expecting that. She stamps on the brakes but nothing seems to happen. The tyres don't seem to be connecting properly with the wet road. With only a few inches to spare, the van finally stops. Then the engine stalls and Julie has to turn the key to start it again.

'Nice driving, babe,' Charlotte says.

'It's this stupid van.' Julie shoves it in first gear and drives across the mini-roundabout. She drops her voice back down to a whisper. 'Anyway, she is a real witch, isn't she?' Julie asks. 'She's not just some kind of smack-head or anything?'

'Witches don't do smack, you idiot.'

'No, but . . .'

'She's definitely a real witch. I could tell you stories that . . .'

There's another roundabout a few hundred yards up ahead. It's a big one, signposted with various choices: M25 East, M25 West, Colchester A12 and London A12. There's no mention of Epping Forest.

'Hang on,' Julie says. 'David? Where now? Which exit do I need?'

'Round to the right,' he says. 'I think . . . Hang on.' He asks Sophie to point to the location of the coven on the map.

'I can't do that,' she says. 'It's secret.'

'For fuck's sake,' he says.

'We do need to know where to go,' Julie says. 'Now, if possible.'

David thrusts the map under Sophie's nose.

'I can point out where to drop me off,' she says.

'Can you do it quickly?' Julie says.

There's some kind of scuffle in the back. Julie glances in the rearview mirror and sees David trying to get away from Sophie, who's smiling strangely at him and waving her finger in the air.

'No fucking way,' David's saying. 'That's unnatural.'

'What's the matter?' says Chantel.

Julie's driving around the roundabout for the second time. There still appear to be the same four choices of exit: two for the M25 and two for the A12. Since she can't go on any of these roads, she heads back the way she came, towards the town centre again. Charlotte's fiddling with the radio as if nothing's happening. So far, all she's picked up is static.

'Get her away from me,' David's saying, almost falling on Leanne.

'Be careful,' Julie says. 'What's going on? What's wrong?'

'Yes, what's wrong?' Sophie asks innocently.

'You know what's fucking wrong. Jesus Christ.'

'David?' Chantel says.

In the mirror, Julie can see Leanne and Sophie exchange a weird smile.

'What the fuck's going on?' Charlotte asks finally, turning the radio off.

'Sophie made the map . . .' David starts. 'She, uh . . . made it . . .'

'What?'

'It *glowed*.'

'Don't be so silly,' says Sophie. 'Why would I want to make a map glow?'

'I fucking saw it, you freak!'

'Must have been the streetlights,' Sophie says.

'Or the rain,' says Leanne.

'Fuck this,' David says. 'Someone else can map-read now.'

'I'll do it,' Chantel says, sighing. 'Sorry about this, Julie.'

David points at the map. 'If her glowing is correct, we're going there.'

Chantel looks up. 'Why are we going back the way we came?'

Julie sighs. 'Because no one'll tell me where I'm going.'

'Oh. OK. You want to turn left whenever you can.'

The next left has a sign to some places Julie's heard of, but never been to.

'Here?' Julie asks.

'Yeah, perfect.'

In a few minutes, Julie's on a tiny country road. It's very wet, very muddy and only really big enough for one car at a time. She didn't even know there were roads like this in Essex. As the streetlights fade in the rearview mirror, she feels scared, then happy. You can't go too fast on roads like this and no one else can either.

Chapter 33

'It's going to be so flooded down here,' Leanne says.

'I didn't know there was real countryside around here,' says David.

'What do you mean, *real countryside*?' asks Charlotte.

'You know, that you can actually go into. Footpaths and stuff.'

'As opposed to what?'

'I dunno. Rape fields next to the A12. Bleak yellow squares.'

'Very poetic.'

'Cheers.'

'I bet people ride horses around here,' Leanne says.

'It's pretty spooky, isn't it?' says Charlotte.

'It's only because it's dark,' Chantel says. 'I bet it's lovely in the day.'

'Not as spooky as Epping Forest, though,' David says. 'I've heard all kinds of fucked-up shit about Epping. Like that road where cars roll uphill, and that headless ghost-woman – have you heard about her? Some of my mates from London got really stoned and went up there for a laugh but it wasn't that much of a laugh, because one of them got lost, saw some kind of ghost, and hasn't spoken since. It was like Blair Witch. No offence, Sophie.'

'Not really, though,' Leanne says. 'You're exaggerating, surely?'

'No, I swear,' David says.

'There is lots of energy in the forest,' Sophie agrees.

'Can you all stop talking about headless women and ghosts?' Charlotte says.

'What time is it?' Chantel asks.

'About half-eight,' says David.

'It feels like midnight out here.'

Luke tries to imagine what they're all talking about. It sounds too weird to look at. He could sit up but he feels too sick. He doesn't know if it's something to do with the motion, or the mouldy smell, or the fact that the outside has got in through his space-suit and he's dying. He can't think properly – this feeling of the ground moving underneath him is too peculiar for his thoughts to stay still. At first it was like a rush – a totally new sensation and he couldn't work out why all the people he's met in his life haven't raved constantly about the delights of moving in an object on wheels. For the first five minutes of the journey the movement was delicious and tingly but now it's making him feel sick. As well as that – who the hell is Sophie and why is she here? Maybe Luke'll sit up when she goes. Maybe then the sick feeling will go.

The movement gets slower and slower.

'Next left, then second right,' Chantel's saying.

'I can't see the turnings,' Julie says. 'There's too much rain.'

Poor Julie, she must be hating this. She hates travelling. Luke wishes they were alone together. If they were, he could make her feel better. He could open his eyes and sit up front with her and tell her she can drive as slow as she wants on whichever roads she wants and he could read the map for her and she could tell him what all the things outside were. But at the moment, Luke doesn't want to know what's outside. It just doesn't feel like his brain will take it – it's still processing the experience of seeing his house from outside. He feels unplugged. He feels weird. He keeps thinking he's left something behind. Then he realises that the thing he left behind is his whole life. All he can do is lie there, hope for the best and listen to the voices in the van.

'*Left*, I said.'

'Oh, shit.'

'You'll have to turn around.'

'I can't. The road's too small.'

'OK. Just take the next . . . uh, left, then left again.'

'All right.' Julie's voice sounds wobbly. 'OK.'

'You OK, Jules?' Charlotte asks.

'I'm fine. I just feel a bit claustrophobic.'

'That's B-roads for you,' says David.

'These aren't even B-roads, though, are they? They're too small.'

'You're like Goldilocks.'

'Huh?'

'Everything's wrong. Too big, too small; too busy, too quiet . . .'

'Yes, well, B-roads would be just right, thanks.'

Everyone's quiet for a few minutes, except for Chantel saying *left*, or *right*.

'Is Epping flooded badly?' Charlotte asks Sophie.

'Not really,' Sophie says. 'It's fine at the moment.'

'Left,' says Chantel. 'And you can stay on this road for a while.'

'Good,' Julie says.

Luke can feel the van lurch from side to side, and wonders what would make it do that. Everything's slower now, though, and the rain has become comforting, and he's almost enjoying the tapping on the roof, and the lazy slosh of the van tyres. There's the steady whir of the car heater, and the cold, comforting smell of Charlotte, Julie and David smoking. Whenever the van goes through another big puddle, Luke thinks of soft drink commercials. Again, the van lurches, then seems to go down, then up very sharply.

'The council should do something about this road,' Julie says.

'This isn't a road,' says David. 'It's a track.'

'Don't worry, Jules,' says Charlotte. 'We'll be there soon.'

'Thanks for doing this,' Sophie says. 'I know it's a bit out of your way.'

'It's OK,' says Julie.

'So are all the witches in your coven girls?' David asks Sophie.

'Yeah,' says Sophie. 'Well, girls and women. The eldest is in her sixties, and the youngest has just turned seventeen. We don't have any men. We're a Dianic coven, so . . .'

'What's a Dianic coven?' David asks.

'All women. Goddess oriented . . .'

'Are you all lesbians?'

'No.'

'Do you run around naked?'

'Sometimes.'

'Pity I'm a man, then. Sounds good.' He laughs, then Luke can hear Chantel saying something like, *David!* then the sound of her hitting him playfully.

'You couldn't join anyway,' Sophie says. 'Even if we did have men.'

'Huh?' David sounds put out. 'Why not?'

'You're not a witch,' Sophie explains.

'Don't you mean a *warlock*?'

'No. A male witch is called a witch.'

'Oh. And I'm not one?'

'Nope.'

'Can you tell?'

'Yep.'

'And does that matter, then?'

'Oh yes. You can't join a coven if you're not a witch.'

Luke shifts in the little bed. The sick feeling isn't so bad now that the van's going so slowly. Inside, he just feels lost. He has no idea where he is, and would have no idea how to get home if he had to. No one ever taught him how to cross the road, or buy a bus ticket, or read a map. If there was an emergency, he wouldn't have any idea how to find, or use, a public telephone. He's a lot further from home than he ever thought he would be, so far away that it's like he's in another world and home doesn't exist any more.

Chapter 34

'Just here is great, thanks,' Sophie says.

For ages there's just been forest. Now there's a little carpark next to the remains of an old church and an old stump that might once have been a tree. Julie stops the van. There don't seem to be any houses around here, just the forest.

Sophie gets her bag from the pile. 'I'll bless the van, then,' she says. Feeling around in her bag, she pulls out a small fabric object, like a pin-cushion. Everyone watches as she attaches a thread to it, then gets out of the van and holds it up to the sky. She turns to face north, then south, east and west, asking each element in turn to empower her charm. Finally, facing east once more, she says: 'I have created this charm to protect this van against all harm. Its power has been created and now let its work be done.' Then she gets back in the van and hangs the charm over the rearview mirror.

'That'll do the trick,' she says. 'Thanks for the lift.'

'No problem,' Julie says, looking at the charm suspiciously.

'Leanne,' says Sophie. 'Can I speak to you outside?'

'Uh, sure, whatever,' Leanne says, picking up her little rucksack from the seat.

They both step out of the van. Julie watches them walk over to the tree stump. She doesn't want to get out of the van in this odd place. It's too dark to see anything very much; anyone could be lurking in the forest, or that horrible old church. But still, she and Charlotte look at each other, then slowly climb out of the van. By the edge of the forest, Sophie has her hand on Leanne's shoulder, and seems to be saying something fast and urgent to her. Leanne's nodding. Then she notices Julie and Charlotte approaching.

'I'm going with Sophie,' Leanne says.

'We thought you might,' Charlotte says.

'I . . .' Leanne bites her lip. 'I have to.'

Julie's not sure whether to laugh – Leanne's sense of melodrama finally has a place – or hug her because she looks so small and scared and like she doesn't fit in here. This place is weird, Julie can feel it. It's weird and full of witches and headless ghosts and other stuff Julie doesn't believe in but can still sense; and Leanne's about to walk off into it with a woman who doesn't seem all there, to somewhere no one knows about. Then again, she is annoying and she does think she's a witch and the customers at Blockbuster will have a better rental experience without her. And she seems to want to do this. Julie realises she can't affect this either way, so she stops worrying about it.

Sophie looks at Charlotte. 'Thanks,' she says.

'What for?'

'Bringing her to me.'

'Sorry?' says Charlotte, but Sophie has already turned to walk into the forest.

'Blessed be,' she says over her shoulder, instead of *goodbye*.

'See ya,' says Leanne, following. 'And thanks.'

'Take care,' says Julie.

Leanne stops and turns around for a second. 'I'm going to put everything right,' she says. 'The rain, and David, and everything . . . I'm going to help Luke, as well. I took a lock of his hair. I'm going to help heal him. And I'm going to help you Julie, and you Charlotte.

I don't know how yet but I will. I'm so grateful you did this for me.'

'What the fuck was she going on about?' Charlotte says, once Leanne's gone.

'Oh. I didn't completely tell you the full story,' Julie says.

'I'm not sure I want to know.'

'Charlotte?'

'Yeah?'

'What the hell are we doing here? I mean . . .'

'What, why are we standing on the edge of Epping Forest with a Scooby Doo van, a Lottery winner, a guy with cancer and someone dressed in a space-suit – that *we* made – having just waved a tearful goodbye to a domineering retail-assistant who's just gone into the woods to "fulfil her destiny" and learn how to channel her humungous witch powers?'

'Yeah,' says Julie.

She catches Charlotte's eye and then, suddenly, they're both laughing so much they're choking, until Julie can't breathe and her stomach hurts. This place suddenly doesn't seen frightening any more.

'Oh God,' Julie says. 'Ow.'

'What are we fucking like?' Charlotte says. 'Come on, we'd better tell the others.'

David and Chantel look worried.

'What was going on out there?' David asks.

'Where's my cousin?' asks Chantel.

'You're not going to believe this . . .' Charlotte says.

'Um . . . Leanne's joined the coven,' says Julie.

'She said she had to be with her own sort,' Charlotte says.

There's a snort from under the blanket on the bed.

'Luke?' says Julie. It sounds like he's laughing.

'Her own sort?' says Chantel.

'She thinks she's a witch,' Charlotte explains.

'Jesus,' says Chantel. 'Will she be all right?'

'Yeah, she'll be fine,' says Charlotte. 'Come on, let's go.'

Julie goes to the back of the van and peers under the blanket at Luke. 'You OK?' she asks.

'Is it true about Leanne?' he says softly.

'Yeah,' Julie giggles. 'I feel like I've just released an animal into the wild.'

Luke giggles too. Then he stops and grips Julie's arm.

'Will I be all right?' he asks.

'Of course you will. You don't have to stay under the blanket, you know.'

'I know, it just feels less strange this way.'

Julie returns to the driver's seat and, after a couple of tries, successfully starts the engine.

'Where now?' she asks.

'Wales!' says David. 'Onwards and upwards!'

'Can someone read the map?'

'I'll do it,' Charlotte says.

Chantel passes it up to her.

'Can you read maps?' Julie asks.

'Sure, babe. I'm looking for yellow roads, yeah?'

'Yeah. B-roads.'

'Through London or around it?'

'Um . . .'

'There aren't any yellow roads going through London,' says David. 'I checked.'

'Yeah, but those London roads aren't, like, motorways or anything,' Charlotte says. 'It'll be all right.'

'What about London traffic?' Chantel says.

'I don't mind London traffic so much,' Julie says. The traffic slows everything down. She likes that.

'What about the Old Bill?' David says.

'What?' says Chantel. 'What Old Bill?'

'They check cars going in and out of the City, don't they? IRA, innit?'

'Oh yeah,' says Charlotte. 'That could be bad.'

'They might want to examine Luke or something,' Chantel says.

'We don't have to go through the actual City, though, not from here,' Charlotte says. 'In fact, having said that, I don't think I even know how we'd get into London coming from here. It wouldn't be the normal A12 way, anyway. In fact . . .' She looks at the map. 'We'd come in much more north. Like, through Walthamstow, then through Islington, and then . . .' She turns the page. 'And then . . . Oh, shit, we'd either have to go through the City or cut down through there to get onto the Embankment so we could go out through West London, but hang on . . . There aren't any actual yellow roads here, just the A4 or the M4.'

'Could you manage the A4?' David asks.

'I don't know,' Julie says.

'Oh. And – fuck – there's only big A-roads going into London from here as well.'

'Maybe London's not such a great idea,' Chantel says.

'Also, what about the fumes?' Julie says suddenly. 'We shouldn't expose Luke to the fumes, should we?'

'So which way, then?' asks Charlotte. 'Under or over London?'

'You don't want to go under,' David says. 'We're already going in the wrong direction for that – aren't we virtually in Hertfordshire or something? Plus there's all the fucking tunnels.'

'OK. Over, then?'

'Yeah,' Julie says. 'Can you see a route?'

'Sort of.' Charlotte looks at the map some more. 'Actually, no.'

'Can I have a look?' Julie asks, switching off the engine.

Charlotte's right. The only B-roads from Epping seem to lead towards Harlow. Oh – but hang on, one of them bypasses Harlow and goes off to the left. At least it's the right direction.

'Here.' Julie shows Charlotte. 'Up here, then along there, then . . .'

'That's a motorway,' Charlotte says, pointing.

'Yes, but the B-road continues underneath it. There must be a bridge or something. Just make sure we don't accidentally end up on the motorway.'

'I'll try. I can't actually see very well.'

'You'll be able to see more when we get going,' David says. 'In the . . . Oh, ignore that. I was going to say in the streetlamps, but there won't be any, will there?' He laughs.

'We should stop at a garage and get a torch,' Chantel says.

'And some sandwiches,' says Charlotte. 'I'm starving.'

'Can I have a look at the map again?' David says.

'Yeah.' Charlotte gives it to him. 'I think you'll have to map-read anyway. My eyesight's not good enough in this light.'

'I see, so we're going here, here, here and . . .' David murmurs. 'Fuck me. *South Mimms*.'

'What?'

'South Mimms. Best ravers' garage ever. Come on, ladies – and spaceman – looks like we're on our way to the greatest service station in the world.'

'Isn't South Mimms on the M25?' Charlotte asks.

'Yep, but there's a little yellow road running right by

it,' says David happily. 'And it just happens to be one of the ones we have to go on.'

'And why are we excited about a service station?' Julie asks.

'I'll tell you on the way.'

Chapter 35

David's on his third South Mimms story and the van smells like skunk weed.

'So this fucking amazing girl, right, the one I just told you about who kissed me by the arcade in South Mimms, she'd said she was going to this rave she knew was being organised the following week, right, somewhere off the M25, and that was the only way I reckoned I was ever going to see her again, even though it was a complete fucking long-shot, because how many raves are there that are "somewhere off the M25"? But I was obsessed, what can I say? So on the Saturday afternoon we're in this pub in north London, and no one knows where the rave's supposed to be. The pirate radio-station's suddenly gone dead, and there's this phone number but we try to phone it and there's just nothing. It was like fucking dead ends everywhere. So we all decide to just fucking bomb it up the A10 and on to the M25 to South Mimms, because we reckoned everyone else in the same boat would just go up there. And we were so fucking right. As soon as we got to the round-about there were Old Bill everywhere, and they weren't letting anyone anywhere near the services, because by then – it must have been '91 or something – they'd been stung so many times with semi-riots and looting at South Mimms that they weren't taking any chances. So everyone congregated by the BP garage instead, and there were so many ravers there it was total chaos. So everyone's stealing stuff from the garage, and no one can do fuck all about it, and . . .'

'You were stealing?' Chantel interrupts, moving and making rustling sounds.

'Oh – is that the spliff? Cheers, mate – yeah, well, we were just kids really. Everyone used to do it. Anyway, we caned a load of packs of Juicy Fruit and mineral water and loads of packets of biscuits for some reason, and the poor guy's just standing behind the counter watching us, almost smiling really because we're all being so cheeky, and then, suddenly, I saw the girl, and then she's gone, but I overheard someone saying something about the A1, so we've legged it out of the garage and back into the car and I've decided to go for a spin up the A1, see what's going on there. So there I am, bombing it up the A1, and this guy in the car goes "Dave, look behind you," so I look in the mirror, and there's about fifty cars following us, because obviously they think I know where I'm going, and then suddenly I realise that the Old Bill think that as well, because I can see a load of blue lights flashing up behind us, so I've just thought to myself, fuck this, and spun the car around across the central reservation – it's just a grass verge on the A1 – and headed back the other way. But sure enough, because that's what I've done, all the other cars in the convoy have gone and done the same thing. What a mental fucking sight.'

'Why were they following you?' Chantel asks.

'Rave culture, innit?' David says. 'You see a bunch of ravers in a car, and if you're lost you follow them. Then you've got two cars with ravers in them, and someone else sees you and thinks – convoy! – so they follow you, and before you know it you are a convoy, but everyone's as lost as everyone else.'

'I missed out on all that,' Chantel says. 'I would have been about seven in '88.'

'How old were you, David?' Charlotte asks.

'In '88 I was fifteen,' he says. 'But when all this shit was going down I was eighteen or nineteen or something. I'd just passed my driving test the year before.'

'My dad does that,' Julie suddenly says.

'What?' Charlotte asks.

'He follows cars for no reason. If he's stuck in traffic and someone turns off, he thinks they know a short cut so he follows them. It's insane, because they could be going anywhere but he assumes they're going to the same place as he is, and he just follows them.'

'Your dad's weird,' says Chantel.

'So, did you ever find this rave?' Charlotte asks David.

'Yeah, of course. We went back to South Mimms, followed someone else, and eventually found where we were supposed to be. That's the thing. Somehow – whether it was through luck, judgement, coincidence, chance, God . . . I dunno, whatever – we always ended up in the right place. It's mental when you think about it, but suddenly, at the right moment, we'd be listening to the right pirate station that had the instructions, or we'd follow the right car, or we'd bump into someone who knew the organiser, or we'd work something out by logic, which is pretty fucked up considering how many pills we used to be on at the time, and we'd get where we wanted to go. Every single time. Or we'd find somewhere better, using the same methods.'

'There's a moral to that story,' says Charlotte. 'But I'm fucked if I know what it is. Give us that spliff, Dave.'

Luke's still under the blanket. He thought he'd come out when Sophie went but it didn't feel right. He's too comfortable and sleepy and outside still sounds too terrifying. If he stays where he is, he can pretend he's in bed at home; that's the plan. Luke's problem: when you see something on TV – because, of course, Luke's seen roads and vans and journeys and everything on TV, so these things aren't alien to him – it's not real. When you see something on the screen, you're in your room. This experience feels like actually being inside the television, which isn't what Luke wanted. Luke wanted to go into the world – the real world that everyone else experiences – but to him it just feels like the inside of a TV, like the glass has sucked him in and now he's banging around in this box, trying to get out. Or – worse – he's escaped from the TV into the outside world like some intrepid neon ray, and now he can't find the way back in. Either way, this is bad. Either way, he wants to go back to where he started. But as long as he stays under the blanket, he can try to ignore it. He's been trying to think about Wei, and being healed, but his imagination won't work any more. He's having trouble thinking about anything apart from being lost and scared.

'Are we there yet?' Chantel fake-whines.

'Yeah, yeah, nearly,' David says. 'Stop moaning.'

'Where now?' Julie asks.

'Next left.'

'Are you sure? That looks like a motorway up ahead.'

'Yeah, that's the A1. Don't worry, we're not going on it.'

Charlotte's found some country-and-western station on the radio.

'I love this,' she says. 'It's so crap.' She starts singing along.

'Hurry up, Julie,' Chantel says. 'This is excruciating.'

'Bitch,' says Charlotte.

'Slag,' says Chantel.

'Ladies,' says David. 'Settle down.'

'We're only joking,' says Chantel. 'Are we *there* yet?'

'No,' David says.

About ten seconds pass.

'Are we there *yet*?' she asks again.

'No, shut up.'

'Is this it?' Julie asks.

'Oh, yeah. We are there. Nice one.'

Luke can feel the van slowing and turning, then turning again. Eventually it goes backwards and forwards a couple of times, then stops. The engine cuts out but Luke's body is still vibrating as if the van's still going. There's the sound of people shifting around, and a door slamming, then a door opening and a blast of cold from outside.

'Luke?' says Julie. She pokes her head under the blanket. 'Hi.'

'Hi. Where are we?'

'South Mimms. We're going to get some sandwiches and stuff.'

'OK. I'll just stay here.'

'Are you sure?'

'Yeah. Well, I can't exactly come in with you, can I?'

'I suppose not. Are you sure you'll be OK?'

'Yeah. Julie?'

'Yeah?'

'What am I going to do if I need to piss?'

She looks alarmed. 'Do you?'

'No, not yet.'

'Oh. Well, we'll stop somewhere when you do.'

'Will I have to get out of the van?'

She frowns. 'Maybe. I don't know.'

'I could use a bottle or something.'

'Don't worry. We'll work something out.'

It's quiet when Julie and the others have gone. The world could have just ended, and Luke wouldn't know. If the world ended and Luke was the only survivor, would his life even change? If Luke and Julie were the only survivors, would he even notice?

As he sits up, he feels dizzy, and sick. Inside the van it's bright with all the light coming in from outside. In fact – what are those lights? What is this place? Luke thinks of his bedroom, and of outer space. Is this place the gateway between them? Could this be like a place he's seen on TV, a no-man's land between reality and fiction; between his bedroom and the moon? Or is it just the outside world, a place where everyone else goes all the time and Luke's been trying to escape into all his life?

Once, Luke cut one of his left fingers on a knife. As soon as he felt pain, and saw blood, he tightened his right hand around the hurt finger and squeezed, not wanting to look and see how badly he'd cut it. But, after a few moments, he couldn't not look any more. And it's the same now. Luke can't not look any more. He needs to see how bad it is, and he's hoping that something about it will be comforting, and that he'll be able to come out from under his blanket for a while at least, and act normal, even if he does have to wear a space-suit, and even if he might just expire any second. He opens the door to the van and looks out. Fuck it; big mistake – this *is* outer space.

In Luke's imagination, the outside world is basically a field with a tree in it and a mountain in the background; maybe a water-feature as well – a stream, river or lake. This isn't that. Luke's head spins. Maybe it's the helmet, or the rain – which has made everything that's not orange look black and wet. Maybe this is a joke. All he can see are cars, lights and concrete, and because Luke has no sense of space or landscape, to him the cars and lights and concrete go on forever. He'd intended to get out of the van and walk around, but now he can't move. This is the kind of place in which you'd find aliens, big men with guns and children dressed in oily rags hanging around in the rain, excluded from the shiny concrete-and-mercury-vapour paradise in the distance.

If Luke had to find his way home what would he do? He wouldn't be able to do anything, because his house isn't in this world, or, if it is, it may as well be as far away as the moon is from the earth. If you wanted to get to the moon, how would you do it? If you were a person, you might dream of building a rocket. If you were a moth you'd fly into a lightbulb. Luke wants the others to come back, because he feels like he'd die out here on his own. But what if they never came back? What then? Luke instinctively knows that left alone in this harsh environment with no computer and no telephone, there'd be only one thing he could do. He'd strip off his space-suit and run towards the nearest bright light, and hope that it would be like the sun and kill him quickly. That would be better than facing death at the tentacled hands of whatever lurks in places like this, or collapsing on some dusty highway, hungry and miles from anywhere, knowing your address but not how to read a map.

Luke puts his head back under the blanket.

He wonders: maybe moths don't think lightbulbs are the moon. Maybe they found out how far away the moon is, and simply chose suicide instead of failure. Wouldn't you?

Chapter 36

'Do we need this many sandwiches?' Julie says.

'I didn't know what Luke wanted,' Chantel says. 'And David wanted loads.'

'Munchies, innit,' David explains.

The girl behind the counter sort of grins at him.

'What kind of torch do you want?' Charlotte calls over from the torch display.

'A big one,' Julie says. 'Just hurry up.'

'Just get the most pretty one,' Chantel says.

Charlotte makes a face and then picks one, seemingly at random. She brings it over to the counter.

'That's £51.98,' the girl says, after she's scanned the torch.

'Jesus Christ,' says Chantel. 'Who can spend fifty-two quid at a garage? We haven't even got petrol yet.' She hands over her debit card anyway.

Outside, it's still raining.

'We'd better get back for Luke,' Julie says. 'He might be worried.'

'Why?' David says.

'We were in there for, like, forty minutes,' Chantel says, giggling

'Fucking hell,' says David. 'You're right. It's eleven o'clock.'

Chantel's holding up her long skirt so it doesn't drag in the glittering orange puddles. Charlotte's walking next to Julie.

'You OK?' she asks.

'Yeah. I didn't realise it was so late.'

'We'll get there. It'll be cool. Don't worry.'

'I'm not.' But Julie can still feel tears welling in her eyes.

Luke doesn't say anything when they get back to the van. He's still under the blanket. David and Chantel get in the back and Chantel pokes at Luke's blanket a bit and offers him a choice of sandwiches and drinks, but he doesn't say anything. Eventually she gives up and gets some beer out of her bag. Julie wonders if she should go and check to see if Luke's OK but everyone's in the van now, and they want to go. It's getting so late. She takes a bite of her cheese-and-pickle sandwich – she doesn't usually buy sandwiches, but felt daring tonight – but then, in her mind, she sees a familiar image of some sandwich maker with blue plastic gloves pressing the slices of bread together in a huge factory with dead flies and dirt and people who are paid so little they probably wipe their arses with the blue gloves.

She stops chewing the mouthful of sandwich. This is why she doesn't buy sandwiches. What if some fucked-off worker put acid in it? Acid's only about £1.50 now. Oh, shit, Julie's got to get this dirty poisoned stuff out of her mouth. She opens the door and gets out of the van, spits out into the gutter and throws away the rest of the sandwich. Back inside, she rinses her mouth with Ribena and lights a cigarette.

'What are you doing?' Charlotte asks.

'Nothing. I was just chucking the wrapper away.'

'Aren't you going to eat anything, then?' Charlotte says.

'No. Maybe later. I'm not as hungry as I thought I was,' Julie says.

'No wonder you're so thin,' says David.

'Where am I going now?' asks Julie.

For the next half an hour or so she just concentrates as David directs her through Radlett towards Watford while he and Chantel eat about three packets of sandwiches each and Charlotte plays with the radio. Luke doesn't say anything and for some reason this makes Julie want to cry.

'Skin up,' says David to Charlotte, as they go through Watford.

Charlotte settles on a local station and reaches for her embroidered bag.

'I thought you were skinning up,' she moans. 'I don't even want to smoke any more. I'm stoned already from that fucking spliff you gave me back at Epping. Dope totally fucks with my head. I've so got to give up.'

'I've run out,' David says. 'You're all right fucking caners.'

'I'll skin up,' says Chantel. 'As long as someone holds my beer.'

There's a rustling sound from the back of the van. Luke is sitting up.

'I'll hold it,' he says. 'As long as I can finish it.' He laughs in a weird way.

'Hey, mate,' David says, reaching over and slapping him on the back. 'We were all a bit worried about you. Glad to see you back in full effect.'

Chantel gives Luke her beer. He reaches in his bag for the straws Julie brought for him so he could drink through the helmet, then he sticks one of them in the can and starts sucking furiously. 'That feels a bit better,' he says, when he's finished. 'Hey, Chan, weren't you skinning up?'

'I, uh . . . Yeah,' she says. 'I was, wasn't I?'

'Luke?' Julie says. He doesn't reply. 'Luke?' she says again.

'I so want to get wasted,' he says to Chantel and David.

Charlotte looks at Julie and raises her eyebrows. Julie just shrugs sadly. She doesn't know what's going on any more. Why is Luke being like this? Why is he ignoring her? Why is he using words like 'wasted'? And why is the van full of sickly sweet smoke and an oniony, beery smell? Why the hell is Julie driving it, and where the fuck are they all going?

On the radio people working late in the Watford area are phoning in asking for requests. At some point, someone from a fire station asks for 'The Look of Love' by ABC.

'I fucking love this,' Charlotte says, turning it up.

Pretty soon everyone except Julie is singing along.

'I haven't heard this for ages,' Chantel says. 'They used to play it in the shop I worked in. It's really old, isn't it?'

'I remember it being on *Top of the Pops*,' says Charlotte. 'Which is depressing.'

'They had it on that tape they used to play all the time in The Edge, didn't they?' David says to Julie.

'I think they have it on tapes in all shops,' she says.

'What shop did you work in?' David asks Chantel.

'Surf & Skate in Basildon,' she says. 'Why?'

'I suppose you weren't a millionaire then.'

She laughs. 'No. I was a total pikey. I lived in a shack with a goat.'

'Oh yeah, Leanne said something about that,' David says. 'What's the story?'

Chantel's twisting a roach for the spliff. 'I dunno. It was my gran's place from just after the war. Me, my mum and her boyfriend, Rob, all lived there with Gran, in this tiny place. Rob was a total speed-head but thought he was going to make it as a songwriter, so he didn't really feel like he had to get a job, and my mum used to work in the pet shop by the market. But then it shut down and she got a bit depressed. Rob was always caning her dole cheque as well as his, and she never even had enough money to go for job interviews. If she did go, there'd always be someone younger who they could pay less so they'd get it.

'So basically they were both unemployed, and my mum used to get fucked off with Rob and try to make him leave and then he'd go and stay at some mate's place for a few days and Gran would be happy – she didn't like Rob – but then Mum would start eating Mars bars constantly and hand-washing everything in the place and crying about the state of the garden, the house and her life and how she'd let Gran down because she couldn't even keep her house nice for her, and how we'd have to move out of there soon – although at that point Gran was really ill and we couldn't leave her – until Rob came back. Then they'd "start again". He never saw anything wrong with the way we lived but Mum used to read *Hello!* magazine and *Homes & Gardens* and dream of having a decent life, and she was always doing things like trying to learn flower arranging or knitting from a library book. But Rob would always just end up treading on the knitting when he was pissed, and Billy would eat any flowers you left lying around.

'I'm glad we left Rob behind, although I wouldn't be surprised if he turned up in Windy Close blagging off me and my mum within a week. He's a fucking nightmare. He worked his way through Gran's savings just before she died, and he's borrowed money off me in the past and never paid it back – I was the only one in that place who ever had any bloody money, apart from Gran. I used to work at Surf & Skate six days a week in the holidays – when I was doing my BTEC at the college – and last year I saved up to go to Spain with some mates, but Rob "borrowed" the money, as in borrowed without asking, and he never gave it back, so I never went.'

'That's out of order,' David says. 'Fucking dick.'

'He wasn't a bad person; he was just irresponsible. Never grew up.'

'Still well out of order, though. What did he want the money for anyway?'

'Drugs, clothes, train fare to London to see potential "agents", more drugs. I don't know. He didn't have the same mentality as me and my mum. We were used to being poor, and we were pretty good at it. We just didn't buy luxuries, and we sort of didn't think we ever would, either. We used to have a Christmas Tin when I was a kid. We used to put spare change in it, and my gran would add to it and stuff, and every Christmas we'd have nice food and everything that we'd lay out on the table for days before, just so we could look at it. The year Rob came to live with us, he invented the IOU system, where you could borrow money from the Christmas Tin as long as you put in an IOU and then replaced the money. At the end of the year there were about forty IOUs in there that added up to about a hundred quid, but no actual money.

'God, do you know what I'll remember most about being poor?' Chantel continues, passing the spliff to David. 'All the invisible barriers – shops you could never, ever go into because you'd never be able to afford anything in them. Gourmet-food shops, department stores, those big toy shops you see in films about Christmas, and you know even if you knew where to find a toy shop like that you couldn't go in there because you'd only ever shopped in pikey shops, or the market . . . Even WHSmith was too posh for us. When I started at comprehensive school we were allowed to use biros and my mum got me a load of Argos pens, the free ones, and she thought she'd been really clever to find free pens, but of course everyone at school just called me a pikey and that was that.'

'I had pens from the betting shop. My granddad got them,' David says, smiling. 'He thought he was being original. In fact, I think when I was really little I used to draw in crayon on betting slips, because they were free and paper wasn't, and I always used to get pissed off because of the lines and writing in the way of my pictures.'

Chantel laughs. 'Oh, God, and I remember when Top Shop and Miss Selfridge seemed totally posh, and I wasn't allowed to go in them. I used to get all my clothes and school uniform from Jackson's Warehouse, where you could get a school jumper for about two quid and skirts for one pound fifty.'

'I remember Jackson's Warehouse,' David says. 'I got my school uniform there as well.' He laughs. 'And I got my first watch from the market – it was a present from my granddad and it cost about three quid. I really loved that watch, though. In my family it was exactly the same – we had no money at all, really – except my old man used to save up and take us to the army-supplies shop every few months, because he thought we'd all become soldiers, even my sister. We all had little army outfits and huge boots and facepaints and penknives and torches and netting, and every Saturday night we used to get a Wimpy, watch *The A-Team* and then pitch a tent in the front room and play Northern Ireland.'

'*Northern Ireland?*' Charlotte says.

David's laughing. 'Yeah. We had two cats. They were the IRA. My mum hated it. My old man spent whole weekends teaching us armed combat – stuff he'd learnt in the marines, like the most efficient way to cut someone's throat, how to crawl in the undergrowth, how to start a fire with no matches and open a tin of beans with no can-opener; and radio signals and command hierarchies and how to kill yourself if you were imprisoned to avoid them torturing the information out of you . . .'

'And now you're doing a law degree,' Charlotte says.

'He hates that,' David says. 'My mum's proud but Dad could never work out why I didn't want to go in the army like he did.'

'Wasn't he actually in the army when you were a kid?' Charlotte asks. 'I mean, how could he be at home pitching tents with you and stuff? Was that just when he was on leave?'

'He was paralysed by then,' David explains. 'Well, from the waist down. Got shot in the spine. We lived on his pension.'

'So he couldn't walk at all?'

'No. But he still made it down the pub every night to meet his mates.' David laughs. 'Electric wheelchair. Used to go where he wanted.'

'So he was paralysed and still obsessed with the army?' Charlotte sounds confused.

'Totally,' David says. 'Mum used to have to dress him and bath him but he was still going on about hand-to-hand combat the whole time, like he was still some sort of expert. You should have seen him when the Gulf War was on. He was obsessed with it all, like a commentator, like some sort of Jimmy Hill of war.'

Chantel and Charlotte laugh at that.

'What did you do on birthdays when you were a kid?' Chantel asks David.

'We always used to have Co-Op Black Forest Gateau and I always got an Action Man from my dad and a book token from my granddad. My mum used to let me choose something from the catalogue a couple of weeks before. The day before my birthday she'd always pretend it hadn't come, but it would always appear, miraculously wrapped up on the kitchen table the next morning. What about you?'

'A trip to McDonald's and a video. We weren't allowed cake in the house because of my mum's diet.'

'A trip to McDonald's?' says Charlotte.

'It was the only time we ever went. It was, like, a huge treat. That was until Rob came, of course; then it would be, like, McDonald's three nights running until there was no money left for the weekend and we'd have to eat out-of-date bread and stuff. Sometimes we couldn't afford tampons and we had to use homemade ones. See?' She laughs. 'That's how much of a pikey I was. Homemade sodding tampons. Jesus.'

'I hate the word pikey,' David says quietly.

'Yeah, so do I actually,' Chantel says. 'I'm just trying to reclaim it. Anyway, where did you grow up, Charlotte?' she asks.

'Cambridge. Well, a village just outside Cambridge.'

'A village,' says Chantel. The way she says the word makes it sound as exciting and exotic as if she'd said *castle*, or *millionaire's private island*. 'That would be well wicked, to live in a village.'

'It wasn't,' Charlotte says. 'It totally sucked.'

'Why?' Chantel asks. 'Wasn't it pretty?'

'Yeah, it was pretty, but it was also small and gossipy, and no one could be different and you had to get a bus into town . . . I don't know. It was just shit.'

'Did you have a nice house?'

'Yeah.'

'Can't have been that shit, then.'

'Maybe not,' says Charlotte.

There's a junction up ahead. Julie doesn't know where to go next. 'Where should I go at this roundabout?' she asks.

'Straight over,' says David, focussing on the map again. 'Then – oh, shit.'

'What?'

'There's no yellow road after the next roundabout.'

Julie starts to panic. 'Where am I going to go, then?'

'You'll have to go on a red road for about two minutes.'

'What kind of red road?'

'It's just an A-road. It's not a dual-carriageway or anything.'

'Oh, shit.'

'It'll be OK, babe,' Charlotte says.

Everyone shuts up while Julie drives around the first roundabout and down a thin road with wet trees and more rain, towards another roundabout with big green signs and white lights.

'So where's this A-road?' Julie says at the roundabout. She's still worried about the sandwich. What if she's on a main road when the acid kicks in? In her head, she sees the van spinning out of control, straight into the path of the oncoming traffic. Or what about drunk drivers at this time of night, haring home from the pub on these fast local roads? What if one of them drove into her? Her head feels weird. She knew she was right about the acid. Now she can't breathe.

'Calm down, Jules, it'll be fine,' Charlotte says.

'You want to go around to the right,' David says. 'The A408 – that's it, that one. Then look out on your right for a turning onto the B470 towards, um, Datchet or Eton. Make sure you don't miss it because the next one's much further down.'

The A-road doesn't look too much different to some of the B-roads they've been on but Julie's still sweating. She doesn't want to have a car crash; she doesn't want to die. She realises she's doing forty miles an hour and remembers what some guy once told her about having a blow-out at forty or over being potentially fatal. She slows down to about thirty-five.

'Can't we go faster?' Luke says.

Julie's hands grip the steering wheel tighter. He's been quiet for ages, drinking more beer through his straw and looking out of the window. He hasn't asked for anything to be explained to him – not that you can see much out of the windows apart from trees, rain and dark, shadowy industrial estates – and he hasn't commented at all on the outside world. Now he wants to go faster. What's the matter with him?

'Why are we going so slowly?' he says.

Charlotte turns around and gives him a look.

'What?' he says. 'I just want a bit more excitement, that's all.'

'Haven't you been paying attention, mate?' David asks.

'Sorry?' says Luke.

'Your friend is doing you a favour. Show her some fucking respect.'

'Leave it, Dave,' says Chantel.

Luke's already retreated back under his blanket.

Chapter 37

'This country's fucked,' David says.

Chantel's asleep and Luke's still under his blanket. It's almost half past four in the morning and Julie's been trying to get beyond Berkshire and into Wiltshire for the last two hours. The flooding's terrible here. All she can see now is a wet kaleidoscope of roads, like mirrors smeared with mud, and the reflection of the van's head-lamps in puddles. By now every road looks the same: wet trees, fallen leaves, dead branches, black fields, damp hedges messed up by the wind.

'Totally fucked,' he says. 'No trains. No roads. Fucked.'

Charlotte yawns. 'I'm knackered,' she says.

She seemed to get bored with the radio about three hours ago and now the only sounds Julie can hear, apart from the others talking, are the sloshing of the van tyres through the water on the roads, the hum of the windscreen wipers and the car heater.

There's another huge branch blocking the road up ahead.

'David,' Julie says, slowing down. 'Branch.'

They've already got a system going for this. If there's a way around via another route, they'll go around. If not, and if it's small enough, David will move the branch.

He studies the map. 'Around,' he says. 'Turn back, then take the first left you see.'

'OK.'

It's not easy turning a VW Camper on B-roads and country lanes. Julie ends up reversing most of the way back down the road until she sees the turning David means. It's an even smaller road, but at least it's not so flooded. Well, the first hundred or so yards of it aren't flooded, then Julie realises it's because the road goes downhill. At the bottom of the hill Julie realises that the space in front of her is filled with shiny black water, collected in the section where the road, she presumes, stops going down and starts going back up again. Unfortunately the up-again bit is nowhere to be seen and the water looks like it goes on indefinitely.

'Fuck it,' David says.

'Shall I drive through it?' Julie says.

Charlotte shrugs. 'What do you reckon?' she asks David.

'I don't know,' he says. 'We can't tell how deep it is, can we? Or where it ends.'

'How deep could it be?' Julie asks.

For some reason, she has remained unafraid of all this water everywhere. In fact, in one way she quite likes it: the roads are clearer; no one's going that fast. The nice thing about water is that if the worst happens, you can always float on it. Irrationally, Julie isn't at all bothered about the floods. She can swim; what's the big deal?

'I'm going to go through it,' she says.

'You might fuck the van's brakes, if it's deep,' David says.

'Or we could get stuck,' says Charlotte.

Julie starts inching towards the huge puddle of water.

'I'm not sure about this,' Charlotte says. 'What about Luke and Chantel?'

'What about them?' Julie says.

'If we get stuck . . .'

'Then they'll have to get out and help push. It won't be that deep,' Julie says.

She stops just before the huge stretch of water and looks at it.

'Low gear,' David says. 'And don't go too fast. But don't stop. If you stop, you won't be able to start again. Just keep going through it, once you're in. In fact, maybe you should reverse back so you can get a bit of momentum going.'

'OK,' Julie says, reversing about twenty yards or so. 'Here goes.'

'Remember not to let the van stop,' David says. 'Second gear.'

'OK.' Julie feels like Evel Knievel about to leap over a line of buses. She glances at Sophie's charm dangling from the rearview mirror, then drives forward, a bit faster than she'd like under these circumstances, and the van eventually sloshes into the water. The incline into the flooded bit of road is a lot steeper than she imagined it would be, and it feels as if the wheels are almost totally immersed.

'Oh, shit,' she says.

'Just don't stop,' David says again. 'Now you're in you just have to get out the other side. Just keep driving.'

Keeping her foot steady on the accelerator, Julie keeps driving the van through the water, trying desperately not to do anything to make it stall. The section of flooded road is even longer than she'd thought, and after a minute or so there's still no end to it. Julie tries to steady her shaking hands and keeps her eyes fixed on the water in front of her. She realises she's been holding her breath, and starts trying to breathe normally again while keeping the van going forwards.

'Oh, shit,' Charlotte says. 'We've driven into a river. I can't look.'

'Shut up, Charlotte,' David says. 'Keep her steady, Jules.'

Julie's concentrating so hard their voices seem to come from miles away. She has to get through this, otherwise there's no way back – or forward. They'd be completely stranded in here. She presses the accelerator a little harder, but it doesn't make any real difference to the speed of the van. Julie has the feeling that they're simply going forward by their own momentum now, and the thought gives her a little buzzing feeling – like fear, but nice. This is one of the most exciting things she's ever done.

'I don't like this,' Charlotte says.

'It'll be all right,' Julie hears herself saying.

Then she realises: Charlotte's scared of something, and Julie isn't.

'Well done,' David says, when they eventually come out on to the road again. 'Top driving, Jules.'

'Jesus Christ,' says Charlotte. 'That was fucking terrifying.'

Julie's shaking but smiling. 'It was pretty fun, actually,' she says.

It was fun but she's stopped the van for a few minutes to have a cigarette anyway. She pierces a new carton of Ribena with a straw and takes several huge gulps. David passes her the map.

'Here's where we are,' he says, leaning over the driver's seat and pointing. 'And this is the only way we can get through now.' He points to a road leading vaguely in the direction of Swindon. 'See, there's where we've been stuck, and here's where we can get back on to that bigger B-road.'

'Isn't that the road that was flooded and had that huge branch we couldn't get past?' Julie asks.

'Yeah, but we'll be joining it higher. See?'

All Julie can see right now are the words *Vale of White*

Horse on the map. And there, almost in the middle: the name of the little village where her mother lives. Julie realises that they must have driven almost right by it already, a while ago, before the huge branch and the flooded road.

'Yeah, whatever,' she says, and wonders what her mother's house is like, and what it looks like, and what *she* looks like now. Julie has a weird pang of something like homesickness, then puts down her drink and switches the engine back on.

'OK. Let's go.'

About a mile or two down the road there's a roadblock just before a village. Two policemen in fluorescent tops are talking to some men in an RAC rescue van. One of the policemen gestures for Julie to stop.

'Shit. Old Bill,' says David, sounding instantly panicked.

'Hide your gear, Dave,' says Charlotte.

'I am,' he says. 'Jesus. Bollocks. Down my boxers. There.'

'I don't think they're going to care about that,' Julie says. 'Look.'

Up ahead, it seems like the whole village is flooded.

'Oh, fuck it,' says David.

Julie stops the van and one of the police officers walks over. She winds down the window to talk to him.

'You're not coming through here, love,' says the officer.

The other one walks up as well. 'Where've you lot come from?' he asks.

'Essex,' Julie says. 'We're going to Wales.'

'Essential journey, is it?' the first one says, and laughs.

'It is, actually,' Julie says, smiling.

'Yeah, all right, love.' He laughs again. 'But you're still going to have to go via another route, because there's no way to get through here at all. I don't know how the hell you got this far anyway. All the roads behind you are very flooded.'

'I know. Are you sure I can't just drive through this water?' Julie's got a taste for driving through water now.

'No, love, sorry. You know how deep that is?' He gestures at the water beyond the roadblock. 'You'd need a boat to get through that. You're going to have to go back, I'm afraid.'

'Back?'

Vaguely, in the distance, Julie can see a wisp of orange in the sky. Sunrise.

'Come on,' says David. 'We'd better go back.'

Julie turns the van around and drives back to the turning she took ten minutes ago. This is like a riddle. You can choose one of three paths: the one with the water, or the fallen tree, or the police.

'We should have listened to the news on the radio,' Charlotte says.

'We did listen to it,' Julie says. 'It said don't travel. We are travelling. This was bound to happen.'

'There's no way out of this,' David says. 'That way's blocked, that way's flooded – and even though we've gone through it once, I don't like our chances of doing it a second time – and that way's got a roadblock and Old Bill. We're trapped.'

'So we're just going to sit here all night?' Charlotte says.

'There's not exactly much night left,' Julie points out.

The sky has turned from black to navy blue, and the orange wisp in the distance is now three orange wisps.

'Sunlight,' says Charlotte. Then: 'Oh, shit. Luke.'

'Yeah,' Julie says. 'It's a problem. A big one.' She lights a cigarette. 'David?'

'Yeah, I'm looking for another route,' he says. 'But

we've tried them all.' He points at the map. 'See up there we had to turn back and come down here, so going back up there isn't really an option. We can't go down, either – see, that was the road with the mashed-up tractor in it, and that one was closed and that one had that huge tree . . . All we could do, if we had time, which we haven't, really, is go back towards London and go higher up, but we'll probably find exactly the same shit up there.'

'In summary, we're fucked?' says Charlotte.

'Yeah,' David says.

'Will the space-suit keep the sunlight out?' Charlotte asks.

'Dunno,' he says. 'It's all right for sunlight reflected off the moon, but . . .'

'Huh?' says Charlotte 'What do you mean, sunlight reflected off the moon?'

'Moonlight is sunlight reflected off the moon,' David explains.

'Oh,' says Charlotte. 'I didn't know that.'

'I wouldn't want to chance it with direct sunlight,' Julie says.

'We're going to have to find somewhere to stay, then,' Charlotte says.

'A hotel?' David says.

'Have you seen any hotels around here?' Julie asks David.

'No.'

'Charlotte?'

'No.'

'Also, we can't be sure that a hotel would be able to cater for Luke.'

'All hotels have curtains, don't they?' Charlotte says.

'Yeah, but we don't know how thick they're going to be. And anyway, we'd have to explain why we're turning up with a guy dressed in a space-suit in the middle of the night. Well, not that it's the middle of the night any more, but still. How many people check into hotels at six in the morning?'

Julie's voice sounds dead but she's panicking. She's cold and it's wet outside and they haven't got anywhere to go. The sun's going to come up soon and then what? Julie's tired. She wishes someone would just rescue her from this.

'We really are fucked,' David says. 'I don't even know how the fuck we're going to go anywhere from here anyway, to be honest. We're going to have to go through that water again, I reckon. Or move that huge branch.' He rubs his head. 'Fuck it. I don't know.'

'We've got to do something,' Julie says.

'Tell me where we're aiming for ideally,' Charlotte says. 'I've got an idea.'

'Where we're aiming for's the problem, though, isn't it?' David says. 'I just don't know. There's nowhere for us to stay, is there? It's all gone a bit Mary and Joseph, hasn't it?'

'My mother lives near here,' Julie says suddenly. 'I haven't spoken to her for years but this is an emergency, isn't it? She knows Luke. She'll know how to get a room ready for him. Do you think I should ring her?'

'*Yes*,' says Charlotte. 'Quickly.'

'Why didn't you tell us about your mum before?' David says.

'I didn't really think about it,' says Julie, getting out her phone. She hesitates. 'Mind you, even if I do call her, I don't know how we're going to get to her place. Maybe I'll see if we can get there, first, then ring her.'

'Drive back to that roadblock, Jules,' Charlotte says. 'Like I said, I've got an idea.'

* * *

Fifteen minutes later, they are on their way with a police escort.

'Skin up,' says Chantel, who's awake again now.

'You can't skin up when you've got a police escort,' Julie says.

'They can't stop us if they're in front of us,' David points out.

'How did you get them to escort us, exactly?' Chantel asks Charlotte.

'I told them about Luke and they were really sweet. They're going try to move that branch for us and then go by routes they know aren't too bad. They said they'll even organise a boat if they have to, to get us to Julie's mum's. I don't think we should do any drugs while they're escorting us. It would upset them if they knew we were like that. Like we were disrespecting their help, or something.'

'I'm too fucked to smoke any more anyway,' David says.

'What were they doing out here in the middle of the night?' Julie says.

'That river back there only burst its banks a few hours ago,' Charlotte explains. 'That village flooded then, basically. The police were there doing emergency stuff: helping old people out of bungalows, distributing sandbags and everything.'

'Didn't look like the sandbags worked,' David says.

'No,' says Charlotte. 'Poor people.'

'You'd better ring your mum,' Chantel says to Julie.

Julie's had her phone on her lap for the last twenty minutes now.

'I can't use it while I'm driving,' she says. 'What about the police?'

'Give it to me,' Chantel says. 'I'll ring her. What's the number?'

'I don't know,' Julie says.

'Isn't it programmed in?'

'No. I've got it written down somewhere . . .'

'You don't know your own mother's phone number?'

'She hasn't seen her for ages,' Charlotte reminds Chantel.

'It's in my address book, in my bag,' Julie says.

Chantel gets the bag and finds it. 'What's it under?'

'M,' Julie says. 'For Mum.'

'What's her actual name?'

'Helen.'

Chantel flicks through the pages. 'God, you don't know many people, do you? OK. Got it. All right, here goes . . . She's going to be very pissed off when we wake her up, isn't she? Does she get up this early?'

'I don't know. She probably won't even answer,' Julie says.

'Keep trying if she doesn't,' Charlotte says. 'The sun's going to come up soon.' She looks at the lump under the blanket. 'Luke?' she says. There's no reply. 'He must be asleep. Make sure he stays under that blanket if he does wake up.'

Chantel's dialling. She puts the phone to her ear, and almost immediately says: 'Oh, hi. Is that Julie's mum?'

Chapter 38

It's about six thirty now and everyone's sitting in Helen's front room. Apparently she was woken at about three a.m. by Doug ringing her to ask if she knew where Julie had taken Luke. Since Chantel phoned, Helen has taped bin-bags to all the windows in the cottage and drawn all her curtains. Since everyone arrived, she has lit a fire and made everyone hot drinks. Now the police have gone and everyone's settled.

'This is very exciting,' Helen says, smiling at Julie proudly. 'You're on the run.'

Luke looks at Julie for a second but she's not catching his eye. No wonder, he was a complete bastard to her in the van.

'We didn't think we were on the run,' Chantel says. 'We didn't mean to cause any trouble.'

'I couldn't believe it when Doug phoned,' says Helen.

'So how come he phoned you?' Charlotte says. 'We didn't even know we were coming here until about an hour ago.'

'Jean was going bananas, apparently. Doug, Dawn and Michelle just seemed to be phoning everyone they could think of. It sounded like they'd also been interrogating someone called Nicky, who seemed to know more details about where you'd gone. But evidently she became rather pissed off and refused to say anything much except that she thought you'd be a few days at least.'

'Nicky's my mum,' Chantel says. 'I'd better ring her in the morning. Well, it is the morning, but . . . At a more reasonable time. Mind you, I'll be asleep then, I hope. Maybe I'll text her.' She pulls her phone out of her bag and starts pressing keys on it.

'I take it you didn't leave that note, then?' Charlotte says to Luke.

'I was going to ring Mum when we got there,' he says. 'I didn't think it would take so long.'

'To get to Wales? In a flood? On B-roads?' Helen says, laughing. 'Why were you going on B-roads, by the way?'

'It doesn't matter,' Julie says.

'And you're off to see . . .' She smiles. 'A healer?'

'That's right,' Luke says. 'He's going to make me better.'

Helen looks unconvinced. 'How?' she asks.

'I don't know yet,' Luke says. 'But he's very good, isn't he, Charlotte?'

She nods. 'If Luke can be healed, he'll do it.'

'Will it cost a lot of money?' Helen asks.

'It's on a donation basis,' Charlotte says. 'You donate to charity afterwards.'

'Well, you'll have to let me know how you get on,' Helen says, yawning.

'Thanks for saying we could stay,' Julie says suddenly.

'No problem. It's been much too long, and all this is very exciting. You should ring Jean, though,' Helen says to Luke. 'Go on. Do it now.'

'She'll be asleep, though . . .'

'I don't think she will. She was very worried.'

'Oh. I thought we'd be there by the time she got home from bingo. I thought I'd call her then . . .'

Luke knows his voice sounds choked. He's got a headache from drinking beer – and he's forgotten something again because of it. Not forgotten, exactly, but if he hadn't passed out in the van he would have known what time it was, and that his mum would be home from bingo and very, very worried. It was late even before he started drinking, though, and he was depressed by everything he saw at South Mimms. That was why he started drinking. So it wasn't even the drinking that made him forget. There's no way he can explain it to himself. He's hurt his mother, and he doesn't even have an excuse. What's wrong with him? Nothing feels right any more. He just wants to go home.

'The phone's in the hall,' Helen says. 'Help yourself.'

Even the phone's wrong. It's not his phone. Luke dials.

'Luke?' Jean answers immediately.

'Mum? Yeah, it's me.'

She starts crying.

'Oh, thank God. Thank God.'

'I didn't mean to worry you,' Luke says.

She cries into the phone for several minutes.

'Mum?' he says.

Eventually she speaks. 'Thank God you're all right. Where are you?'

'I'm not sure. On the way to Wales.'

'Wales? What the bloody hell . . . ?'

'There's a healer . . . I wanted it to be a surprise.'

'A surprise?'

'Sort of. Well . . .'

'You mean you weren't going to phone me at all?'

'No, I was, I mean I am. Look, I'm sorry.'

'I almost died when you weren't there. A *healer*?'

'I'm sorry. Look, I'll be OK. I'm in a house now, with no sunlight.'

'What about your allergies?'

'I'm OK, Mum. They seem to be OK. I've got my Ventolin and my adrenaline. Julie knows how to do the adrenaline if I accidentally eat a peanut or something.'

Jean is silent for a few seconds.

'Mum?' he says. 'Are you still there?'

'I suppose you're not coming home, then?' she says.

'What? Of course I'm coming home!'

'You won't come home. I can feel it.'

'Why are you saying this?'

'I felt it when your father left. You're just like him.'

'Mum, for God's sake. I'm not like my father, and I am coming home. I've just gone away for a few days to try to get myself better. It's not a big deal.'

She sighs. '*Not a big deal*. Luke, I'm so tired. I've been up all night.'

'I'm sorry,' he says again.

'Good luck,' she says, in a weird voice.

'What with?'

'Everything. Your life.'

'Mum, are you saying I *can't* come back?'

'Of course not. This is your home.' She pauses portentously. 'But I saw it.'

'Saw what?'

'I had a dream. I saw you walking down a long path and never coming back.'

Luke can't handle this right now. 'For God's sake. I don't need this, Mum. I've had the most fucking awful night, and Julie's not speaking to me because I acted like a dick, and I don't know where I am, and I've wanted to come home all this time, but I wouldn't know how to get home and everyone's being so nice to me and looking after me and I can't let them down . . . And this healer, he sounds so genuine and it's my one chance to get better and I'm so fucking scared, but I'm trying to be brave and I miss you and . . .'

'Please don't swear at me, Luke. I'm tired.'

'How do you think I feel? I'm tired too.'

'It's always about you, isn't it?' she says.

'No, Mum. Do you know what? I don't think any of this is about me.'

Luke puts the phone down.

He pretends he's on TV. 'That went well,' he says to himself in a low voice, as if there's an audience. Then he laughs like canned laughter but this isn't funny. Maybe she'll be in a better mood tomorrow. She's always like this when she's tired. But . . . Why does she have to be so fucking horrible to him? Nevertheless, Luke still wants to go home.

Helen comes into the hall. 'Everything OK?' she asks.

Luke notices that Helen looks older. The first time he saw her, when he was nine, she couldn't have been that much older than Charlotte is now. And when she lived in Windy Close, he didn't notice her change, particularly since he didn't see her much. Her hair seems to have more grey in it now, and her eyes have more lines. But what he really notices are her clothes. This is the first time he's seen Helen wearing anything other than what would count as 'young people's' clothes – jeans, denim jackets, hippy scarves from the market, purple DMs. This morning she's wearing a cardigan that looks, well, grown-up, and when she held her mug of hot chocolate in the sitting room before, Luke could almost imagine her as an old lady, with greyer hair, a bit smaller and sunken and in some way frail. Will Julie be like that when she gets older? Or do you have to actually live life before you can look like that?

'Fine,' he says. 'Well, Mum was weird.'

'In what way?'

'I don't know. She . . . She thinks I'm never going home.'

'Oh, ignore her.'

'She makes me really sad, Helen.'

Helen just smiles sympathetically, but she doesn't know that's the first time Luke's said anything negative about his mother to anyone.

'Shall I show you your room?' she says.

'Thanks,' says Luke.

Everything's TV again. All he can manage all the way up the stairs are TV responses: *Thanks, that would be lovely; don't go to any trouble; in here?* He's never really had to use any of these phrases before. When Helen shows him the bathroom he can't listen to what she's saying because the room smells so different to his bathroom at home, and he can't identify the smell, because smells – particularly ones that imitate nature – are not something he's familiar with.

Helens explaining something about how to flush the toilet.

'What's that smell?' Luke asks suddenly.

'Smell?' she says, in an odd voice.

'Have I said something wrong?'

'No, but . . .' Helen smiles. 'Is it a nice smell?'

'Yes. It's . . .'

'What does it smell like?'

'I don't know. It's amazing. I've never . . .'

'Oh, God. You don't have smells in your house, do you?'

The way she says this makes Luke think she's criticising his house in some way. But she's right, his house doesn't smell of anything, really, just his house. Nothing. But the smell of Helen's bathroom is indescribably beautiful.

'Is it this?' She opens a small bottle and holds it under his nose.

'No, not completely,' he says.

Helen puts several more bottles under his nose for him to smell. It turns out to be a combination of rose conditioner, mint shampoo, rosemary bath-oil, pine-fragranced bleach ('I shouldn't use bleach, because of the environment, but how else do you clean the toilet?'), toothpaste and three different kinds of soap: rose, orange blossom and heather.

'These are from flowers, aren't they?' Luke says. He thinks of vague smells on the few girls who've been in his bedroom over the years. Occasionally there was a small whisper of something like this, but mostly the smells were faint and slightly poisonous. Luke's never smelt a flower before, on a soap or on a girl or anywhere.

'Yes,' Helen says. 'These are mainly made from essential oils.'

'Do the real plants smell like this?'

'Oh, yes. I've got mint in the kitchen and a few roses left in my garden. I can show you, tomorrow.'

'Tomorrow?'

'Well, when you wake up.'

'Cool. Thanks, Helen.'

'You've really missed out, haven't you?' she says sadly.

Luke thinks about this. 'I don't know,' he says. 'I don't know how much more than this there is. I've no idea what there is out there. Whatever it is, I guess I've missed out on it.'

His bedroom smells and looks different to anything he's seen before. Often, on TV, bedrooms look very similar to one another. They don't usually have every wall covered in books or slightly ragged folded-up towels lying on the dresser ('They're for you. Help yourself to the bath or shower.') This room also has an old-looking mirror standing against a dusty fireplace, and lying at its foot, old copies of magazines Luke's never seen before – *City Limits*, *Spare Rib* and *Time Out*. There are also lovely pieces of thick printed fabric thrown over the bed, which actually looks like a sofa.

This room is dark, like his room at home. The only place he's ever seen sunlight is on TV. Were he ever to see sunlight in real life, it would surely be as different as everything else he's seen on this journey. Would it have a smell? What would it feel like? There's a small wooden wardrobe in the corner of this room, by the dresser. Luke walks over and runs his hands over it. Wood comes from trees. Luke knows that. But he's never felt wood before. This is wood, but it's surely not real. Would a tree feel different? And, hang on, there's something else here – something amazing – a piece of fabric hanging through one of the handles in the door. It's the softest thing Luke's ever felt in his life. It's a square, a red square of this incredible fabric, with pictures of flowers on it.

He touches it to his face. Chloe had some knickers that were made of fabric that felt a bit like this – he remembers that, and that he wasn't allowed to touch them once she'd taken them off because she thought it was weird. Maybe that was one of the reasons she never got in touch again: Luke wanted to rub her knickers in his face. This material smells of a flower, maybe one from the bathroom. It's so soft. He can't stop touching it. He puts it down while he takes off his space-suit and most of his clothes underneath, but then, like an addiction, he can't leave it alone. It's better than fleece. He takes it to bed with him and rubs it on his legs.

This is lovely, but he still wants to go home.

Chapter 39

Downstairs, Chantel's totting up all the ways in which Julie looks like her mum.

'It's, like, different colour hair, but the same kind of hair.'

'So not the same at all,' David says, yawning.

'Same eyes,' Chantel says. 'Well, the shape.'

'So still not the same, then,' David says.

'You do look like her,' Charlotte says to Julie. 'You can tell you're mother and daughter.'

The cottage looks a bit like Julie's house in Essex used to look before her mother moved out, but more so. Julie recognises the Indian rug on the sitting-room floor – it is their old rug from the house in Bristol years ago. She never saw it in Windy Close; her dad never liked that sort of thing. The two bookcases in this room are more familiar, though. Her mum took those from Windy Close when she left, and most of the books in the house – her text books from her days at the Poly, and books with titles that Julie remembers from being a child: *Woman on the Edge of Time*, *Feel the Fear and Do It Anyway*, *Fat is a Feminist Issue*, *Women Who Love Too Much*; and novels by Ursula Le Guin, Alice Walker, Toni Morrison and Maya Angelou. Julie remembers lying on the sitting-room floor, colouring, watching TV or eating jam sandwiches, and gazing up at the bookshelves that she thought would always be there. She must have read the titles hundreds of times but she never opened any of the books. Then they were gone.

* * *

Helen comes in, asks if anyone wants another drink before bed, then goes into the kitchen to make them. She looks tired, but as if she's still trying to get to grips with what's going on here, and who all these people in her house actually are.

'So . . .' she says, when she comes back. 'You're all Julie's friends?'

'David and I used to work together,' Julie explains, 'and Chantel just moved into number 14 on our street. She's Leanne's cousin – you must remember Leanne. And Charlotte used to live there before. She moved in with Mark and his family a few years after you left.'

'Oh, yes. How is Leanne, and how's Mark?'

'Um . . . Leanne's gone to become a witch and Mark's . . .'

'Dead,' finishes Charlotte. 'He died.'

Helen looks shocked. 'He died?' she repeats. 'That's awful. How . . . ?'

'A brain haemorrhage,' Julie says, glancing at Charlotte.

'And you were his girlfriend?' Helen asks Charlotte.

Charlotte nods. 'Yes.'

'How do you feel about that? About him dying?'

'Feel? Oh. I don't know. At the time I was a mess, but you know . . .'

Helen speaks in a slow, gentle voice. 'Time makes it better?'

'Yes. I don't know. A bit. It's more the coming to terms with loss, and the guilt and all the questions you ask yourself about whether you did the right thing, or thought the right thoughts or behaved the right way.'

Helen's nodding. 'Hmm, hmm,' she says. 'Absolutely.'

Julie feels uncomfortable. Although she hasn't seen or spoken to her mother for more than seven years, in essence she doesn't seem to have changed very much. Her idea of getting to know someone has always been to zero in on the most life-changing, horrible thing that's ever happened to them and make them talk about it in excruciating detail, and quiz them on exactly how it makes them feel. Charlotte doesn't seem to mind, particularly. Then Julie realises maybe that's because Charlotte does the same thing. In fact, now Julie thinks about it, Charlotte's probably got more in common with Helen than Julie has.

David yawns, which makes Julie yawn. The light in the sitting room seems brighter, even though it's almost totally blocked out by the bin-bags and the curtains. The clock on the wall says it's almost eight in the morning. Helen makes some more *Hmm, hmm* noises in Charlotte's direction before she gets up, stretches and suggests that everyone might like to go to bed.

'You can sort yourselves out however you'd like,' she says, providing them with a stack of blankets, pillows and sleeping bags. 'One or two of you might want to go in Luke's room with him – you'll need sleeping bags if you do. Now. That –' she points to one of the sofas – 'is a futon. I've never actually pulled it out before but I'm sure it's very simple. That other sofa's big enough for whoever's smallest, probably Julie, or you, Charlotte, and whoever's left over will probably have to go on the floor in here, or in Luke's room, or wherever.' She laughs. 'I've never had five guests before.'

'I think I'll go upstairs, then,' David says, when Helen's gone.

'I'll come with you, then,' says Chantel.

They gather various bits of bedding and go.

'That leaves us, then, babe,' says Charlotte to Julie. She gets up and seems to be assessing the bedding options. 'Shall we pull out this futon?' She drags off the large throw and pulls at the futon from a couple of directions. 'How the fuck do you get this out?'

Julie examines it. It's pretty simple. 'There,' she says when she's done it.

'It's cold now,' says Charlotte. 'We may as well both sleep on here.'

'It is big,' Julie says. 'OK, whatever.'

What else can she say? *No I don't want to sleep with you because I once had a crush on you?* Yeah, right. Girls sleep together all the time, though, don't they? It's one of those girly things. It'll seem stupid if she says she doesn't want to.

They arrange blankets on it, and a couple of pillows.

'Do you think I can smoke in here?' Charlotte asks.

'I don't know,' Julie says. 'I don't know if Mum would mind or not. Open a window or something if you can; I'm sure it'll be fine. Use the fire as an ashtray. I'm going to smoke too, so . . . If she says anything we just won't do it tomorrow.'

'OK.'

'I'm hungry. I might go and see what there is in the kitchen.'

'OK, cool.' Charlotte starts rolling a cigarette. 'If you find anything good, bring some for me.'

'Sure.'

'You must be starving,' Charlotte says, as Julie goes through the sitting-room door into the kitchen. 'You never ate those sandwiches, did you?'

The kitchen is small and has two window boxes filled with herbs. The window itself has a bin-bag taped over it, so Julie opens the back door for some air and some light. Outside there's Helen's small garden, crowded with shrubs, autumn leaves, more herbs and a little path that doesn't seem to go anywhere, except to a tiny shed. Just outside the door, in a covered alcove, is a bucket, a trowel and some gardening gloves. It's raining. Julie's had enough of rain. She shuts the door.

She wants chocolate but there's none in the kitchen. The small fridge contains hoummus, bean sprouts, organic cow's milk, sheep's cheese, carrot juice, organic vegetable cocktail and a small loaf of brown bread. There's also some Safeway organic eggs, some Safeway yoghurts, a Safeway cucumber, several jars of Safeway olives and two bottles of white wine. Nothing edible there, although Julie remembers liking hoummus as a child, and carrot juice. The cupboards contain things like herbal teas, vitamin supplements, Echinacea, honey, lentils, uncooked beans in packets (one of Julie's greatest fears – everyone knows that if you don't cook beans exactly right they'll kill you), rice, tinned soup and various bags of organic oats. There are no crisps or sweets anywhere. Desperate, and feeling slightly faint, Julie cuts a piece of dense brown bread from the fridge and spreads honey on it.

She sticks her head through the door to the sitting room. 'Do you want bread and honey?' she asks Charlotte.

'No, I'm all right, thanks. I'll have a cup of tea if you're making one, though.'

'Normal tea?'

'No, chamomile, please. That's what your mum was making for me.'

'OK.'

Julie puts the kettle on and replaces the lid on the honey. As she's putting it back in the cupboard she strains somehow and the next thing she knows, she's got the hiccups. She holds her breath. When was the last time she had the hiccups? Maybe when she was a kid. Holding her breath doesn't work, and the next hiccup catapults from inside her with startling force. Having hiccups is to do with your diaphragm going into spasm, isn't it? That's actually pretty scary. Whatever is spasming inside her is bigger than her heart . . . Would a heart attack feel like this, only smaller? Oh, God. There's a glass on the draining board. Julie fills it with water, leans over the sink and tries to do that thing where you drink the water backwards. It doesn't work. And now she's drunk tap water. God.

Julie tips the rest of the water down the sink and closes her eyes. She tries pulling her tongue, but that doesn't work either. She's got to get rid of this before she becomes like that guy in Iowa who hiccupped for more than sixty years. If you can make yourself concentrate on something else, really hard, that can cure hiccups – that's a theory, isn't it? Maths. Maths can solve anything. 2 times 2 is 4; 4 times 3 is 12; 12 times 4 is 48; 48 times 5 is 240; 240 times 6 is 1,440; 1,440 times 7 is 10,080.

The kettle boils. Julie's hiccups have gone.

'Here,' she says to Charlotte a few minutes later. 'Tea.'

'Cheers, babe. You OK?'

'Yeah.' Julie smiles. 'I had hiccups. Freaked me out. I'm all right now.'

'Cool.'

Charlotte's sitting cross-legged on the big futon. Julie sits on it too.

'Does your mum live here on her own?' Charlotte asks.

'Looks like it,' Julie says.

'You don't know much about her, do you?'

'Not since she moved, no.'

'She left when you were in sixth form, didn't she?'

'How do you know that?'

'You told me ages ago.'

Charlotte's always been so into herself Julie wouldn't

expect her to remember a conversation she had with her yesterday, and certainly not one they had something like three years ago. Charlotte's blowing on her tea and looking at Julie while she does it.

'She seems OK,' Charlotte says. 'Nice. I like her house.'

'Yeah, it's very her.'

'Why did she leave?'

'My dad was having an affair.'

'Oh. Why didn't you go with her?'

'She didn't ask me.'

'Would you have gone?'

'I couldn't, could I?'

'Why not?'

'Luke, of course. And my exams.'

'Oh, yeah. Of course.' Charlotte sounds unconvinced.

'Anyway, she didn't ask me.'

'Is that why you're all thingy with her.'

'All thingy?'

'Yeah.'

'Am I?'

'Yeah. Totally. She looked like she was scared of you.'

'No, she didn't. Don't be stupid.' Julie doesn't like this conversation. She sips her tea. 'I hate hiccups,' she says. 'I had to do this weird thing with numbers to cure it. It worked. You have to start at two and multiply the next whole number by the answer to the last multiplication . . .'

Charlotte looks blank. 'Numbers,' she says. 'What is it with you and numbers?'

'I just . . . I just like them. I know it's weird.'

'It's not. It's interesting. It's just . . . You freaked me out in Homebase, though.'

'What, when I added up the shopping?'

'Yeah. To the last fucking penny.'

'Addition isn't exactly complicated,' Julie says. 'I told you that. It's just a party trick. No big deal. It's not exactly like working with imaginary numbers or anything . . .'

'What is an imaginary number exactly?'

'It's pretty complicated.'

'So? Explain it to me.'

Julie sighs. 'It's . . . Oh, how can I explain? Um . . . you sure you want to know?'

Charlotte sips her tea. 'Yeah. I like the idea of imaginary numbers.'

'OK. It's like . . . All right . . . What's the square root of 4?'

'Huh? The square root of 4?'

'Yeah, what number do you have to multiply by itself to get 4?'

'Oh. 2. Yeah, that's right; 2 squared is 4.'

'OK, so what's the square root of 36?'

'Um . . . 6. Yeah, 6 times 6 is 36.'

'Yeah. Good. So what's the square root of 1?'

Charlotte thinks for a second. 'Is it 1?'

'Excellent. 1 times 1 is 1. So what's the square root of minus 1?'

'Huh?'

'Minus 1? What's the square root?'

'Um . . . minus 1?'

'No. Minus 1 times minus 1 is 1.'

'Is it?' Charlotte frowns. 'No, it can't be.'

'A minus number multiplied by a minus number is always a positive number. Don't you remember that from school?'

'No. Well, maybe vaguely. This is where maths loses me. That sort of thing just doesn't make any sense. It doesn't seem logical.'

'It is, though,' Julie says. 'A negative value multiplied

with a negative value must be positive. The negative values cancel each other out. It's like with English, if you said, "I didn't do nothing", you're actually saying you did do something. The two negatives cancel each other out.'

'I get how that works in English, but I don't get it with maths. It's too theoretical. It fucks with your head. It makes you feel stoned all the time.' She laughs. 'Well, maybe that's a good thing, but still . . .'

'It's not theoretical, though,' Julie says. 'It's what actually happens. Um . . . I'm trying to think of a good example . . . OK, say you smoked a pack of 20 fags every day. We'll call that a value of minus 20, in the sense that you're taking 20 cigarettes away each time you smoke them. You see what I mean? You had them. They're gone. Minus 20. OK? But say you gave up smoking for 5 days, and you therefore didn't smoke your normal packet a day for those 5 days. So if we multiply the minus 20 cigarettes by the minus 5 times you have smoked them, you get 100 cigarettes. Do you see what I mean? You haven't smoked 20 fags a day for 5 days, so you're left with 100 unsmoked fags. Do you see that? So minus 20 times minus 5 equals 100.'

Charlotte looks confused. 'I sort of get it.'

'It's like when they say you'll save money by giving up smoking. By not spending it you're saving it. It's the same thing. "Not" is a negative. So is "spending". Not spending means you have the money you haven't spent. So you've saved money. A negative multiplied by a negative is always a positive.'

Charlotte's rolling another cigarette. 'OK,' she says, frowning. 'Yeah, I get that.'

'So minus 1 times minus 1 is actually 1. If you usually drank one bottle of vodka a day and you did that for minus 1 days – in other words, if you didn't do it for a day – you'd have 1 bottle of vodka as a result. So if 1 times 1 is 1, and if minus 1 times minus 1 is also 1, then we can say that 1 has 2 square roots: 1 and *minus* 1. Similarly, the square root of 36 is 6, and also minus 6.'

'What's this got to do with imaginary numbers?'

'Well, we're still looking for the square root of minus 1, remember. So if it's not in fact minus 1, because minus 1 squared is actually 1, then what is it?'

Charlotte lights her cigarette. 'Pass,' she says. 'I don't know. If it's not minus 1 – and I get that, now – then what else could it be?'

'Exactly. There isn't anything else that it could be, so it doesn't exist.'

'This is pretty interesting, actually,' Charlotte says, sipping more tea. 'Right. So if it doesn't exist, then . . .'

'Basically, mathematicians invented imaginary numbers to function as the square roots of minus numbers. So that's what they are. You write them as values of "i", which is the square root of minus 1. The square root of minus 4 is therefore 2i.'

'So what's the square root of i, then?' Charlotte asks, after thinking about this for a few seconds.

'You so don't want to go there,' Julie says, laughing. 'Can I have a roll-up?'

'Yeah, sure. So how do you know all this stuff?'

Julie shrugs. 'School, reading, the Internet.'

'You never went to university, did you?' Charlotte says.

'Nope.'

'Why not?'

'I failed my A levels. Didn't I ever tell you that?'

'No.' Charlotte wrinkles her forehead. 'So what did you do, fail them on purpose so you wouldn't have to leave Luke and your safe life, and to punish your mum for leaving you or something?' She laughs. 'That would be so you, babe.'

Julie can feel her face going red. This is typical of Charlotte. Things that everyone else somehow misses are always completely obvious to her.

'Why are you saying that?' Julie says.

'Well . . . you're too clever to have failed. But you are fucked up enough to fail on purpose and probably get some kind of cheap anarchic thrill out of it. I know you.'

'Yeah. You do.'

'So you did, then?' Charlotte says, her eyes wide. 'You did fail on purpose?'

Julie looks down. 'It doesn't matter what I did, does it? This is my life.'

'Does anyone else know?'

'No.'

'Wow. So did she notice?'

'Who?'

'Your mum. Did she notice you'd failed and make a big fuss about it?'

'Not really. She didn't do anything.'

Charlotte shakes her head. 'You poor thing,' she says.

It's cold. Julie gets under the covers. When Charlotte puts her cigarette out she does the same. They lie there in silence for a few minutes, not touching.

'Did you miss not going to university?' Charlotte says eventually.

'I don't know, do I? Since I've never been, I don't know what I missed.' Julie suddenly laughs. 'Oh, God, I sound like Luke now.'

Charlotte laughs too. 'Seriously, though, did you want to go?'

'I don't know really. At the time, I suppose I did.'

'And now?'

'Now? No, I don't think so.'

'Why not?'

'Aren't you tired?' Julie asks, ignoring Charlotte's question.

'A bit. I'm still a bit psyched from the journey and everything. So why not?'

Julie sighs. 'I just like being a waitress and reading about other stuff in my spare time. I wouldn't want to do a maths job or a chemistry job. Did you know I was good at chemistry as well? I liked the equations. But anyway, I'm scared of chemicals, so I definitely wouldn't want to do a chemistry job. I liked physics, too, although I'm hardly going to become an engineer or anything. And maths? I don't want to be in business or do economics or accountancy. I'd like to solve a theorem, or a problem that's never been solved before. I suppose that's my dream, even if it is a bit of a stupid one.'

'Like thingy – that French one?'

'Fermat's Last Theorem? Yeah, that's been solved now. There's a maths institute offering million-dollar prizes for solving certain other unsolved problems, though. There's one problem in particular – I think about it when I'm waitressing. That's basically it. I'm a waitress trying to solve maths theorems and I'm happy with that. No one knows about the maths, by the way, so you've got two secrets out of me tonight.'

'You like having a secret life, don't you?'

Julie hasn't ever considered the idea of a secret life in relation to herself before but she does have one. She suddenly thinks about Chantel's grandmother.

'I suppose so,' Julie says. 'Although it sounds a bit weird when you say it like that.' She frowns. 'I suppose it's the only thing that's completely mine. Plus, Luke's my only real friend apart from you – and I haven't seen you for ages – and he's not interested in maths or numbers or physics, so it's not like it's a total secret, because I haven't actually got anyone to tell who'd be interested, or understand what I was going on about. But . . . Yeah, I do quite like it that way. I like having my own thing.'

'So why are you so sad,' Charlotte says, 'if you're so happy?'

'Other stuff. Luke. My dad. My mum. Just stuff, you know.'

'Do you think you'll be able to solve this problem or theorem – or whatever it's called?'

Julie laughs. 'Yeah, right. Me and the other zillion people working on it.'

'Do mathematicians use words like "zillion"?'

Julie laughs again. 'Look, there's a very, very small chance I could apply for a maths scholarship without needing A levels – please don't tell anyone about this – and when Luke's better I might think about it.'

'That would be really cool.'

'I also know four computer-programming languages. I learnt them for fun last year. So I don't have to be a waitress. I just enjoy it. So I might do maths, or I might continue being a waitress. Who knows? I might decide to sell flowers by the side of the road. Well – it would have to be a B-road, but still.'

'Wow, babe.' Charlotte laughs. 'You're a total free spirit.'

'I have to be, don't I? I haven't had any other choice. Also, I've been taught by the best.'

'What do you mean?'

'Well.' Julie moves slightly in the bed. Her breathing feels different. 'You.'

'Me?'

'I was really depressed before you came to Windy Close. I learnt how to be a free spirit – if that's what it is – by copying you. You were the one who taught me that it doesn't matter what your job is, or how much money you've got, or how many people you employ or have power over, or even how often you wash your hair or what clothes you wear – what matters are the books you read, and the thoughts you have, and being true to yourself, whoever you are. I've never bought into that corporate bullshit of going to university so you can get a good job and move to London and spend all your money on rent and lunch and tights just so you can feel important. I like being down to earth. I've always been like that but meeting you made me realise I'm not a freak, and that it's OK.'

'I taught you that? Fucking hell.'

'Well . . .'

Charlotte laughs. 'When you put it like that my life doesn't sound like such a fuck-up.'

'Your life isn't a fuck-up.'

'It so is.'

'How?'

'Where do I start? Me and Mark ditched university to go travelling, so I haven't even got a degree. We did too many drugs. He died – and I bet you all the drugs I made him take didn't exactly help him to not have a brain haemorrhage. I drowned in guilt. My parents disowned me. I did more drugs. I have no future. My life totally sucks . . . I could go on.'

'Come on, Charlotte. If I'm a free spirit, you definitely are.'

'Maybe we should be free spirits together, then,' she says, really quietly. 'It would be a whole lot more fun.'

'But you're going to India.'

'And you're going to do some kind of weird maths thing.'

'Only if I can get there on B-roads. They probably won't even accept me.'

Charlotte laughs, then turns over. She falls asleep breathing into Julie's hair.

Julie dreams about driving fast through water.

Chapter 40

By three o'clock the next afternoon everyone's up except Luke. David and Chantel have been talking in low voices to each other for most of the day so far and Charlotte's been pottering about with Helen, pestering her about her time at Greenham Common. Luke's going to stay in bed until it gets dark, and Julie's vaguely reading the *Independent on Sunday*, eating toast and marmalade, and thinking that she wishes she was in motion again, like yesterday.

'Where's the nearest big town to here?' Chantel asks Helen suddenly.

'What for?' Helen asks.

'Stuff . . . I'm not sure. A bookshop, big shops in general . . .'

'There's Wantage but for a good bookshop you'd need to go to Oxford.'

'Oxford's a city, isn't it?' Chantel says.

'Of course it is, stupid,' says David, smiling.

'I want to go there, then,' Chantel says. 'Can we get a cab there?'

Julie looks up from the paper. 'I'll drive you,' she says.

'Super cool,' says Chantel. 'I was hoping you'd say that.'

'Are you sure?' David says to Julie.

'Yeah. I might even try a red road.'

It's not raining.

'Fucking hell, what's that?' David says once they're outside.

'What?' Julie says.

'Up there. Blue sky. Fuck me.'

'You scared me then,' Chantel says. 'I didn't know what you meant.'

In daylight, the van just looks like a van. Last night it felt like a mini-universe; their whole world, like an orange womb on wheels.

'You sure about this red-road stuff?' David says, as they get in.

'Yeah,' Julie says. 'Bring it on.'

'So what's happened to you, then?' Chantel asks once they're on the A338.

'Huh?' says Julie, concentrating.

'Why aren't you freaking out?'

'She drove through this big puddle yesterday when you were asleep,' David explains. 'It gave her a buzz.'

'How do you know it gave me a buzz?' Julie says.

'I was there, mate. You were well buzzing.'

Julie smiles. 'I wanted to do it again afterwards.'

'I know you did.' David looks at Chantel. 'You should have seen it,' he says to her. 'Me and Charlotte were fucking bricking it and Julie's like some kind of fucking kid going down a slide or something – *again, again*. It was mental.'

'I like water,' Julie says.

The red road isn't too bad. It's a single-lane main road, and there's a lot of traffic, so Julie just has to concentrate on following the brown Sierra in front of her. And she's already decided that she's just going to follow the signs to Oxford from now onwards and not worry about which roads she goes on. She's fucking terrified but it can't be that bad. She looked at the map before she set off anyway and the bit of dual carriageway into Oxford looks a bit like the section of the A12 that goes into London. Julie's hoping for a similar forty-mile-per-hour speed limit, lots of traffic lights and plenty of slow-moving traffic. As they get closer to the city centre, Julie remembers she likes town driving and that something about the density of the traffic and the lack of open spaces around her makes her feel almost invincible. Without really noticing, she finds she's driving more like the way she used to drive when she was eighteen, nipping out to overtake slow Metros and buses at two-lane junctions, cutting it fine, getting a thrill from occasionally cutting it *very* fine. Julie had forgotten she was even capable of this – and in a VW Camper, as well.

Why? Something about the floods, and Charlotte, and telling secrets. And maybe something about seeing her mother. Not that seeing her mother has been great so far, but it's been real, and comforting, and she still exists, and Julie knows what her house looks like. At the next set of lights, she races a Mini and wins.

David shakes his head. 'You've gone feral,' he says, smiling.

It's almost four o'clock when they get to the centre of Oxford.

'Where are we going, then?' Julie asks Chantel, when she's parked the van in a multistorey carpark.

'A bookshop first, then a travel agent.'

'A travel agent?' Julie says. David and Chantel just smile.

'Why don't we all meet back here at five?' Chantel says.

Oxford.

Julie sits in the van and looks out at the dirty concrete walls of the carpark. She's been to Oxford once before: to do the entrance exam for mathematics & philosophy, the course she probably would have done if she hadn't failed her A levels. They offered her a place conditional on her obtaining three A grades as long as two of them were maths and further maths. She could have got those grades easily but she didn't. Would she still be sitting here if she'd got the grades and gone to Oxford? Probably not. She'd probably know a better place to park.

Coming to Oxford to sit the test was one of the last things she did with her mother and father together. They all drove up in her father's Volvo. While Julie took the test her parents went for coffee and cakes in a nearby teashop and looked around some of the city.

'Would you really want to come here?' her mother asked her as they drove through the old city on their way home.

Julie looked at her mother's face. Helen was frowning as if she thought there was something wrong with Oxford University. Julie knew that look very well. Her mother was objecting to some whiff of patriarchy, power and influence she could sense in medieval-looking honey-coloured buildings all around them.

'I'd love it,' Julie said.

The rest of the way home Helen read a magazine she'd picked up in an alternative bookshop and Julie replayed the maths test in her mind as if she'd just taken part in an exciting sporting event or theatrical production. Her dad listened to a Stone Roses tape over and over again. Later it would be discovered that his art-student girlfriend had given him the tape as a birthday present.

Julie gets out of the van and finds a small newsagent a couple of streets away. She buys three cartons of Ribena and lots of sweets. Then she goes back to the car-park. She drinks two cartons of Ribena and eats all the sweets while she scribbles numbers on an oily scrap of paper from the glove box in the van. At about five she stops and rubs her eyes. The light isn't very good here. At ten past five, Chantel and David walk towards the van, holding hands. Julie looks at them as they get closer. She does a double-take. They're actually holding hands? God.

In her free hand, Chantel's carrying a Waterstones bag. She and David get into the van and Chantel starts taking items out of the bag. She gives David two envelopes, then hands three book-shaped packages to Julie, each in a paper bag, sellotaped shut. One has a C written on it, one has an L, and the last one has a J.

'Don't open these until you get back,' Chantel says.

'Huh?' says Julie. 'You sound like you're not coming back with me.'

'I'm not,' Chantel says. 'I mean we're not. Me and David.'

'Oh . . .' Julie frowns. 'Where are you going?'

'We're going to America,' David says, waving the envelopes. 'Get my balls fixed. Go surfing. Chan's just got the tickets, look.'

His eyes sparkle as he waves the tickets around in the half-dark of the van.

'America?' Julie says, grinning. She looks at Chantel. 'Really? You're going to America so David can get cured?'

'Yep.' Chantel grins. 'David's taking a year off university, if he can. We've been planning this all day. We're going to go and stay in a hotel for the next couple of nights so we can have our passports sent to us – I hope your mum doesn't mind us not going back there, but David's never stayed in a hotel, so I thought it would be nice. Also, your poor mum doesn't really have enough room for us all. I've spoken to my mum and she thinks I'm a bit mental but she's OK about it. I've just got to spend this money. It's pissing me off now.'

'Oh, wow,' is all Julie can say. 'That's . . . amazing.'

'Tell me about it,' David says. 'I thought she was winding me up this morning.'

'That's the most romantic thing I've ever heard,' Julie says.

Chantel laughs. 'Well, we'll see. Dave'll probably ditch me in a month.'

'Might give it two,' David says.

Chantel's still laughing. 'We'll just see how it goes,' she says.

This is still the most romantic thing Julie's ever heard.

'Neither of us have ever been abroad,' Chantel says. 'It'll be an experience, anyway. I like the idea of travelling. I suppose our journey's going to be a bit longer than yours, but if it wasn't for you, we wouldn't be on a journey at all, so we wanted to say . . .'

'Thanks,' David finishes, leaning over and kissing Julie awkwardly on the cheek.

Chantel hugs her next. 'Yeah, thanks,' she says. 'And say thanks to the others as well. I got you each something – only something small. Well, it's books, you can probably guess that.' She laughs. 'But still don't open your package until you get back. I'll be embarrassed, because I'm shit at choosing books.'

David and Chantel are both getting out of the van. This is happening so quickly.

'What about the van?' Julie says, getting out and standing next to them. 'It's yours and . . .'

'Just look after it for me,' Chantel says. 'We'll be back. Don't worry about that.'

'OK,' Julie says. Her voice echoes in the half-empty carpark. 'Well, have fun.'

'We will.'

'And send me a postcard,' Julie says.

Chantel throws her arms around Julie again. 'I'm doing the right thing, aren't I?' she whispers into Julie's hair.

Julie thinks about Chantel's grandmother. 'Yes,' she whispers back.

'Well,' Chantel says, pulling away and smiling at Julie. 'See ya.'

'Yeah, bye,' says David.

Then David and Chantel walk off with their little bags and their travel tickets without looking back.

Chapter 41

'So what was it like going back to Windy Close once you'd been at Greenham Common for a year?' Charlotte asks Helen.

Luke's in the kitchen reading one of the Sunday supplements. He's wearing the same fleece and tracksuit bottoms he had on yesterday. But no space-suit today, thank God. Charlotte and Helen are standing by the sink, sipping tea and talking. Helen's been describing how, after her degree, she desperately wanted to be 'free', and went travelling to India and then spent some time at Greenham Common. She bought this house from one of the Greenham women, a few years later, and her connection to Greenham was the reason for her wanting to settle in this area. She's working as a therapist now.

'It felt incredibly strange,' Helen says. 'I never felt comfortable there. It was too . . . I don't know. Too trivial and money-obsessed and, well, too Essex for me.'

'Why did you move there in the first place?'

She shrugs. 'Doug liked it. He's from Essex and he always wanted to move back there. One day he inherited some money; the next he started looking for jobs in the southeast. He spent the money on the house. He said we had to grow up.'

Charlotte raises her eyebrows. 'Grow up?'

Helen laughs. 'Yep. We were about your age at the time.'

'God. That's insane.'

'I know. I was just starting a college course as well. I wasn't quite ready to grow up and play house and worry what the neighbours thought. It was like living in a soap opera. I kept expecting people to come round with a casserole or a cake recipe or something. At that age I still wanted to smoke dope and listen to John Lennon.'

'I suppose having a kid didn't help?'

'What, Julie? I wanted to take her to Greenham with me – in fact, I wanted to take her everywhere with me – but Doug said she couldn't afford to miss all that school and I'd probably get into trouble for taking her away in the middle of a term and so on. Also, she wasn't interested in any of that sort of thing. Do you know her name's really Juliet? She shortened it to Julie when she was about eight because it was more normal. She always wanted normal clothes and to be just like everyone else. To be honest, we didn't completely click when she was a child.'

'*Juliet?*' Charlotte says. Luke catches her eye. 'Did you know this?' she asks him.

He shakes his head. 'Nope. Juliet? Huh.'

'Does anyone get on with their kids, though?' Charlotte asks Helen. 'I mean, if you're a – excuse the expression – hippy parent, in particular. Don't all kids just want to be normal and embarrass you by wanting to go to McDonald's and wear Adidas and listen to pop music?'

'I don't know,' Helen says sadly. 'I had friends who had great kids.'

'And Julie wasn't a great kid?' Charlotte says. 'I can't believe that.'

Helen looks thoughtful. 'It wasn't just that,' she says. 'You know the most terrifying thing about having kids? It's that you could fail, somehow, and lose them. And then one day it happens; you realise that your worst fear is coming true and you are losing your child because your relationship's completely breaking down and you don't know where it went wrong or how to put it back together again. How do you pick up the phone and talk to your daughter when you haven't seen her for seven years? Especially when you feel like you've tried your best, and when she'd rather live with her father than with you, and she never makes contact. And then there was the Barcelona thing . . .'

'The what?'

'I arranged for us to go away on holiday – to Barcelona – after her exams. I was going to ask her to come and live with me here or at least use the time to explain to her that this could be her second home. I wanted to make the effort, to try to get to know her properly, because Julie's not actually an easy person to know. But I was willing to try. She never turned up at the airport.' Helen sighs. 'She just couldn't be bothered, so I gave up. I went to see her when she got her exam results but she wasn't interested in me being there. By then I'd given up on her, to be honest. So I stayed for a cup of tea then came home.'

'But . . .' says Charlotte.

Luke's quicker. 'Hang on,' he says. 'That's all complete rubbish.'

'I'm sorry?' says Helen. 'What do you mean?'

'The "Barcelona thing". She actually came home in tears because she was scared of flying. She almost had a complete breakdown because of it. It hadn't been the easiest year for her anyway – you leaving, her A levels and everything – and she couldn't handle the train, and she definitely couldn't handle the idea of going in a plane. I rang the airport. They said they'd make an announcement and get you to call me.'

'Well, I never got that,' Helen says.

'It took her hours to get home because suddenly she

couldn't handle any motion at all. All she was saying when she came back was that she'd let you down. I think, to be honest, she thought you might come and see what was wrong with her . . .'

Helen frowns. 'So she was trying to get my attention?'

'No,' Luke says. 'It would have been nice for her to have it but she wasn't trying to get it deliberately. She was very frightened.'

'Of what? Trains? Flying? Why?' Helen looks confused and upset.

'Julie's had a problem with travelling for ages,' Charlotte says. 'That's why we came here on B-roads. It took absolutely hours. And it's not just travelling – she's scared of almost everything. Didn't you even know that? Didn't you care when she failed her A levels? It was really important to her that you cared but . . .'

Helen's face hardens. 'I'm sorry,' she says. 'Let me get this right. My daughter's messed up and you're both saying it's my fault? I'm sorry. I don't think either of you actually know what you're talking about. I did care, and I do care, but when your daughter hates you, there's not much you can do about it. Excuse me.'

She leaves the room. A few seconds later, Luke can hear her going up the stairs.

'That went well,' he says.

'Oh, fuck it,' Charlotte says. 'What have we done?'

'We?'

'Shut up, Luke. Stop talking like you're on TV.'

Charlotte leaves the kitchen and a few seconds later Luke hears her going up the stairs too. Is she going after Helen? What's she going to say? Poor Julie, poor Helen. They've spent all this time thinking they don't care about each other, but they do, surely? Luke thinks about his own mother. Is it better to care too much or too little? And who knows how much anybody really cares about anything anyway?

At about half past six, Julie comes back. David and Chantel aren't with her.

'You'll never guess what,' she says to Luke.

'Are you speaking to me again?'

'What? I was never not speaking to you, silly.'

'But in the van. I was a dick to you.'

'Yeah, you were. But that was yesterday.'

'And?'

'Well, it was yesterday. You didn't mean it, did you?'

'No. I, uh . . .' Luke wants to tell Julie about South Mimms and how he felt but he gets the impression that something's going on upstairs that's more important than that.

'You don't need to explain,' Julie says. 'It's OK.'

Luke smiles. 'Thanks.'

'There is one thing, though. It's just . . . OK, look. It wasn't so much the go-faster stuff that bothered me. It was the drinking and smoking, like you were trying to kill yourself.'

'I wanted to escape.'

'Yes, Luke, I think we all did.' Julie frowns. She has an expression Luke hasn't seen before. 'You know, Chan and David and Leanne made you a space-suit, and we got a van, and Charlotte found you a healer and we've all gone to a hell of a lot of trouble to get you here. You don't know what it was like last night, when we were trapped and we couldn't find a way out of the floods. And I know you don't like it and I know you want to go home but we're all trying to help you. Before we left, you wanted to go out more than anything in the world. You wanted to be healed. Right? Now, I'm only going to say this once, Luke. Just be nice to everyone because we're trying to help you, and in order to help you some of us are really doing things we're not enjoying very much. For example, do you think I really wanted to come here? Just think about it. Anyway, lecture over.' Julie smiles. 'I've got some amazing news.'

'Is that Julie?' Charlotte shouts from upstairs.

'Yeah,' Julie calls back. 'Hi, Charlotte. I've got some news.'

'Can you come up here for a second?'

'Why?'

'Can you just come?'

'You'd better go,' says Luke.

Charlotte comes downstairs a few minutes later and puts the kettle on.

'I think we'll be making a move soon,' she says.

Chapter 42

'You stupid girl. You stupid, stupid girl.'

Helen's sitting on her bed with a purple shawl wrapped around her. She's been crying. Now she's stopped. Evidently, Charlotte's told her about the A levels, and Luke's told her about Barcelona, and between them they've told her about Julie's fears. Julie's not sure what else has happened or why her mother would have been crying.

'It doesn't matter now, does it?' Julie says. She's standing limply by the door. She doesn't know what to do; whether to come further into the room or run out screaming. She didn't want to have this conversation.

'I suppose you can do them again. But you're twenty-five, for God's sake. What a waste of seven years – well, nine, when you count the two years of studying you threw away. What a waste. And you did all of this to get my attention. Why didn't you just pick up the phone?'

Julie looks at the floor. 'I did it because of Luke,' she says. 'Not because of you.'

'That's not what your friend said. Charlotte said that . . .'

'Look, Mum, I didn't do it consciously because of any one thing. Yes, I failed on purpose. I didn't want to go to university and I didn't want to leave Luke. I didn't want my life to change . . . And I guess I wanted to hurt you as well, because I knew how much you wanted me to do well. But also, I didn't know what I was doing. I just wanted to do something dramatic because my life felt so horrible. But it didn't work, so I moved on. I know it was childish but I was just a kid at the time.' She looks at her mother, small and sad on her purple bed. 'I'm sorry,' Julie says.

But why is she apologising? This is confusing. Julie remembers that the one thing about her mother was that she always felt like apologising to her – for who she was, for being less cool than other kids they knew, for liking maths more than reading, for preferring Pepsi to carrot juice. But she remembers a time before that, when she just loved her mother so much, when Julie used to automatically cry when Helen did, when they used to bake cakes together and have flour fights, when if anyone said anything bad about her mother, Julie would cry for the whole day. Then Helen gave up baking cakes, because, as she explained to Julie when she was about eleven, 'Real women don't bake cakes. They change the world.' Julie bets that her mother bakes cakes now, though. And she hasn't changed the world – well, not much.

'It's all because we moved there, to that horrible place,' Helen says.

'Why? What do you mean?'

'If you'd never met Luke . . . I like him but boy, he messed your life up.'

'Please don't say that, Mum. He didn't mess my life up.'

'And those people, those Essex people . . .'

Julie thinks of Chantel, and David, and Leanne. 'I like Essex people,' she says.

Neither of them says anything for a minute or so. Julie walks a couple more steps into the room, then stops.

'Oh, God,' Helen says eventually. 'This is all my fault, isn't it? I've been a crap mother. I've been a crap mother and I've screwed you up, and I ruined Doug's life – as he's always telling me . . .'

'It's not your fault,' Julie says quietly. 'It's no one's fault.'

'But I'm a terrible mother.'

'No you're not, Mum.'

Julie walks over to the bed and perches on the edge of it. She notices that there is only one bedside table in the room. On it there's a lamp and several books stacked haphazardly. One of them is called *You Are a Good Person*. There's a small chest of drawers facing the bed. There's a vase of fresh flowers on it and several new-looking candles. Is Helen lonely in here? Or happy on her own? Julie wouldn't have a clue.

Helen's voice drops almost to a whisper. 'You would have been OK if you'd had a different mother,' she says.

'No! Mum, stop this. I loved having you as a mother. I thought you were cool. When you were on TV that time at Greenham I was so proud I almost cried. I thought everything you did was brilliant. I didn't want a mother who'd stay at home cooking and know how to do laundry properly and stuff. I wouldn't have wanted Luke's mum, or Leanne's, or anyone's. I thought you were great. The only thing is that I didn't think you liked me very much and I wanted to try to impress you so you'd like me but you never did.'

Helen looks down. 'But that's ridiculous,' she says quietly.

'You never asked me to go anywhere with you.'

Helen looks at Julie. 'You never wanted to come!'

'I was shy, Mum.'

'Oh . . . But you could talk to me, couldn't you?'

'Until you left. When you left, I just thought you really hated me.'

'See, I am a crap mother. I didn't even know that.'

Julie looks at the way her mother is clutching her shawl with both hands, as if she'd die if she didn't have it. 'Dad was there. He could have told you what was happening.'

'He always said you were fine.'

'That's pretty typical,' Julie says.

Helen manages a weak smile. Julie smiles back.

'What happened to us, Julie?' she says. 'Why didn't you just phone me? Just once? Some nights – like on your birthday, or around Christmas, or on my birthday – I just sat looking at the phone, convinced you'd call me. But you never did.' She shakes her head. 'You never, ever called me. I ended up telling my friends I didn't have a daughter any more. I was so ashamed that I had a daughter who didn't love me. How horrible do you have to be for your own daughter to stop loving you?'

'I never stopped loving you. God, Mum. I just . . . I didn't phone because I wanted to sort myself out first. I wanted to get rid of all this fear – I knew you wouldn't like me like this. And I wanted to get Luke better. In my head I had this plan where I'd be able to travel again and I'd call you and ask if I could come and visit . . . Anyway, you never called me either. I used to watch the phone on those nights as well, in case you called. Eventually, I just thought I was right and you didn't like me, and I didn't blame you because I'm a bit messed up and I know you always wanted me to be strong . . .'

'I was scared,' Helen interrupts. 'I was scared that, if I phoned you, you wouldn't want to know me. That would hurt a lot more than you not phoning, so I just waited.'

'Ditto,' says Julie.

'What a waste,' Helen says. 'What a stupid waste.'

'I'm still not the daughter you wanted, though, am I?' Julie says.

In her head she can see a well-proportioned girl with long black hair, eating rice and drinking wine and laughing over some politically correct joke. She can see rainbow rugs and organic food and a campsite with colourful tents and women with colourful hats. The girl with long black hair is reciting poetry now and everyone's listening. Now she's flying in a plane and it doesn't scare her. In fact, now she's parachuting and she's an aid worker or a traveller or a CND ambassador, and she's in Africa or Asia travelling with a threadbare rucksack and a big smile. And she's not scared of anything.

'And I'm not the mother you wanted, am I?' Helen says. 'You know, I only ever wanted you to be happy, Julie. I wanted you to be happier than me, happier than I ever could have been. I was so jealous of you, you know? You were born in the right generation and you genuinely had the chance to have a great life and make a difference. Me? I married the wrong man and got pregnant at nineteen and it felt like my life was over. When I started putting my life back together, I was doing it because I wanted you to see how your life could be better than mine. I was angry when you failed your exams. I thought you hadn't worked hard enough or that you'd been wasting all your time with Luke and I thought that was so stupid because you had all these opportunities that I never had. I never even had the chance to take exams when I was at school. I was sent to the local technical college because I was a girl. I was pissed off because you could have been anything. You could have been a company director. All I was qualified to be was a secretary. You could have been a doctor. I could only ever have been a nurse.'

'I'd rather be a secretary or a nurse, though,' Julie says. Helen looks so horrified by this that she has to pause and think. 'But I know what you're saying. I'm glad we live in a world where I have that choice but it should still be a choice. I mean . . . well, it's all down to your generation that we have a choice in the first place but . . . Anyway, I don't think I'll ever get married,' Julie says, smiling. 'If that makes you feel any better.'

'Thank God for that.' Helen shifts on the bed. She takes off the shawl and crosses her legs, leaving it draped loosely on her lap.

'And I might change the world but in a way you might not notice.'

'You don't have to change the world, Julie.'

'Good, because I probably won't.'

They laugh awkwardly. 'I'm glad you came,' Helen says.

'Me too, kind of.'

'Will you come back? I'd like to introduce you to my friends and . . .'

'What, you're not embarrassed about me?'

'Embarrassed? Don't be so silly. Look, I know you're on an important journey at the moment, but one day, just ring me up – or don't even ring – and just come. We'll get to know each other. If we hate each other, then fine – at least we tried. But we might not.'

Julie smiles. 'No, we might not.'

Helen clutches Julie's hand, then lets it go. Julie gets up from the bed.

'So are you off to Wales now, then?'

'Yeah. This seems like a good time to go.'

'Will you say goodbye to Charlotte and Luke for me?'

'Sure.'

'And tell Luke I hope he finds what he's looking for.'

'I will. Bye, then.'

'Bye, Julie.'

Chapter 43

'*Juliet?*' Charlotte says for the fifth or sixth time.

'Shut up,' says Julie.

'I think it's a cool name. You should start using it again.'

'I like just being Julie, thanks.'

It's still not raining. Luke's sitting in the back of the van and Charlotte's up front again with Julie. They're driving through the country roads towards the bigger B-roads that will take them to Wales. Julie has told Charlotte she might be able to manage the odd red road on the way but Charlotte's style of map-reading is somewhat unusual, so who knows where they're going to end up.

Julie's been explaining vaguely what happened with her mum, and about David and Chantel, and how she managed a red road on the way to Oxford, and how happy David and Chantel looked, and how she almost cried when they walked off together. Since then, Luke's been fiddling around in the back redoing his tin foil with the rolls David left, and Charlotte's been taking the piss – in a nice way – out of Julie's name.

'Parents really fuck you up, don't they?' Charlotte says suddenly.

'My mum meant well,' Julie says. 'It was just a misunderstanding, really.'

'Pretty big misunderstanding.'

'Yeah, well.' Julie sighs, then focuses on the road for a few seconds.

Charlotte laughs. '*Juliet*.'

'Shut up,' says Julie, smiling. 'Why don't you try to work out the square root of i or something.'

'Ha ha,' says Charlotte, putting her feet up on the dashboard.

'Are you OK?' Julie asks Luke, trying to catch his eye in the rearview mirror.

'Yeah,' he says. 'I'm fine. Just trying to see out of the window.'

'There's not much to see around here,' Charlotte says.

'I wonder how Leanne's getting on,' says Luke, sitting back down.

'She's probably gone home by now,' Charlotte says.

'No, I bet she's still there,' says Julie. 'She was serious about wanting to do it.'

'Hmm.' Charlotte starts rolling a cigarette. 'Oh, shit,' she suddenly says. 'I should ring Wei, shouldn't I, and tell him when we're arriving and find out where we actually need to go. Can I borrow your phone, Jules?'

'Sure. Luke, have you got the phone?'

He's been using it to check his e-mail. 'Yeah,' he says, chucking it over to Charlotte. 'Here.'

Once, in Windy Close, there was a power cut that lasted almost a whole night, and Luke had to check his e-mail on the mobile phone then, as well, even though he's not really supposed to use mobiles. He remembers the absolute dark of that night, when even the street-lamps in the road outside went off, and there was no vague glow from the industrial estate and no lights from any of the other houses on the street. Leanne's mum often fell asleep with the TV on in her bedroom, and sometimes you could see strange moving lights casting shadows on the street all night. Luke remembers suggesting to Julie that she was actually being abducted by aliens or interfered with by some sort of sex ghost. Now, when he tries to look out of the window, he sees pretty much the same as that night, except that tonight there's sometimes a hint of grass or a hedge as the headlights briefly pick things out then move on.

'Weird,' says Charlotte. She tries to shut the phone. 'Jules? How do you do switch this thing off?'

'Give it to me,' says Luke.

'What's weird?' says Julie.

'We've got to meet Wei in a Travelodge, in this place I've never heard of . . . Hang on, let me have a look at the map. Oh, I see. It's in Wales, but . . . Not where I thought we'd be going.'

'Where did you think we'd be going?'

'Jemima and Walter's house. I thought we'd meet him there.'

'Why?'

'He's been staying with them. I told you they flew him over to do Walter's book.'

'Oh. So what do you think's going on?'

'Dunno. I'll phone Jemima. Luke? Can I have the phone back?'

'Yeah, here.'

Charlotte dials a number. 'There's no reply,' she says. 'Oh, wait, hang on, there's an answerphone message with a mobile number. I'll replay it. Have you got a pen?'

Luke scrabbles around in the back. 'There was one here . . .'

'Just read the number out,' Julie says. 'I'll remember it.'

'You sure? Oh – here it comes.' She says a long number. Then she sort of fiddles with the phone to try to end the call and start a new one. 'Fucking thing. OK, what's the number, then, babe?'

Julie recites it back. Charlotte punches it in wrong, so Julie recites it again.

'It's amazing that you can do that,' Charlotte says.

'Oh – hi, Jem, it's Charlotte here . . . Yeah, cool, thanks . . . Yeah, we're on our way . . . Hmm? . . . Yeah, we just spoke to him. He wants to meet us in a hotel . . . Oh, really? . . . Oh, no, you poor things . . . Yes, sure . . . OK . . . Huh? Oh, right . . . Actually I've been thinking about that . . . I'll talk to you about it when we see you, or I might ring you later . . . Are you? . . . OK, well, we'll check into the Travelodge as well, then . . . No, no problem . . . OK . . . Cheers. Bye.'

'What was that?' Julie asks.

'Their house got flooded so they're staying with Jemima's parents. They checked Wei into the Travelodge, because there was no more space at her parents'. I guess you don't take an important guest you've flown over from America to stay with your parents, do you? So we're going to have to check into the Travelodge as well or sleep in the van. Wei is going to see us just before dawn tomorrow morning, i.e., later tonight, in his room at the Travelodge.'

'Oh, shit,' Julie says. 'I've hardly got any money left.'

'Same,' says Charlotte, sighing.

'We'll have to sleep in the van, then.'

'Yeah.' Charlotte lights a cigarette. She sighs again. 'Oh, bollocks. Chantel goes and you realise that stuff actually costs money. And Leanne could have magicked us some sort of tent or something but she's fucked off. All the useful members of the group have gone. This is like one of those videogames where you accidentally take a party member out of the group and they run into the forest and never come back and then you get killed by a load of bandits because they had all your best weapons.'

'Things are going a lot better now, though,' Julie says. She laughs. 'Maybe Leanne's working some magic from afar. It has stopped raining, for one thing.'

'Like she caused the rain in the first place,' Charlotte says.

'What's all this?' Luke says. 'Have I missed something?'

'No. Well, Leanne thought she caused the floods, that's all.'

'Oh.' Luke laughs. 'OK.'

'Oh, God,' Julie says suddenly. 'The packages.'

'What packages?'

'Chantel got us all presents. I completely forgot.'

'What presents?'

'Books, I think. They're in the glove box.'

'Presents?' says Luke.

If this was a story, there'd be money in those packages. There'd be money in the packages and they could stay in a hotel and Luke would get cured and everyone would live happily ever after. But, Luke's realising, life isn't actually a story.

Chapter 44

There's money in the packages. Three cheques, hidden in three books.

'Fucking hell,' Charlotte says. 'How much have you both got?'

The van is in a service station just outside Cirencester. About five minutes ago, Charlotte got out and bought coffee for everyone, and then they all unwrapped their packages together, like Christmas.

'Loads,' Julie says, passing her cheque around. 'Too much. She shouldn't have done this. This is too nice.'

'Luke?' says Charlotte.

'Same,' he says, showing her. 'She's given us all the same.'

'She's so lovely,' says Charlotte. 'I would have been happy with just a book.'

'Me too,' Julie says.

'We are such liars,' laughs Charlotte. 'Wow, this is amazing.'

'This is lovely,' agrees Luke.

'I do like my book as well, though,' says Julie. She shows the others. It's a survival manual. 'It tells you what to do in a plane crash, if a snake bites you, in the sea . . .'

'Very you,' says Charlotte. 'What's yours, Luke?'

Luke's is a lot bigger. It's an illustrated hardback called *Nature's Miracles*. It has pictures of caves with stalactites and stalagmites in shapes of rabbits and dolphins and dragons; the highest mountains; the deepest oceans; the night sky; glaciers; insects; tsunami; and rare birds.

'This is amazing,' Luke says. 'I want to go to all these places and see all these things.'

Charlotte's got a book on creative writing. 'Fucking hell,' she says, looking through it. 'I told Chantel I wanted to be a writer but I didn't totally mean it. I mean, everyone on my English course wanted to write. Why else would you do an English course? They were all pretentious wankers. That was one of the reasons I left. Anyway, I'd be shit as a writer.'

'Why?' Julie says. 'I think you'd be a good writer.'

'Well, I suppose it is the only thing I'm qualified for, apart from yoga teacher,' she says, laughing. 'But I haven't got anything to write about. I had a short story published once – did I ever tell you that? Anyway, that was shit, too, all self-conscious angst and taking myself too seriously. Still, with this money . . . Oh, I don't know. It's all too easy, isn't it? Really I should use this money to totally fuck myself up. That's what I'm best at.'

'You know that isn't true,' Julie says. 'Come on, we'd better get going again.'

It's just gone eight o'clock. Julie checks the map and then sets off again, trying to stick to small roads. Having money suddenly makes her want to live even more than before. But she also feels weirdly superstitious – surely all this good luck can't continue? She vaguely remembers Leanne promising to put everything right and then the rain stopping and Chantel saying she was pissed off with having the money. Then Julie reminds herself that she's a scientist not a fucking palmist and what she's thinking is utterly ridiculous. Maybe a butterfly flapped its wings in Kansas. Who knows?

Charlotte's fiddling with the radio again. Somehow she finds a station playing 'Heaven Knows I'm Miserable

Now'. 'Cool,' she says. 'My all-time favourite song.' She starts singing along.

'So can we stay at the hotel now?' Luke asks when the song finishes.

'Not really,' says Charlotte. 'We can't spend this money till it's in the bank, can we? Unless . . . Jules, have you got any actual money that we can use? I mean, I know you're skint but have you got a credit card or anything?'

'Huh? Yeah, I might have enough emergency money to pay for the hotel, I suppose, if we all share one room. I mean, if I know I'm putting this cheque into my bank account, it'll probably be all right. We need to get petrol as well, and food.' She thinks for a moment. 'Yeah, it should be all right. I'll just draw out the last of my wages and use what's left on my credit card and hope for the best.'

'You're not going to have to find another job for a while, anyway,' Charlotte says. 'You can spend all day doing maths or something.'

'You make that sound so exciting,' Julie says, smiling.

Chapter 45

It's almost eleven when they get to the Travelodge. Luke's been reading his book since the service station. He's seen pictures of elephants that can live to more than seventy years old, beautiful birds that fly in intricate formations, and cats with no tails.

'We're here,' Julie says to him.

The van stops and Julie reverses into a parking space.

Luke puts down his book and looks over Julie's shoulder out of the window. He has to stretch to see properly. There are little trees everywhere in the carpark. Luke had never seen trees before yesterday. Now there are so many of them all at once. Everything outside seems so green and beautiful, shining in a hazy glow. Beyond the carpark and the trees is a big building – bigger than Luke's house, anyway. It looks like a palace. There are amazing lights all around it – the source of the glow on the trees. This place is beautiful.

'Is Wei in there?' Luke asks Julie.

'Yeah,' she says. 'If this is the right place.' She sort of laughs.

Luke panics. 'It is, isn't it?' he says. 'This is the right place. It has to be.'

'It is,' Charlotte says. 'It's the one Wei said, Jules. It was on the map.'

'Yeah, I know,' she says. 'I just thought we got lost at one point.'

'No. This is definitely the place,' Charlotte says.

'God,' says Luke excitedly. 'He's in there. Wei is in there.'

'OK,' says Charlotte sensibly. 'How are we going to do this?'

'Do what?' Luke says.

'Get you out of the van, check in . . .'

'Let's just do it,' Luke says. 'I feel OK. This place seems magical. I know I'll be fine.'

Julie gives him a funny look, but says nothing.

'What about when we get in there?' Charlotte says.

'Oh, shit,' Julie says, looking back at Charlotte. 'The receptionists. Luke's dressed like a spaceman.'

'Won't they let me in?' Luke says. 'They have to let me in. We've come all this way . . .'

'Calm down,' Julie says. 'It'll be fine.'

'We'll tell them it's a dare,' says Charlotte. 'Or a stag night or something.'

'Some more of my tin foil's coming off,' Luke says.

Charlotte and Julie both give him a hand threading new bits through the loops Leanne made. Luke can't stop looking at this mesmerising place and the huge white tower he's about to enter.

Inside, there is a vast green carpet leading to a desk. The carpet has sparkling flecks in it like jewels. There are plants everywhere. It seems like outside, inside. Everything's green. Everything sparkles. This is a magical place, all right.

Julie and Charlotte walk towards the desk, where there's a male receptionist smiling at them oddly. Luke stands by a plant, looking at it. It has big leaves that look thick like plastic. Luke wants to touch them but he can't with his gloves on. He puts his hands behind his back and looks down at the floor.

'Where've you lot been, then?' the guy behind the desk asks. 'Fancy-dress party or something?'

'Yeah,' says Charlotte quickly. 'We changed. He didn't want to.'

'He likes being a spaceman,' Julie adds.

The receptionist laughs. 'OK. What can I do for you?'

'A smoking room for one night?' Charlotte says.

The receptionist taps some keys on his computer system. 'Yup,' he says. 'I think we can manage that.' He taps again. 'One room.' More taps. 'For one night. Smoking.' He taps some more and something starts to print out. 'Are you all sharing?'

'Yes,' says Julie. 'Is that allowed?'

'That's fine. Maximum of three adults, so long as you haven't got any other spacemen hanging around . . . ?' He laughs. 'Right, so that's one smoking family room with en suite. Maximum occupancy three adults and one child under twelve. You've got one double bed, one sofa and one pullout. All OK for you? OK, here is your bill. Please pay now.'

Julie takes the A4 sheet of paper. 'Is that all?' she says. 'God.'

'Is it cheap?' Charlotte asks her.

'We don't say cheap,' says the receptionist. 'We say good value.'

Julie hands over her credit card. 'Do you do food?' she asks.

'No. But we have a Häagen-Dazs machine right over there and also a newsagent kiosk which will open again in the morning. Alternatively, we can call out for pizza to be delivered to reception. But if you want pizza you should say so now because they shut at midnight.'

Charlotte looks at Julie. 'Shall we get pizza?' she asks.

Julie shrugs. 'Yeah, OK.'

As far as Luke knows she hasn't eaten pizza for months.

'Luke?' says Charlotte.

He nods. He's wishing he could touch the plant and he's wishing he could talk to the receptionist and interact with people like everyone else does. He feels less like a TV character the longer he's out in the world. If this scene was on TV he probably wouldn't be in it. Well, why would he be? He hasn't even got a speaking part. They'd just cut the stupid spaceman and focus on Julie and Charlotte. Then again, if this was a TV show it would be about him and he'd have to be in it. So why isn't he cracking jokes and having fun like everyone on TV does?

'I think I'd better get him up to the room,' Julie says. 'Can you stay here and sort out the pizza?'

'Sure, babe. What do you both want?'

'I'll just have a plain one. Cheese and tomato, I suppose, or Margherita or whatever they'd call it . . . And Luke always has a Hawaiian – that's ham and pineapple – from The Edge, so get him one of those.'

Luke shakes his head at her.

'Oh, no – wait,' she says. 'He went vegetarian recently. Get him whatever their equivalent of a Vegetarian Feast is. And you'd better get a bottle of Coke or Pepsi if they do them; it'll be cheaper than using the machines here.'

'Do pizza places do that?' Charlotte asks.

'Yeah,' Julie says. 'We did a take-away deal at The Edge – two medium pizzas, a garlic bread with cheese and a one-litre bottle of Pepsi for £9.99. They all do some sort of deal like that, therefore they all sell bottles of Pepsi, or Coke. Here's some money.'

Julie gives Charlotte the last of the cash from her purse.

'Can I borrow your phone?' Charlotte asks. 'I need to make a call while I'm waiting.'

* * *

When Luke steps into the lift, he may as well be stepping into some sort of time-travel machine, or a space-pod. Sure, he's seen lifts on TV all the time but he never ever thought he'd actually go in one. In a way, he wasn't sure if they actually existed or whether they were just the invention of TV companies, as if every drama or sitcom he watched was always set a few years in the future, with improbable inventions that only exist in TV-land, because no one's invented them in the real world yet.

'Are you OK?' Julie asks.

Luke nods. 'I think so. Is this actually a lift?'

'Yeah. We can take the stairs if you want,' she says, sounding slightly hopeful.

Luke thinks of Escher's stairs and they don't seem more weird than the lift. 'What's the difference?' he asks.

'Well, the stairs will take longer, and we might meet people on them, and there'll be dust and stuff. The lift will take about a minute. But I don't mind taking the stairs. I'm not all that keen on lifts anyway.'

'The lift's fine. Unless . . . ?'

'What?'

'If you're scared . . .'

'I'm trying not to be. Come on.'

Luke steps into the lift with Julie and waits. This really is like being in space. Julie presses a number on a panel and then the doors close. Luke hadn't been sure what to expect – maybe something like the movement of the van – but as the lift starts to go upwards, he feels dizzy, then sick, then terrified.

'Oh, God. Stop it doing that,' he says to Julie.

'Luke? What's wrong?'

'Stop it doing . . . Oh, Jesus . . .'

The lift stops and the doors open. Julie steps out. Luke means to follow her but somehow his legs don't work. By the time she looks around, presumably to see where he is, the doors are closing again.

'Help,' he calls to her.

'Press the button for opening the doors,' she says.

He has no idea what she means. He looks at the panel, wondering what the numbers mean, and then the lift feels like it's gone into freefall, and it's going down. Luke feels like his body's going down too but all his insides are going up and this is the worst thing that's ever happened to him. He's lost, in this moving cube, and he has no idea how to find Julie again. Gasping for breath, he looks at the numbers. The sensation of moving is starting to feel less horrible now but Luke's still lost. He tries pressing '1', thinking that might take him back to the place he stared this horrible up-and-down journey, but when the lift stops and the doors open, it looks exactly like the place he last saw Julie standing but she isn't there. Luke tries some other numbers randomly, hoping that one of them is going to be the lucky-prize door and Julie's going to be there behind it. But each number seems to take him to the same place and Julie is never there. Paralysed with frustration, Luke gives up pressing the numbers. They're obviously not the key. The next time the lift stops, at the same floor again, he stumbles out, hardly able to breathe. Is he having an allergic reaction? Oh, God. He must keep moving.

There's a sign saying 'Stairs'. Luke remembers that Julie said you could get where they were going by the stairs. There's an arrow pointing out of a door. Luke remembers teaching himself what arrows mean and proudly walks in the direction of the pointed bit rather then the thick end. So here are the stairs. There's some going up, and some going down. This is fucked up. Which way should he go? Panicking, he goes down, running, and for a few moments this is amazing because he's never had a space like this to run in before. But then the terror comes back; this is like that videogame he tried to play and he just wants to be back at the starting point. In desperation he calls, 'Julie?' and his voice sounds weird in this space, and there's no reply.

A couple of flights of stairs later, there's a sign saying 'Lifts'. Julie was standing by the lifts, so Luke follows the arrow, again, still pleased he knows how. And there are the lifts he's just come from. How can that be? This hotel must be circular, or something. Julie's not there, of course, because she wasn't there when Luke was just here, so that makes sense. The only thing that changes is the number on the wall. It said '3' before. Now it says '2'. Maybe it changes depending on the amount of times he comes here, counting down, or something. Luke turns around and again sees the same 'Stairs' sign and the same arrow and again he follows it. This time he decides to go up. Again, when he follows the next sign for 'Lifts', he seems to be back where he started, except this time the number on the wall is '3'.

OK, Luke, *think*. He thinks. There must be a knack to this. This time he keeps going up. Maybe it's better to stay constant and not change direction. At the next sign for the lifts, he almost goes down again, doubting his strategy, because he knows he's going to end up again at the same horrible dead end. But instead, he follows the arrow and Julie's there smiling.

'Where did you go?' she asks.

He runs towards her and embraces her. 'Oh, God,' he says. 'That was horrible.'

All he can manage as Julie walks him to the room are words like: *maze*, *lost*, *circle* and *Escher*. He doesn't think she understands what happened to him, but then maybe she's never made that mistake and got lost in one of these weird places before. The card-key she's holding has a number on it, which is obviously what Luke should have punched into the lift. If he'd had the card-key, he'd have known that.

Inside the room, Julie pulls the curtains and puts a blanket over the windows.

'Why don't you take off your helmet?' she suggests.

While he does that, she fiddles around with things in the room, and pulls out something that doesn't look like a bed, until suddenly it does look like a bed. That must be what a 'pull out bed' is. Luke takes off the whole space-suit and then lies on it. Julie takes off her trainers and sits cross-legged on the big double bed.

'You poor thing,' she says. 'So what happened, exactly?'

Luke explains.

'Oh, God, sorry,' she says, laughing. 'I know it's not funny.' Then she explains to him how hotels are laid out, and why every floor looks the same, and that Luke was in a different place every time – it just looked as if he wasn't.

'If you get lost again,' she says. 'I'll always be at the number 0. OK?'

'OK.'

'That'll always be our emergency plan.'

'OK.' Luke's still worried.

'It won't happen again, Luke, honestly.'

'I feel like an idiot now,' he says. 'I was terrified.'

'I would have been too,' Julie says. 'If I didn't know how hotels worked.'

Luke looks down at his feet. 'I want to get better. I want to get better so much.' He knows he sounds like he's about to cry but he doesn't care.

'I know,' Julie says, frowning. 'Oh.' She smiles suddenly. 'I just remembered – when I was a kid I went to a department store for the first time, with my mother, and got lost. It's so easy to do in those places. One minute my mother was looking at some skirts and it was boring, then I walked off somewhere, looking for the toys. All I could see were massive skirts and trousers like a forest around me and before I got to the toys it became clear that I was lost and had to get back, but whichever way I went, it was impossible to find my mother. Every time I thought I was going one way, I was actually going another way. I remember going on two escalators before one of the women who worked there asked if I was lost, and I cried and said yes. Then they gave me a lollipop and put out a special announcement for my mother to come and collect me.'

'Why were the skirts so big?' Luke asks.

'They weren't, silly. I was just really small at the time.'

'Oh,' Luke says. 'Of course.' Although he can't really see it in his mind.

'You just learn how to find your way around places, how the codes work. You'll work it out, too, when you're better.'

'Do you think I'll get better?'

'Of course you will. Well, I hope you will.' She doesn't sound very sure. Maybe she's just trying not to get his hopes up too much.

'Jules?' Luke says.

She looks at him. 'Yeah?'

'What do you think Wei will do?'

Luke's been thinking about this for a while. He can see a room with a lot of white light and a shiny white examination table with a lamp. He can see himself lying on the table, covered with electrodes, and a man with goggles is looking at him, maybe adjusting something on his computer monitor, and there's something in the room – some specialist equipment – making a low-pitched humming sound. The door to the room has a glass window. A nurse with a mask comes in and whispers something to the doctor, while Luke lies there being cured by the electrodes.

'I don't know,' Julie says. 'But I suppose you'll find out soon.'

There's a TV in the room, and Luke's been aching for TV, but he doesn't ask for it to be switched on. He has a funny feeling that he's going to be upset if the TV here looks the same as his TV at home, but just as upset if it doesn't. What is TV now anyway? Will it even make sense any more?

He lies down on the bed and closes his eyes. About five minutes later someone knocks on the door and he jumps. It's Charlotte with the pizzas.

'I've got some news,' she says.

Chapter 46

'So you're not going to India, then?' Julie whispers. 'Not at all?'

She and Charlotte are in the double bed together. Luke's under a blanket on the pullout bed. They've had pizza and Charlotte's told them her news: she's not going to India. It's warm and comfortable in the bed, which is why they're both there. No one wanted the sofa, plus Luke seemed very attached to the pullout bed.

'No,' Charlotte whispers back. 'Cool, huh?'

'Yeah. I mean, if that's what you want, it is.'

'I was just running away, really. I mean, that's the only reason I was ever going to go. I still want to run away, of course, but I'm doing a pretty good job of that with you and Luke. I thought . . .'

'What?'

'Well, you don't want to go home, do you? Maybe we could just keep on running, together. We'll have to look after the van until Chan comes back anyway. It could be like *The Adventures of the Orange Bus* or something.'

'We'll have to go back to Essex at some point, though,' Julie says, smiling.

'That's a yes, isn't it?' She semi-squeals in the darkness. 'You're so cool, babe.'

'Yeah, well, we'll have to see what Luke thinks. I think he wants to go home.'

'We'll just have to go the long way.'

They both giggle.

'We've got to stop doing this, though,' Julie says.

'What?'

'Sleeping together.'

'Why? You smell nice. Like peppermint.'

'Thanks. What time's dawn, by the way?'

'About quarter to seven or something. Wei said he'd see you both at seven.'

'OK. Cool.' Julie sets the alarm on her mobile phone.

At seven o'clock, Julie and Luke are standing outside a room on the second floor. Luke's wearing his space-suit and Julie's carrying a blanket for Wei's window because the curtains in this hotel are quite thin, and the sun's coming up. Julie feels tired and achy. She knows Luke didn't sleep well either; she heard him sighing and fidgeting all night in the little pullout bed. It must have been strange for him sleeping in a different bed for the second time ever.

It's quiet and dark in the corridor. Wei's door looks like all the others. Julie stands there for a few seconds just looking at it, not able to believe that there's a person behind it who has claimed to be able to make Luke's dream come true. Everything's so quiet and still. Is this all a big mistake? Julie's hands are sweaty. She knows that after she knocks on this door nothing's going to be the same again, ever.

'OK,' she says. 'Here goes.'

She knocks, and for a few moments nothing happens. Then she hears a man's voice saying to hang on a minute and that he's coming. Her heart thumps at the sound of the voice and she feels the uncomfortable tickle of adrenaline in her stomach. She almost wants to be sick. This is him. This is it.

The door opens and a tall man with black hair is standing there.

'Hello,' he says warmly. 'Hey, I like the space-suit.

You must be Luke.' He offers his hand, and Luke takes it uncertainly. 'And you are Julie?'

Julie takes his hand. 'Yes. You must be Wei. Thanks for agreeing to see Luke. It's so . . .'

Wei smiles. 'Actually, I would like to see you first.'

'Me?' Julie says.

'Uh huh. Perhaps, Luke – you can come back in half an hour?'

'Oh, um . . .' Luke says. 'I don't know the way back to our room.'

'I'll have to take him back,' Julie says. 'Are you sure you want to see me first?'

'Yes. Certain.'

'OK. I'll be five minutes taking Luke back. Is that OK?'

'Sure.'

When Julie gets back, Wei's left his door ajar. 'Come in, come in,' he says enthusiastically. 'Sit.'

Julie comes in and sits at the small table by the window, where Wei is pointing. There's another chair facing it and Julie wonders whether Wei's set up this arrangement specially for his meeting with Luke. It's very tidy in here and there's no smell of stale cigarette smoke like in the rooms upstairs. This room smells of coconut oil and, very slightly, of earth. Wei seems to have personalised his room in a few small ways: the TV is covered with a scarf, and one of the pillows on the bed has a different pillowcase from the others, with thin pastel stripes. On the wall by the bed, there's a picture of a small boy who looks like he could be Wei's son. Wei himself is tall and angular, dressed in a black polo-neck jumper and loose black trousers. He seems like a pop star or a politician and Julie feels slightly awed by him. There's nothing Crystal Ball about him at all, which she didn't expect. She gets comfortable on the chair, then Wei explains that he wants to help her and that Luke told him about her 'problems'.

'OK,' she says, uncertainly. 'Thanks. I'm not sure how you'll be able to help, though. I may be a bit of a lost cause.' She laughs nervously. She hadn't expected this. She thought he'd want to talk about Luke – that's why they're all here, after all.

'We'll see,' says Wei. He sits down facing her. 'So. You have fear.'

This is very direct. How does he know this? Luke must have told him a lot. Still, there's only one answer. 'Yes,' Julie says. 'Well, maybe slightly less now.'

Wei rests one of his arms on the table. 'Well, I'm pleased to hear that,' he says, smiling. 'How was your journey?'

Julie laughs. 'Wet, dangerous, time-consuming.'

Wei laughs too. 'And did it teach you anything?'

'I learnt that I like water. And I seem to have slightly less fear.'

'But still some?'

'Of course. I mean, if a journey to Wales could cure fear, you wouldn't be able to get here, there'd be so many people coming.'

Wei frowns. 'Do you think so? Most people don't do very simple things they could do to conquer their fears. It's as if they actually like their fears and want to nurture them and care for them.' He tries to cross his legs but they don't seem to fit under the table properly. He looks at Julie. 'Still, I can already see that you are too clever. That's one big problem we have to overcome.'

'Will I have to become more stupid?'

'No. You have to become more clever.'

'Oh.'

'Yes. Oh.' Wei laughs. He seems uncomfortable on

the chair and pushes it further away from the small table and then manages to cross his legs. Then he clasps his hands together and balances them on his knee. 'So anyway, you are generally afraid, yes? Is that a fair statement?'

'Yes.' Julie's tracing the pattern in the false wood on the small table in front of her. 'That's a fair statement.'

'And it's mainly that you're scared of death?'

'Sort of.' She looks up, uncertain about how to explain everything but suddenly feeling she has to; that if this man thinks he can help her, she should at least tell him the truth. Truth is a problem, though. Does Julie even know what the truth is? She knows what she feels, at least. She could try that. 'I think I'm just as scared of losing control,' she says. 'I mean – I am terrified of death, but it was only recently that the absolute finality of death dawned on me. Before that I was still terrified of everything, so it can't just be death.'

'So it's control, and it's death?' As Wei says this, he raises his hand and holds up first one, then two fingers, as if he needs to count these items.

'Yeah.' Julie stops examining the table and puts her hands in her lap. Her palms are sweaty.

Wei puts his hands back on his knee. 'Give me some examples.'

Julie tells Wei about how she can't eat prepared food like sandwiches or pizza – even though she managed a pizza last night, she still waited an hour in fear that the acid was going to kick in – and how she also can't stand the idea of natural foods, because they might have earth on them, and she's scared of E. coli and dirt and fungus and fertilisers and cancer. Then she explains all her travel phobias: the way she feels about planes, trains and boats; then she tells Wei about her fear of the weather, bacteria and freak accidents in general. He nods enthusiastically while she talks. Then he laughs.

'Well, you may as well be dead,' he says.

'I know. I've thought that myself.'

'And you're not in control.'

'No, but I try to be. Like if I only eat heavily processed foods, I'm controlling what goes in me, and I know I don't have a very healthy diet but at least I control it. If I do that, I can't be killed by someone else's mistake, or sabotage, or by a rogue spore in some clump of earth.'

Wei scratches his head. 'So which fears have you overcome?'

'Well, I haven't exactly overcome anything, but . . .' She tells him about the flood she drove through, and how excited she felt, and how different that was for her.

'So you felt the joy of life once?' He raises a finger, counting again.

'The joy of life? I suppose you could put it like that. Yes. I did.'

'Only once?'

Julie frowns. 'Sorry?'

'When was the last time you felt that joy?'

'Um, oh, last night, actually, in a way.'

'Last night?' Wei raises his eyebrows. 'What happened?'

'My friend who came on the journey with Luke and me – Charlotte; you know her, I think – she was due to leave the country, but now she's staying so she can travel around with me and maybe Luke if he gets healed and doesn't want to go home afterwards.'

'So you have friendship?'

Julie thinks about this. 'Yes.'

'And you're continuing on your journey?'

'I hope so. I'm not so good with roads, but there's always more than one way to get somewhere. And if I hadn't been on the small roads, I'd never have been able to drive through the flood.'

Wei stands up and walks across the room, with his back to Julie. She can see him counting on his fingers again. 'So you have two good friends, you're on an exciting journey, and you are healthy. But you are still afraid.'

'Stupid, isn't it?'

He turns around and looks at her. 'Julie, if somebody did put LSD in your sandwich, what's the worst thing that could happen?'

She frowns again. 'Well, that would be the worst thing, it being there.'

'But people take LSD for fun, don't they?'

'Yes, but I never would.'

'Well, that's good.' He pauses and looks at the blanket covering the window. Julie gets the impression he would actually like to look out of the window at the dawn but the blanket is there ready for when Luke comes and there's no sunlight coming through it at all. He stops looking at the blanket and looks back at Julie. 'But still, these things don't usually kill you. So, it terrifies you because it's not your choice. But you accept that some people take it and have fun?'

'Yes, but some people take it to have fun and then try to fly by jumping off a bridge or something. That terrifies me.'

'But you wouldn't do that, would you?'

'I don't know. I might.'

Wei starts walking back towards the table. 'Look, these drugs don't change your whole mind, they just confuse it. You are still the essential person inside, just a little bit muddled. You would never get so muddled that you'd kill yourself. You want to live so much. A drug would never make you stop wanting to live. The feeling's too dominant in you.' He sits down and crosses his legs again. 'Julie, I want to ask you: what would you actually do if there was LSD in your sandwich?'

Julie's embarrassed. Her fear sounds so stupid when he puts it like that. Terrifying still but totally stupid. How does her mind come up with these things? Mind you, people do spike other people all the time. Once in The Edge, someone's ex-girlfriend came in with another guy and got an E in her Pepsi. Julie's fears are grounded in some sort of reality. She stares at the table again, trying to think how to answer. She can't lie; there's only one response to Wei's question.

She looks up at him. 'What would I do? I'd panic.'

'OK. So you've panicked. What then?'

This throws her. 'I don't know. I've never thought beyond the panic.'

'Try.'

'OK, well, I suppose if I was driving, I'd pull over. But I'd be scared that I'd start hallucinating and there'd be monsters on the road and it would be dark and I'd go mad . . .'

Wei leans forward. 'So the monsters come. What would you do?'

'Tell myself they're not real, maybe. Put the radio on. Keep drinking fluids. Have a cigarette. Maybe I'd phone someone and get them to pick me up. But what if I couldn't remember their number or I thought my phone was crawling with insects or something? Mind you, you don't really get acid that strong, do you? I've heard people at work talking about it. In fact, some of the people I used to work with would do acid and other drugs then go out clubbing – or even come into work. So, logically, I wouldn't get completely out of it. I'd be able to do something, like phone for help. Or, I could phone for help as soon as it kicked in, before it got too bad. Then my friend would pick me up, and I'd get them to call a doctor to give me a sedative. Or, I suppose if I really was so out of it that I couldn't phone anyone, then I'd just have to sit it out. Anyway, hopefully I'd just be sedated and wake up OK, and then in the morning I'd call the police and report what had happened.'

Wei looks amused. 'In the morning, eh?'

'What's funny?'

'You just survived.'

'Oh, yeah. So I did.' Julie smiles.

'If surviving is the worst thing that can happen to you, I don't think you have much to worry about. I think you need to think through the ways you'd cope if some of these things happened, and not just stop at the idea of you panicking. Assume that once you've panicked for a while, you'd have to do something else, and work through the scenario until you either survive or you don't. Most times you will. Who cares if you get a little sick, or a little muddled . . . You've survived! Not that I'm recommending you eat packaged sandwiches – they really are horrible.' He laughs. 'But you could if you wanted to. It's so unlikely that you'd get one that someone had deliberately put LSD into anyway . . .'

'It's a possibility, though.'

'Not a very convincing one. I think the odds would be very remote.'

'I don't know about that. Oh, dear. I, uh . . . I have a bit of a problem with probability,' Julie says, knowing she's probably about to really piss Wei off, but not able to stop herself. 'It's that whole quantum-physics thing where you have infinite possibility and infinite universes, and therefore everything has a probability value of one. In a sense the probability of getting acid in my sandwich is the same as not getting it, and it would be just my luck to be stuck in the scenario where it happened. If there were infinite universes, I just know I'd be stuck in the one where everything goes wrong.'

'Are you a mathematician?'

Julie blushes. 'Sort of. It's my hobby.'

'Explain this idea of infinite possibility.' He makes this sound like an order.

'OK,' Julie says nervously. 'It's basically the idea that every known outcome to every possible event not only exists but actually happens somewhere, in a parallel universe or another world. The probability of anything happening therefore simply has a value of one, because if you accept multiple universes and infinite outcomes, everything possible actually happens. In that sense everything exists: millions of versions of this conversation, millions of outcomes of the throw of a pair of dice, square circles, zombies, God and the devil . . . They all exist somewhere. In some universe somewhere, when you asked me to come into the room before, I instantly turned into a lemon. In another, I tripped and fell, in another I went off with Luke and never came back. You've probably heard those ideas before. It's all to do with wave-function . . . I'd better not explain that bit, it gets a bit complicated.'

'OK, OK,' says Wei, smiling. He sighs. 'So it's just as likely that you'll get acid in your sandwich as it is that you'll turn into a lemon. I have heard about this before, although not phrased in exactly the same way, but I see how it works. It's connected with that unfortunate cat, isn't it?'

'Schrödinger's cat?'

'Yes, that's the one.'

Julie smiles. 'Yes, it is.'

'The cat was in a box, I think?'

For some reason Julie thinks of the mice she saw in the pet shop last week. 'Yes. It's a thought experiment

– there's no real cat and no real box, of course. In the thought experiment the cat is sealed in the box with some radioactive material and some cyanide. There's a fifty per cent chance that the radioactive material will break down and start a chain reaction that releases the cyanide. So the question is this: is the cat alive or dead while the box is sealed? Since you can't observe the cat, you can't know. Therefore the cat is in a "superposition" of the alive and dead states as long as the box is closed, and only becomes actually dead or alive when you open the box to make the observation. Until you look at it, the cat is both dead and alive, or fifty per cent alive, both of which are impossible. Nothing can be alive and dead at the same time; and there isn't a state between life and death. Schrödinger's thesis was a paradox that he used to illustrate problems with the way quantum theory treated the observation of atoms. The cat *must* be alive or dead. It can't be alive and dead, or fifty per cent alive, which is what the experiment suggests.'

Julie suddenly thinks about Luke, and about how he's been sealed in his box for so long. Before he left his room, was he alive, dead or fifty per cent alive? Or was he some sort of paradox, a trick, or something imaginary like a number you make up because it answers your impossible question? If something's not there you invent it. If you don't have an answer, you make one up. Is Luke imaginary? Is his life – full of narrative and perfect fiction – just imaginary?

Wei strokes his chin. 'This is an imaginary cat, is it not?'

Julie nods. 'Yes. It's a thought experiment, like I said.'

'So it can be neither alive nor dead anyway.' Wei smiles. 'Or even fifty per cent alive. And if the cyanide is imaginary it can't kill anything, can it? And you think you are like the cat. You always think you are going to be killed by imaginary cyanide.' He shakes his head. 'So, do you believe in all this quantum theory?'

Julie freezes. Is she the cat? No. Luke's the cat. Isn't he?

'Julie?'

'What? Oh, do I believe in quantum theory? Well, not really. I accept the possibility of it being there, but it doesn't actually mean anything, apart from the fact that probability is a stupid concept. It never works, and bookmakers are sometimes wrong, but not often, and you can cut a pack of cards fifty times and get the same card every time, particularly if you're cheating. Probability can only ever truly be considered in the context of infinity, because once you start talking about probability, you have to consider infinite outcomes, which makes it all a bit tricky. That's all I was trying to say. Infinity always creates its own paradoxes. In fact, if you had infinite possibility and infinite universes one of the possibilities would have to be that infinite possibility doesn't exist. That would cancel the others out.'

She sighs. 'Anyway, the point is that I still believe in weird things happening and no one's going to use probability theories to convince me otherwise, because once you start talking about probability, you have to accept that anything's as likely as anything else, including stuff that's a lot weirder than the weird thing you were worried about in the first place.'

Wei gets up again and walks around silently for a few moments. 'For someone so clever, you are not the wisest person in the world, are you?' he says eventually. 'You are right but you're not using this knowledge you have. You have to get to the point where you do not do these calculations in your conscious mind. Let your spirit handle chance and probability and calculation – those decisions you make in milliseconds are usually the best ones; for example when you "automatically" swerve out of the way when someone steps in front of your car. As you know, when you do that, your brain does thousands of calculations to do with distance and time and velocity and so on, and you are not even conscious of those calculations. If you knew the joy of playing sport you'd know that your mind is able to calculate the effects gravity has on a ball. When you fall in love, you have to let your internal world handle that. Your unconscious mind – or your spirit – makes wonderful calculations. You should not override it all the time.'

Wei turns, looks at Julie then sits in his chair again. 'Anyway, going back to our discussion, then: whatever happens to you, there are two possible outcomes, apart from the infinite ones where you turn yourself into a die, throw yourself a billion times and come up with the number six every time.' He laughs. 'You must realise that, in your predicament, when you have too much fear, even the infinite outcomes boil down to two basic ones. Essentially, you'll either survive, or you won't. Even the Schrödinger experiment demonstrates that. There really is no such thing as being fifty per cent alive. You accept that?'

Julie has to accept elegant maths. 'Yes.'

Wei looks at her. 'So if you survive, that's OK. But what if you died?'

Julie feels a chill go through her. 'That's what I'm trying to avoid.'

Wei frowns. 'But what frightens you about death?'

'Not existing any more. Nothingness.'

Now he speaks gently. 'And you're sure death leads to nothingness?'

'Huh? Of course it does.'

'What about all the other – I'm tempted to say infinite – possibilities? There are many ideas about the afterlife, and there are notions of reincarnation, or there's what I believe: that your spirit lives on in life and in nature. Many cultures believe that there is an afterlife. In fact, millions of people all around the world believe it. There are so many different versions of the afterlife.' Wei laughs. 'The one thing there couldn't be is nothingness.'

'Why not?'

'Come on, Julie. Nothingness cannot "be". Therefore it cannot exist. Use your own logic.' He smiles. 'You like using your logic. Come on. Infinity might have problems but it is more believable than nothingness. We use our being to contemplate infinity, because it exists. It is the concept of existence, multiplied to the highest factor. It is absolute being. But how can we contemplate non-being? Have you heard the phrase *nature abhors a void*? Of course you have. You should look to nature for some of your answers. Nature is all about being. Even death leads to life in nature. You shouldn't need me to tell you these things.'

Julie smiles. 'OK, but I'm still scared of dying. I know it's selfish but I don't want to make way for new life right now. I just want to carry on being me for a long time, at least until I'm very old.'

Wei sighs. 'People who have had near-death experiences say it's nothing to be scared of, you know. They see wonderful lights, happiness.'

'I know. But isn't that actually just some hallucination to do with the optic nerve closing down or something?'

'Is it? I heard of an experiment in which it was proven that the person's spirit was able to float above the body, or at least move outside it in some way, because people reported seeing objects that were placed in the room outside the range of vision anyone would have at ground level. In fact, the human spirit is a well-travelled thing, if you believe all the accounts. Ghosts, spirit guides, shamanic flight, dreams. If your spirit can travel, surely it can live on after death?'

'Really? Do you believe in all that?'

Wei smiles. 'I believe life is good and life has meaning. Look, my words aren't going to instantly cure you – as you can see, I don't work like that. But you can create for yourself a better sense of well-being if you simply ask yourself: "What's the worst that could happen?" and realise that only in rare circumstances will it be death, and even if it is, so what? If death's the worst thing that can happen, you can cope with it! You are a strong, beautiful woman, Julie. Do you really think death will be the end of you? Of course not. And even if it was, which I doubt, and there was no heaven or any sort of spirit world or afterlife, it still wouldn't be, because you will leave behind some wonderful things: maybe some children, or some ideas. Perhaps a nice garden, or a beautiful picture, or a song you made up. These are the important things. But you can't create these things, or live life, when you are so scared.'

Julie sighs. 'I know. You're right. It just might take a while for me to accept that.'

'Look, Luke's going to be waiting for you to collect him, so unfortunately our time is up, but I have enjoyed talking to you.' Wei gets up and walks over to his bedside table, from which he takes two pieces of yellow paper. One of them is blank. He gives it to Julie, along with a pencil. 'I have prepared some guidelines that I think will help you. I think you'll find these are the only reasonable precautions you'll need to take to keep healthy, which is all you're really worried about, so you can go on your journey, and have fun with your friends, and do your strange maths. Some of these are from the Tao, but most are things your grandparents could tell you, in that they're just common sense. And Julie, do not be afraid of illness – you will be ill, then you will get well, and you may read a wonderful book while you are in bed. Illness can be a blessing.'

For the next couple of minutes, Wei recites a list which Julie writes down. Then he gives her the other piece of paper, which has something from the book of Chuang Tzu written on it that he tells her to read later. When she leaves, she has the excerpt from Chuang Tzu, and the following list:

Wash food before preparing it
Wash your hands before eating or preparing food
Keep cold food cold and hot food hot (never eat reheated rice)
Look each way twice before crossing the road
Be kind to people, animals, plants and the earth
Relax like a baby does, and you will not be harmed
Learn First Aid
Follow the Highway Code
Exercise regularly
If you have a problem, make a journey; you will find the answer
Stop thinking about infinity

Chapter 47

When Julie comes to pick up Luke, she looks different in some way that Luke wouldn't be able to describe. Wei must truly be a wonderful healer. Perhaps now Julie is completely free of fear.

'So can you go on motorways now?' Luke asks.

Julie smiles. 'I have no desire to go on a motorway,' she says.

'Oh.'

Then she shows him a piece of yellow paper with something written on it about fish. One man is saying something to another man about how happy the fish are when they're playing in the river. Then the other man asks the first man how he can know that, since he's not a fish. Then the first man asks the second man how he can know that he cannot know what the fish are thinking, since he is not him . . . This is too confusing. Luke can't understand this right now, and he's not really concentrating anyway, because he's thinking about seeing Wei. Without finishing reading it, he gives the piece of paper back to Julie.

'It's interesting, isn't it?' she says, but he doesn't reply.

As Luke, covered in a fleece blanket, walks down to Wei's room with Julie, he thinks about the moment he will be able to take off the blanket and his space-suit. It'll be like an uplifting film and he'll dance around, full of gratitude, and he'll give Wei all (or almost all) his money to give to his charity and then he'll go and climb a mountain. Of course, right now, Luke's terrified of the idea of mountains. After all, he couldn't even navigate his way around a hotel. But he knows that Wei is going to do something to make all that go away, and Luke will be normal just like everybody else.

Before he enters the room, he thinks to himself: *This is my last moment as a freak.*

About ten minutes later, he leaves the room and slams the door. He's angry.

'Take me home,' he says to Julie.

'But what about . . . ?'

'He isn't a proper healer. He can't heal me.'

'But what did he say?'

'He said, "The answer is inside you," or something.'

'And?'

'That's stupid. He said something about how I'd always had the answer and I knew what it was, but he's just fucking insane. I don't want to talk about it. Take me home.'

'But we've come all this way.'

'And now I want to go back.'

'Oh, Christ. OK. We'll have to go and tell Charlotte.'

Julie throws the fleece blanket back over Luke and he knows this is it: he'll never see light, not natural light, ever. The blanket feels like death to him; a soft shroud. He wants to cry but he can't. He can't rub his eyes because of the helmet. But who cares? His life may as well end now anyway. Under the blanket and the helmet Luke does cry and the blackness in front of him smears and he can't see any more. He doesn't care. He wants to choke on his tears and his snot and his sadness.

Julie's leading him by the arm, gripping him too hard. He likes the pain.

'There are stairs now,' she warns in a cold voice.

Luke stumbles but he doesn't care.

When they get back to their room, Charlotte's still asleep.

'You'll have to wait while I get her up,' Julie says. Her voice still sounds weird and cold.

Luke sits on the pullout bed holding the fleece blanket in his hands. Through his tears he can see Julie moving around, collecting things in the room, trying to wake Charlotte, lighting a cigarette. Luke thinks of those commercials that show how economy batteries run down quicker than branded ones. Julie looks an economy-powered toy about to stop or break.

'What's wrong with you?' Luke says.

'I wanted it to all get better,' she says, staring at him for a moment.

'Well, it isn't,' Luke says.

'Oh, yuck,' Charlotte says, when Julie wakes her up. 'What time is it?'

'Almost eight,' Julie says. 'Luke's upset. We have to go.'

'Go?'

'Home. Sorry.'

'Shit.' Charlotte sits up in bed and starts rolling a cigarette. 'What happened?'

'I don't know. I think it just didn't work.'

'Has he tested it?'

'I don't think the "healing" actually took place at all.'

'The guy's an idiot,' says Luke. 'That's why.'

'He's not an idiot,' Charlotte says. 'Are you sure you understood what he was saying to you?'

'Yes, I understood,' Luke says. 'Can we go soon?'

He lies down on the pullout bed until Charlotte's ready. While he's there, Julie and Charlotte say nothing, and all he can hear are the sounds of them folding things up, and then Charlotte putting her clothes on. Luke can't even think any more; he's just aching to go home, back to the horror of what he knows, which is better than the unfamiliar, lost horror of being outside. At least he can't get lost at home. And he knows he's being horrible again and he knows Julie's upset, but this is probably the most depressing thing that's ever happened to him.

Out in the van, no one's saying much.

'Do you mind map-reading?' Julie says to Charlotte.

'Sure. The short way, yeah?'

'You'll have to stay under the blanket,' Julie says to Luke. 'It's light outside now.'

And that's all they say. Luke wants one of them to say something else, but they don't. Maybe they don't know what to say. Maybe Charlotte's pissed off with him for thinking Wei was an idiot. Maybe even Julie's pissed off with him; she was before. He goes under the blanket and cries again. And as he cries, and feels more and more pathetic, the answer comes to him, just as it did at the service station at South Mimms. He has no life. So: he has no life.

'Stop the van,' he says to Julie, coming out from under the blanket.

'Stop the van?' she says. 'Luke, why aren't you under the . . .'

'Stop the van,' he says again, unable to stop his voice sounding slightly mad.

'We'd better do it,' says Charlotte. 'We'd better stop.'

'Where?' says Julie. 'This is a main road. You can't stop here.'

'Hang on, Luke,' Charlotte says. 'We have to find somewhere to stop.'

'Oh, God,' says Julie.

'There's a big park coming up in a second,' says Charlotte, looking at the map. 'Look out for the sign and pull in. Can you wait two minutes, Luke?'

'I guess so,' he says.

'You'll have to,' Julie says. 'It's illegal to stop here.'

Luke doesn't even feel that scared of what he's about to do. When the van eventually stops, he simply opens the door and steps out. He can hear Julie shouting at him to stop, and Charlotte stupidly telling her it'll be all right. Then he takes off his helmet.

As soon as he does he feels cold, fresh air on his face and he can smell something. It's a damp smell, new and exciting like flowers, but different. Ahead of him he can see an amazing wash of green, and it's grass – he recognises it, but it's bigger in real life and there's so much more of it. Luke can't believe he ever thought the whole world was made of concrete when it's so obviously made of this. He walks forward, breathing in the air and staring at the grass, and he sees tall trees and a bird flying and a small lake in the distance, and then he starts ripping off his space-suit.

And he doesn't die.

He doesn't even unzip the suit; he pulls at it until the seams burst open and he's throwing bits of ripped-off material and tin foil behind him on the grass. He kicks off the wellington boots and takes off his socks so he can feel the grass under his feet. The cold, wet, soft feeling is so intense and pure that he almost stops breathing. This one feeling of grass under his feet is the reverse of all the pain he's ever felt in his life. He wants to touch the ground with his hands now, so he gets down on his knees and presses both his palms into the grass. Then he's rolling on it but he doesn't want to wear these clothes any more. He strips off his fleece top and tracksuit bottoms and his T-shirt and flings them behind him. Then he lies face-down in the grass, breathing it in, wanting to live in this moment forever.

And then he sees a ladybird, shiny with the morning

dew. Could this be real? This joy is too much. He has to get up and run. So now he's running, trying to remember how to breathe, and Julie and Charlotte are running after him. He's still running – not away from them, but because he can – and he's never felt anything this soft beneath his feet before, and he wouldn't care if he died if these things were the last things he ever saw and he could die with that wonderful smell all around him. This is some sort of paradise. Everything here is a miracle; more beautiful than the pictures in his book, more bright and soft and real than images on TV. He gets as far as the edge of the lake, and there are ducks, and Luke doesn't know how such perfect creatures could ever exist. They float perfectly on the surface of the water, which is a blue Luke's never seen before, rippled with orange from the sun, the colour he never thought he'd see.

He still doesn't die. He doesn't even feel ill.

He doesn't want to go home any more. Everything's wonderful; everything's changed. Julie and Charlotte look beautiful walking towards him now with their straight brown hair, like twins. But he's never seen women's hair do *that*. It's shining in the sun, and they both look like angels with haloes.

'How could this happen?' he asks Julie as she catches up with him. 'I don't understand. I'm healed but Wei didn't heal me.'

Julie looks at Luke and the grass and the lake and she seems to be thinking about all the different answers to his question. Then she looks at him and smiles.

'Didn't he?' she says.

Then it starts to rain.

The Scarecrow and the Tin Woodman and the Lion now thanked the Good Witch earnestly for her kindness, and Dorothy exclaimed:

'You are certainly as good as you are beautiful! But you have not yet told me how to get back to Kansas.'

'Your Silver Shoes will carry you over the desert,' replied Glinda. 'If you had known their power you could have gone back to your Aunt Em the very first day you came to this country.'

'But then I should not have had my wonderful brains!' cried the Scarecrow. 'I might have passed my whole life in the farmer's cornfield.'

'And I should not have had my lovely heart,' said the Tin Woodman. 'I might have stood and rusted in the forest till the end of the world.'

'And I should have lived a coward for ever,' declared the lion.

The Wonderful Wizard of Oz by L. Frank Baum

Acknowledgements

Thanks to my family and friends. Special thanks to Leo, Simon and Tom.